"With its themes of creativity and art, *Write My Name Across the Sky* is itself like a masterfully executed painting. Using refined brushstrokes, O'Neal builds her vivid, complex characters: three independent women in one family who can't quite come to terms with their fierce feelings of love for one another. O'Neal deftly switches between three points of view, adding layers of family history into this intimate and satisfying study of how women make tough choices between love and creativity and family and freedom."

—Glendy Vanderah, *Washington Post* bestselling author of *Where the Forest Meets the Stars*

THE LOST GIRLS OF DEVON

One of *Travel + Leisure*'s most anticipated books of summer 2020

"A woman's strange disappearance brings together four strong women who struggle with their relationships, despite their need for one another. Fans of Sarah Addison Allen will appreciate the emphasis on nature and these women's unique gifts in this latest by the author of *When We Believed in Mermaids*."

—*Library Journal* (starred review)

"*The Lost Girls of Devon* draws us into the lives of four generations of women as they come to terms with their relationships and a mysterious tragedy that brings them together. Written in exquisite prose with the added bonus of the small Devon village as a setting, Barbara O'Neal's book will ensnare the reader from the first page, taking us on an emotional journey of love, loss, and betrayal."

—Rhys Bowen, *New York Times* and #1 Kindle bestselling author of *The Tuscan Child*, *In Farleigh Field*, and the Royal Spyness series

T0036209

"*The Lost Girls of Devon* is one of those novels that grabs you at the beginning with its imagery and rich language and won't let you go. Four generations of women deal with the pain and betrayal of the past, and Barbara O'Neal skillfully leads us to understand all of their deepest needs and fears. To read a Barbara O'Neal novel is to fall into a different world—a world of beauty and suspense, of tragedy and redemption. This one, like her others, is spellbinding."

—Maddie Dawson, bestselling author of *A Happy Catastrophe*

WHEN WE BELIEVED IN MERMAIDS

"An emotional story about the relationship between two sisters and the difficulty of facing the truth head-on."

—*Today*

"There's a reason Barbara O'Neal is one of the most decorated authors in fiction. With her trademark lyrical style, she's written a page-turner of the first order. From the very first page, I was drawn into the drama and irresistibly teased along as layers of a family's complicated past were artfully peeled away. Don't miss this masterfully told story of sisters and secrets, damage and redemption, hope and healing."

—Susan Wiggs, #1 *New York Times* bestselling author

"More than a mystery, Barbara O'Neal's *When We Believed in Mermaids* is a story of childhood—and innocence—lost, and the long-hidden secrets, lies, and betrayals two sisters must face in order to make themselves whole as adults. Plunge in and enjoy the intriguing depths of this passionate, lustrous novel, and you just might find yourself believing in mermaids."

—Juliet Blackwell, *New York Times* bestselling author of *The Lost Carousel of Provence*, *Letters from Paris*, and *The Paris Key*

Praise for Barbara O'Neal

THE SCENT OF HOURS

"With great insight Samuel explores the many problems facing newly divorced women and offers hope and inspiration in the form of one gutsy heroine."

—*Booklist*

THIS PLACE OF WONDER

"*This Place of Wonder* is a wonderfully moving tale about four women whose journeys are all connected by one shared love: some are romantic, some are familial, but all are deeply complicated. Dealing with loss, love, hidden secrets, and second chances, this stirring tale is utterly engaging and ultimately hopeful. Set along the rugged California coastline, *This Place of Wonder* will sweep you away with the intoxicating scents, bold flavors, and sweeping views of the region and transport you to a world you won't be in any hurry to leave."

—Colleen Hoover, #1 *New York Times* bestselling author

"Kristin Hannah readers will thoroughly enjoy the family dynamic, especially the mother-daughter relationships."

—*Booklist* (starred review)

"Barbara O'Neal's latest novel is simply delicious. Engrossing, empathetic, and profoundly moving, I savored every sentence of this story of several very different women who find solace and second chances in each other after tragedy (though not before facing some hard truths and, yes, a few rock bottoms). *This Place of Wonder* is one of the best books I've read in a long time."

—Camille Pagán, bestselling author of *Everything Must Go*

"I have never much moved in the elevated circles of California farm-to-table cuisine, but O'Neal makes me feel like I'm there. Rather than simply skewering the pretensions, *This Place of Wonder* pinpoints the passions. Some of these characters have been elevated to celebrity, some are newcomers to the scene, but all are drawn together by the sensuality, the excitement, and ultimately the care that food brings them. Elegiac but also forward-looking, this is a book about eating, but more than that, it's a book about hurt and healing and women finding their way together. I loved every moment of it."

—Julie Powell, author of *Julie & Julia* and *Cleaving*

WRITE MY NAME ACROSS THE SKY

"Barbara O'Neal weaves an irresistible tale of creativity, forgery, family, and the FBI in *Write My Name Across the Sky*. Willow and Sam are fascinating, and their aunt Gloria is my dream of an incorrigible, glamorous older woman."

—Nancy Thayer, bestselling author of *Family Reunion*

"*Write My Name Across the Sky* is an exquisitely crafted novel of three remarkable women from two generations grappling with decisions of the past and the consequences of where those young, impetuous choices have led. A heartfelt story of passion, devotion, and family told as only Barbara O'Neal can."

—Suzanne Redfearn, #1 Amazon bestselling author of *In an Instant*

"In *When We Believed in Mermaids*, Barbara O'Neal draws us into the story with her crisp prose, well-drawn settings, and compelling characters, in whom we invest our hearts as we experience the full range of human emotion and, ultimately, celebrate their triumph over the past."

—Grace Greene, author of *The Memory of Butterflies* and the Wildflower House series

"*When We Believed in Mermaids* is a deftly woven tale of two sisters, separated by tragedy and reunited by fate, discovering that the past isn't always what it seems. By turns shattering and life affirming, as luminous and mesmerizing as the sea by which it unfolds, this is a book club essential—definitely one for the shelf!"

—Kerry Anne King, bestselling author of *Whisper Me This*

THE ART OF INHERITING SECRETS

"Great writing, terrific characters, food elements, romance, a touch of intrigue, and more than a few surprises to keep readers guessing."

—*Kirkus Reviews*

"Settle in with tea and biscuits for a charming adventure about inheriting an English manor and the means to restore it. Vivid descriptions and characters that read like best friends will stay with you long after this delightful story has ended."

—Cynthia Ellingsen, bestselling author of *The Lighthouse Keeper*

"*The Art of Inheriting Secrets* is the story of one woman's journey to uncovering her family's hidden past. Set against the backdrop of a sprawling English manor, this book is ripe with mystery. It will have you guessing until the end!"

—Nicole Meier, author of *The House of Bradbury* and *The Girl Made of Clay*

"O'Neal's clever title begins an intriguing journey for readers that unfolds layer by surprising layer. Her respected masterful storytelling blends mystery, art, romance, and mayhem in a quaint English village and breathtaking countryside. Brilliant!"

—Patricia Sands, bestselling author of the Love in Provence series

The Scent of Hours

ALSO BY BARBARA O'NEAL

The Starfish Sisters

This Place of Wonder

Write My Name Across the Sky

The Lost Girls of Devon

When We Believed in Mermaids

The Art of Inheriting Secrets

The All You Can Dream Buffet

The Garden of Happy Endings

How to Bake a Perfect Life

The Secret of Everything

The Lost Recipe for Happiness

Lady Luck's Map of Vegas

The Goddesses of Kitchen Ave

A Piece of Heaven

No Place Like Home

In the Midnight Rain

The Scent of Hours

a novel

BARBARA O'NEAL

LAKE UNION
PUBLISHING

Text copyright © 2006, 2014, 2024 by Barbara Samuel

Published by Lake Union Publishing, Seattle

www.apub.com

Amazon, the Amazon logo, and Lake Union Publishing are trademarks of Amazon.com, Inc., or its affiliates.

ISBN-13: 9781662521379 (paperback)
ISBN-13: 9781662521362 (digital)

Cover design by Shasti O'Leary Soudant
Cover image: © Lumina, © Laura Stolfi / Stocksy; © Vesnushka.art / Shutterstock; © John Elk III / Getty

Printed in the United States of America

Tori\real 'Barlow,
just as you are:
rare as a unicorn,
steady as a mountain.

BASE NOTES

1

Nikki's Perfume Journal Entry

SCENT OF HOURS
November 22, 1978

Definition: Chypres
Chypres is a highly original group that is based on contrasts
between bergamot-type top notes and mossy base notes. Chypres perfumes tend to be strong, spicy, and powdery. This perfume group was named after the famous perfume from Cyprus of
Roman times. It is used primarily for women, and is appropriate
for both day and evening wear, especially during winter.

I told the insurance company I was sleeping when the house blew up.

In actual fact, the cold woke me. I stood at the top of the stairs that led
to my basement at three a.m. on a morning in late winter, daring myself
to go down and find out why the furnace was not working. Puffs of dust-
scented air wafted around my ankles. The narrow wooden steps disappeared
into yawning darkness, and even when I turned on the light, it wasn't particularly inviting. I hate basements—spiders and water bugs and the possibility of creepy, supernatural things lurking. *Ammie, Come Home* scared the
holy hell out of me when I was seven, and I've hated basements ever since.

Standing there with my arms crossed over my breasts, frozen in every sense of the word, I thought, This was so not in my script.

I made a bargain, to love, honor, and cook all the meals, while he promised to love, honor, and do things like go down into the basement in the middle of the night. This was not strictly gender role stuff—I was a good cook and I liked it. Daniel was not the slightest bit afraid of ghosts or spiders.

Cold air swirled around my ankles. I couldn't move. Frozen, just as I'd been for the past seven months.

A vivid picture of the house blowing up in a blaze of noise and fire flashed over my imagination (and wouldn't they all be sorry then!). Experimentally, I stuck my head into the stairwell and took a long, deep sniff. No smell of sulfur, and I have a very good nose. Of course, it wasn't exactly an airtight basement.

I shuffled forward three inches.

Halted.

A shuddering hitch caught in my throat. I realized that I could not do it. Could not physically force myself to go down into that creepy, cold, spidery cellar and then get down on my hands and knees and look for a pilot light, and maybe even have to put my hands into a place where there were spiderwebs.

No. Way.

In the morning, I'd call someone to check it out. For now, I'd just have a cup of tea and play with my computer. Instantly, my heart stopped fluttering. Decision made. I stepped crisply back from the yawning mouth of doom and closed the door.

From the linen cabinet by the downstairs bathroom, I took a blanket that smelled of the lavender stalks that I tuck into all the drawers and closets. The pale purple scent eased my tension as I carried the blanket into my study, where the computer was breathing steadily, softly, its lights blinking comfortingly in the darkness.

I turned on the small art deco lamp I'd found on eBay and settled into my chair, blanket around my shoulders, and opened a novel I'd checked out of the library. At least some things were reliable.

Unlike the furnace. Which exploded exactly one hour later with a noise you can't even imagine.

Obviously, I lived.

The house, on the other hand, did not fare quite so well.

~

My mother used to say, "When the student is ready, the teacher will appear." I was pretty sure I was ready after blowing up the house, but no Mary Poppins of the over-forty set magically appeared to rescue me.

Instead, I sat for six more days at the Motel 6, drowning my sorrows in pints of Dove chocolate raspberry ice cream while I played the television for company and pretended I wasn't panicking.

The day I met Roxanne for the first time, I gave my Visa to the girl in the Albertsons line and she shook her head. "Do you have another one?"

I did, but it was the last one. I'd maxed out all the rest—four of them, if you want to know the truth. As I handed over number five, even I, queen of denial, had to admit it was time for a change. I had to find a place to live and a job to keep me in ice cream until the insurance settlement came through.

Back at my clean, uncluttered room, where I didn't have to worry about anything at all, not even vacuuming or dishes or whether I'd remembered to buy shampoo, I faced myself in the mirror. Squared my shoulders.

Time to rescue myself.

First, clothes, since I was wearing an ancient skirt that had been in a bag of things I'd collected to go to Goodwill. I drove to Target, which was, once upon a time, one of my monthly stops. Today, the excessive light and acres of red—on signs and walls and the T-shirts of clerks—dazzled me. Music, modern and unfamiliar, poured out of the loudspeakers.

There were so many jeans. Did I want low-slung or high? Was I too old for acid-washed? Would my expanding butt look stupid in the wide pockets?

How could I choose? In the end, I took the pair that fit, and rushed out of the store because my throat was starting to close. It was an oddity, the hitch I kept getting in my throat. It was as if I couldn't quite swallow.

Sometimes, I was afraid that what I was holding back was a long banshee scream. As I stood there in those polished aisles, it was way too easy to imagine throwing back my head and letting go, maybe in the men's department beside the boxer shorts and socks, where I spent so much time and money lovingly picking out underthings for Daniel. He'd liked funny boxers—Tasmanian Devil and Bugs Bunny in particular, said it made him remember the kid he was inside—and sensible white cotton socks for the heavy boots he had to wear on jobsites.

When he turned forty, he started wearing silky, black-spotted socks and colored bikinis. Should have been a clue, I guess, but you're not really thinking your husband is going to fall in love with someone else. That's what other husbands do.

Yes, I could scream a really long time.

Instead, I grabbed an advertising circular from the racks outside Target and headed for the Village Inn near my motel, where I ordered a cup of coffee and some eggs and toast, like a normal person.

I opened the flyer. There were a lot of apartments in town. Hundreds and hundreds. Again, I felt that fluttery sensation in my throat. Stirring too much sugar into my coffee, I took a long, soothing sip, and promised myself ice cream if I at least looked at some of them.

~

The Scent of Hours

The first one I chose was stacked on a hill, a place of in-betweenness. I hadn't lived in an apartment since I was twenty-three years old, and I never much liked them even in the old days. This one was a gigantic complex, three and four stories tall. I liked it, though, much prettier than the old boxy places I remembered. There were french doors opening onto little balconies that boasted views of King Soopers, and the mountains beyond.

I was scared to death, sitting in the parking lot. So nervous, my elbows felt weak, and there was no logical reason for it. Not even as much logic as spiders in the basement—just general life terror, the same fear that inflicts you the first day of school or starting a new job.

Some sensible part of my brain said with a slap, Get over it! Get out of the car! Stop being such a wimp!

I didn't know what was wrong with me. This was not 1952. It wasn't like divorce was uncommon. It wasn't as if I didn't have resources and brains. I'd led committees of fifty, headed up fundraisers, organized the busy lives of my ex and my daughter, planned parties for a hundred. My garden was one of the most envied on the block, and I made perfumes. Beautiful perfumes. I was quite accomplished.

But it didn't matter. Divorce was making me feel like a worm dug out of the nice, loamy ground and flung out on the sidewalk—I was writhing and wincing and struggling to get back into the earth.

Since I couldn't, I stepped out of the car, carefully locked the door behind me, and walked across the pavement to the office. In the reception area, which was very modern and clean, with a huge arrangement of flowers that reminded me of a hotel, I waited for a girl to get off the phone.

She waved a finger at me: just a minute. I turned to read the notices on the bulletin board: hand-printed ads for house sitters and babysitters with individual tear-off flaps with phone numbers; a flyer for a lost cat with the sullen face of a Persian; couches for sale.

There were the predictable empty promises: MAKE MONEY AT HOME!! LOSE 30 LBS IN 30 DAYS, GUARANTEED!!! Feeling my gut billow out beneath my crossed arms, I thought I ought to give that one a call.

The rest were odds and ends, mostly odds: a drumming circle met on Thursday evenings (women only, please!). A tarot reader in Building 4 offered her services for $45, call Roxanne. There was Sufi dancing at the Unity church; shaman-ism classes, call White Wolf Woman, 555-4309.

A slight buzzing roar blazed through my head, and I took an airless step backward. I was divorced, not weird. There had to be a better place to rent an apartment.

The girl materialized beside me, her wash of thick, glossy hair swirling over her shoulders. "Sorry. It was my boss." Sticking out a thin white hand, she added, "I'm Monday. How can I help you?"

"Monday's child?" The rhyme ran through my head. "Fair of face."

She looked confused. "No, you know, like the Mamas and the Papas song?"

"Oh. Right. Nicole Carring—I mean, Bridges." I blinked the embarrassment of my name change away, squeezed her hand too hard.

"Did you want to look at an apartment?"

"Um, well. I . . ." With a grunt, I glanced back toward the flyers stuck with pins and thumbtacks, blue and yellow, white and red, to the corkboard. "Maybe this isn't the right spot for me."

Following my gaze, she waved a hand. "Oh, don't worry. People just do some different things when they're free for the first time in ages, you know? There are lots of different kinds of people who live here. Lots around your age, too, which is always nice, right?"

My age. Like a class of children to play with at recess. "Sure. All right."

She picked through a set of keys on a ring. Her cheeks were that natural blushy rose some fair-skinned girls have. With her dark hair and dark eyes, it made her look like Snow White. "What would you like to see? Two bedroom? Three?"

"Um." Another choice. "Let me see them both, I guess. I'm not sure."

"Great." She gestured toward the parking lot. "We also have an exercise room, a pool in the summer . . . and, of course, a shopping center right across the street. Grocery store, videos, gas . . . all right there at your fingertips, and the best views in the city."

"Mmm."

She wore pointed black plastic boots on slightly pigeon-toed feet, and even on this cool day, a slice of white skin showed between her blouse and the top of her jeans, which were what we would have called hip-huggers. I had a pair with three tiny snaps in front, long, long ago. Something about her, the sweet awkwardness of her, made me long for my daughter, though Giselle was not at all like this girl.

I tried to imagine Giselle, doing this job. Since she was driven toward medical school with a ferocity that surprised both her father and me, it wouldn't happen, but I liked the sunniness of Monday. Traitorously, I wondered if Giselle would be easier to deal with if she weren't so ambitious.

"Let's look at the three-bedroom first," Monday said. "Hope you don't mind a little climb."

There was a smell of bacon in the air. The stairs twisted upward, solid concrete rimmed with wispy-looking wrought iron. When we stopped on the landing, stupendously high above the street, a tiny wave of vertigo moved over my brow. I clung to the railing, trying to steady myself, and focused on the horizon.

"Wow!" I said, a reflexive response to the view.

The mountains this afternoon were the color of a plain blue Crayola, jagged peaks dusted with snow above the timberline. Above them, the sky was softly gray. Pikes Peak, blue and white and burly, spread his shoulders across the horizon, exactly centered—the father mountain stretching his arms to the north and south. The tourist literature called it America's Mountain, a moniker that irked me. Daniel used to tease me about my possessiveness, but on this I was unmovable: it was not America's mountain, it was mine.

"It's great, isn't it?" Monday said over my shoulder. "You never get used to a view like that either. How could you?"

"I know."

A door slammed and the sound of heels clicking against concrete came toward us. A woman said, "Hey, Monday," in a voice as throaty as Elvira. I turned around to see a thin, leggy woman with dark hair cut in urbane choppy layers head down the stairs.

"Good morning, Madame Mirabou," Monday said.

The woman laughed. It was a rich sound, knowing. "How did it go Friday night?"

"You were right," Monday said.

"Excellent." I watched her descent, her knees showing in tan stockings beneath a green dress. "Maybe I should hang up a shingle."

"Madame Mirabou's School of Love."

"Not bad." The woman looked up as she made the last turn, and her eyes were bright, bright blue as they met mine. I could see she was my age, more or less. "It's a good place to live," she said. "I'd be your neighbor, though. Ask Monday if that's a good idea."

"Thanks."

Monday said, "Come on in and let me show you the apartment."

The tension in my chest built as we circled the rooms. It was an inoffensive place, with good closets and good views and a certain upscale beigeness that shouldn't cause so much anxiety. I paused in the windowless kitchen with my hands over my middle, noticing how green my skin looked in the fluorescent light.

It made me think of a spot I loved in the old house, a niche in the kitchen set beneath a leaded glass window. I'd found a battered cherry-wood table at a garage sale, and refinished it myself, and put it below the window with a blue glass vase on top. I liked it best if there were sunflowers available at the florist, but any yellow flower was fine.

I didn't love the house, but I'd loved that spot.

Now it was gone.

The hitch in my throat made me cough. Suddenly the idea of going around looking and looking was more than I could bear, especially when I had nothing to put inside any of them anyway, and I could better use the time trying to find a job to see me through until the insurance company approved my claim. I didn't love this apartment, but it would do for now.

I reached for my purse. "I'll take it."

Monday looked surprised, but she was no dummy. "Come on downstairs and we'll write up the contract."

Looking out the window, I said, "Will she be a good neighbor?"

"Who?"

"The one we saw out there. Madame whoever."

"Oh, Roxanne." Something flickered in her young eyes, gone before I could pinpoint it. "Yeah. She's divorced with two kids, a son and a daughter in their teens—but they're not noisy. I never get complaints or anything."

"Has she been here long?"

"A year or so." She waved me toward the door. "Let's get back downstairs, all right?"

I wrote out the check a little later, my hands were shaking, but I was relieved to have made some kind of decision. The first one.

2

Nikki's Perfume Journal Entry

Time: midnight
Date: Tuesday, February 12, 1985

Scents: dryer sheets, faint mildew, pepperoni pizza, semen,
lemons, white wine, hint of sulfur, touch of chocolate
Bottle: aquamarine cracked glass
Notes: the night I first made love to Daniel

The whole divorce business would have been much easier if I could have said afterward, "Oh, you know I never really loved him." Or, "Well, we were having problems for a long time. I wasn't happy and neither was he." It would have been easier for me and easier for everyone around me if I could have said, like a woman on television did one day: "I'm happily divorced."

But in my case, it just wasn't true. I was happy. I loved him, and our rituals, and our family, and our life. I liked the startling couple we made, he so tall and dark, me curvy and fair. I loved how Giselle blended us in a way that was a cut better than either one of us, like a café mocha. I liked going to movies on Sunday afternoons and having dinner together every night, going on vacation every June and rubbing his shoulders when he was tired.

The fact that I loved him and did not want to be divorced and did not—no matter what anyone *says*—see it coming, seemed to make a lot of people very uncomfortable. It was almost as if my newly unrequited love was in bad taste, that I should get to the truth of the whole matter and figure out why my marriage broke up. Find all those signs that were lurking that I should have paid attention to.

Right. I'd get right on that.

Some of the worst offenders in this were my friends from the old neighborhood. The Wednesday morning after I moved into my new apartment, I had plans to meet them all for lunch at Annie's Organix, which is the restaurant Pamela often chose when it was her turn. She also shopped exclusively at Wild Oats and ran sixty miles every week. There wasn't enough fat on her body for even little breasts, just a teeny rise for a couple of nipples.

Not exactly my problem today. My blouse was gaping badly. As I tried to safety pin the placket over my breasts, the doorbell rang. I jerked reflexively and the pin jabbed into my skin. A minute bead of blood appeared, which then soaked instantly into my light pink blouse, which meant I'd have to change, and it had already taken all morning to decide on this one!

In sudden panic, I plucked at my hair, which was too long and raggedy, and suddenly realized that they were going to see me like this. My friends. The girls. My old gang. The well-tended mavens of the old neighborhood.

Damn. I dipped a washcloth in cold water and rubbed at the bloodstain. To the universe at large, I said, "Would it kill you to let me look decent for one hour?"

I was nervous. Pam, Kit, and Evelyn were my best friends in the old neighborhood and I knew they'd been worried. They wanted me to stop wallowing now. Move on.

Which, really, I wanted too. But how?

As I rubbed at the spot on my blouse, I felt myself erecting careful barriers for my squishy self to hide behind. I wasn't entirely sure why

I'd agreed to go to lunch, but in fact, I hadn't made new friends, and I was sick to death of being alone all the time.

The bell rang again, and I dashed into the living room, startled anew—as I was every time I passed through it—by the room's absolute beigeness.

"Coming!" I cried.

But when I opened the door, it wasn't Pamela. It was my next-door neighbor, Roxanne, the one I'd seen the first day. We'd spoken, politely, when we met in the halls, but nothing more.

"Hi," she said in her throaty voice. "Sorry to bother you. I'm Roxanne, from next door?"

"Sure, hi."

"Do you have a cup of flour? I was making pancakes for the kids."

"Isn't this a school day?"

She inclined her head, and gave me a smile. It tilted her features, making her look very young and mischievous, like an elf. "It's our family tradition to take a day off to shop for spring clothes."

"Oh! Fun!" For a minute, I ached to have Giselle with me, so I could make her pancakes, go shopping at the Citadel, maybe. London, which is where her father had taken her, was no doubt more interesting. I was still fairly sure he'd done it, offered the trip over spring break, so Giselle would stay with him, not come to see me as we'd planned. He was furious with me over the house.

"Flour?" Roxanne prompted.

"Right." I blinked. "I honestly have no idea if I have any. Come in and let me check."

"Thanks." She looked around the naked living room, with the row of garden plants in clay pots marching around the baseboards. "Minimalist style! I like it."

I chuckled. "That's one way to look at it."

"Reality is fluid."

"I'll try to remember that." I paused. "By the way, I'm Nicole Carrington . . . er, Bridges." I shook my head. "I keep doing that."

"It takes a while," she said, and flicked bangs away from her face. She wore her thick black hair in a choppy, trendy cut that was flattering, but added to the tough, take-no-prisoners air around her. Her shoulder blades were sharp as wings. "How long have you been divorced?"

"Almost five months," I said, stinging with it. "How did you know?"

She lifted one shoulder, and leaned on the counter when I pulled open the pantry door. "You're living in Splitsville, honey."

"Splitsville?"

Her smile was sad. "Yeah, that's what we call this apartment complex."

"Are you divorced too?"

She nodded. "I can't afford to buy a house yet, so here we stay."

There on the cupboard shelf was an untouched five-pound sack of flour. "Aha! Success." I gave her the whole bag. "Just take it. I won't be using it anytime soon."

"Yeah? All right. I'll bring you one back when I go to the store later."

Pamela's voice sailed into the room from the front door, "Yoo-hoo! Anybody here?" She came around the short wall, putting her sunglasses on her head, the exquisitely foiled blonde of her hair setting off the ice-blue eyes. She looked like a travel poster for skiing in Aspen, where in fact, she and her athletic corporate lawyer husband kept a condo. "Jeez, Nicole, this place is empty as a tomb. Where's the furniture?"

I gave her a look with raised eyebrows. "Hello? Nothing much survived the explosion."

"Explosion?" Roxanne asked.

"Oh yeah," Pam said.

"Long story," I said to Roxanne.

Pamela extended a hand. "Hi, I'm Pamela."

"Roxanne." Her voice was cool. "Thanks. See ya."

We watched her leave and then Pamela leaped around the breakfast bar. "Give me a hug! I miss you!" Her lean arms were strong and familiar, and she smelled of something citrusy and clean. "You look great!"

"I do not, but thanks anyway." I brushed at the bloodstain on my blouse. "I'm going to have to change. I'll be out in a minute."

"Okay."

I paused. "You are not allowed to make up lies to make me feel good, Pam. Let's not do that, okay?"

"What?" She grinned. "You look better than the last time I saw you."

"Ha ha!" It was the middle of the night, when I blew up the house. "I'll be back in a minute."

~

Pamela parked behind the famous old arcade in the center of Manitou, and we walked across the wooden slats over the creek, toward the restaurant. Annie's Organix was on a side street just off the main drag, but even before we turned the corner, I could smell peaches and cinnamon.

"God, that smells fabulous," I said, breathing in. "I wonder what her secret is—that's the best peach crisp in the known world."

"How do you know it's not *apple* crisp? She does both."

"Because I can smell the peaches."

"I'll take your word for it." She pulled open the door to Annie's and a spill of scents poured into the street—peaches and cinnamon and coffee; a powdery sort of perfumed bread; and the sharp, astringent scent of dill. "How's Giselle doing?" she asked.

"Fine, I guess." A sore spot. "I haven't talked to her much the past couple of weeks, but she seems to be settling in very well. Straight A's last semester."

"It's killing you."

If I spoke of it, I'd cry, and I was tired of crying. "Let's not talk about my daughter, all right?"

It was killing me, the absence of Giselle. I missed my daughter. Not just the presence of her, but all the things I was missing about her life, the dailiness of her coming in from school, chattering or complaining

16

or yawning. The simple grace of her long back as she leaned into the fridge to get milk, serenely talking in the full confidence that I would listen no matter what she said. And she was right, of course.

I miss the smell of her clothes, piled pungently in the laundry room, redolent with her sweat and sleep, a scent I know so intimately you could give me a thousand blouses smelling of a thousand girls and I could pick Giselle's. I miss the sight of her shoes lying in a tumble by the door and the stacks of her books on the dining room table and the surprising, guttural earthiness of her laughter. I miss the shape of the bridge of her nose and the flutter of her hands and the way she would come into the kitchen and say, "Hey, Mom! Did you know . . ."

She loves me, my daughter, and I love her, and our bond is something I thought could not be breached, not ever, which is why I let her go with her father. Who has loved her more than anything on earth from the very moment of her arrival on the planet. I sometimes think it was his love of her, globalized, that is what led to his lack of faith in us. In me. How could he love me, when I represented the kind of woman who could—theoretically, politically—deprive her?

It's a twisted logic, but that's what we get for having such a twisted class structure in this country—all graded out according to a strict point system of coolness.

Oh, wait. America is a classless society. I forgot.

"Are you okay?" Pam asked.

I cleared my throat, trying to dislodge the bitterness clotted there. "Fine." Spying Kit and Evelyn sitting at the bar, I waved. "Let's just not make my miserable life the sole topic of conversation at lunch today?"

"No problem. We can talk about me, me, me."

I gave her a wry smile.

It was busy, and we had to make our way through knots of waiting customers around the old, heavy wooden bar. Kit and Evelyn pinned down the west side of the bar. Kit, a petite blonde with very short, tousled curls, wore a crisp pink blouse and khaki skirt, her legs tanned year-round. She taught fitness classes at the Y, and her forearms were like tiny rectangular planks.

"Hey, sweetie!" she said, kissing my cheek. Her makeup was always so good, I felt slightly skuzzy, and today I wish I'd paid more attention to foundation and powder. She held me at arm's length. "You look tired. This has been hard on you."

I want to say, "Duh," as if I were my daughter. Instead, I lifted one shoulder. "I'm okay."

Evelyn was the mother of our group, plump in her expensive, ethnic tunic and faux-faded jeans, as bosomy and comfortable as her slightly twangy Texas accent. Beneath the facade, however, was a barracuda, the wife of a mild-mannered computer engineer who'd stumbled into gold in the boom of the eighties. "Hi, Nicole. I'm so glad you could come today!"

"Thanks. Me too." I plucked at my bangs, smoothed my shirt. Couldn't think of anything more to say. It seemed, suddenly, that we didn't have anything in common anymore.

"How's everything going?" Kit asked brightly.

"The apartment? I'm in. Got the cable hooked up, everything settled."

"No, I meant the job hunt."

"Not great." Which was a slight understatement. It was not only not great, I had not had one single nibble on anything I'd sent out. Since I hadn't worked in twenty years and didn't have much experience before that, it wasn't a big surprise. Depressing, but not surprising. I'd worked the usual restaurant jobs as a student, then worked in Daniel's office in a variety of capacities over the years.

Then he hired a secretary. Who applied for, and landed, the job of wife.

"I've sent out quite a few résumés," I said, "but it's not like I have a lot to offer the market."

"Oh, don't say that!" Kit exclaimed. "You've done all that fundraising for the school, and the soccer league."

"Garage sales, Kit," I said gently. "People don't hire you to put on garage sales."

The bartender set down our mimosas, served in big bowls of wineglasses, with giant strawberries in them. "Enjoy."

Evelyn lifted her glass. "To fresh starts!"

I snorted. "Be careful what you wish for."

A small ripple of uncomfortable laughter went around the group as we touched rims. My sense of humor seems to have morphed into something a little brittle. Evelyn's cheeks reddened. "I meant for you, silly."

"I know. I'm sorry."

The hostess, a willowy woman with a longish skirt, came up to us clutching menus in her thin, long hands. "We have a table for you, ladies, if you want to follow me."

We gathered our drinks and purses and traipsed through the multi-windowed rooms, by little alcoves looking out to the sunny spring day. The light made me long for lilacs, banks and banks of lilacs blooming in the May air, making the air so thick with scent that walking through the neighborhood could perfume your clothes for the evening.

Spring. Fresh starts.

I could use one.

As we passed one alcove, a boisterous round of male laughter exploded out of the room. We four women all turned our heads to look. The men were mostly our age, in their forties or so, a few somewhat younger, all dressed in polo shirts and khakis, with a few wool sweaters. They glanced at us, but we were boring, just like the wives they had at home. A balding redhead with a freckled pate stood up and started talking.

"Blip Data, I bet," Kit said, mentioning a computer company in town.

"Or Oracle," Pam offered.

"No, definitely Blip Data." Evelyn waved at someone. "I recognize half of them. Must be a reward meeting. I heard they're doing that."

Since getting divorced, I'd been trying to remember to notice what men look like again. You just get out of the habit, you know, not noticing, unless they're Morgan Freeman or Russell Crowe or a particularly dashing cellist in the symphony.

I'd been finding it illuminating to notice them now—at the grocery store, at the gas station, restaurants, even in traffic. They tended to get a little too thin or a little too soft in their forties, with only a handful working hard to keep their figures. Many of the best-looking ones were balding, and the ones who had good hair preened about it.

These were computer geeks, and it was easy to pick out the skiers and the runners with their sharp shoulders; the plump dads with their exceedingly white arms. One tall bearded fellow had very good shoulders, and there was a man beside him who was very dark, with black curls. My type, always. Who knows why? It's been that way as long as I can remember, since I walked into third grade and sat down next to Alan Medina, the sexiest bad boy to walk the halls of Lincoln Elementary.

The hot guy looked up, saw me admiring him, and gave me a friendly smile. It shocked me to be caught. I ducked my head without acknowledging him.

Which made me feel like an idiot. I was relieved to be swept into the alcove where our table waited. The hostess left us with menus, and a busgirl rushed over to fill our glasses with water and lime and breathlessly rushed out the specials, a mushroom quiche and a chicken salad sandwich. Soup of the day was a savory pumpkin.

"Aha," I said to Pam. "There's the cinnamon, I bet."

"Right." She doesn't care. No one does.

I asked the girl, "Is there cinnamon in the soup?"

"I think so," she says. "Oh, and the other special today is peach cobbler."

At that, Pam grinned. "You're just weird, Nicole. That's all. Weird."

Kit plucked out her springy little curls that shone blondely even in the dull light. "By the way, Nikki, I am nearly out of my perfume. Can you make me some more, maybe a bigger bottle this time?"

"I can make some more, but not in a bigger bottle. It won't work as well."

"I still say you should open a perfume shop," Kit said.

"Not practical," Pam argued. "It would be impossible to make any real money."

"I think it's a great idea," Kit said. She was my main supporter in the group. Evelyn was almost religiously anti-perfume, even when I proved to her that she could wear my perfumes if I knew her list of allergies.

Kit genuinely loved perfume—real perfume, and especially classics like Chanel N°5 and Joy—and blending one for her had been a challenge and a delight. It took me three years to find exactly the right blend, and when I gave it to her several years ago for her birthday, it was such a hit that she found an antique Lalique perfume bottle on eBay to put it in.

"Pam is right," Evelyn said. "You need to find something with some security. You really are a good fundraiser. What about museums, those kinds of places?"

All three looked at me. "I don't know," I said. "Offices make me feel claustrophobic."

Kit leaned over the table. "You got a settlement, didn't you?"

Pam ducked her head, touched her upper lip. "Ahem."

"Very funny." I rolled my eyes. "I did get a settlement. Unfortunately, it was the house, which I blew up."

"Oh, you didn't do it. The house was old! The furnace blew," Evelyn said, and shuddered as delicately as a woman of her size could. "That's why I hate vintage anything—houses, clothes, whatever. Too much trouble."

"Well," I said with a shrug, "it blew up, and the insurance company is investigating, so until they rule out arson and negligence, I don't really have anything but a small"—I used my finger and thumb to illustrate—"stipend, most of which was spent on the move."

"He didn't have to be a cheapskate," Evelyn said. "Why did he do that? He should be shot anyway."

I hated to have to defend Dan, considering, but it had to be said. "Evie, we had a lot of equity in that house. He gave it to me, free and clear."

"Blood money," Pam said.

"Yes, but it was what I asked for. It was fairly good of him to send me more."

Kit put her hand on mine. In the sunlight, the diamonds in her wedding set sparked fire. Of the four of us, she was the wealthiest, and probably the happiest. Everyone who saw her with her husband assumed she was a trophy wife. Her husband was an enormously wealthy corporate executive twenty-five years older than his tiny, fit, blonde wife.

"It's nice that you want to avoid bitterness, Nicole," she said, "and I'm glad you have a good attitude, but he's a bastard and we all know it. You don't have to stand up for him."

"How can a woman just waltz in and take somebody's husband anyway?" Evelyn asked rhetorically.

Here we go. My divorce was the only thing we talked about now. "Let's not—"

"I knew that night we saw them in Aspen—" Evelyn halted.

Deep, dead silence swallowed the table. No one met my eyes. Beneath her fine white skin, Evie's jaw showed a wash of purple. The other two faces were ashen.

It was very hard to tell if it was a deliberate or a genuine slip of the tongue, but it was out.

"You knew?"

I looked at Pam. She rubbed a finger along the rim of her mimosa glass. Kit touched her upper lip with an index finger, as if she was about to say, "Shhh."

"You all knew? For how long?"

"Nikki—"

I held up a hand. "No, wait, I think I can figure this out. You went to Aspen together and I never even bothered to talk to Dan about my going because I knew he had a conference that weekend and I couldn't get away." Inclining my head, I counted backward in time. "That was more than two years ago."

They still didn't look at me.

I leaned forward and said, very quietly, "So my supposed best friends knew for at least a solid year that my husband was cheating on me, and none of you told me?"

"Nicole—"

I raised a hand to stop the protestation. Pam fell silent. I lifted a hand to my face, rubbed my forehead. "You know, there you are, thinking you've just about gotten through the mortification of this kind of thing, and then you get some new bit of information, and you're slammed all over again."

They looked miserable. But I thought of all the times we'd gone to lunch, to dinner at one or another of their houses, to school carnivals and soccer games, and they'd had this secret. How many times they sat there and made polite conversation, looked me in the eye over chicken Caesar salads, and knew.

I stood up, threw my napkin down on the table. "I hate this."

Pam put her hand around my wrist. Hard. Her fingers were cold. "Nikki, wait."

I yanked away from her, not enough to make a scene, just trying to get her to let go. "Please, Nik. Listen."

It felt as if there was something caught in my throat. With a panicky sense of airlessness, I sucked in a breath.

She took it as a sign. "What could we do?" she asked.

"Tell me?"

"It's not that easy. Maybe it would burn out, and he'd get tired of her, and then we'd have been in trouble too. Maybe it wasn't a big deal."

Kit said, "We didn't know what to do. It always seemed like you loved each other a lot."

"And what if," Evelyn, ever the practical one, added, "you did know, and were pretending not to, which would be a perfectly valid choice, and then you found out everybody knew?"

I sighed. Sank down into my chair. "You're right." I still felt like I'd swallowed a gallon of vinegar. I covered my face for a moment. "It's always tawdry, isn't it? Predictable and tawdry and degrading."

Kit rubbed my shoulders. "I'm so sorry, babe."

I raised my head. "Can we just not talk about me anymore for today? I'm sick of the subject of my divorce, frankly. I'd like to hear about something else. Anything else." I looked at them. "Deal?"

"Deal."

"I'll drink to that," Evelyn said, and raised her glass.

"Where the hell is our waitress anyway?" Pam said.

"Here I am!" A brunette with dishpan hands and black slacks rushed into the room, pencil at the ready. "Very sorry, ladies, but we are swamped and two servers quit last night."

"Two?"

The woman waved her hand. "They ran off to get married in Las Vegas. We'll be up to speed in a day or two when they can hire someone new, but today, I'm begging your patience."

Hire someone new. I looked at her, looked back over my shoulder toward the kitchen doors. A swift yearning burst in my mouth, as sharp as a pomegranate seed. I'd loved the restaurant business as a young woman, and had waited tables for quite a few years while I put myself through school. I could do it again. The bustle and hustle appealed to me. And it wasn't like everyone here was fresh out of school.

"I'm ready to order," I said, prompting the others.

3

Nikki's Perfume Journal Entry

Time: 11 a.m.
Date: July 2, 1972

<u>Scents</u>: root beer, coppery river water, bananas, earth, moss, blood, bubble gum, pines
<u>Bottle</u>: brown soda bottle with a cork
<u>Notes</u>: picnic in Cheyenne Canyon with my sisters, when Molly stubbed her toe

After lunch, I was restless. There wasn't much to do in the empty apartment. I called the insurance company to nag them again. Picked the dead leaves from a few plants. Checked email and found the predictable nothing. Went out to the balcony and leaned on the railing, my heart hollow with longing—a longing for my old life, the things I used to do. Hollow, echoey, empty.

A lot of it was missing my daughter. Her quicksilver laughter, the way her eyes turned up at the corners, the fierce, concentrated attention she gave to something that caught her. When it grew too terrible, I told myself it was the predictable hunger of an empty-nester. I'd had to let her go a little early, but it was the right choice.

Or at least I thought so most of the time.

And, okay, the rest of it is, I missed Daniel, too, damn it, whether anyone wanted me to say it or not. His big laugh. His twinkling eyes. The way he sang gospel music in the shower.

A thousand things. A million.

Before she'd dropped me off, Pam said, "I know this has been hard, Nicole, but you need to get over the divorce and get moving. I think they have a class at First Presbyterian Church and you could—"

"No." I knew about it. I wasn't going to go and sit around and whine with other divorcées. That was just pathetic.

How long did this part last? The grieving? Would I just wake up one morning and realize it had been ages since I'd thought about it?

I felt raw over the realization that my friends had all known he was cheating on me. How could they have kept quiet for so long? What kind of friends did that?

It wasn't that they were bad people. It just suddenly seemed to me that there wasn't much room in their world for anyone who wasn't just like them.

Worse to realize I'd been the same.

On the horizon, clouds billowed in over the mountains. The wooden railing dug into my elbows, and I felt the rich lunch in my belly, and it suddenly occurred to me that I was thinking of the job at Annie's Organix. I needed money, and it would at least give me something to do.

A swoop of anxiety went through my chest. Was this the answer I was looking for? Or was it just some foolish midlife crisis answer that would make me look like an idiot?

I paced inside, looked at the empty rooms. I hadn't bothered to go looking for furniture. I hadn't gone shopping for clothes. I ate frozen meals and cold cereal because it seemed like too much trouble to shop and cook.

I was sick of being frozen. Sick of being stuck. Even if I did something stupid, it would be movement. I should go apply.

In the living room, the phone rang, and hoping it was Giselle, calling to tell me about her adventures in London, I dashed back in to answer. "Hello?" I said breathlessly.

"Nicole?" my mother said.

Hope burst like an overfilled balloon. "Hey, Mom."

"I was just calling to see how you're doing."

"Feeling sorry for myself at the moment, honestly. Wishing I were in London with my daughter."

"I can understand that. Don't let it get you down too much, though. No point in indulging negativity if you can avoid it."

"Right." My throat felt tight, and I had to clear it. Our relationship was, at best, uneasy, but I did love her. "How are you? How's Bob?" Bob was her fourth husband—my father had been her first—and she and Bob had actually stayed married for more than a decade. He'd been diagnosed with colon cancer and was about midway through the first round of chemo.

She sighed. "All right. He's been pretty sick, but he's got a good attitude."

"How are you doing?"

"Oh, I'm fine." Her voice sounded thin. "Just a little tired."

"Are you sure you don't want me to come down there, Mom?" Not that I wanted to go, you understand. They'd moved to the Phoenix area four years ago, and loved it, but none of their children was anywhere close. My sisters were in Hawaii and LA, the first with her army husband, a major and safe from the current fracas in Iraq; the second an actress in a soap opera. If my mother needed help, there wasn't really anyone else to go.

"Don't be silly," she said. "You have enough on your plate. Bob's daughter Carole is going to come next week."

"Really." It was comment more than question, since Bob's children were not exactly fans of my mother—a.k.a. The Hussy Who Stole Their Father. "That's a surprise."

"She's worried about him. We all are."

"I thought it was going well, that they caught it early?"

"Well, sure, but it's still cancer, Nicole. It's still chemo."

"I'm sorry. You're right."

"Anyway, I called to see how you're liking your new apartment. Settling in?"

I looked at it. The walls were still bare. The plants lined up in a row against the wall gave it a little warmth anyway. The clay pots caught the dying embers of afternoon. "I guess. I'll have it in shape by summer."

"I'm sure you will. I think you're going to like the fresh start, really."

"I guess."

"You know who I dreamed about the other day?"

"Nope. Who?"

"Your friend Mark, remember him? The one who died?"

Prince Valiant hair, blue eyes, freckles. "Yes."

"He was picking carnations," she said. "Pink carnations. I always have liked the way they smelled."

"Me too." A little plucking ache pierced my lungs and I walked across the room and rapped on my door. "Hey, Mom, there's someone at the door. I have to go."

"All right, sweetie. Take care."

"You're the one. Do something nice for yourself today, huh?"

I hung up, and stood for a moment looking at the horizon from my patio. She seemed distracted, tired, aging. The aging was no mistake—I'd been trying not to think about it, but she was nearly seventy. Not young.

There was too much on my plate to think about that, too, so I turned on the radio to the local classical station and wandered into the spare room with a watering pot to tend the scented geraniums with their lemony and cinnamony deliciousness; a plant called Cuban oregano with spicy, velvety leaves. Pots of carnations, in all colors, an ordinary flower with an extraordinary, peppery scent.

I'd grouped the sun-loving herbs—hyssop and thyme and pots of ferny French lavender—where they captured the most light, and they were thriving. I poured water into the pots and watched air bubble up from the dirt, distractedly wondering if I was just going to keep them in pots all summer. Maybe I needed to at least get some whiskey barrels for the balcony, repot some of them out there.

No. What I needed most was a job, to get me out of the house, get some money flowing. Before I could chicken out, I sat down at my desk and wrote a letter of application for the job at Annie's Organix. Maybe it was crazy. Maybe I was too old. Whatever. It was at least some forward movement. When I finished proofing it, I printed it out, carried it to my car, and drove back to Manitou.

The day was getting dark and blustery as a storm moved in, the clouds lowering hard on the blue peaks all around the tiny town. I had to duck my head against a gust of wind as I got to the front door of the restaurant.

A sign?

"Don't be stupid," I muttered aloud, and yanked open the door. The lunch rush was well over, and the bartender from earlier was wiping down the stools with a damp cloth.

"Can I help you?" she asked. "Did you forget something?"

Suddenly, I felt foolish. She was close to my age, I thought, but with a lean, youthful suppleness to her body that made me think she was probably a runner. Fit, in other words, youthful in body if not face. But I blurted out my wish anyway. "I was hoping to fill out an application. If you haven't filled the waitress positions."

"Oh." She hid her surprise quickly, her glance flickering down my legs, to the jeans, to the shoes. "Sure. Annie's not here—she's gone to do some shopping—but you can fill out the application and I'll give it to her when she gets back."

I filled out the simple application, and asked for a paper clip so I could attach the brief letter explaining my background and the reason for the outdated work credentials.

"Thanks," the woman said. "We really need help. Do you have a second telephone number?"

"No. But I always have my cell with me."

"Cool. I'm sure she'll call you."

Outside, I felt oddly buoyant. It was a little crazy. It would probably be a terrible job and I'd quit in a blaze of disaster and despair. If my friends found out, they'd be horrified. I was almost certainly too old to do that kind of work, to brutalize my ancient body that way.

But standing there on the street in Manitou, which I'd loved all my life, with a wind blowing down from the mountains, carrying the taste of snow that still covered the Peak, I felt a whisper of hope. It might not be the answer, but it was an answer for the moment.

I didn't have to be anywhere. The rain hadn't arrived yet. Manitou was one of my favorite places. A tiny hamlet built on the outskirts of Pikes Peak, it was named for healing springs that had drawn tuberculosis patients at the turn of the century. When I was a child, my father brought my sisters and me here on hot summer evenings to eat ice cream and play games in the arcade.

I tucked my hands into my pockets, thinking of the days when my friends and I skipped high school to come to Manitou on the city bus; when the castle was a warren of apartments with red-painted floors; when my father, before his breach, had driven a tourist bus to the top of Pikes Peak. The town was eclectic and odd and beautiful; it attracted bohemians and dreamers, runners and eccentrics.

I passed a real estate office with notices plastered in the picture window, and slowed down to look at them. Not much available in what would be my price range, and I wandered on. Above the street, elbows and shoulders and knees of brilliant blue mountain rose from the strip of quaint shops—the saltwater taffy bar, the tourist traps with cheap copper bracelets, the boutiques and T-shirts.

Between the real estate office and the tourist store was a vacant little shop, no more than ten or twelve feet wide. A kitten snoozed inside the dusty window, standing up straight, only his head bowed. His serene oblivion snared me and I paused. Daniel was allergic to cats, but I'd always loved them, and this one had the kind of fur I most liked—not quite long hair, not quite short, just that medium length that was so very, very silky. I could imagine exactly how he'd smell, curled up on my shoulder, the soft fur against my neck.

Something must have alerted him to my presence, because he startled awake, and dashed into the back of the shop.

It was only then that I noticed the shop itself. It was a narrow little thing, perfect for something so esoteric and what some might—had—called ridiculous as my hand-blended perfumes. It seemed a place tourists might wander into, and because they'd never see anything like it again, they'd slap money down on impulse for a rare, hand-blended perfume, a single ounce that smelled exactly like the afternoon of their wedding.

My throat started to close, and I turned away. One thing at a time. As if to underscore that idea, my phone buzzed against my leg. I didn't recognize the number, but answered hopefully. "Hello?"

"Hi, this is Zara Holsworth, from Annie's Organix. Annie asked me to call and see if you could come in tomorrow at ten-thirty for an interview."

"Yes!"

"All right. See ya then."

A wind brushed my face, blew my hair across my mouth. I smelled rain, and any minute now, there would be a downpour. But I didn't move. For a minute, I only stood there next to the car with the phone in my hand, letting pleasure creep through me.

One step.

~

The next morning, I put on the new clothes I bought when I heard I had an interview—a pair of black slacks, a neatly pressed white shirt, a long, thin scarf looped around my neck. My hair, grown well past my shoulders now, much to my amazement, fell in good waves instead of a zillion uncontrollable curls. I put on my good silver-and-turquoise earrings, and a silver cuff bracelet, and the slightest of lipsticks. It seemed a place where too much makeup would be frowned upon.

In the post-breakfast hour, Annie's was quiet. A small group of people who looked like mountain bikers or runners in CoolMax T-shirts and high-end athletic shoes ate muffins and free-range eggs in the first dining room. The rest were a quiet lot who read or stared out the windows at the view. I heard the clink of flatware against plates. It smelled of coffee and coriander.

I looked for a hostess, but there was no one at the little stand, and I headed toward the bar area. It, too, was underpopulated. Only a single man sat there, reading a newspaper.

But—oh! Hadn't I seen him the day before? He was dressed in a simple, business-casual way—long-sleeved shirt, khakis, good leather loafers. His hair contradicted the simplicity of the clothes, riotous and complex, black hair that tumbled in ringlets around a strong, Mediterranean sort of face.

As I sat down, he glanced up from the paper and gave me a polite nod. A pot of tea sat in front of him, served the English way, in a plump ceramic pot with a small pitcher of whole milk. Annie, a European, was known for that, pots of good English tea, served with scones and exquisite pastries and fresh cream.

I took a stool three seats down from the man, settled my purse on the bar. Folded my hands. Tried to pretend I wasn't nervous. That I didn't want this job very badly.

The scent of the man wafted over to me. Very strong. I focused on trying to pinpoint the elements—ginger, coffee, cinnamon, and below those things the elusive note that's as unique to each person as a fingerprint. His smelled of summertime. I let it wash over me, taking it apart: pine needles drying in the high-altitude sun, very clean water chuckling somewhere nearby, an earthiness of mushrooms, and one astringently sour note, like sticky sap, to bring it all into focus.

Heady. The mix came off him in waves, a little too strong, really, as if he might be sweating. It made the back of my neck ripple.

I didn't look at him. He turned a page of the paper. Soft classical music played over the speakers of the restaurant, cello, something I couldn't quite place. The barista/bartender, a youngish man this time, came over. "Can I help you?"

"I'm here for an interview," I said.

"Oh, good! You must be Nicole."

"Nikki."

He smiled. "I'm Jason." A little plump, with kind blue eyes, he said, "Annie is concocting the last of her soup of the day, and told me to get you something to drink and apologize profusely."

"No problem."

He put a napkin down in front of me. "What would you like? A latte? A chai, maybe? Mine is very good."

"All right, I'll try it." I caught another snip of the music. "What is this music, do you know?"

"I don't know. Something classical."

"Right."

The man next to me said, in a voice as mysterious and layered as twilight, "Marin Marais."

"Sorry?"

"The music," he said, "is Marin Marais." The accent was British, but something a little more than that.

Glad for the excuse, I looked at him, aware of a pleased little ruffling along my nerves, on my shoulders and my arms, the small of my back—all places that hadn't been touched and remembered it. He was a delight to look at, my type exactly, those curls, that beautiful nose. He had excellent hands, too, long and dark with well-tended nails. A weakness of mine, good hands.

"Of course." I nodded. "Thank you."

"Are you a fan of classical music?" he asked. There was a delicious, slight rolling of the *r*, along with the open British *a*'s. Wonderful. "Or Marais in particular?"

"Well, especially cello. I studied it as a girl."

"Ah. My instrument was clarinet."

"Were you good?"

"No." A twinkle lit his dark eyes, the faintest hint of a smile on those beautifully shaped lips. "You?"

"Terrible." I grinned back. "But I love music anyway."

"So do I."

It was small talk, something I'd forgotten. I'd forgotten that the words lent a moment to connect in other ways. His eyes flitting over my face, touching eyes, hair, lips. Mine gathering details of wrist, neck, mouth.

The bartender ambled away to make my drink, presumably. The man said, "Did you know that 'chai' is just the word for tea in Hindi?" His accent made me think of PBS imports, of London broadcasters in worn-torn lands. Very British, a little reserved.

The word came to me: "posh."

"I didn't know that," I said now. "That's kind of funny, isn't it?"

"Yes." His mouth quirked. His eyes were luminous, the lashes so black they seemed dewy. "English is a very greedy language."

With great originality, I said, "That's true."

"Did I see you here yesterday?" *Hyeah* in British.

I was startled into a blush. "I was here. Were you?"

"Yes," he said simply.

In a flash, I remembered the group of computer geeks, the beautiful man. "You were with the Blip Data people."

"And you were wearing a turquoise blouse."

A pleased flush ran through me. He had seen me! He'd obviously liked what he'd seen.

Boy, did I ever need that.

He smoothed his newspaper, picked up his cup. "Are you applying to work here?"

"I hope so."

"It's a good place. Very good tea." He smiled, and it was an understated thing, a little smile in his eyes, poking fun back at himself. "And chai."

Jason brought my chai, but he didn't put it down. "Annie is ready to talk to you, if you want to follow me."

"Oh!" I stood up. Butterflies whirled around in my stomach. I really wanted this job, and wanting things too much had not been particularly good for me the past few years.

"Bye," I said to the man.

He lifted a hand.

The boy led me through a pair of swinging doors with round windows in them. With a swish-swish, we left the world of the diners behind and entered Kitchen World. A smell of carrots and soap and sterilizer and faint rot—I thought there might be a bad drain somewhere—and just now, pickles.

Restaurant kitchens are wonderful, mysterious, glorious places, and this was a particularly good one. Old, with wooden floors mopped pale, and a row of high, multipaned windows in the rear that let in light. The back door was propped open to a view of thick trees, and I could hear the creek.

A thin, sixty-something woman with a sleek pixie of silver hair chopped dill pickles on an acrylic cutting board. Her hands were strong, tanned, adorned only with a plain, narrow wedding band. Behind her on the enormous stove was a twenty-quart aluminum pot.

"Is that coriander?" I asked, stopping to breathe it in.

Annie lifted a brow. Her skin was largely unlined and her eyes were quite startlingly blue, almost turquoise. "Very good," she said with a slight German accent. "Most people do not recognize that scent so quickly."

"Oh," I said dismissively, "I just have a good nose."

"Do you cook?"

I shrugged. "Not much. Not anymore."

"Ah." She scraped pickles into a clear glass bowl. "Why do you want to work here?"

"I need a job."

"Clearly. Why here?"

Inhaling, I cocked my head. "I like it. I like the food and the organic angle. It feels nourishing. And—" I smiled. "It smells good."

She liked that. "How long since you worked?"

"Is it obvious that I haven't for a while?"

"I read your application, dear," she said, not unkindly, "but yes, there is that air about you, that sudden fling into the world."

"Oh," I said, stung. I plucked at the buttons of my blouse. "It's been a while."

She put the knife down, wiped her hands on a white towel tucked into the waist of her bibbed white apron. "Women in their forties usually prefer other work. Less physical. A bank teller, maybe. A secretary. Why pick a restaurant?"

It was not the kind of question I had anticipated. "I hate sitting inside an office. A bank—" The idea made me feel strangled. "No, thanks. I did some secretarial work for my ex and really hated it, honestly. When I heard you were shorthanded, it seemed like a lot more appealing job."

"Why should I hire you?"

I met her eyes. "For one thing, since I have no life, I'll be reliable. No running off to get married to another server."

She grinned. "And?"

"And I love food, taking care of people, being in movement, instead of sitting around." I lifted a shoulder. "I don't know how long it will take for me to get up to speed, but I'll work as hard as I can."

"Your base pay is not much," she said. "But the tips are quite good. You'll make a good wage."

I nodded.

"Can you start tomorrow?"

"Yes!"

"Then we will try, shall we?"

My heart squeezed. "Really?"

"Yes." She picked up her knife again. "We cannot function with only six servers."

"I'll be here."

"We'll start you at breakfast, which is a little slower, as you see out there. Do you have a problem with mornings?"

"No! I love them! What time?"

She raised an eyebrow. "Five-thirty."

"No problem."

Taking a peeled, boiled egg from a bowl, she said, "Have Jason give you a shirt and the training book."

"Thank you." I wanted to shake her hand, but she waved me on.

"Don't worry," she said. "You'll be all right."

I wandered back into the restaurant, feeling buoyant, almost giddy with accomplishment. I had a job! It was hard to keep myself from grinning ear to ear, like a little kid with a new finger painting.

The dark-eyed man was still at the bar, and he shook his paper, smiled at me. "It must have gone well."

I let the smile out. "Yes, it did."

"Congratulations." He held out a hand. "I am Niraj." The *j* was soft, buzzing.

"Cool name." Grinning in happiness, I accepted the gift. "I'm Nicole."

"Both *N*s," he said, as if it joined us. "Nice to meet you."

Even in my giddiness, it was impossible not to notice his scent piercing through the heady thickness of freshly brewing coffee, and the cinnamon tea, and the undernotes of soap and bar cleaner, and a thousand other restaurant smells—there was his skin. The perfumer in me tried to pin it, and failed.

Jason came over, his arms full. "Annie said to give you these—shirts, manual, menu, basic stuff. You don't need to get too wrapped up in all of it just yet—she won't quiz you or nothing."

I took the load. Blinked. "Thanks. I guess I'll see you tomorrow, first thing."

"Cool."

The British man said, "See you soon, Nicole."

"All right. So long!"

4

Nikki's Perfume Journal Entry

Time: 10:30 a.m.
Date: Wednesday, April 12, 2006

Elements: fresh coffee brewing, ginger, pine needles drying in the sun, tangy sweat, tea
Bottle: dark green
Notes: the man sitting at the bar at Annie's Organix

One thing that startled me, post-divorce, was how much hostility some widows direct toward divorcées. I'm not particularly comfortable with married women, either, but their sins of ever-so-subtle superiority can be forgiven since they're born of cluelessness. Widows should know better.

Two months after Daniel moved out, I'd been hustled to an ice-cream social at the gigantic First Presbyterian Church, where one of my former neighbors, Evelyn, was a member. She had insisted it would be good for me to get out, talk to other people.

I didn't know until I arrived that it was for newly single adults. We were all dressed like teachers, with sweaters and skirts and loafers. I'd tried to make myself presentable, though there wasn't a lot I could do about the pallor that comes of sitting inside on your couch and crying for eight weeks.

Daniel had moved to California and taken our Giselle with him, a decision we'd all made together, and one that had left me alternately hating myself for my cowardice and congratulating myself for being a big person. Either way, it left me echoing around that big house alone. It was good, in a way, to be out in the world, even if it was some dippy ice-cream social. In the eyes of some of the others, I saw the same shell-shocked robotic movements, as if we'd all forgotten how to move and someone programmed us. Walk. Talk. Smile.

Evelyn deserted me to go help in the kitchen. I carried a strawberry sundae over to a long table and sat down next to a woman who looked nearly as miserable as I felt. She was older than me, perhaps her mid-fifties, and her long salt-and-pepper hair was pulled back sharply from her face. "Hi," I said. "Mind if I join you?"

She half smiled. "Who dragged you here?"

I nodded toward Evelyn, talking with a group of other women near the door. "How about you?"

"My daughter. She's worried that I am giving up my will to live."

Curiously, I asked, "Have you?" The thought had crossed my mind. Not to do anything to actively kill myself, but giving up my will to live and pining away held a certain Victorian appeal.

"No. I just want everyone to leave me alone and let me get over this in my own way."

"Me too. How long has it been?"

"Eight months. He died on the golf course, unexpectedly. We were supposed to leave for a trip to Scotland the next day."

"I am so sorry."

She lowered her eyes. "Thanks." We poked our ice cream. "How about you?" she asked.

"Two months ago. Another woman."

"Oh, divorce," she said. "Well, maybe you'll work it out eventually."

"Since he's moved to another state with this other woman, I seriously doubt it." A half strawberry slid down the mountain of ice cream and I caught it with my spoon, struggling to keep my voice even. "It was a shock. Never saw it coming."

"There's always signs of a breach like that coming," she said.

"Are there?" I raised my head. "I didn't see them. And I feel like—" I struggled. "Like I woke up one morning in somebody else's life, and I don't have any instructions for how to live this one."

"You'll be all right."

Her faint dismissal stung in a place I'd not felt before. "You know, it's not that different, losing a husband to divorce or death."

"Yes it is. You can pick up the phone and call him if you want to. You can see his face again. You know he's still in the world, somewhere."

"Yeah," I said, "and yours still loved you when he died, didn't he? You don't have to deal with loss and betrayal, just the loss."

"You don't understand."

"Did your husband die of a heart attack?"

She nodded.

"There must have been signs. Why didn't you do something to save his life?" I stood up, trying to hide my tears, and walked out of the stupid room and out of the stupid reach of well-meaning friends, and walked all the way home through the stupid wind that at least dried my stupid tears.

~

After getting the job at Annie's, I could hardly wait to get home and call my daughter. The ringer was a song I didn't recognize, and it played the same little bar three times before it flipped over to voice mail.

"Hello, this is Giselle," she said in a voice that enunciated her consonants clearly. "I'm in London, so leave a message and I'll call you when I get home."

Damn. I'd forgotten. With a swift, sharp stab of jealousy, I imagined her on a red double-decker bus, with daffodils blooming in clouds, while a soft drizzly rain made the world cool and damp.

I thought of her with her father and his proper Southern belle of a wife seeing Trafalgar Square and the conservatory at Kew Gardens, which I'd always, always, always wanted to see, and the Thames, and—

"Argh!" I cried, and wished for an old-fashioned kind of phone to slam down hard. Instead, all I could do was flip the cell phone shut and throw it—harmlessly—on the counter.

My resentments rose, fluttering through my chest like bat wings. Trying to escape them, I hauled open the patio door, stepped between the pots and their new fronds, and leaned on the balcony. The light was fading, leaving behind only a long line of gold over the top of the mountains.

Twilight settled on the landscape, darkening the line of mountains, making me think of winter suppers and families gathered around a table in a humid kitchen. A howl burned in my chest. Loneliness, yes, but this one was particular: missing my daughter was a constant pain, as if fingernails were being yanked out, say, or nails pounded into my heart.

I clenched my teeth. This wasn't about me. It was for Giselle, for the education she could receive, for the lifestyle her father could give her. Even with all the money in the world, I couldn't give her the education she was getting in California.

Lately, I sometimes thought about moving there. If I lived nearby, I could see her more often. We'd have a chance to be easier with each other, not so much on, as happened with the noncustodial parent. I needed long stretches with her sleeping too late and huffing over having to do dishes and all the other dear, normal details that went along with teenagers.

My beautiful, brilliant daughter. The best thing I'd ever do in my life, no matter what else happened. Think of her, not myself. Today, Giselle was in London, breathing in the air of that lovely city, gaining experience and culture. Hooray for her.

Below me, in the parking lot, a young mother carried a baby on her hip and held the hand of a toddler, and shepherded another with her voice. She had the look of an army wife, of which there were a number in the buildings, many whose husbands were in Iraq.

Which made my situation look pretty whiny in comparison.

Get over yourself, Nikki.

I turned on the radio to the local classical station and was about to fill up my watering can when the doorbell rang. Surprised, I carried the can with me, fully expecting it to be a flyer delivery or other such excitement.

Instead, it was my neighbor, Roxanne. She wore simple jeans and a paisley turquoise peasant blouse that showed a slice of elegantly slim collarbone. "Hi," she said, holding up a grocery bag. "I'm returning your flour, and"—she held up the other hand, which obviously held a bottle of something—"I've brought a welcome gift." She spied my watering can. "Unless you're busy?"

"God, no. Come in!" I swung the door open, gestured her in. "There's still no furniture, but we can sit on the stools at the breakfast bar. Do you want some coffee or something?"

"I could drink some coffee," she said. Again the luscious, Lauren Bacall smokiness of her voice snared me. "Or"—she raised the bottle—"I have wine."

I grinned. "Oh, chardonnay wins every time."

"I thought you looked like a chardonnay kind of girl." She settled at the counter. Her smile was warm and somehow mischievous. "My ex is going to pick up my children for the weekend and I thought it would be a nice chance for us to get to know each other a little."

From the drawer, I took out a heavy-duty corkscrew, passed it over, and took down some glasses. "This is a treat. I was just feeling sorry for myself."

"It gets easier," she said, taking cheese and crackers out of the bag too.

"Oh, I'm pretty good at it already," I said.

Roxanne grinned. "If you can make jokes, you're doing pretty well."

I settled on the stool beside her. "I'm so glad to meet someone else who is divorced."

"This is a very married place, isn't it?"

"It is."

She poured wine into each of our glasses, and we raised them. "Welcome to the neighborhood, Nikki."

I clinked my glass with hers, feeling almost absurdly grateful for the possibility of a friend. "And to you, for being the welcoming committee."

"You're welcome." She put her glass down. "It was really hard for me at first too. It's like that little stretch of time after you've had a baby, and you want to tell everybody about the delivery?"

I laughed in recognition. "Yeah."

"Women," she said, "need to tell stories about what happens to them. That's how we get it to make sense."

"Interesting. What do men do?"

"Have heart attacks, and sex with strange women."

I snorted.

"So tell me about yourself, Nicole. Does anyone call you Nikki?"

"Yes. Please. I like it better."

"So you're divorced. No children?"

"No, I have a daughter. She's fifteen."

"She lives with her dad?" My face must have given some sour signal because she waved a hand. "Sorry. Tell me to back off if I get too personal."

"No, it's fine. Giselle lives with her dad."

"And you don't mind?"

I closed my eyes. "I mind a lot, but he has a lot more money. They live in Malibu, and she's having a great time."

She nodded. "Do you mind if I ask what the explosion was that your friend talked about?"

"Oh, that." I turned my wineglass in a circle. "I had a house over on Wood Avenue—"

"Nice!"

"—and the furnace exploded. Which is why I'm here."

"No insurance?"

"Oh, yeah, there was, but—" I cleared my throat. Took a sip of wine. "Uh . . . an inspector had told me to have the furnace replaced, and I just didn't get to it, and now the insurance company is trying to avoid paying."

"Ah." Roxanne's dark eyes glittered. She looked at the empty living room, then back at me. "It will be great fun to buy new furniture. You'll get to make all the choices yourself."

The words blew a sense of possibility through my chest. "I never thought about it that way."

"Well, now you can. What kind of furniture do you like?"

I thought of the living room in the old house. "I had a lot of over-stuffed, chintzy things, but the rooms sort of required it. Daniel liked all that heavy wood and sturdy stuff that weighs a million tons."

Roxanne nodded, her delicate features patient. "And what did you pick?"

I thought of the niche in the kitchen. "I had a blue glass vase I liked to fill with sunflowers, and this tiny art deco table."

She smiled and spread her hands. "That sounds like an easy place to start."

"It does," I said in some wonder. "Thank you."

"No problem."

"What did you buy, the first thing?"

She took a teeny, tiny sip of wine. "A garlic press. I love garlic, and my ex hates the smell of it. Now whenever I'm pissed at him, and I know he's going to come get the kids or something, I eat like a whole head of roasted garlic."

I laughed. "So the divorce isn't that friendly?"

She widened those blue eyes, which were, I suddenly noticed, almost exactly the same color as that blue glass vase I'd loved. "You mean I'm actually sort of hiding my bitterness a little now?" Her mouth was rueful, that pained mix of ashamed and furious that seemed so much a part of the game. "No, it's a very unfriendly, unhappy divorce."

"It's been two years?"

"Yep. That's actual final divorce, now. We were separated and going back and forth, trying to make it work for a couple of years before that."

I wondered how that would feel, a year from now. Three years from now. "Tell me it gets easier."

"It does." She took a delicate sip from her glass. "Takes a while, though, so don't beat yourself up if you're not over it in five minutes. People kept telling me to get over myself, and it pissed me off. It was hard." She lowered her eyes. "It's still hard."

"Thank you for saying that."

"People just don't understand. They mean well."

"I'm sure."

"To good times," she said.

"To understanding," I replied.

We touched rims and drank.

~

Not even the slight leakage of dawn had begun when I set out for Annie's the next morning. It felt like having a secret to start my day when the streets were still empty. I loved the glimpses of other lives I saw through windows lit with lamps. At a traffic light, I sat for a long time, and no other cars ever showed up.

The front door was locked at Annie's. I knocked on the glass, and the young man—Jason—from yesterday opened it, smiling cheerfully. "Hi, Nicole. I've been watching for you—forgot to tell you to go around to the back in the mornings."

"Thanks."

"We'll go to the kitchen first," he said.

"Okay."

He led the way through the restaurant. I heard laughter and women's voices coming from the kitchen, along with the sound of dishes clattering, water being run, a radio playing quietly over the sound system, something baroque, though I couldn't quite pin down the composer. Each dining room was lit up, and a girl about twenty-one or twenty-two had a fistful of pink carnations in her hands, which she was putting in tiny vases on the tables.

Passing into Kitchen World, we were met with a blast of sound and light and scent—the overhead lights were bright and strong, the radio was louder, the dishwasher was running. Annie and another woman stood at the butcher-block cutting area, and a skinny girl with multiple facial piercings and tattoo sleeves on both arms washed a giant steel bowl.

"Hey, everybody," Jason said. "Here's Nicole."

"Nikki," I said, lifting a hand in a wave.

"Hi," the dishwasher said. "Cool earrings."

I touched them. A Spanish-style silver and amber pair, not expensive, but pretty. "Thanks."

Annie smiled. "Good morning, Nicole." Her German tongue lingered slightly on the *l*. "We're glad to see you. This is Mary." She waved to the other woman, an African American somewhere between forty and midfifties with perfectly unlined skin and an Alfre Woodard mouth. She didn't smile. I felt my measure being taken.

Mary dried her hands on a bar towel. She was preparing something from a cookbook I vaguely recognized, and I paused. "Do you mind?" I asked, pointing to the cookbook.

She waved a hand. "Go ahead."

"Thought so," I said, looking at the cover, which showed two attractive, middle-aged black women. "*Spoonbread & Strawberry Wine*! I have such a battered copy of this cookbook. I absolutely love it."

"What's a white girl like you doing with this book?"

I raised one eyebrow. "Sorry, I didn't bring my credentials with me." When she had the grace to look at least slightly abashed, I said, "Somebody gave it to me."

"Somebody black, I reckon."

"Yeah, it was."

Mary grinned. The expression gave her face an entirely different aspect, made her look a lot younger. "You have favorite recipes?"

"The sweet potato salad with pineapple, by far. But I also love, love, love the triple-decker butterscotch pie."

"Damn. Me too. Love it. Won't be eating that around here, but I'm making the potato salad this afternoon. This crowd likes it a lot."

"Cool." I thought it funny that a Southern-style cookbook could be adapted to the Colorado healthy-lifestyle organic cooking that Annie's offered, but why not?

"We'll have to talk some more about food, but this mornin', let's get you started."

She took me around the kitchen, illuminating various stations. There was a giant blackboard on the wall with the day's specials, with ingredient lists—which I presumed was for the allergy prone—and the choices available. The morning's breakfast special was an egg casserole with scallions, swiss and gouda cheeses, and layers of spinach, served with whole grain walnut muffins, or oatmeal made with fresh berries and served with raisin toast. My stomach growled.

"It's a small operation back here, just me and Annie in the morning, with another girl who comes in at lunch," Mary said. "So you do your own garnishes. You'll pick up your plates here," she said, and showed me the pass-out bar, traditional and old, with lights and a metal shelf. "This'll get very hot after a couple hours, so don't burn yourself." She turned around to a long counter against the wall. "Breakfast has a garnish of fruit—usually grapes, one strawberry, and an orange or grapefruit slice, and you'll get your own breads. Penny will show you all of that."

"I should have brought a little notebook."

She nodded. "Tomorrow. For now, just remember two things: you do your garnishes, and keep your eye on that board. If I erase something, we're out of it. I can't be bothered trying to remember which girl I told. We're out, I just walk over there and erase it."

"All right. Seems simple enough."

Her rich-looking mouth quirked. "Yeah, well, you'd think so."

Mary continued the kitchen tour—dish and trash, walk-in fridge, which I wouldn't have much call to enter, and the little door beside the big one that opened to a series of shelves with little silver pitchers on trays, and a box of whole oranges, grapefruits, clusters of red grapes.

The waitress who had been in the other room came up. "I'm stealing her now. We have a lot to cover." She smiled at me. Her face was pricelessly fresh, her skin dewy, no makeup and none needed. Freckles were scattered across her nose, and her hair was braided tightly into plaits that fell down her back. "Ready?"

"Sure."

"I'm Penny," she said. "You're Nicole?"

"Nikki."

"Let's go out front. We open at seven, and I want to get you oriented as much as possible before then."

"There's more than just us, isn't there?"

"Barely," she said, and gave me an apologetic lift of the eyebrows. "There will be three servers—you, me, and Janny—but I'm not going to lie, there should be four. Zara—the blonde barista, you met her?"

I nodded.

"She can take a few tables, but usually she's pretty busy at the bar, so we try not to overload her too much."

Panic sucked the air from my lungs. "You know I haven't done this in years. I'm going to be terrible."

She smiled. "No you won't."

"You don't know! I feel way over my head. Maybe this was—"

Penny laughed, and put her hand on my arm. "Breathe. Trust me, you're going to be fine. I'm not going to throw twenty tables at you—only a couple to get started, and you can do it. I'll let you have the easy customers to start with, all right?"

I sucked in a deep breath, let it go. "Okay. Right. Breathe."

"The truth is, we are desperately shorthanded, and just having you take two or three tables is going to help tremendously. We've closed one dining room for a few days, and we've got a fourth waitress coming in at lunch, so we'll be all right, okay?"

I nodded.

"Let me show you where everything is." We went to the service area, and she showed me the coffee machine, the pots of milk and empty tin pots for milk, and the butter, condiments, baskets for bread. There were rows of industrial gray plastic bins for forks, spoons, knives, and above them, shelves for tiny bowls.

I barely heard her over the roaring panic in my ears.

What could I possibly have been thinking, coming to work in a restaurant? I was going to be a terrible, flaming disaster, and I'd never be able to come into Annie's again.

But I was stuck just now. I had to stay for today anyway.

~

By the time the first customers arrived, I felt better. Penny had walked me through everything. I would have only a few tables.

I could do this.

It was quiet to start with—the table of regulars Penny had described, a genial pair who read their newspapers and sipped coffee in the sunshine coming through the windows.

After an hour, close to three-quarters of the tables in the restaurant were full, and I had just had my third turnover on two tables. There were tips in my pocket. I had worked up a light sweat, and had been a little flustered trying to remember things a couple of times, but mostly felt okay.

After two hours, I felt like the queen of the world, fully in control of my little three-table section, and it was nearly nine-thirty. The rush—such as it had been—would no doubt be done very soon, and then I'd have a chance to regroup and train for lunch.

I could do this. With a sense of optimism, I went to the coffee area and started to make a new pot and then deliver the two tickets in my pocket. Penny bustled into the alcove, and I remembered to tell her, "We're out of oatmeal."

"Thank you," she said, and slammed metal teapots on a tray. "No more muffins either. Just give them another biscuit."

The bell on the door rang, and we both looked over our shoulders. "Uh-oh," she said.

There was a little knot of women at the door, from their thirties to their sixties, outfitted in Gore-Tex fleeces and Land's End cotton turtlenecks and sturdy walking shoes. "What?"

"Annie's Amblers," she said. "They have a longer name, but I can't think of it now. They're one of the walking clubs."

"One of the walking clubs?"

"There's a bunch of 'em around here." She sighed. "This is one of the larger groups. We're about to get slammed, I think."

As we stood there, two more came in. They were the kind of women who lived in my old neighborhood: well-to-do, healthy, clear-sighted. I wondered suddenly what it would feel like to wait on someone I knew from, say, the PTA or soccer club or violin recitals. "Is there something I should be doing to get ready?"

She nodded. "Here's the plan," she said, and laid out my instructions.

~

It went well enough. I made some small mistakes—forgetting to bring juice to one man, and nearly mixing up the orders of two tables another time, realizing I'd left the coffeepot empty another.

But for the most part, I handled the small number of other tables that came into the restaurant, as well as ran backup for Penny, garnishing plates, pouring refills on coffee, refilling the little bowls of butter.

It was weirdly empowering, to master something. Do something new. Take a step forward and do okay with it.

Zara showed me the ropes for lunch. The specials were corn chowder and a layered phyllo-and-spinach casserole. Sandwich was goat cheese and tomato on olive bread. The baskets switched over, too, to warm servings of small, hefty brown rolls.

By noon, there was a waiting list, and Zara started taking tables here and there, and Jason did a lot of backup, and I was feeling the strain of serving five tables. Penny was handling twice as many tables as she ordinarily would have, including the lingering walking group.

I was starting to feel it. The heavy trays, the constant movement, the mental stress of trying to remember everything. I was getting tired.

About midway through the lunch rush, I forgot we were out of the spinach casserole, and put in an order for it. Mary spied it and said, "Nicole! Look at the board." She slid the ticket back toward me. "Go find out what else they want."

"Right, right," I said, glancing at the board. The casserole had been erased, but everything else was the same. "Sorry." I hustled back out. To the man at the table by the window, I said, "Sir, I'm sorry, we're out of the spinach casserole. Would you like to look at the menu again?"

He sighed in enormous irritation. "No, thank you. I'll just have the sandwich, but I don't want the olive bread. How about whole wheat?"

"Sure. I'll have that right out."

He didn't bother to acknowledge me, just went back to his newspaper, which he flicked with a crisp annoyance.

I had to struggle not to roll my eyes. But I'd lost that luxury, hadn't I?

In the kitchen, I hung the order and called out the change. "Special sand on whole wheat."

Mary spooned soup into a heavy pottery bowl. "Sorry. We're out of whole wheat too."

I looked at the board. "Did I mess up again?"

"No, babe, that was me. The olive just didn't go over that well, so we've run out of whole wheat. Tell them we'll give them a free dessert."

Relieved that it had not been my mistake, I took the ticket again and went back out. As I came around the breakfast bar, Penny was rounding her corner with a tray full of food. It was only through a quick dodge from both of us that disaster was averted.

"I'm sorry, I'm sorry!" I cried, reaching out to steady her.

"No, my fault." A lock of hair had come loose from her braid, and her cheeks were flushed. "Can you take the coffee around?"

"Yes." I grabbed the pot and headed to find out what else the man would want. "Sir? The cook offers her apologies—we're out of whole wheat. Would you like some fresh rye or maybe sourdough?"

"Christ!" He slammed the paper down on the table. "What kind of place is this? It's not even one o'clock."

"I'm sorry for the inconvenience," I said as mildly as possible. "I'm happy to give you a free dessert for your trouble."

"Why? So you can be out of that too?"

I took a breath. "Would you like a different bread for your sandwich this afternoon, or shall I bring you a menu?"

"No, just give me the rye."

"No problem, sir. Thank you."

I swung the coffeepot around, filling cups as I went. A spot in my gut stung, but I ignored it, went back to the coffee station, started a fresh pot, and headed back toward the kitchen. Penny slammed out of the swinging doors with a wide tray laden with plates on her shoulder. "Coming through!"

I plastered myself against the wall to let her by.

She said, "Bring that tray table, will you?"

I grabbed it and followed her. I opened the tray, then backed out of her way—and slammed right into a customer sitting at the table behind me. I felt the heavy thud of it, heard her little choked, "Ulp!" and turned around to comfort her.

Which put my hip against the edge of the tray, and the whole thing swayed dangerously. Luckily, I saved it, just in time, and I saw Penny's wide-eyed relief.

I turned back to the woman I'd slammed into, bent down, and put my hand on her shoulder. "Are you all right? I'm so sorry."

"Fine, fine," she said irritably, flinging her fingers at me to make me go away. I flushed.

I straightened and headed back to my station. There was a new table, one that had obviously been seated at least a minute or two, because they'd already laid down the menus. I spied the man who'd asked for rye for his sandwich and realized I hadn't turned in his revised order.

I swore under my breath. What to do?

I'd brazen it out, I decided, take the order of the new couple, then revise his as well.

At the new table, I said breathlessly, "Hi, I hope you haven't been waiting long."

"No. We'll have the soup, thanks."

"Excellent choice. Would you like anything to drink?"

"Just water."

It was easy enough to go back to the kitchen, ladle up the soup from the server's station, fill a basket with rolls, and carry it quickly back to the table. It restored my equilibrium.

Except the man was still waiting, and he glared at me as I passed. I winced, realized I still hadn't turned in his order. I went directly to the kitchen, turned in the order, and felt a chill go down my back when Mary said, "Nikki, read the board."

I did. Out of rye. "This man is going to be so mad at me!" I winced and turned back to Mary. "What kind of bread, then? Only sourdough?"

"No," she said with a hand on her hip, as if I were stupid. "We got white too."

I braced myself and went back to the table. "I'm really sorry, sir," I said, "but we're out of rye too. No one liked the olive and that's meant everything else is running out. Can we make the sandwich on white bread for you?"

"Fine," he said. "Whatever. Just bring me something to eat so I can get back to work."

I took his order directly to the kitchen. "This is the one I keep screwing up," I said.

"Give me two minutes," Mary said.

"I'll be right back." I swung by the coffee maker to make sure there was enough coffee, checked on the progress of my other tables, delivered a ticket to the soup folks, which did make me feel guilty.

Mary had the plate ready when I went back in—and it was a beauty. The gorgeous sandwich, piled high, a side salad looking like an ad for farm-fresh produce. "Take him a brownie," she added. "No one can hate you with a brownie in front of him."

"I have my doubts, but it's worth a try." I carried the sandwich carefully, and picked up a brownie on the way out. The man was checking his watch as I arrived. "Do you know that I've been here for half an hour?"

"And at last, here it is," I said as cheerfully as I could. "Along with a brownie, compliments of the chef."

"No, I don't want it," he said. "Just bring me some more tea and the check and we don't have to talk to each other anymore."

I picked up the brownie. "I really do apologize, sir. It's my first day and I'm just making every possible mistake with you. Sorry."

He just looked at me.

"Right. Tea."

I put the brownie on the sidebar, where it was understood mistakes went, for the servers and kitchen help. Pitchers of tea with ice stood in a row and I grabbed one, swirling into the dining room, thinking it was going to be very, very good to get off work. I picked up the man's check and carried the tea out to him. "Is it all right?"

He nodded dourly. If he hadn't had such a sour expression, I thought, he could have been good-looking. But I suspected he always had that pinch around his mouth.

I put his check down, and reached over to pour tea into his tall, empty glass. Small cubes of ice tumbled out, and amber tea. And then, in slow motion, I saw a big chunk rush out of the pitcher, into the glass, and in an agony of extra-super-slow motion, I saw the big chunk of ice hit the glass just right, and it very, very slowly fell over, splashing right onto the plate with the finally-made sandwich, and pouring like a river right over the edge of the table.

Into his suited lap.

He jumped up and threw his napkin on the table. "Fuck!" he cried. "You're the worst waitress I've ever had in my life."

"I'm sorry, sir, let me—"

He waved me back. "Just stay away from me." He stormed out.

The area around me was dead silent for an agonizingly long time, customers staring down at their own plates, those at a distance wondering what the heck had happened. To the table closest to me, I said, "Sorry about the disturbance," and bent over the table to start cleaning up the mess.

5

Nikki's Perfume Journal Entry

August 1, 1978

THINGS I LIKE TO SMELL
The seeds of the rue plant. Sharp, pungent, resiny. Old world, protective against witches.
Notes: not so good when the seeds are green. Have to be ripe and dry.

I left the restaurant at two and headed for my car. Every muscle in my body ached with a kind of twisted tension, and I smelled of sweat and grease and bread. At the car, I unlocked the door and tossed my soiled apron inside. A breeze swept down from the mountain and over my hot face, and instead of getting in the car, I slammed the door and headed up the hill toward Barr Trail instead.

It was a hard uphill climb to the base of the trailhead, but it felt good on my overstressed body. As I walked, blips of the day fell away— the walking club, the tangle of going back and back and back to get the order of the businessman wrong over and over. The slow-motion spill of tea—

Ugh!

There were a handful of cars in the parking lot, but no visible humans. At the foot of the path, I read the sign, carved into wood, that warned hikers of the climb to the top of Pikes Peak:

WARNING

BARR TRAIL CLIMBS 7300' IN 12.6 MILES. 8 HOURS TO SUMMIT AT BRISK PACE. HIKE EARLY IN THE DAY TO AVOID DANGEROUS AND COMMON AFTERNOON THUNDERSTORMS. EXPECT WINTER ON TOP, DRESS FOR IT. HOW ARE YOU GETTING OFF THE MOUNTAIN? COG R.R. MAY NOT, SUMMIT HOUSE WILL NOT, PROVIDE DOWNHILL TRANSPORTATION. ROAD CAN BE CLOSED BY SEVERE WEATHER.

I stepped on the path, which was dark red mud, and started walking. Just a little way, that was all I needed to do. Just walk a little way uphill.

The breeze tasted sharper here, cooled by the snowy shadows up higher. At city level, the snow melted fast, but in the mountains, it lingered a long time. There were times there was snow on the Peak in June.

But I wasn't going to the top. I'd heard the walking club volleying dates for their annual walk up the mountain, but that wasn't me. I was just—I didn't know what. Walking on the hems of the mountain. Trying to get away from my failures, failures that seemed to be piling up like dead moths. I'd failed as a wife, as a mother, as a productive human being.

I wasn't even a good waitress.

I could walk, though. It was a vigorous incline, with switchbacks to make it more manageable. A wooden rail fence protected hikers from tumbling down the side. I climbed for about ten minutes, then paused to look at the view. I could see down over the city of Colorado Springs, stretching endlessly between hills and bluffs, crawling up and down the terrain. Behind me, above me, rose the mountain, which made my problems look small.

And there, alone on the mountainside, I could let go of some of my tears. I was embarrassed at how badly I'd performed. Furious with Dan for putting me in the position of having to wait tables at the age of forty-three. Despairing over my bleak-looking future. Everything in the past six months had been a lesson in mortification, and I was getting sick of it. Enough already!

A figure on the path below made me wipe my eyes, take a deep breath. The man wove in and out of view, visible, then not. It was safe enough here, but I had my cell phone in my hand just in case.

When he rounded the last switchback, however, I saw it was the man from Annie's, the beautiful British guy. "Hello," he said, dipping his head in greeting as if to underscore the formality of his speech. "Do you remember, we spoke yesterday?"

"I remember." I wanted to be wary, but it was difficult. His glossy curls, those dancing eyes with their sooty lashes, the slightly amused lips.

"Am I interrupting something?"

"No." I resisted the urge to wipe my face, make sure there were no tears there. "Just didn't have the best day."

"I hope you're not climbing far in those shoes."

"What?" I looked at my feet, shod in white tennis shoes now smeared with reddish mud. "Oh, no. I wouldn't. I mean—" I halted. Just stop stuttering, Nikki. Close your mouth.

He smiled.

I took a breath. "Sorry."

"Don't be." With one long-fingered hand, he gestured to a spot next to me. "May I join you for a moment?"

"Please." And I just had to add, "Yes."

"It's beautiful here, isn't it?" He leaned easily on the fence, his arms beside mine. He wore a long-sleeved shirt, the palest imaginable shade of green, with tiny darker green lines making a grid of squares on it. The sleeves had been turned up twice, to show his chai-colored wrists, square and polished-looking. His hands were long, with smooth oval nails.

I focused on the view. "Yes. It calms me down."

"I followed you here," he said. "Do you mind?"

With a slight frown, I looked at him. "Why?"

His nose was wonderful—hawkish and strong, high-bridged. He smiled, showing his big, very white teeth. "Why did I follow you or why would you mind?"

"I don't mind. I just don't know why."

"I saw you leaving Annie's, and wanted to see how you'd done."

With a snort, I scraped mud from the bottom of my shoe onto the rock sitting there. "Very badly."

"That is not what Annie said."

"No?"

"She said you'd done very well in terrible conditions."

"Really?"

He touched my hand. "I followed you because you looked so . . . sad."

It suddenly didn't matter in the least if he was lying. There was kindness on his elegantly handsome face, and anything that made me feel less like dog puke was good. Tears sprang to my eyes again, and I bowed my head quickly to hide them. Blew out a short breath. "I'm too old for this," I said. "It was a stupid idea. I should have just applied at a bank or something."

"No, no!" he protested, and his hand stayed with mine, anchoring it. "New things are always hard. It will get better."

Not in my world. Things had been going from bad to worse for quite some time. "I guess we'll find out."

"In six months, we'll have a cup of coffee," he said, "and we will laugh about this. What do you think of that?"

It was hard to hold on to my despair in the face of that cheery good humor. I held out my hand to shake on it. "A cup of coffee—it's Niraj, right?"

"Yes." He clasped my hand in his, and his palm was taut and cool. "Niraj Bhuskar. You're Nicole."

"Right." We stood there on the sun-warmed side of the mountain, beneath a brilliant blue sky, with clasped hands. A ripple of something cool and hungry went through me. I looked at his mouth, his brow, wished to put my hands in his thick, glossy hair.

He looked back at me and it seemed to me that some of the same things were in his eyes, in his face. "You have beautiful eyes."

"Thank you." I tried to think of what you said when you first started liking someone, how you let them know, what was stupid and what would be sophisticated.

He let go of my hand before I could think of the right phrase. For a long moment, we stood side by side, looking at the scenery, and I felt pressure in my chest, a wish to say something. "What sort of work do you do?" Lame, but better than nothing.

"Computers. I work at home, which is why I go to Annie's so often. It breaks up the monotony of my own company."

"No family?"

"No." He dipped his head in a way that telegraphed his disappointment. "I followed a woman to Colorado, but she proved to be"—he gave the hesitation a smile—"the wrong one for me."

"Where did you follow her from?"

"London."

"Is that where you're from? Don't laugh if that's wrong—I'm not that good with accents."

"You are correct with mine. I was born in London. My family is still there." He paused and gave me a crooked, halfway smile that conveyed a pleasurable wickedness. "Which is one reason I am here."

I chuckled. "My mother is in Arizona, and I'm glad."

"Do you have siblings?"

"Two sisters." A Steller's jay, dark blue with a darker head, flew across my field of vision. "One is a soap opera actress in LA. The other is an army wife in Hawaii." Something in me was easing in his company. Tension drained down my spine, softening my neck. "How about you?"

"Two brothers and two sisters. They all live in London. My father runs a grocery. One brother helps him. The other"—he shrugged—"doesn't do much. I have one sister who will likely not marry, and the other is a writer and runs her family with an iron fist."

"What sort of writing?" I asked.

"Serious nonfiction about the problems of society. Essays, books. My parents are very proud of her."

"Are you?"

He pursed his lips ruefully. "I'm proud of her, but I do not read her. She's too serious about everything."

I smiled. "And you are not serious?"

"No." He leaned on the railing, looked across the vistas. "I'm afraid I'm a man of pleasures. Give me fresh air, good company"—he inclined his head my way—"good food, and I'm happy enough. My sister needs to save the world."

I discovered I liked the slight lilt layered atop the proper British phrasings. I liked the angle of his cheekbones and the way the wind ruffled his hair. My breath came easier in my not-so-tight chest. On the top of my head, sunlight baked the part of my hair. "I know a lot of people like that. Who want to save the world."

"And what about you? Do you have a family?"

"I did. I'm divorced. I have a daughter who is fifteen—she lives with her father." A pang stabbed through my heart. I rubbed it.

"You miss her."

"Like a hand," I agreed.

"I'm sorry."

I met his eyes. "Thank you." Behind him, purple clouds had eased over the mountains. "The thunderstorms are coming. I guess I'll get off the trail now."

"Do you mind if I walk back down with you?"

"No, please do." Still too formal. Why was I speaking like a Victorian heroine?

The footing was treacherous—slippery logs and mud. I stepped carefully, but even so, my foot skidded out from under me, and I went down on one palm. I hopped up immediately, unhurt, and patted the mud off my left hand with the other one.

"Are you all right?" Niraj asked.

"Yes. Thanks." I laughed. "It's just been that kind of a day."

"You've kept your sense of humor anyway." He touched my elbow, a gentle assist, then let go.

"I'm better at it some days than others."

"Aren't we all?"

He really was spectacularly attractive. The silky curls, the deep eyes, that ease of movement. I couldn't make up my mind how old he was. Forty? Forty-five? Lines fanned out from his eyes, and there was a certain look to his hands that made me think he was around my age somewhere.

This vivid awareness flustered me, and I turned and went down the path, holding out my hand to dry the mud on my palm. We made it to the bottom without further incident, then headed down Ruxton Avenue to the main part of town.

"Do you like to hike, Nicole?" he asked.

"I used to. Haven't done it much over the past few years for some reason." I paused, wondering suddenly why that happened—and a dozen reasons crowded in: soccer with Giselle, Saturday afternoons in my garden, dinner parties to plan or to attend, shopping with the rest of the world. "How 'bout you?"

"Oh yes. My father always walked when I was a child—he would go to a small lake nearby our home, and walk around it nearly every day. It seemed a good habit to me, and it has kept him fit, and well."

"That's how it was with my grandmother. She used to march us all over town. It was sort of shameful in my family to take a car if it wasn't a very far walk, like to the store or the post office or something."

"That's very healthy."

"I suppose." It made me remember holiday dinners. "At Christmas or Thanksgiving, we'd all spill out into the street and go ambling around the neighborhood after lunch."

"It is a good city for walking, once one adjusts to the altitude."

"Did the altitude bother you when you got here?"

"Yes. I lost quite a lot of weight at first, too, which I liked." He smiled, patted his lean middle with that elegant hand. "But now it's come back."

I rolled my eyes. "Oh, please. It annoys me how easily men lose weight."

"Women always diet, diet, diet. You strike me as too sensible to eat badly."

I looked at him for a clue to what he might mean by that. "I'm not always this plump," I said in my own defense. "I wasn't doing much for a while there but feeling sorry for myself and eating ice cream."

A glitter lit his dark eyes, and he imitated my stance by putting his hands behind his back. One eyebrow lifted. "You do not seem plump to me, only female."

Oh! Feeling like Marilyn Monroe, I tried not to preen. "Thanks."

We made it to the main stretch of shops. Next to my car, I paused. "This one's mine."

"Look at your hand," he said, pointing.

Across my palm, where the mud had dried in light smears, was a shimmer of gold flakes. "Is it mica? Fool's gold?"

"I don't know." He grinned at me. "It's beautiful."

I wiggled my fingers, and light glinted off the thin gold flakes. "Amazing."

"The mountain must like you."

"Maybe." I smiled at him. "Thanks. You made me feel better."

"You're welcome. I will see you again."

Words froze in my throat. Any of the ordinary words that adult women used to encourage men they found attractive, like *I hope so*, or *Would you like to see a movie*, or any number of other possibilities. Gone.

I just nodded. "Well. Bye."

"Do you have email?" he asked.

"Um. Yes."

His eyes crinkled. "May I email you?"

I laughed a little. "Yes. It's easy: nikki@scentofhours.com."

"Do you have a pen?"

From my back jeans pocket, I produced a stick ballpoint. He spread his palm and said, "Tell me again?" When I repeated it, he wrote in tiny block letters across the heel of his palm.

"I haven't seen anyone do that in a long time."

He raised his eyes, and it seemed, suddenly, as if he might be embarrassed. "Old habit."

I looked at his face, at the high bridge of his nose, the darkness of his eyes, and still couldn't add, *I look forward to your email.* It seemed too much to want. "I'll see you," I finally said.

He nodded. "Good."

I climbed into my car and drove home. I was imagining a nice hot bath in my oversize oval tub, a tall glass of wine, some takeout from the Chinese down the street, paid for with my tips.

But the universe wasn't finished with me yet.

6

Nikki's Perfume Journal Entry

Time: 5:30 p.m.
Date: Any November weekday in the 1990s

Bottle: frosted silver glass. Moon-shaped stopper.
Elements. cold silvery twilight, roast baking, dark falling around rooms cozy with yellow lamplight, the sweet reassurance of child safely doing homework upstairs, onions perfuming the air
Notes: How do you make a scent that smells like supper? Cinnamon, apple notes, no florals, a little woodsmoke, snow. Hmm. Costus blend number one as a base. Middle notes: black pepper, cinnamon, green tea. Wormwood? How do I reproduce the scent of snow? Clary sage, a hint of lime for the freshness? What does security smell like?
Call it: WINTER SUPPERS

I climbed the stairs to my apartment, threw my keys on the table, and carefully scraped the mud with gold/mica flakes onto a piece of paper. It sure looked like gold. It didn't matter, particularly, except that it was cool. It did seem like a kiss of approval from the lady of the mountain.

My cell phone rang, and I reached into my purse to see who it was. Pam's Aspen smile showed up on the viewfinder. I flipped the phone open.

"Hi!"

"Hi, Nicole. Are you home?"

"Yep, just got here. What's up?"

"I'm at Kit's house. We'll be there in a minute."

I scowled. "Who's 'we'?" I didn't want to deal with Evelyn.

No answer. I looked at the phone and saw she'd hung up already. Argh. I smelled like cooking, like old grease and stale coffee, and any makeup I'd applied this morning had worn off by now.

People would find out eventually that I was working at the restaurant, but I wanted to preserve the illusion of my self-sufficiency at least a little longer. And who knew, perhaps the insurance inquiry would go fast enough that I would have a settlement pretty soon, and then I could quit before anyone knew.

I hurried into the bedroom and stripped off my work shirt and bra, and rushed into the bathroom. I ran water into the sink, soaped a washcloth, and prepared to give myself a quick sponge bath. At second thought, I stripped off my jeans, too, and kicked them into the corner.

By the time the doorbell rang, I had combed my hair, washed the day off me, and put on a pair of khakis with a fresh, summer-weight sweater.

I flung open the door, and there was Pam, carrying a lamp. It looked vaguely familiar. "Surprise!" she cried.

Behind her was Kit, hauling a small table up the stairs. The effort showed in her ropy forearms. I blinked, standing there at the door as two burly guys came up behind, a sofa balanced between them. "What's going on?"

"Lady, this is heavy. You want to tell us where to put it down?"

"I don't—"

"Let us in, silly goose, and I'll explain." With her usual air of mastery, Pam pushed by me. I was forced to leave the door and get out of the way of the men. Kit followed behind them.

"This all right?" the man said, indicating the empty space along the wall.

"Sure, I guess. Put it down." When he pulled the protective blankets off the couch, I recognized it immediately. It was a slightly battered sofa with the peach and green swirly patterns of the late eighties, and recliner options at each end. To Pam, I said, "That's from your family room, isn't it?"

"I know, I know." She put down the floor lamp, which I now realized had arched over the couch. "It needs to be cleaned, and I have a certificate here for you to call them and have them come in to take care of it." She patted her purse. "There's more stuff downstairs. I'll be back."

I didn't know what to do. Or feel. Or think. My cheeks burned as the guys headed out with burly swaggers to get God-knew-what-else.

Kit put the end table down by the wall and gave me a bright, false smile. "We should have done this before. I just didn't realize how dire the situation was." She tossed a curl off her forehead and looked around the room. "This is cute! I like it. And what a great view of the mountains!" She put her hands on her hips and looked at the horizon, an exaggerated pleasantness in her expression.

I stared at the table, which I thought I remembered from the downstairs hallway in her house. "Thanks," I said. "I guess I'll . . . um . . . put on some coffee."

"Great. I'll go help with the chairs. That's a lot of steps, isn't it?"

Through the door, I saw Roxanne, smoking in the open-air hallway. She leaned against the wall, frankly observing the commotion. Her choppy haircut and short skirt made her look much younger and hipper than Kit, and I saw Kit notice.

Roxanne blew out a stream of smoke and raised her eyebrows at me. I lifted a shoulder and went to make the coffee.

~

Pam and Kit didn't stay long. They'd hired the movers and cleaned out their houses of unwanted furniture to help me, and once it was placed, they seemed to be in a hurry to get out. Back to their lives, their little families, where nothing untoward had yet shattered their safety, where they'd all eat supper prepared from fresh, whole foods and not too much fat, and sip wine as they served up leafy green salad.

I was left standing in my newly furnished apartment, smarting from throat to gullet. The smell of coffee lingered, but there was no wintertime dark flavor of onions cooking, of supper calling everyone in from their chilly corners. I turned away from the open door after waving them down the stairs, and stared at the stuff in my living room.

I recognized every single thing they'd brought in. The couch from this family room; the lamps from a back bedroom where we often dumped our coats during parties; the dining room table that had been in Evelyn's garage since she'd bought a new one two years ago. There was a white twin bed, night table, and dresser set painted white with gilt, which would furnish Giselle's bedroom, and I knew had once belonged to Crystal Merriweather, the daughter of one of the soccer coaches, who'd gone on to medical school.

I knew they meant well. I could just imagine how the conversation had gone, too, could hear the concern in Pam's voice as she'd said to the others, *Nicole is doing so well after all this drama*—she'd praise me first—*but I was at her apartment the other day and she barely has a stick of furniture.*

They would have all clucked and tsked and said, *Oh, I feel terrible for her*, and *We need to do something*. They would have fallen silent, drunk some more wine or coffee or eaten another tidbit of salad, and then someone had come up with this plan, made a list of what would be needed: *She'll want a couch, and lamps, and a table. Oh, and don't forget Giselle's room.*

They meant well. So why did I want to cry? Or take an axe to the lot of it? I had never felt so humiliated in all my life.

From behind me, a voice said, "It's just their voodoo, you know."

I turned around, and Roxanne was standing in my doorway. "What?"

"They're afraid," she said, leaning on the threshold, looking like the dangerous divorcée in every single inch of her slinky body, "that they'll end up like you. After all, your husband loved you, right? And you guys were the couple everybody thought would stay together forever."

I crossed my arms against the burn of anger in my chest. Even more so. Everyone just loved being able to pepper their parties with a mixed couple. It gave us more cachet than PhDs or Ivy League or a job in the arts. "Yes."

"So," she continued, "they have to find some way to make you different from them, so they bring you their cast-off furniture and pretend they're safe."

I met her eyes, wishing I was not dripping tears of bitter fury, that I was the kind of woman who would beat somebody up when she was mad instead of standing there crying. "I could just kill them."

She nodded. Her hair was fantastic, moving in glossy shifts that left little choppy pieces around her sharp jaw and cheekbones. "My kids are watching videos. I could bring over a bottle of wine."

The whole day suddenly seemed as if it weighed about nine hundred pounds. "You know, that sounds great. I'll order a pizza."

"Good idea. I'll pitch in. And how about if I go get Wanda too? She lives downstairs. Her husband is in Iraq, and you want to talk about miserable! She has three kids under six."

"I don't really want kids around tonight. I worked my ass off today."

She gave an earthy laugh. "Oh, honey, I'm a third grade teacher. No fucking way I want kids around. Why do you think I want to come to your house? I'll send my daughter down there to babysit."

"Now, that I can live with. Go get Wanda."

∼

Wanda turned out to be a wren of a girl, slightly plump with white skin and brown hair and a very pretty mouth. She wore rings on every finger and her eyes were tired. "Hi," she said. "I brought string cheese and Ritz crackers and some grapes. Not so elegant, but we live on child food in my house."

I chuckled. "Been there. Come on in. I miss string cheese." Roxanne, who'd been gathering things in her apartment, slid out of her door carrying three bottles of wine, two red, one white.

We settled around the newly set table and I brought out the cheap wineglasses I'd bought when I replaced my dishes. "This is a nice table, you have to admit," Roxanne said, rubbing her hand over the grain. "Is it cherry?"

"Probably. I think it might have been inherited from somebody's mother or something."

"You don't like it?" Wanda asked, rubbing her hands on the grain. "It's a heck of a lot nicer than my dining room table."

"It's a weird situation," I said, and gave a three-second overview as I worked the corkscrew out of the wine bottle. "So I'd probably love it under other circumstances, but I hate being the charity of the week."

She nodded, but plainly didn't get it. I didn't bother to go into it. None of these things were my taste—not the apartment or the life, so what difference would it make if the furniture was wrong too?

"Did you talk to your husband today?" Roxanne asked her.

"Yeah. We talk every day, mostly."

"How long has he been there?" I asked, pouring wine.

"Eleven months this time. A year the first time."

"This is his second time?" I asked.

Wanda nodded wearily. "He went with the first wave, and then came home for a while and then went back."

"Jesus," I breathed. Wanda winced, and I apologized. "I just don't know how you stand it, worrying like that."

"What choice do I have?"

I felt chastened. "Right."

"It's worse for him anyway," she said. "This tour has been hard on him. Two of his friends have been killed, and they don't really get enough relief time, and he's sick of the food, and, well, it's just not ideal conditions."

"How long till he comes back?"

"Five weeks." Her smile was wan.

"You're not happy?" I asked.

"Well, there's an adjustment period. It's kind of hard, that first little bit. It was rough the first time, but I'd been living with my mother in Nebraska. This time, I decided I wanted to be with the other wives from our battalion and I've been on my own out here in Colorado."

Roxanne leaned forward, and I settled in with my glass. "So what kind of adjustments?" She wiggled her eyebrows. "Don't you just spend the first few weeks in bed, making up for lost time?"

It shocked me. "Roxanne! That's personal."

Wanda rolled her eyes. "You'll find out that nothing is too personal for Roxanne."

Roxanne shrugged. "I don't understand why sex is such a big deal—I mean, why not talk about it? What are we all thinking about all the time?"

"Sleep," Wanda said.

"Money," I said at the same time.

"See? That's the trouble. If you shift your focus, you don't have to worry about sleep or money. You can just enjoy yourself."

"Easy for you," Wanda said. "I'd rather not think about it, because I'll just feel frustrated."

"Ditto," I said, and took a deep sip of the wine, which was a simple, busty Italian red.

I couldn't remember the last time I'd had sex. It had probably been at least a year. You'd think you'd remember the last time you'd had sex with someone you'd then broken up with, but the trouble was, while we were doing it, I didn't realize it was the last time.

"Surely you have a vibrator?" Roxanne said.

Wanda choked. "No!"

Neither did I, but I wasn't about to say so. The idea made me feel pathetic. Needy.

"Oh, we need to go shopping, then."

"Where?" Wanda asked. "What if I see somebody I know?"

"Like one of the soldiers' wives who've also gone damned near a year without sex, you mean?"

Wanda shrugged.

The doorbell rang and I jumped up, stack of one-dollar bills in hand, to answer it. A girl as skinny as a cattail stood there in her ill-fitting uniform, two steaming pizzas in her hands. She gave the total and I tipped her generously. "Thanks, ma'am."

Without fuss, I popped open the pizzas, handed out napkins, and we started eating. I took a big bite of pepperoni and the tension in my shoulders eased slightly. "I can't believe I'm waiting tables at my age. So much for college."

"Do you have a degree?" Wanda asked. Wistfully, I thought.

"A sore point, actually. No. I have three years of chemistry. Not terribly useful."

Roxanne grunted in sympathy. Then gave me a pained look. "Chemistry? Were you headed for med school or something?"

"No. I wanted to study perfume. Go to Grasse."

"Perfume? Really?" Roxanne inclined her head. "How wonderful!"

"I've been there," Wanda said. "To Grasse? Just for a day, driving through. It was kinda neat."

"I'm jealous!" I said.

"And I'm jealous of you going to college. I'd love to go. I'd study anything, I mean it."

"C'mon. Not anything," Roxanne said. "Mechanics? Botany? Anthropology? All equal? I don't think so."

Wanda chewed thoughtfully. Her eyes were a very clear, deep blue. "No, not anything, I guess. But I like the idea of being on campus, you know? Like with other people who like the same things and maybe like to read and, you know, talk about stuff?"

She was capturing my mother side, this girl. "Where are you from?"

"Nebraska. I met Tommy, my husband, when I was seventeen. He swept me off my feet and we got married three days after I graduated."

"And you've been married how long?"

"Eight years come summer. The first four were so great! We were in Germany, and we didn't have any kids yet, so we were pretty free, and got to go all over—Paris, Ireland, and even Rome."

"Wow," I said, taking a gulp of wine. "That kind of travel equals college any day. My ex and my daughter are in London right now. I've always wanted to go."

"Do you think that's why he took her now?"

"Probably," I said, pursing my lips. Shrugged. "Whatever."

"And how old is your daughter?" Wanda asked.

"She's fifteen. Her dad is living in Malibu, so she's happy to go live with him."

"And his new wife?" Roxanne drawled, not really a question.

"Yes." It burned. "You too?"

"Oh yeah. I would have thought my intense bitterness would've broadcast that fact all by itself."

"You're not bitter," Wanda said.

"Believe me," Roxanne answered, pinching off a two-centimeter measure of crust and tucking it between her lips, "I am."

"No," Wanda said. "What she is, is crazy."

Roxanne looked at me, and I saw the tightness around her mouth that she was trying to hide with her smirk. "I'm also, as all the divorce recovery workshops will tell you, an example of everything not to do."

"Really." That made me smile. "Now, that sounds interesting. How so?"

"Well, I have been known to stalk them, follow them around town in my car, or go to restaurants where I know they'll be, or sit in front of their house."

"Why? Doesn't it end up making you feel bad?"

"No," she said, and took a long, deep swallow of her wine. "But it makes them crazy, and that makes me happy."

"That's not the bad part, and you know it." Wanda plucked another slice of pizza from the box. She picked off the mushrooms and looked at me. "Ask her how many men she's slept with since she got divorced."

"How many?"

Roxanne looked at the ceiling. "'Slept with' is not the right term here. I've fucked forty-seven."

A blister of heat worked its way down the edges of my ears—shock. Her language shocked me and the number shocked me. I blinked, put down my pizza, took a deep swallow of wine. "That's pretty hostile."

"It's not, though," she said, and poured us each some more wine. I was surprised to realize I'd got to the bottom of my glass already. "I started out just being curious. I had a high school boyfriend, a college boyfriend, and then my ex, so I just wanted to see what other men were like."

"Still. Forty-seven?"

"That's not even one per week."

And for one brief second, I had a flash of desire to know what that would be like. A new man every week. Different skin, different kiss, different hands. "Where do you meet them?"

"All over the place." She waved a hand. "Supermarket, bars, restaurants, dating services, internet, work. All over."

A ripple of curiosity pulsed in my chest. I thought of the men I'd noticed in the restaurant the other day. "And you just tell them you want to have sex with them?"

She gave me a look, like, *Get real.* "Have you ever met a man who didn't want to have sex?"

"Well, no." I thought of Dan, the last few months of our marriage, but in that case, he was having sex with someone else, wasn't he? So it didn't count.

"I've only had sex with one person in my life," Wanda said.

"I am so surprised," Roxanne said dryly.

"Don't be mean." Wanda tore the dough very carefully, picked up the empty bread. "It's not like I didn't like guys. They just don't like me that much."

"You just never thought you were pretty, that's all," Roxanne said.

"That's because I'm not."

"You have beautiful eyes," I said.

Wanda shrugged that away.

Roxanne reached out and brushed a lock of Wanda's hair away from her cheek. "You're beautiful, sweetie. I wish you knew that."

"Thank you, but you think everyone is beautiful."

"No, I don't! That woman down in the building on the corner, with the black mustache, is definitely not beautiful." I laughed.

Roxanne looked at me. "Have you had your post-break fling yet?"

I thought, fleetingly, of Niraj. His walnut-colored wrists and inky curls. "No. It's only been six months since we were officially divorced."

"Perfect."

"Tell her about penises," Wanda said, her eyes glittering.

"I'm sure she knows all about them," Roxanne said.

"No, I don't think I do!" The wine was tickling my brain, melting my rigid worries about everything, everything, everything. I looked around the room at the stupid furniture and rolled my eyes. "Tell me about anything to keep my mind off the fact that my old best friends all just gave me their castoffs." I slammed my head on the table. "God, I could just die."

"Give it all away," Roxanne said.

I raised my head. Turned my lips downward. "That's a good idea. Wanda, do you want this table?"

"Yes! It's gorgeous."

"Done."

Roxanne smiled like a cat and spread her hands—*See?* I suddenly loved her more than I'd loved another woman in all my life. I would kiss her. I loved her so much I wanted to be gay. But— "What about penises?"

"Nothing!" she said, but she grinned. "I just like them. Like, all of them."

"Big ones, you mean."

"No, not necessarily. They're all beautiful in their own special way." She fluttered her eyelashes and put her hands over her heart in mock modesty. "Big fat ones and little bitty skinny ones and plump short ones." She grinned. "Black ones and white ones, and crooked ones and straight ones."

I laughed. "I hear a song coming on."

Roxanne laughed too. "Big cocks, little cocks," she sang to the hot-dog song. "Cocks that list to the left! Ripe ones, sad ones, clipped ones, squishy ones, scared and lost and silly ones!"

Wanda and I snickered. Roxanne kept singing a little under her breath, working out the rhyme, and then broke out, "I love hot dogs, all those hot dogs, and they love them so much more!"

She ended with a grin, and celebrated by eating an entire bite of pizza.

"You are so bad," Wanda said. Her cheeks were red as cranberries.

"They do love them," I said. "More than anything, they love their penises."

"You know what I really do like?" Roxanne said. "Uncircumcised."

"Really? I've only seen one. Why?"

"More sensitive," Wanda said slyly.

"Exactly!" Roxanne laughed. "Aha! That's kind of unusual, a white boy from Nebraska who didn't get clipped. Is his family conservative Christians? Southern, maybe?"

"Yep. The Evangelical Church of Jesus and the Holy Spirit, in Cedar Grove, Alabama."

"How did you know that?" I asked.

Roxanne shrugged. "Most American men of our age are circumcised, because it was the fashion when they were babies. The exceptions are some black men, and hard-core Christians."

"Why? I don't get it."

"Muslims and Jews are all circumcised. The Gentiles are not."

Dan was not circumcised, but I'd never really thought about why. I laughed, a little uncomfortably. "Never thought about this before."

"Me either, until I met Roxanne," Wanda said. Her eyes were shiny with wine. "Now, though, watch—when you meet certain men, it'll be the first thing that pops into your mind."

"Oh, that's terrible!"

Roxanne laughed. "Glad to know I'm doing my part to further the cause."

We fell into silence, all of us no doubt thinking about a particular man, maybe even a particular penis.

Abruptly, Roxanne said, "So what happened?"

"What?" I said. "To my marriage, you mean?"

She nodded, a slight heavy-liddedness giving away her inebriation. "What else?"

"I don't know," I said, and struggled for an answer that sounded more substantial. "Like, there should be something, right? Some moment of unhappiness, or a fight, or a really bad day, or even some sense that we were sort of drifting apart." I peered into my wineglass, seeing a point of reflected light glowing in the pool of merlot. "But all I can say is, if it was there, I didn't see it."

"Right," Roxanne said. "Me either."

Wanda said, "That scares me. If you don't know, how can you do anything to stop it?"

Roxanne lifted an eyebrow.

Wanda's expression of panic made me say, "I'm sure there were lots of things, if I wanted to look hard. Like, we never did anything together, really. Well, except movies and special meals. I liked those."

"Not helping," Roxanne said.

"I know." I shook my head. "Maybe there is no reason. Maybe it just doesn't make sense to one person anymore, and then there you are, dead to it."

"Sorry, but it was bad character," Wanda said.

"Bad character?" Roxanne echoed. "Have you been hanging out with those Baptists again?"

"I'm a Presbyterian."

"Same difference."

"They aren't, actually, but that's beside the point." Wanda's chin jutted up stubbornly. "I know it sounds old-fashioned, but I mean it. It's not right. If you give a vow, you're supposed to keep it."

Something in me shifted. A sensation of cool relief wafted through me, erasing some of the heat of my confusion, my fury, my despair. "That's a good point, Wanda."

"Oh, I don't buy it," Roxanne said irritably. "Just because a person falls out of love doesn't mean they're a bad person."

"If you stick with it, you'll fall back in love eventually," Wanda said. "That's what my mother says."

I blinked. "Have you fallen out of love?"

"It's not that." She turned her wineglass around in a perfect circle. "I hardly know him now. He was gone with the first deployment for over a year, then he came home, then he was down-range, then he went back. It's been like three or four years that we've barely been together at all. What are we going to talk about when he comes home?"

"Oh, sweetie!" Roxanne said, and put her hand over Wanda's. "It's going to be just fine, you'll see."

I wondered. Sometimes, it probably wasn't all right at all. "I bet it's hard for everybody. What do the other wives say? What did you say last time?"

"I don't know." She brushed bangs from her eyes. "I don't really want to talk about this. Do you have cards? We could play rummy."

"Rummy!" Roxanne rolled her eyes. "Poker is what we need."

"I don't think I have any cards."

"I do," Roxanne said, standing up. "I'll get them. Pull out your change, ladies."

When she came back, she had donned a velvet shawl in many colors. Wanda said, "No readings, Roxanne. You know how I feel about that!"

"I won't read for you, then." She put a large cookie tin down on the table, and pulled the lid off to reveal ceramic poker chips and two decks of Bicycle cards, one blue, one red.

I picked up one of the chips. "These look old."

"They belonged to my ex's grandfather," she said, raising one pointed eyebrow. In her other hand, she carried a bundle wrapped in something fringed. "We'll play in a few minutes, but first, do you want a reading?"

"Reading?"

"Tarot." She unwrapped the bundle to reveal a much-used deck of tarot cards. "I am Madame Mirabou, darling, and I can see the future."

Recklessly, I said, "Oh, sure. Pull a card."

She shuffled, her sleeves sweeping over the cherry tabletop. Wanda shook her head. Roxanne gave her a look. "It's just a party game," she said. "Lighten up."

"It's tempting fate."

"Whatever." Roxanne turned over three cards. "Past. Present. Future," she said. Then, "I hmm, check it out." With a fingernail, she tapped the past card that showed a castle on fire and somebody falling out of a window.

I snorted.

"The Tower," Roxanne said. "Quite right." The middle card was a picture of three women dancing, cups held high. "Appropriate, isn't it? Here we all three are, celebrating."

"Cool."

The final card, a single hand reaching out of a cloud, like God's hand, holding up a branch. "Fresh starts," she said. "In many ways, but it's especially a spiritual fresh start." She fixed her eyes on me, and there was a fierce penetrating blaze to them, as if she really could see into my heart. "What have you left behind that you need to bring into your life?"

My first thought was, My daughter. The next was a vision of my perfumery. "I'm not sure. I'll have to think about it."

"You do know. Trust yourself," she said, and there was authority in her tone. As she gathered the cards into her thin hands, I wondered at the disparate angles I'd glimpsed of her in a very short time: a teacher, a tarot reader, a mother who fixed her children french toast and gave them a day off the day before spring break, a woman who'd slept with forty-seven men since her divorce.

Oh, sorry. Fucked forty-seven men.

"I'll just do a quick one for myself and we'll play poker."

Shuffling, shuffling. Her sleeves swept back and forth, and then she plopped the deck down, divided it, and put three cards down in a row, slap slap slap. She scowled.

I knew tarot a little. It was something my mother loved and used. This was not a good string of cards. The Lovers, reversed, which made sense—the divorce. Then the present-day card: Page of Wands, reversed. Then Temperance, reversed.

Wanda tapped the third card. "See? You're supposed to practice moderation in all things."

Roxanne rolled her eyes, but it was clear she wasn't pleased with the cards. She slapped down three more in a row. Wheel of Fortune, reversed. A woman tied up and blindfolded. The ten of Cups, the family happiness card, reversed.

"Oh, never mind," she said, and swept the cards into a pile. "Let's play poker."

"Oh no you don't, Madame Mirabou," Wanda said, putting her hand out. "If you want to play with fate, you have to pay attention when it gives you a warning."

Roxanne looked at her. "I haven't had any sex in a month, okay? I haven't followed Grant or Lora-Lies-a-Lot in at least two months. I'm actually seeing a counselor, and she's helping."

Wanda's expression cleared. "Really?"

"Cross my heart," she said.

"Good. You're a good person, Rox. I want you to be okay."

"I want you to have this table."

"Me too."

I poured more wine. "It's yours, honey. First thing tomorrow."

HEART NOTES

Hast thou not learn'd me how
To make perfumes? distil? preserve? yea, so
That our great king himself doth woo me oft
For my confections?
—William Shakespeare, *Cymbeline*

7

Nikki's Perfume Journal Entry

Magazine clipping, dated August 8, 1999

The Max Factor Sophisti-Cat was a big hit with girls in the mid-sixties. The perfume came in ¼ oz. bottles held by a flocked cat with rhinestone eyes, a necklace, and a feather boa, all covered by a clear plastic dome. The perfume came in several varieties, including Golden Woods, Hypnotique, and Primitif, but the true lure was the cat, sitting mysteriously, an example of all things female. The colors of the rhinestone eyes matched the feather—blue, pink, yellow—and each one had a necklace of pearls or ribbon. —*Vintage Perfumes, vol. 3*

I must have dreamed about Daniel, because when I woke up, for one long moment, I was confused. My hand reached for the place he used to sleep, as it had done for six thousand mornings all in a row. When my fingers found smooth, cool sheet, I remembered all over again.

Oh yes. We divorced.

How did that happen? We were so in love. Everyone who ever knew him always talked about how insanely attached to his family my husband was. Lying in my bed in the dim, empty apartment, I rolled onto my back and put the backs of my hands to my eyes, willing the images to stay away, to leave me alone.

But they didn't.

We met when I was twenty-three. A cook at the restaurant where I worked had helped me fill out all the financial aid and application papers to go to school at UCCS, the local branch of the University of Colorado, and I had a year under my belt in chemistry, which made me feel like maybe I was about something, after all.

Daniel was taking business courses, but I didn't meet him at school. He worked for a remodeling company that had been hired to overhaul the apartment building I was living in. He showed up one afternoon when I had an exam the next day, to take some measurements and make appointments to fit our windows.

The minute I opened the door, I was knocked sideways. I'd had plenty of boyfriends by then, but Daniel was in a league all his own, and I was tongue-tied in his presence. As he took measurements, I pretended to study. He didn't make small talk, but I felt him looking at me. Finally he said, "You look familiar."

I raised my eyes. "I went to Doherty High School."

"So did I," he said.

"I know. You played basketball. They gave you a scholarship or something, right? That was the worst year for football, but a great one for basketball, and largely because of you."

He half smiled. His best expression, so surprising in that serious face, and it lit up his eyes, gave him a practically mischievous look. "You had your eye on me, huh?"

"Maybe," I said. But it had gone way beyond that—God, I'd lusted after him with a kind of narcotic deliriousness I couldn't admit to anyone. Not then. Not in our school, not a white girl lusting after a black boy. The black girls would have kicked my ass.

But seeing him again, I remembered it instantly, the way he moved through the halls, taller than anyone, his Afro combed out to twice the size of his head, all fluffy and soft-looking. He carried a comb in his back pocket to keep it neat. It was never squished on one side. He loped, like a tiger or something, and those slightly hooded eyes gave him a faintly dangerous look, as if he were sizing up the prey skittering before him. Everyone got out of his way. He sliced through the halls cleanly, never stopping to chitchat, to smile at a girl, anything. Once in a while, he'd raise his chin slightly at a friend, stop to open a door for a teacher. Only once had he ever spoken to me, when I found myself startled to absolute flustered blushing heat to realize he was right behind me in line at the cafeteria. I nearly couldn't breathe for the scent of him, cleaner, less spicy than I had imagined, and a thousand times more narcotic. I stared at his giant hands, the clean oval nails, the length of his thumbs, the gleaming red-mahogany shade of his silky-looking skin, and just wanted to faint.

It was a bad crush.

He said, "Excuse me. Would you mind handing me that last piece of pie?" His voice was much lower than I expected. His enunciation as precise as his daughter's would be twenty years later.

Startled, I looked up at him. Into light brown eyes flecked with gold, looking right down at me. "Pardon?"

He looked at my mouth. Back up to my eyes, and for the most fleeting of seconds, a boy's quick peek, to my breasts, unbound as always beneath my seventies peasant blouse, my nipples no doubt perfectly erect, since my ears were as hot as the steam table right in front of us.

The boy who would become my husband smiled ever so slightly. "Can you hand me that pie? Unless you wanted it?"

I swallowed. "Uh. No. Sure." I reached for it, nearly overturned a line of iced teas, slammed it onto his tray.

"Thank you," he said.

"Sure." I felt his eyes on the side of my neck, glanced back up, snared in his eyes for one long, burning, melodramatic moment, and then the woman behind the cash register bellowed, "Next!" and I had to scramble to pay.

Which is what was in my memory the first night we went out and he'd cleaned his car for me, and worn a sport coat, and took me to dinner, real dinner, at Castaways restaurant. He told me about his dreams, his big plans, his eyes glowing. He wanted to build an empire. I wanted to go to Grasse to study perfume. By the time we headed back out to his car, we were in love. He took me back to his apartment and poured white wine. His hands smelled of the lemons he'd squeezed onto his crab, and his skin was silkier than anything I'd ever felt, and he kissed like he had nothing else to do for the rest of his life.

We were inseparable afterward, and married almost exactly two years later.

Thinking of it, so many years later, I could still remember how it was that night. That perfect laughter, that sweet dance. He loved me, almost instantly, and I loved him back.

And yet, here I was, lying in my bed with a vague hangover, that slight tightness over my brows, and a creeping sense of disappointment in—what? Myself? The world? For a long time, I didn't move, just laid there, cocooned in my quilts and pillows.

I could tell the sky was overcast because there was no glare of sunlight against the blinds. Wind blasted against the building, catching a loose piece of shingling that whistled sharply, then abruptly stopped. Between gusts, it seemed almost eerily quiet. No dogs barked. No child clattered dishes in the sink. No voices came from a man on the phone in the other room. No televisions, left on by someone going to answer a phone, played to empty sofas.

Nothing. Just that wind blasting the windows. I curled up closer under the quilts, realigned the pillows. There was nothing to do today. I might as well sleep.

But even with a touch of a wine headache, I couldn't stay there very long. A lark I was born, my mother used to say grumpily, peering at me through eyes smeared with old eyeliner as she clasped her mug of strong, hot coffee; a lark I remain.

Which is the only thing that has remained the same these days. As I laid there, wishing I had the capacity, like my sister Gina, to sleep through the trials and tribulations of life, I felt an overwhelming sense of disconnectedness.

Whose life was this?

How did I end up here? Shouldn't I be fixing someone's breakfast? Shouldn't I be going to a soccer game or washing clothes or cursing the mess someone left in my kitchen or planning what I was going to do with the garden?

Instead, I was lying in bed by myself in an unbelievably still apartment, with a hangover, and there wasn't even any sound of traffic outside.

It finally dawned on me that so much silence was a little odd. I flung back the covers and winced at the soreness in my legs, arms, back—oh, and feet!—as I stood up. My feet might as well have been clubs, and my hips ached as I hobbled across the room. The job at Annie's was going to take some getting used to.

Peeking through the slats of the blinds, I discovered there was snow blowing like Antarctica across the deserted landscape. A lone car crawled along the snow-packed street. The parking lot across the way held barely a handful of vehicles, most the sturdy four-wheelers that could actually get through the mess, Outbacks and Jeeps and SUVs. I thought of Roxanne's plans for a walk in Ute Valley Park this morning and shook my head. We wouldn't be going anywhere today.

Not that I particularly felt like it. I hobbled to the bathroom, felt more sore muscles down my spine as I bent over to brush my teeth, limped into the kitchen to make my coffee.

The sight of the furniture startled me all over again. The table was littered with the detritus of the night before, glasses with red wine pooled at the bottom in a sticky mass, the empty bottles standing in mute commentary to our wine-soaked musings.

It depressed me. Terribly. As the coffee brewed, I cleared off the messy table with a sense of displacement. I didn't belong here! This was not my world!

But I had no idea what my new life was, where I did belong. The disconnectedness felt like a black hole in the middle of my chest.

Over the breakfast bar, I could see through the patio windows. To snow blowing hard across the morning landscape, obscuring everything. I would not be leaving, and even if I did muddle out into the blizzard, there would be nothing open, no place to go.

Trapped! What in the world could I do with myself?

And into the chaotic, frenetic churn of my thoughts came a word: perfume.

It had been a while. Something in me broke with the divorce, as if all the things I loved were collected in the same corner of my heart, and it was smashed to bits, along with everything inside.

But my love of perfume had been there longer than my husband or my daughter. Longer than I could even remember, really. From the time I was small, I noticed the way things smelled. The rubbery burn of tennis shoes in my uncle's bedroom. The ink and man-sweat of my mother's boyfriend when he came home from work as a pressman at the local newspaper, which was very different from the delicate soap-sweat tang of my mother when she came in from the garden. I liked a corner of our stairs, which smelled of dust and glue and grass my sisters and I tracked in from the backyard. There was a sharp juniper bush outside my bedroom, a scent I disliked, and I'd close my window on summer days when the sun heated it and burned it into my bedroom. I have since learned I was quite ill with the measles the summer I was three years old. I must have wanted to scream, trapped by that smell in that small bedroom, unable to escape. I don't really remember it. And perhaps it is the memory of illness that I associate with juniper.

As coffee brewed in the kitchen, I went into the study and pulled out my perfume journal, bound in heavy leather binding with pale green lined pages that gave off the scent of a thousand experiments.

Riffling through it, I caught a hint of tangerine, another of musk. It looked like a grimoire, as if it would contain magic spells and potions.

I'd been writing recipes in it since I was nine, when I received a chemistry set and the journal one Christmas. The earliest entry was a record of making perfume from the chemistry set, which had outlined the need for recording steps and observations.

Written in a loopy schoolgirl hand, it said:

PREFUME EXPERIMENT #1

Ingredints: 1 cup flower blossoms. ½ cup alcohol. Cheesecloth. Soak flwrs in alchol overnight.
Results: I tried to get my mom to take me to Safeway for roses, but she said no, so I used some daisies that didn't have much smell. STINKS!

PREFUME EXPERIMENT #2

Ingredints: 1 cup carnations. ½ cup vodka. Cheesecloth. Soak overnight.
Results: Much MUCH BETTER! My mom suggested putting a drop of vanilla in and it was nice!!

Reading the early notes always made me feel hopeful, alive. I'd been so heedless in those days, so ready to smell anything. That carnation/vanilla combination was the first one that hooked me, and I'd spent the following summer trying to find the best method of extracting the scent of roses from their petals.

As I turned the pages, one part of my brain was dancing with the perfume I hadn't realized I had been thinking about for days, a scent that had gelled last night.

How could I replicate the poker game with Roxanne and Wanda? Not an actual, specific reproduction, but something that carried the spiritual essence of it? A snowy spring night with wine and women and cards?

Camaraderie, I thought. The heavy grape smell of wine. A hint of smoke from Roxanne's cigarette breaks. The lurking promise of snow in the air. Pizza and cheese. The laughter of women.

And don't forget Roxanne's Ode to Penises. Alone in my apartment, I laughed. From the study in the closet, I brought out my perfumery, housed in a wooden box, a miniature version of a perfumer's organ that opens up to showcase the rows of essential oils, absolutes, tinctures. I keep thinking it's probably time for a new box, but I've had this one for so many years now that replacing it would almost be a sacrilege.

And, too, Daniel made it for me for Christmas the first year we were married, an act of love that honored my passion. It was hinged, folding out in thirds to reveal the tiers designed to hold the small bottles of common and rare substances required for the perfumer's art.

I treasured it even more now, as it had survived the explosion and only three bottles were broken. Me, the perfumery, and the computer were all in the corner of the house farthest from the furnace, and closest to the street. The room survived almost entirely intact, though much of the furniture was ruined by water from the fire hoses or smelled so strongly of smoke they were a complete loss. My laptop computer was knocked to the floor, had been protected by the desk. The perfumery supplies, along with my precious notebook, were tucked in a closet, and fell on a pile of blankets. Only three bottles broke—lime, fir, and a nearly empty bottle of oakmoss. The trio soaked the wood and made it smell of a particularly pungent chypres, which I liked.

I opened the box on the counter. Within were thousands and thousands of dollars' worth of oils, absolutes, solids, resins. Most of the women I knew in my old neighborhood collected something crafty— fabric for quilts or cross-stitch patterns; yarns and needles for knitting or crocheting; candle molds; or whatever. I never had the knack for needlework, but I had my magical box of potions, and I added to it gleefully as the years of my marriage housed me. Dan always made a comfortable living, even in the beginning, and eventually made quite a lot. There was always enough that he would not notice the amounts I paid out to various markets for my precious supplies.

And they were not inexpensive. A half ounce of many absolutes ran $20–$40; carnation absolute ran to $100 per quarter ounce, and it was something of a signature note for me. Compared to many of the hobbies of my friends, that was nothing. His prosperity allowed me to amass a top-tier collection of essences, to seek out rare and hideously expensive items, and indulge experiments beautiful and lovely and odd. Blue chamomile and blood orange and civet. Rose absolutes from Turkey and France and Morocco; patchouli from India; vanilla from Madagascar. There were bottles of lighter notes like lime and grapefruit; florals like orange flower and jasmine; herb and spice essences like tarragon and black pepper and clove.

Beyond the essences, there were drawers of various sizes to hold other supplies. Glass eyedroppers and small brown glass bottles for mixing; grape seed and jojoba and sesame oils; rubbing alcohol and perfume alcohol; blotter strips for testing; and test tubes. Pulling out bottles of absolutes and concretes from the box, I lined them up on the counter.

I measured perfume alcohol into a beaker and nestled it securely in its metal stand. Something earthy and female for the base note; twenty-five drops of a custom blend of civet and oakmoss, very strong, even unpleasant until it was mixed with other elements. As the dark essence dropped into the alcohol, it unfurled like a living being, lacing the clear liquid with its power. I inhaled happily, a sense of tension easing away from my neck. Under my breath, I started to hum—the standard perfume soundtrack, a breathy bit of Bach.

Into the mix of base notes and perfume alcohol, I added a few drops—a very few—of patchouli, a very dark brown, and let the notes blend for a minute or two. As the elements swirled around one another, I made a cup of coffee, narrowed my eyes, and bent to the beaker to wave my nose over the combination.

From there it was a very instinctive thing. I had an idea of what I wanted, but opened several bottles and closed them again without using the essences contained within—all too tame. This would not be a simple or easy perfume, and I'd rather ruin one with recklessness than be too cautious. And for this, yes, it needed to be intense.

Into a second beaker, I mixed Moroccan rose, a waft of bergamot, and paused for a moment, trying to let my subconscious toss up the element I could almost sense. Grapefruit? Hmm. Not quite. Ylang-ylang. Yes. I let them blend a little, breathing in the oxygen and crispness of snowy morning air. Opening to a clean page in my perfume journal, I made several notes on both base and heart notes, then blended the two combinations together in the first beaker.

I bent in to smell it, and reared back. Whew! Very intense, and not one that would even out easily. Carefully, I added lavender, one of the greatest perfume absolutes of all, for the work it could do—sometimes sweeten something too bitter, sometimes soften a hard-edged scent; sometimes, as in the case of such strong others, it became nearly invisible itself, while illuminating the rest of the blend, like sunlight falling on a forest floor.

I smelled it. Perfect. I dipped in a strip of blotter paper, noted the change, walked away for an hour, and read a book while it breathed. To finish, I added top notes of spicy clove to give it Roxanne's laughter, and a splash of ginger. Oddly, carnation asked to be included, and I hesitated, then did it anyway. It was something of a signature, my pleasure in carnation. It was elusive, like memory, not always favored.

I closed my eyes and breathed it in, smiling at the heady mix. Not just anyone could wear such a perfume. Not everyone would even find it appealing, but I liked its complexity.

It was also missing something. I sensed it as a hexagon of emptiness near the edges. A top note, then, but though I squinted and thought, smelled it again and tried to let the answer float in, I wasn't sure. Heaven knew I'd ruined a great many perfumes by adding one drop, one element too much. Not this time.

Heady, I wrote in my journal. Almost dangerous, like Roxanne. Like drinking three bottles of wine, one for each of us, except I think Wanda only drank two glasses, so how much did we have? A lot.

For now, I'd let it rest. Glancing at the clock, I noted the time, poured a cup of coffee, and went to check my email. I'd come back in an hour or so and check it again.

While I waited for the computer to warm up, I drank my coffee and looked at the swirling snow. Amazing. There was probably three feet of snow in drifts across the road, and I knew from experience that once the skies cleared, the snow itself would be melted in a day or two.

Waiting in my inbox were six actual emails. Three were obvious spam, which I deleted. One was from Giselle, one was from a name I didn't recognize. One was from my sister Molly in Hawaii, forwarding pictures of my nieces. THOUGHT YOU'D LIKE THESE! said the subject. I opened them and smiled at their freckled noses.

Eagerly, I opened the one from Giselle, written from her Hotmail account.

TO: nikki@scentofhours.com
FROM: gisellegiraffe@hotmail.com
SUBJECT: hi from London!!!

Hi, Mom! Not a lot of time left. I'm writing from a café and Dad's going to be back to pick me up any second. I'm sitting here listening to all the accents around me and you'd just love it so much I can't stand it that you're not here! I'm sending some pics I thought you'd like. London is AMAZING!!!!! I'd like to live here someday, maybe. Thinking of you lots and I'm bringing back presents. Love you!

Giselle

I scrolled down to look at the photos. There was Giselle, tall and skinny, her hair as curly as mine and just as unruly, blowing out from beneath a striped hat. She stood before the Tower of London with her father, mustached and looking happy and trim. His new wife must have snapped the picture.

An unexpected pinch of hatred stabbed my chest, and I clicked the X to close the email before the evil feeling took over my body.

And yet—how dare he? How dare he look so cheerful and happy? In London? Without me? The pinch rose from my chest to my throat, closing off joy, happiness, the small contentment that had been mine while I made perfume and forgot—for a few minutes anyway—that I was divorced and alone and everyone else was having a good time while I was sitting here, sore, broke, and hungover in a soulless apartment furnished with other people's furniture.

God, it was so not fair.

I hated admitting it, but I was also forlorn. He looked good, my handsome ex. I'd genuinely loved him from the moment we met, when he'd stomped into my world like a big-footed bear, brown and burly and fierce. He thought I was privileged and spoiled—I was neither—and gave me a hard time. His arrogance, his ambition, his burning wish to prove himself to the world captured me.

And I'd been a good wife to him. It wasn't fair that somebody else was in London, had a good house and my own daughter, while I was suffering these outrageous losses.

Unable to resist, I opened the photo again. Peered at his face.

There were a lot of disturbing questions that arose out of this whole divorce mess. For one thing, if we were soulmates, as I'd always believed, then something had definitely gone wrong with the Great Plan.

If we were soulmates, did that mean I would be alone forever?

If we'd been soulmates, how could he be so happy with someone else?

And if karma rewarded good, and punished bad, why was he full of joy and delight while I was mewling around here like a lost kitten?

I jumped up and went to the kitchen. Gulped my coffee and poured another cup, stuck my nose into the beaker again for a quick sniff. It calmed me down, but the hexagon of emptiness still waited for me to fill it.

When I was calmer, I went back to the computer, opened the final email.

TO: nikki@scentofhours.com
FROM: niraj.bhuskar@blipdata.com
SUBJECT: you are not alone

Dear Goldfinger(s):

Here is a link to a blog I thought you would enjoy.

www.workingforaliving.timeblog.net.

I had hoped to go walking today, but like everyone else in this city, I am trapped within my walls by the blizzard. What is it like where you are?

Warmly,
Niraj

Something unfamiliar fluttered in my throat. A man had emailed me! A very attractive man. It had escaped my notice that men might talk to me. That the post-divorce period might hold something positive.

I clicked on the link and read the tale of a young woman in London working in a restaurant for a temperamental chef she called The Ogre, and all the terrible things he did to make her life miserable. She was a good writer, and funny, and plainly liked the job, aside from the evil chef. I laughed aloud three times.

TO: niraj.bhuskar@blipdata.com
FROM: nikki@scentofhours.com
SUBJECT: at least she's young!

Hi, Niraj.

Thanks for the link. I really enjoyed reading it and now I don't feel so terrible about spilling an entire glass of tea on a very grumpy businessman.

Like you, I was planning to walk this morning (with a woman I've met in my apartment building; she likes to go to Ute Valley Park—have you ever walked there?), but the snow is awful here too. I'm at Filmore and Centennial, and there isn't a single car in sight, except the one that's buried in a snowdrift up to the windshield. Obviously, it was abandoned last night. You wouldn't even know there were mountains out there.

Nikki

(Niraj is a great name, BTW. Never heard it before you.)

I sent the email and went back to the kitchen to decide what I wanted for breakfast. Everything sounded like too much work, and I ended up making peanut butter toast.

The perfume needed to rest until tomorrow morning, I decided, which left me nothing whatsoever to do for the rest of the day.

My cell phone, sitting on the counter, rang and spun itself around in a circle. I grabbed it and saw that the call was from my mother. I did not particularly want to talk to her, and my heart fell. Sighing, I picked up the phone, prepared to open it—and then suddenly realized I didn't have to if I didn't want to. I put it down.

From the other room, I heard the bing of email arriving, and curiously went to see what it was.

TO: nikki@scentofhours.com
FROM: niraj.bhuskar@blipdata.com
SUBJECT: how to use the hours

Dear Nikki,

I like your name too. Nikki suits you better than Nicole. Less formal. You do not strike me as a formal sort of woman—you are a Westerner, and I like that very much.

So how will you spend your day instead? I am making a very elaborate meal for my supper—rack of lamb with shallots—which I learned from a friend who lived in New Zealand.

What does your email address come from? Scent of Hours—it sounds like a movie.

Cheerfully,
Niraj

P.S. You needn't feel you must answer quickly. There are obligations with my work that require me to monitor email carefully, even on a snow day. Not everyone is as chatty as I.

~

TO: niraj.bhuskar@blipdata.com
FROM: nikki@scentofhours.com
SUBJECT: scent of hours

Dear Niraj,

Your emails are very welcome. There isn't much to do in a little apartment—I'm used to much more space, and many more toys. I've only been living here for a week and I'm not used to it. The perfume is resting. There are not many ingredients in the house to cook with, or like you I'd likely make something elaborate and warming for supper. The lamb sounds fantastic, and I think you must be a wonderful cook if you undertake something like that. Unusual for a man!

Where in the world do you get lamb in Colorado Springs?

Scent of Hours is a business name I dreamed up a while back. I make perfume and would like to have a business devoted to it someday, so I reserved the domain name. That's what I did this morning, instead of a walk. I made perfume. It's brewing on the counter, still missing something. Not sure what.

What is your work? Computers, of course, but what sort of work?

I guess I'm babbling and will stop now.

Best,
Nikki

In the middle of the afternoon, I turned on the tiny television in my living room, and watched old movies on AMC, dozing for hours. It was oddly healing. When at last I roused myself, there was one more email from Niraj.

TO: nikki@scentofhours.com
FROM: niraj.bhuskar@blipdata.com
SUBJECT: lamb and perfume

Dear Nikki,

You make perfume! How unusual! Did you find the missing ingredient? I buy lamb from a rancher in the East. He sells his own stock—it's very good.

My work: I've done many things with computers over the years, but now I write compression algorithms for transmitting video images across the web.

It is not unusual for a man to cook if he has spent much of his life alone and he enjoys good food. Both are true for me. I have often lived alone and did not want to spend all my pennies eating out, which is not as pleasant as one's own kitchen. Do you like to cook? If you were making something elaborate today, what would it be?

Would you like to take a walk with me this week sometime?

Cheerfully,
Niraj the Nerd

~

TO: niraj.bhuskar@blipdata.com
FROM: nikki@scentofhours.com
SUBJECT: walk

Dear Niraj the Nerd,

I ordinarily don't allow myself to be seen in public with geeks and nerds, but in your case will make an exception. I would enjoy walking with you. My schedule is pretty flexible at the moment, so let me know when a good time would be.

If I were to cook something elaborate, it would be a turkey dinner with all the trimmings, which I love.

I've never eaten lamb, by the way. Just saying.

Sweet dreams,
Nikki

8

Nikki's Perfume Journal Entry

<u>Ingredients</u>: Clove
<u>Category</u>: Spice
Through steam distillation of the dried flower buds (called cloves).

The flowers are hand-picked when the buds are ready to open out and turning pink. They darken and take on their unique final shape after three days in the sun. Clove essence is extracted through steam distillation of the leaves. The crown, which holds the clove, yields yet another essence characterized by a dry and spicy smell.

Each day I worked things went a little more smoothly. Annie had hired another new waitress, a round-faced girl with elvin eyes named Tabitha, and there was enough staff, enough bread, and crowds that were not too demanding. I started to find my rhythm, and when it got busy and I found myself losing my sense of humor, I'd remember the blog link that Niraj had emailed me, and felt better.

It also helped that I started to get the hang of the job. I liked the people I worked with, learned some of the signals that meant I needed to back away from Mary, the dragon of the kitchen, and started to understand who my allies would be. I left the job pleasantly spent, which meant I could sleep through the night and didn't wake up at three a.m. freaking out.

The insurance company was still stalling, and I started to wonder if I needed to hire a lawyer. Until this was settled, I couldn't sell the land, which was enormously valuable even without the house on it.

Wednesday, I worked the lunch shift, and didn't leave the restaurant until nearly five, which put me right in the thick of rush hour. I was able to avoid the highway by taking back roads, but I still had to stop at the grocery store across the street from the apartments at the worst possible time of day.

It was the usual five p.m. zoo, the well-tended occupants of the lush condos around the corner popping in for their fresh greens and imported cheeses; the harried mothers from Holland Park stocking up on Rice-A-Roni and hot dogs, and macaroni and cheese in a box; the singles like me, from the dozens of apartment complexes in the area, coming in after work to buy frozen dinners and quarts of milk.

I felt tired and frazzled in the store. I'd stepped in a giant puddle left over from the blizzard a few days before, and my right shoe squished uncomfortably when I walked. It also made a loud squeaking noise on the shiny floor, which was more than annoying. I had my list and tried to be methodical about the aisles, but I still didn't know this store very well, and had to keep backtracking. It seemed there were awful children in every aisle, too, which always made me upset at the mothers who ignored the poor kids until they were hysterical, then over-disciplined them with sharp jerks or spats to the bottom or other physical reprimands, and then had the nerve to apologize to other adults for the child's behavior. Dan used to complain that I was a nosy parent, and it was true. I hated to see kids get the blame for things that were not their fault.

Not all kids were awful or all parents either. Every so often, you ran across a genuinely miserable child. An overburdened mother trying to soothe a miserable baby or toddler.

Or both, in this case. As I passed the pharmacy, knee-deep with customers, I saw my neighbor Wanda in line, a baby on her shoulder crying softly in obvious pain, a two-year-old in the cart, a boy a few years older leaning on her leg. All three bore the raw, oft-wiped noses of colds, and the toddler in the basket stared glassily toward nothing, his thumb in his mouth.

Wanda swayed back and forth with the baby, whispering to him. The boy on her leg was crying softly, miserably. "I just want to go home!" he said. "My head hurts. Please!"

"I know, honey," she said, her hand smoothing the hair on his crown. "We're just going to get your medicine and then we'll go."

"Wanda," I said. "Do you remember me?"

She looked up. Dark shadows ringed her makeup-less eyes. "Hi, Nikki! Yeah, of course I do. Much wine the other night." She grinned. "That's the most fun I've had in a year. How could I forget?"

"Me too, honestly." I gestured toward her babies. "Looks like you have your hands full. Let me help you."

"Oh," she said. "It's okay. I don't know what you can do, really."

"How about if I stand in line for the medicines and you take the boys home and I bring it over when it's done?"

Her ice-blue eyes filled with tears. "That would be so great. They're starved and sick and we've spent the whole afternoon at the doctor's office."

"Give me the info and I'll bring it over when they get it filled. Can I bring anything else? Chicken noodle soup? Juice?"

"Chicken and stars!" said the boy on her leg.

"You don't have to shop too," she said. "The medicine will be fine." She pulled a list and money out of her purse. "We just got paid, and that's the cough syrup they need, too, over-the-counter stuff. Just forge my name. They don't know me."

"Got it."

"I owe you big," she said. "Come on, guys, let's get you home." Forty-five minutes later, I climbed the stairs to Wanda's apartment with two bags of groceries, plus the medicines. I'd just picked up a few things—several cans of soup, milk, apple juice (which, as I recalled, was easier on young sore throats than orange), some small snacks and easy things to cook. I'd only used her money for the medicine, since I didn't know her budget. My tips had been good—a few extra groceries would hardly be noticed.

She opened the door, looking even more exhausted than she had at the store. Waving me in, she said, "Welcome to my nightmare."

The apartment was almost the same as mine, a little bit larger in the kitchen area, with no fireplace. All three boys were howling, two in the living room, the baby on her shoulder. The room was wrecked; not dirty but strewn with toys and discarded clothing and dishes stacked on the counter as if waiting to be loaded into the dishwasher. A basket of clean laundry sat on the dining room table. Another pile looked as if it had been dumped there to make room for the other.

"I so remember this," I said, laughing softly, "and I only had one. You really have your hands full." I put the bags down on the counter. The two-year-old was yanking at his tennis shoe and I knelt to help him. "Where do you want to start?" I asked Wanda. "What needs to be done? Medicine? Baths? Supper? What?"

"Let's do medicine, supper, baths. Maybe then they'll all crash for the night. Which I could really use."

"I bet."

~

With two adults to split the chores, it wasn't such an impossible undertaking, and within an hour, I was helping the two older boys, Tommy Jr. and Ricky, put on their pajamas, while Wanda sat in the living room and nursed the baby. Spying the books along the wall of the boys' room, I said, "Do you want me to read you a story before you go to bed?"

"Yay!"

"Go kiss your mom good night and I'll read to you when you're under the covers."

"Can she come kiss us when she puts Pete to bed?"

"Is that what she usually does?"

"Yeah."

"Okay." I read *Goodnight Moon* and the first two pages of *Owl Moon*, and they were both out cold before I got to page three. Wanda was putting the baby down, and came out of the room shaking her arms.

"You," she said, "are my guardian angel today. I was about ready to burst into tears in that grocery store."

"I understand. It's horrible when they're sick. I don't know how you do it."

"Do you want some wine? I have some. I can only have about a half a glass in case the boys need something, but by golly, you've earned it."

Her "golly" made me smile. "I'd love that." I looked around the apartment. "Why don't you let me help you put things away first so you can wake up to a little more order? I was never particularly neat, but I can tell you must be."

"Can you? In all this mess?"

"Yes." I pointed to dusted windowsills, sparkling counters except right by the sink. The only real clutter was books, and she obviously liked reading a lot, but even the bookshelves were very neatly tended. No books stuck in sideways, or in front of others. I suspected if I examined the shelves, they'd be alphabetically arranged. "It'll only take a few minutes if we work together."

"I feel guilty, but I want it neat again so bad, I'm going to let you help."

When that was done, we sat at the table beneath a set of family photos—the boys as babies; a family shot with Wanda, her sturdy, swarthy husband, and the two older boys when they were very small. A wedding photo showed two much more relaxed-looking humans, with sunny smiles.

"I never thought about how hard things like this would be for the wives of the soldiers. My mother did it, when my dad went to Vietnam, but I was little. I don't really remember."

"It's usually not that horrible. With all of them sick and nobody to help, it was pretty crazy today." She touched my hand across the table. "Thank you. Really."

"No problem."

She poured wine into my glass. "So you must have children if you managed all that so well."

"I do. A daughter."

"That's right. You mentioned she's in London with her dad. Will she live with you when she gets back?"

"No." I sighed, feeling the weight of it pressing against my chest. "The truth is, I didn't fight as hard as I should have for full custody, and he has a lot more money, so it seemed like it would be better for Giselle."

"Is that her name, Giselle? That's very pretty."

"Thanks."

A rap sounded at the door, and Wanda jumped up to answer it. Roxanne stood there, obviously freshly home from work. "How you doing, hon?" she asked. "Got everything you need?"

"I'm great, thanks to Nikki rescuing me at the grocery store." She shifted to point at me, and I waved.

"Good for you," Roxanne said. "I just wanted to make sure you hadn't killed anybody. Y'all have fun now."

"We will." Wanda gave Roxanne a quick hug, and then closed the door.

Wanda sat back down. "She's really in trouble, you know. You don't have to tell her it was me who said it, but I worry about her all the time. And I worry about her kids. She's sleeping around all over the place and not for the fun of it."

I nodded, not sure whether these were the judgments of a young, protected woman who was shocked by multiple lovers or the concerns of a woman who was nearly thirty and had lived all over the world. "Why do you think she's doing it?"

"Because she's not over her ex." Wanda narrowed her eyes. "You know what I think is weird? She really likes to sleep with married guys. It's almost like she's getting back at her ex."

I nodded. "It's hard stuff, you know. My ex is remarried too."

She pursed her lips. "I'm sorry."

"Thanks." I sipped my wine. "He was an all right guy, just kind of lost at the end there. He thought he needed something else, I guess."

"How long were you married?"

"Almost eighteen years."

"That is long! How did you meet him?"

I took a breath, smiled. "He came to do repairs at the apartments I was living in with a roommate. Back then, he had his first renovation business, him and one other guy, and he was only twenty-three, which I thought was amazing." I grinned, moved my arms. "He had the best arms you ever saw, just sleek and muscled and very nice."

"Mmmm."

"But the reason I ended up going out with him was because he was smart. He talked about politics. He read the paper every morning. He knew geography and culture and all kinds of things like that that I didn't know. I thought he was amazing." I paused. "He is amazing, I guess. Not was. If he's not a millionaire, he's pretty close now—he's worked really hard."

"Wow." She rubbed her forehead, and I saw in the gesture her absolute exhaustion. With an embarrassed little shock, I realized she was being patient with me, letting me stay because she probably sensed my loneliness. Heat burned around the edges of my ears.

"You are so tired," I said, standing. "I'm going to take off and let you get some sleep."

"Drink your wine! I'm not that tired."

"I appreciate it, but I'm going to get home. If you need anything, please call me, all right? It's hard work to be a single parent, even if it's only technically single-parenting."

She gave me a very sweet smile. "You must have sisters."

I laughed. "Yes. Two. And I'm the oldest."

"I can tell."

On my way out, I touched her shoulder. "Be good to yourself, kiddo."

"I will."

Back in the silence of my apartment, I made a cup of tea and settled in front of the little gas fireplace, an ache in my chest. It didn't seem that long ago when Giselle had been a little thing, her hair wild, her laughter the best thing in our world. We'd been in love then, too, me and Daniel. In love with each other and our baby daughter.

When had it changed? I thought of grade-school plays and recitals, parent-teacher conferences. Still solid, still solid, still in love. We worked together. We went to business functions to hustle up more contacts and clients. We rented movies on Saturday nights and ordered pizza and drank wine in bed. We did it in the old house, and even when we moved to the house on Wood Avenue.

My tea was deep red, tasting of hibiscus, and I sipped it slowly, admiring the flames on the grate.

When did it change?

It wasn't one moment, but if I was honest, I could think of little things that had started to bother me. One night, as we got ready for a fundraiser for the Urban League, Daniel frowned at my hair, lying loose on my shoulders as always. "Have you ever considered dyeing your hair dark?"

I snorted. "I thought all men wanted blondes?"

"I like it," he said, straightening his tie. "All that yellow sure does stand out, though, doesn't it?"

The wind of change chilled me for a moment, washing over my white collarbones, my blue eyes, my very, very white arms. "Are you embarrassed to have a white wife, Daniel?" I said incredulously.

"Don't be ridiculous."

But he was. He was the president of the African American Businessman's Association, and more and more often he did not take me with him to anything connected to it. It was still fine for us to be a couple at white dinner parties and at fundraisers arranged by white folks, but in the African American world, not so.

But even now, after he'd married a perfect little African American princess, if I would have accused him of dumping me for the sake of his public perception, he would have denied it.

At least, I thought now, taking my cup to the sink, I'd never caved in to pressure and cut or colored my hair. Blonde it was, and curly and bright.

Hooray for me.

On Thursday morning, there was an email from Niraj.

TO: nikki@scentofhours.com
FROM: niraj.bhuskar@blipdata.com
SUBJECT: walking

Dear Goldfingers,

Would you like to go for a walk this afternoon? I was thinking about the Garden of the Gods—it might be very muddy, but beautiful anyway. It will soon be too busy with tourists to enjoy. What do you say?

Niraj

I wrote back:

Yes. Call me at work around one p.m.

So I was expecting his call when Zara, the beautiful blonde bartender, came to the kitchen to find me. "Niraj is on the phone," she said with a little smile. It seemed secretive. Maybe mocking. "Do you want to take it?"

"Yes." I pushed the box of lettuce back into the fridge and hurried behind her. She gestured to the phone and again I caught a little edge of something in her attitude. I picked it up. "Hello?"

"Hello, Nikki," he said. He really did have the most extraordinary voice, dulcet and smooth. "Will you have time to walk this afternoon?"

"Yes. I should be finished in about half an hour. I could meet you around two-thirty?"

"That will be fine. Shall we meet at the main parking lot, then?"

"Great. I brought old shoes in case it's muddy."

"Good for you. I'll see you then."

"Fine. Bye."

I hung up, feeling suddenly fluttery and nervous. Was this a date? Or were we just friends? Even the fact that I asked the question was embarrassing—what in the world would a man like that see in someone like me?

"Niraj, huh?" Zara said with a smile, wiping down the bar.

"We're just going for a walk."

She smiled. "New to dating, are you?"

I felt color in my cheeks. "No, it's not that. I mean, we just got to talking and he likes to walk and so do I, and well—"

"Interesting," she said, inclining her head. "You're not his usual type."

"His type?" I suddenly imagined him cruising the local bars and hot spots for easy marks.

"He tends to go for a country club brunette. A tennis babe."

"You're right. That's not me." Realistically, did anyone's taste run to pudgy, middle-aged blondes? I added some figures on the computer, and tried to seem casual when I asked, "Does he have a reputation or something?"

She lifted a shoulder. "Maybe a little. He's dated a few women around here. I don't think he's a player, though, I think he just likes women and they like him back."

"Well," I said dismissively, "we're friends, that's all."

"You don't have to justify it to me, sister. I'm all for dates, friends, lovers, whatever." She grinned. "Have a good time."

~

I'd brought a change of clothes with me, and after my shift, I washed my face and hands, reapplied some blush and mascara, and combed my hair. The blouse was one of the first new things I'd purchased after the official divorce, a floaty blouse in greens and blues in a pattern that reminded me of things I'd loved when I was twelve. It was a good color for me. I was feeling fairly cheerful as I headed for my car, my restaurant clothes in a bag.

It was a beautiful day, with a light, fresh wind whispering through the narrow street. I swung the bag at my side as I walked, my spirits light. Maybe Niraj was a player. It had been so long, maybe I needed the reminder that men were not uniformly nice. But it didn't matter. Maybe nothing would come of it. Maybe we were only friends, even though I was more than a little attracted to him.

Whatever. A little tangle of annoyance rose in me. Stop it! Not everything was life and death. In the period when I'd been trying to save my marriage, when I'd been trying every possible variation on magical thinking, it had often seemed that if I just did the one right thing, or figured out where the one bad thing was that I could undo, everything would be all right.

But even then, it hadn't been life and death, had it? It only felt like it was.

Coming up on my right was the narrow, neglected little shop for rent. I slowed. In the window, sunning himself in perfect contentment, was the black kitten. He'd startled so badly the first time I saw him that this time I paused and looked at him from a few feet away. Not more than three or four months old, with glossy black fur and a white chest. His back was dusty, as if he'd been rolling in the dirt.

As a girl, I'd always had cats, but Dan was allergic, and to have the man, I gave them up. For the first time, I realized I could have one if I wished. I could have three! Ten! Who would stop me?

It was weirdly exhilarating.

Cautiously, I approached the window and let my shadow fall on the cat. He seemed to realize now that the window was protection, and instead of bolting, he only lifted his head and opened bright yellow eyes. I put my fingers against the glass and he rubbed against it. I smiled. "You should come home with me, little one."

He bent down and stretched, then jumped out of the display window and disappeared into the dusty bowels of the shop. I wondered what he lived on. Mice? The creek was right behind the store—probably all sorts of little things lived down there.

I thought of Niraj. Our walk. Butterflies swept through my belly.

The Garden of the Gods was only a couple of miles from the restaurant. Although it was not yet tourist season, there were a fair number of cars in the parking lot, and I didn't immediately see Niraj. I didn't know what he drove, either, and imagined he might have a Toyota or Nissan, something reliable and clean. I didn't know why. He didn't strike me as an SUV sort, or someone who'd drive a sports car to impress, but then, what did I really know about him?

I smeared Carmex on my lips and checked my reflection in the rearview mirror before I got out. The butterflies fluttered wings in my belly again. I touched the spot, surprised and a little embarrassed, but also pleased. How lovely, to anticipate the company of a man! How long had it been?

As I closed my car door, I raised my face toward the sky, happily. It's an impossible vista to feel jaded about, the hot cerulean sky, the stark white snow on the Peak, the vivid orangey-red rocks dotted with sage and yucca and juniper in various shades of grayish green. Ash green, I often think. It should be an official color.

And against such a backdrop, Niraj was beautiful too. He waited for me at the opening to the park, wearing a white T-shirt with three-quarter-length sleeves and a placket of three buttons at the neckline, which somehow gave him a Continental look. His feet were clad in boots with good socks, and he wore khaki shorts with plenty of pockets. He had spectacular legs, a cinnamony color with silky scatters of hair and splendid calves.

I was so out of my league!

My cheeks grew hot with it, the recognition of how much better-looking he was than me. Zara's spiny comments poked me—*You're not exactly his type.*

As I approached, however, he straightened, gave me a smile. "Hello, Nikki," he said. "How are you?"

"Hello, Niraj," I said, feeling that awkward sense of formality with him. "I am very well, and you?"

He had a small CamelBak over his shoulders, and shifted so he could take a sip. "Do you have water?"

I lifted a liter bottle in my hand to show him. Was he a little nervous too? How could that be? "I'm good."

"This way, then," he said, and led the way across the parking lot. A path ran between stands of trees, headed away from the main area. We walked in silence for a few moments, Niraj in the lead, which gave me a chance to admire the working of his strong calves. He wore gray-and-white wool socks. The day was warm, the sun high-altitude strong against the top of my head, even though it was only April.

When the path widened to let us walk side by side, he paused to let me catch up. "You're a very serious hiker, aren't you?" I said.

"I am not sure 'serious' is the correct word, but why do you say so?"

I grinned. "The boots, socks, backpack—even the shorts. All the right things."

"Ah." He grinned, too, and leaned a little closer. "That is only the habit of a bachelor with simple tastes and disposable income. I go to the store and say, 'What is the best you have?' And they show it to me."

I chuckled. "And you buy it."

"Mostly. And you, the native, you don't have special things?"

"Not because I wouldn't want them." I eyed the water-filled back-pack. "That's very cool. I'd like one of those."

"I do like it."

I kicked a rock and it skittered up the path, glittering with mica. "When did you start hiking seriously?"

"In college. It was a girl."

"Of course." I smiled.

"She liked trekking, which is what we call it in the UK. We traveled many places, exploring. Always on foot."

"Really? Like where?"

"Scotland, Greece, Turkey, the Verdon Gorge in France."

I imagined a sturdy English girl, all enormous eyes and breasts. "You must have been with her a long time to see so many places."

"Five years," he said. "We planned to marry."

"And?"

He looked at me with a small smile. "We did not."

I grinned. "Is she the one you followed to Colorado?"

He met my eyes. "You are a good listener."

"I try."

A slight hesitation. "The answer is no. It was another woman I followed here."

There was some small something that made me think it was unre-solved, or at least his feelings were. His face showed nothing. I let it go.

"And what about you, Nikki? How long were you married?"

I told him, and wondered if he would realize that I hadn't dated much. At all. How embarrassing would that be?

We reached a tight place on the path and he gestured for me to precede him. I led the way around a turn and stepped over a hay-clogged pile of horse manure, then down the hill a little ways. I was conscious of the fact that he could now look at my behind; the backs of my thighs, which might not be as smooth as they once had been; the slight roll of flesh beneath my bra. All the bad spots.

"I like your hair," he said. "It looks like cotton candy."

I looked over my shoulder. "I like yours too."

"No! Mine is wild and mischievous."

"That's why I like it."

He caught up with me on a wider space of the path. "Do you have a rebel heart, then?"

"No. Never really have." I looked at the mane of his curls, the loose ringlets falling. It made me think of a prince. "You have medieval hair," I said, "from a painting." I wanted to touch it and instead unscrewed the lid of my water bottle, took a sip. "So what happened to the fiancée, if you don't mind my asking?"

"I don't mind." He gestured for me to go ahead around a rock in the path, then caught up with me when we'd passed it. "My fiancée dumped me for a man with a very posh accent and a pretty face."

"It's so English, that you mentioned his accent."

"No, it's English that she would choose it." A shrug. "She was not a rich girl. I don't blame her. And in those days, I was not a handsome lad."

"Impossible."

He smiled. "Thank you. But I assure you, I was not. I was a computer boy, a little bit fat from my mother's cooking." He gestured with his fingers. "Very thick glasses. Black ones."

"I can't tell if you're pulling my leg or not."

"Sorry?"

"Teasing me. Seeing if you can fool me."

He smiled. "I assure you, I was quite a homely child."

I tried to imagine him a doughy Indian computer geek in thick glasses. "Well, you grew out of it very nicely."

"Thank you."

"What happened to the glasses?"

"Lasers."

"Ah. Good idea. My mom had it done, years ago."

"And you, Nikki-Nicole, what were you like as a young woman?"

"You mean I'm not one anymore?"

He looked slightly abashed, then realized I was only kidding. "You're pulling my leg."

I danced around a spot where melted snow had made a pool the color of blood from all the clay. "Yes."

"So?"

"I was ordinary," I said. "My mother is beautiful, and I have a beautiful sister who became an actress, but my other sister and I were just the ordinary ones." I realized that it would sound as if I were fishing for compliments, that he might feel obliged to comment on my not-ordinariness now, and I rushed to add, "Not that I think I'm ordinary, necessarily," which was worse, "or beautiful, either, but my sister is really, really pretty and—well, that's just sort of the cornerstone of deciding what everyone else looked like."

He listened to this long babble with patience. "I have a very, very beautiful aunt," he said. "When she comes into a room, everyone feels a little bit less. They're all looking at her."

"Exactly."

"Aside from having to endure a beautiful sister, what else were you like?"

"Serious. Quiet. A little bit on the outside—an observer, I guess."

"You liked kittens and pretty things? Or were you a tomboy?"

Surprised, maybe embarrassed, I glanced at him. "Both. I loved kittens, and ribbons in my hair, and flowers and perfume. But I was also a daredevil on my bike, and I liked climbing trees. I liked being outside.

I had this friend, Mark—" I stumbled for a minute, surprised to hear his name on my lips. I didn't speak of him, as a rule. Not because it was some hidden trauma or wound I wanted to keep secret—I just didn't.

"Mark?"

"We used to try to find horny toads by the creek."

He chuckled. "I don't think I know what that is."

"It's an ugly little frog."

So it went. We fell silent, then spoke again in small washes of words. Our feet crunched over rocks. A light sweat had formed on my skin. I liked the look of his knees, lifting so sturdily, the cording in his thighs. The sun was hot on my head. I liked the feeling of fresh air in my lungs. The sense of healthy movement.

And Niraj—I liked the way his name rolled around in my mouth— he smelled of sun-heated hair and faintly of ginger. A wind blew the flavor of pine needles over us, and I liked that too.

It wasn't a long walk, only an hour. As we headed up the sidewalks toward the parking lot, with the Kissing Camels towering over the land-scape from the left, I wondered how we would end it.

"I think they look like kissing squirrels," he said, pointing.

"Like clouds—open to interpretation." I pointed at another rock formation. "A gargoyle."

"So it is." He smiled, met my eyes, and I felt a quick, hot flash of something over the darkness, the twinkle in his irises, what seemed to be a frankness of admiration—though how would I know, it had been so long? The backs of our hands brushed and we swayed closer, then farther apart, focused on the ground, the red concrete beneath our feet.

"I really needed a walk today," I said. "Thank you."

"My pleasure. We shall have to do it again soon."

"Yes."

We reached the parking lot and stopped, facing each other. A breath of breeze ruffled his hair, teased mine into my eyes, and I caught it back. I cocked a thumb over my shoulder. "I'm parked over there."

"I'll walk you."

"You don't have to."

He gave me a very small smile. "I know."

It took all of thirty seconds to get there, even weaving through the knots of walkers and rappellers crowding the lot on such a beautiful day. "Here's my car," I said brightly, and opened the trunk to get my purse. A waft of restaurant odors, embedded in my clothes, sailed out.

"I am leaving for San Francisco in the morning, so I won't be seeing you at Annie's."

"Forever?" I said, surprised at how disappointed I felt.

He laughed. "No, no. Only a week. I will be back next weekend. Perhaps we can think of some walk to do then, hmm?"

"Okay." I slammed the trunk, held my keys in my hand. He stood there in front of me, not really doing anything, either, and I wondered if I should offer my hand or something. "Um . . . I guess I'll see you then. Have a good trip."

He took a slight step back, as if he'd been waiting for some sign, and raised his hand, palm out, in a wave. "All right, Nikki. You have a good time working. Take care."

I climbed in my car, buzzing. I watched him walk away in the rearview mirror, strong calves and a loping grace. I should have given him a sign, shouldn't I? But what?

Or maybe I was imagining things. Zara's words came back to me: *You're not exactly his type.*

I sat there with my hands on the wheel for a full minute, filled with an agonizing insecurity I hadn't experienced in decades. I thought of my best friend from junior high, Holli Bradish, and how we would sit in my bedroom listening to 45s and eating M&M's, examining every detail of a boy's behavior—*Do you think he likes me?*

With a groan, I threw the car into gear and backed out. You would have thought at least something would have become easier over the years. Apparently not.

On the seat beside me, my cell phone rang. I didn't recognize the number, but picked up anyway. "Hello?"

"Hi, Nikki," said a husky woman's voice I didn't immediately recognize. "This is Roxanne, your neighbor? I just found out my kids are going to see their dad tomorrow night. You want to go to happy hour somewhere, maybe?"

The car idled beneath me, and in a Land Rover, Niraj drove by, his hair blowing. Hmm. "I have to work Saturday morning, so I can't stay out too late."

"That's all right. It's only happy hour. Over at seven-thirty."

Happy hour. "All right."

9

Nikki's Perfume Journal Entry

Time: 1:30 a.m.
Date: June 30, 1982

Bottle: something that calls up the excess of the eighties
Elements: Aramis cologne, sour beer, martini with too much vermouth, cigarette smoke, onion rings, glass sterilizer, Double-mint gum
Notes: the apartment over on Academy, with all the mis-matched glassware

My mother's first husband was my father, a Fort Carson sergeant she fell in love with when she was sixteen. They married when she was eighteen, and he sowed three daughters before heading out to his second tour in Vietnam, which was just before the Tet Offensive. He was a good soldier, they say. Not that he died there, not physically anyway.

Her second husband was a mechanic at the shop next to the real estate office where she worked as a secretary. He only lasted a little more than a year, which is when my mother decided he was a bum, like every other man she met in those days, and she kicked him out. We three girls secretly cheered. I thought he looked like a caveman with his hairy back, and my sister Gina hated the way he chewed with his mouth open.

After that, my mother did without male companionship for quite a while. Or if she had lovers, she kept them off-screen. Her daughters didn't see them. She worked her butt off, bought a smallish house in the suburbs so we could go to good schools. She kept herself up, and the other mothers were often jealous of her figure.

She met her third husband at a Parents Without Partners meeting, and moved to LA with him and my youngest sister—the beautiful one—the summer after my high school graduation. My sister Gina had already met the soldier who would be her husband, and she'd gone to live with him in Germany.

I was left to my own devices. In my working-class world, nobody went to college, so it didn't even occur to me at that point to even explore the possibility—not then. It took a couple of years.

Right out of high school, I took a job as a waitress at Coco's Hamburgers—waitresses made more than secretaries or receptionists—and found a place with a girlfriend from school. We lived in an anonymous strip of apartments on the north end of town and went to happy hour at a dozen spots along Academy Boulevard.

In those days, Colorado still had a 3.2-beer drinking law for ages eighteen through twenty-one. We'd put on our eyeliner, our Danskins and jeans, and head out for the Odyssey or D.J.'s or Giuseppe's to drink watery beer and dance with soldiers and cadets from the Air Force Academy, and others who were just as young and bored as we were. The Odyssey had floors with squares of flashing lights. I had a crush on a drummer who played at D.J.'s in a band called the Wumblies that earnestly seemed as if it might make it someday. He had long dark hair and full lips and I couldn't think how to talk to him. I don't remember why we went to Giuseppe's, other than the fact it was close and we could walk if gas money was an issue.

My roommate, J.J., was a little fast, and sometimes she'd spend the night with a guy she'd met, or bring him back to our apartment, which was hung with posters of Peter Frampton—hers—and the Rolling Stones—mine. There were plants crowded into every available space, coleus and purple velvets and Swedish ivy, and a hanging macramé table J.J. had woven that attracted much admiring comment. We lived on boiled eggs, coffee, potpies, and copious amounts of 3.2 beer.

Twenty-five years later, as I checked my lipstick in the rearview mirror, nervously eyeing all the cars in the parking lot at Ruby's, I thought of J.J. and my old apartment with a sense of exhaustion. Was this the answer, going the happy hour route? It seemed idiotic and impossible to do it without the freshness of young skin or a spectacular waistline or even a sense of optimism. How could I stand it?

What did women do when they found themselves widowed or divorced at middle age? What had my mother's friends done? They'd gone to bars, I knew. I'd babysat for them sometimes.

Now it seemed that women in the magazines had women friends, book circles, cooking classes, travel. They went on walking tours of Tuscany, or trained for marathons. They had careers, most of them. Good lives.

I patted my hair and got out. That was my problem. I should have had a career, and then I wouldn't need a man. I wouldn't have to be headed across the parking lot in a pair of jeans that were a bit too tight, trying to remember to keep my stomach pulled in, to meet a girlfriend for happy hour when I was well past the traditional age.

At the door, seeing all the people crowded around the bar, I nearly turned around and headed right back to my car. Only the sight of Roxanne, smoking a cigarette as she kept an arm protectively around an empty stool she was presumably saving for me, made me take a deep breath and pull open the door.

An instant slam of laughter, voices, smoke enveloped me. Roxanne waved, and I made my way through the room.

Ruby's was a restaurant I'd passed a zillion times, just down the hill from the apartment complex. Once it had been an upscale steak house, and it had that slightly outmoded sense of the seventies about it, a giant flagstone fireplace with a copper hood, and heavy wooden tables. The bar section had been redone, the windows opened to the view of the mountains, the chairs upholstered in a purple-and-blue fabric, which made it cheerful enough.

I felt people looking at me as I settled on the chair Roxanne had saved for me. "Hi!" she said. "What do you want to drink? It's all two-for-one."

"Um. Chardonnay?"

The bartender, a good-looking young man with red hair in a brush cut, said, "House white?"

"Sure."

Roxanne leaned over. She was wearing black slacks with a red shirt that showed off her shoulders. Her eyes were smokily lined, her hair freshly washed and swingy. I'd done my hair and face and ironed a fresh blouse I usually liked, but next to her, I felt like a worn-out old mama wolf, coat molting, tummy swinging with my walk.

"It's not usually this crazy in here," she said in my ear. It wasn't like screaming over the music, but we had to tuck our heads together. "But it's a pretty good crowd, huh?"

I looked around. There were a few tables of mixed guys and girls in their mid-to-late twenties, dressed as if they'd just got off work. Some couples shared appetizers. The surprise was in the numbers of people my age, forty- and fifty-somethings in little knots. I had had no idea middle-aged people went to happy hour. In my old neighborhood, we were too busy with dinner or soccer or phone calls to think about taking time to go have a cocktail with friends.

I leaned over. "Where do they all come from?"

Roxanne shrugged, lit a cigarette. Her smoke joined the low cloud hanging over the room. It was weird to see so many people smoking. Before this, before going to work at Annie's, I hadn't known anyone who smoked anymore. At all. Ever.

"All over," she said. "There are a bunch of computer companies around here, and some manufacturing, that kind of thing." She eyed a man who came in the front door. "There's Alan. What do you think?"

"Is he your date or something?" I asked, prepared to be miffed.

"Not at all. He's a regular. He used to be dating one of the bartenders here, but she quit and went back to Detroit, or wherever it is she was from."

The man was in his late thirties or a little more, with the artfully messy look of a country-western singer—sun-streaked hair raggedly cut and a little too long around a good-looking face he hadn't shaved. "He looks like he'd be a headache," I said without thinking. "Too much trouble."

The bartender delivered my wine. Two of them. He slapped the ticket down on the bar in front of me and rushed away. "Two?"

"Yeah." She gestured, and I noticed lots of stacked-up drinks around me. "They mean literally two-for-one."

Maybe, I thought, I wouldn't be driving home, after all. "Is it hard to get a cab from here?"

"You can always get a ride. Nearly everyone lives right along here somewhere. A lot of them live in the same apartments we do."

"I still can't stay out late." I looked at my watch and made a mental note to be out the door in two hours—at eight, sharp. "I have to work at six."

"Ugh!" She sucked on her cigarette, wiggled her fingers at the guy across the bar. "Too much trouble, huh? Probably is. But I bet he's good in bed."

"Maybe." He did have a good mouth, lush and sullen.

"What's your type, then?" she asked.

"I don't know, really. It's been so long that I'm just now realizing I can even look at them." I sipped the wine, and it was crisp, cold, refreshing. "I went on a walk yesterday with a guy from the restaurant."

She lifted her eyebrows. "Yeah? Was it a date?"

"Good question. I don't know." With a sheepish smile, I shook my head. "It's all so new and weird and I don't have my signals straight yet."

"Yeah? What's he like?" Her gaze was direct, interested.

"He's really nice. Great hair. Sort of formal—he's British, and his manners are very good."

"Cool! An accent is always good. Very sexy."

"Right."

She took a deep drag off her cigarette, politely blew it away from me. "Do you think that's partly why it's hard to tell if you're reading his signals right?"

"Maybe." A teeny sense of pressure drained away. "I hadn't thought of that."

"You'll figure it out."

"I'm sure."

"You will. At first, I didn't even remember how to flirt, or what to do, or—oh, it's just so weird at first, you know?"

"It's hard to imagine you feeling that way."

She lifted one finger and reached into her purse, which was sitting on the bar. It was a big leather bag, not at all what I would have imagined her to carry. "Check it out," she said, and gave me a picture of a family—a mother, father, and two children in soccer outfits. "That's me the year before he met his hoochy-kootchie girl."

The mother in the picture had long dark hair and straight-cut bangs. She was somewhat plump through the middle, but still very pretty in a denim jumper and T-shirt. She looked like a third grade teacher and suburban mom, and her husband had his arm around her and one of the children. His face said he was exploding with pride over them all.

For a blistering second, I was transported to my own past, to a morning of gilded sunlight, my own husband happy beside me, everything in its place as children kicked a ball around a green park.

I shoved the photo back to her. "You look so happy."

"Happy!" she barked, and looked at the picture. "Fat, you mean!"

"Maybe a little, but not much. What were you carrying there, an extra fifteen pounds, maybe?"

"About that," she said, and peered hard at the photo. "I've lost around thirty-five." She was painfully thin, but it gave her a chic look.

"I mean, I've never worn more than a size ten my whole life. It's not like I've ever been obese."

I wanted to cross my arms over my middle and resisted. My top was never smaller than a twelve, and that was on a good day. Dan's new babe was much smaller than me—if I'd been thinner, would our marriage have lasted?

I didn't know. Maybe it didn't matter either. I'd loved him even though he'd started losing his hair, even though his ears sprouted hair and he snored. "He didn't leave you over fifteen pounds, Roxanne," I said.

"I know." She shoved the picture back in her purse and lit another cigarette, her foot swinging restlessly. She blinked hard, sucked the smoke, gave me a rueful smile. "Don't mind me. I'm just PMSing. Let's talk about something else."

I looked at her, seeing the vulnerability beneath her eyes, the fragile line of her collarbone, and felt suddenly protective. "I think you're one of the most beautiful women I've ever met," I said. "Don't let him take that away from you."

She looked at me. "That was so nice. Thank you."

~

We ordered a mixed appetizer plate, made up of things I ordinarily never allowed myself to eat, like potato skins and fried cheese (fried cheese!), and savored them. In the spirit of indulgence, I even put sour cream on the potato skins. Roxanne asked about my walking date, and I told her a little, just that we'd walked around the Garden of the Gods, that he was good-looking, that we hadn't kissed or touched or anything.

"He sounds nice," she said, and it sounded like she meant boring, but that was all right. She liked something other than what I did.

Witness her mark, Alan, who came over and took the chair next to her. I tried to see what she was excited about, but even the mouth really just looked surly to me. He looked like the kind of man who was used to getting his own way all the time. Like the petted, celebrated youngest brother in a family.

A friend of his, a dark-haired construction worker who was called—of all things—Wolf, joined him. Roxanne gave me a sly look I tried to ignore, but I did like him quite a lot better than Alan. He was unapologetically a workingman, a construction supervisor for a concrete firm, and it showed in his build. He smelled of clean laundry and sunshine, and his eyes were lively. The pair of them played off each other in an attempt to charm us.

It wasn't so bad. A lot better, actually, than sitting alone in my apartment thinking about my ex-husband and my daughter touring the city I'd most wanted to see my whole life. I drank the first wine too fast and made myself slow down for the second, and that was when I made Roxanne split the appetizer plate with me. Plenty of fat and carbs to soak up the alcohol.

Wolf downed a huge cheeseburger with fries, along with two tall pints of some dark beer. His lusty appetite fascinated me. His forearms were tanned a dark brown, even in spring, and they looked like they'd ring like steel if you tapped them with a hammer. Wiping his mouth delicately, he sighed. "Damn, that was good. Since I got divorced, I live on nothing but Swanson's potpies."

Alan chimed in. "No, I like Marie Callender. Macaroni and cheese, and beef stew."

I laughed, raised my hand. "Lean Cuisine."

"Welcome to Splitsville," Roxanne said. She pointed to her chest. "Cracklin' Oat Bran and Lucky Charms."

We all laughed. As if it was funny. As if there weren't a thousand things funnier than that. And there was more along the same lines, the same inane little conversations.

But really, how different was it from the polite conversations I'd had a thousand times at dinner parties at Pamela's house, or Kit's? Not much. If you were lucky, there was a raconteur who held up your end of the table. In this case, it was Wolf, who seemed smarter than his muscles would have suggested. He was verbal and funny and never seemed to show the beer he was drinking. His speech stayed steady, his eyes clear.

They bought Roxanne and me another round—a second two-for-one. "That's too much for me," I protested.

"We'll just split a cab," Roxanne said. "It won't cost that much if we split it."

It seemed like a waste, since I wouldn't drink it, but whatever. I shrugged.

Taking a slight, tiny sip of the first glass, I said, "If you could go anywhere, where would you go?" It was no less stupid than any of the other things we'd been discussing.

"Cairo," Wolf said without hesitating. "I gotta see the pyramids before I die."

I raised my eyebrows. "Really."

One side of his mouth lifted in a wry smile. "You look surprised, sister. What'd you think I'd say?"

I shook my head. "I don't know. Not that, I guess."

"Make you feel better if I said Branson, or something?"

"No." I met his eyes, which were vividly blue, and challenging. "Why the pyramids?"

"Because they're so old. Because I'd like to see if they have any kind of vibration in them, you know? Secrets." He plucked a piece of lettuce from the bar and dropped it on his plate. "I used to love to read about them when I was a kid."

"I'd go to Rio," Alan said. "All those beautiful women."

I just barely stopped myself from drawling, *What a surprise.*

Wolf said, "Don't be a cliché, man. Come up with something better than that."

Alan looked into his beer. "Las Vegas. Even though I been there."

I dipped my head to hide my amusement. Roxanne kicked me under the table and I looked at her. Her eyes were glittering with amusement, and I couldn't believe she meant to have this guy. Under her breath she started singing the hot-dog song. My nostrils quivered with my attempt to keep the giggle out of my voice.

"How 'bout you, sister?" Wolf asked. "Where would you go?"

"Are you calling me sister because you can't remember my name?"

He grinned.

"It's Nicole."

"All right, Nicole," he said, and I liked the ease in it. "Answer the question."

"London," I said. "I was a history fiend when I was a teenager and I want to see all the places I read about."

"What she's not saying," Roxanne piped up, "is that her ex took her daughter there for spring break, even though it was the place Nikki wanted to go more than anywhere. Isn't that just like an ex?"

"Dude," Alan said, shaking his head. "That sucks."

"I'll get there," I said. "Now you, Roxanne. Where would you go?"

She tapped a cigarette out of her pack, drew it out, held it in her fingers. "Around the world. One of those cruises where you get on the ship and it takes you all the way around in one hundred and eighty days or something. I'd love that."

I smiled at her. "You should do it."

She bent into the match Alan held for her. "Maybe I will," she said, and blew out a stream of pale blue smoke. "Maybe I will."

～

At seven-thirty, I excused myself and went to the ladies' room. In the mirror, I stared at my face and saw the wine flush on my cheekbones, the excessive brightness of my eyes. It was very hot and smoky in the pub area, and it was making me feel dizzy and overwrought. I told myself I should go home, but there was something enjoyable about it too. Forgetting. Immersing in the noise.

I soaked a paper towel in cold water and held it to my forehead, then each temple. My chest at the neckline of my button-down was flushed, and I unbuttoned it a little more, pressed the cold towel to that flesh too. The one good part of being a little overweight right now was the extra cleavage it gave me. It looked nice, I thought, blurrily.

Time to stop drinking. Well past time, actually. Maybe I ought to just go ahead and call a cab and go home. Except then I'd need a ride down here in the morning before work. Why hadn't I thought of that?

Stupid, stupid, stupid.

I could call another cab in the morning, but that would cost even more, wouldn't it, and it wasn't like I had tons. I could walk, couldn't I? Leaning into the mirror to reapply my makeup, I thought, Yes. Walk. Good idea. It couldn't be more than a mile, maybe not even that much. A half mile.

Good plan.

Time to go home. Hmm. I'd have to figure that out. When I went back out to the bar, I said to the bartender, "Will you call me a cab, please?"

"Sister, you don't have to get a cab," Wolf said. "I'll drive you."

I shook my head. "I don't think so. You've been drinking too."

"Nah. I had beer with my dinner, but that's it." He pointed to the two inches still left in his last pint. "Ask Andrew."

The bartender nodded. "He's sober. I know him."

Which left another dilemma. "Er . . . I don't really know you."

Roxanne put her hand on my arm. "He's all right."

Truth was, I liked the idea of getting into a car with him. He was big and solid and smelled of Tide detergent, and I was really ready to go home before I drank yet another matched set of chardonnays. "All right."

We paid our separate bills, and as I waited for my change, I asked Roxanne if she was ready to come now too. She shook her head. "My night's just getting started."

In the old days, I wouldn't have left a girlfriend alone at the bar with a guy, not when she'd been drinking, or I had. She wouldn't have let me go off with another guy either. In those days, that was the rule: girls stuck together.

We were grown-ups now, I thought blurrily, following Wolf out. The air outside was crisp and bracing. I liked the feel of it on my face. "Better," I said, pausing to take a deep breath. "It was really smoky in there."

"Yeah, it is better. I work in Pueblo sometimes, and they've killed indoor smoking. It's great." He took keys out of his pocket. I noticed he had a very nice rear end in his blue jeans. "You ever go down there?"

"No."

He led the way to a modest-size pickup, nicely kept and clean inside, but not a monster-size gas guzzler. A workingman's truck, with a toolbox in the back and the obvious dust of concrete in the bed. "You're a concrete man," I said.

"Yeah."

"My ex was a contractor." I rethought it. "Is." I sat in the truck and let him slam the door. I hoped it wasn't obvious that I was feeling the wine. "Not is husband, but is a contractor."

"Right. I got it."

Stop talking, Nikki, I told myself. Less said, less regretted.

He climbed in on the other side. "Where to?"

I told him the name of the apartments, and he started the engine. The radio came on, playing old-time rock at a fairly high volume. "The truck and the music fit," I said.

"Not Cairo, though, huh?"

"Sorry, that probably seemed snotty."

"'Elitist' is the word I was thinking of."

I looked at him again, and felt ashamed of myself for thinking the things I was thinking. That "elitist" seemed not a word a guy like him would drop in casual conversation. "Well, I'm kind of new to the world of not snotty."

"I can tell. What are you doing over here slumming?"

I lifted a shoulder, dropped it heavily. "Same thing you are. Divorce."

He turned into the apartments in less than two minutes, and I directed him to the lot behind my building. He pulled into a space and turned off the lights. "I hate it when people shine their lights into my bedroom window."

I was suddenly aware of the intimacy of the cab, of the look of his hands on the wheel, competent and strong, and I wondered what it would be like to kiss him. To kiss anyone. I had been in my twenties the last time I'd kissed someone who wasn't my ex-husband.

Wolf just sat there, his hand resting on top of the wheel, the engine idling. Which made me feel like an idiot for thinking anything at all.

"That's nice of you," I said. Did I slur that *s*?

I tried to unfasten the seat belt, but it seemed stuck or something. I pushed the button and nothing happened. Pushed again, harder. Still nothing.

"I seem to be unable to release myself," I said primly. "Which I swear is not my way of trying to get you to come over here and put your hands on me or something."

"No?" He chuckled, and the sound filled every molecule of empty space in the cab, as warm and scented as an evening campfire. "It gets stuck." He released his own belt, stamped down on the emergency brake, and scooted over a little way to push the button on my belt.

It released, and I took a breath. "Thanks."

"I wouldn't mind kissing you," he said.

"Oh," I said, and looked up. But I didn't have to say anything to Wolf. He leaned over and put his hand on my jaw, and I caught the silhouette of his lashes against a faraway glow of streetlamp before his lips touched mine.

Just touched. Full lips, fuller than Daniel's anyway. I found my mouth going softer in response, and he scooted a little closer, the hand on my jaw sliding down the juncture of neck and shoulder.

His tongue nudged my lips. Something told me to notice this, this very moment, this first kiss after my divorce. His tongue was pointed, hot, wet, nudging along the parting of my lips, wiggling inside, teasing my tongue to come out and play.

And with sudden release of heat, I did. I opened to him, let his tongue dive into my mouth, and I thrust mine into his, dancing, swirling, rubbing lips, tilting heads.

Here was a man, smelling of laundry, his body hot and urgent beside me, and I didn't protest when he pulled me closer, putting our chests into contact. "Mmmm," he breathed. "You taste good." His hands smoothed down my back, slid into my hair, and shivers rustled over my skin in their wake, the starved skin rippling in response.

I touched him in return. Sucked on his tongue and pushed my hands through his short, thick hair, and traced the bristling of beard on his jaw. When he slid his hands around to touch my breasts, I didn't stop him, and an involuntary little noise came from my throat. Taking his cue, he plunged his tongue deeper into my mouth, and I pushed back, and he pulled me into his lap, so I straddled his erection.

He unbuttoned my blouse a little in the front, and kissed the skin there, and I rocked against him a little, aching for his fingers or his mouth on my nipples, which felt engorged and irritated. Without much thought I reached up and unbuckled the front clasp of my bra. The flesh spilled out, bare and—even I knew this much—pretty. "God, you've got beautiful breasts." He sighed, and cupped them, lifted his face.

I pressed into him, harder. "Kiss them," I whispered.

He did. Opened that hot mouth, put it over the tip of my right breast, and suckled. I moaned and he did it again, and we moved into a rocking rhythm, me pushing against his erection, his lips, tongue, mouth playing with my nipples. I felt the heat building between—

A door slammed somewhere close by and I was shattered out of the moment. Wolf went still beneath me, his hands still cupped around my breasts. I realized the engine was still running. That I was drunkenly making out with a guy I just met, in his car, as if we were teenagers.

"Let's take this inside, baby," he said.

"No." I squeezed my eyes closed, finally ashamed of myself. "No. This is a mistake." I pulled away from him, tugged the edges of my blouse together. The voices of the people who'd slammed a door faded away. "Sorry," I said, and pushed wild hair out of my face.

He looked up at me, his eyes starry and beautiful in the dark, his face square and working-class and wry. "You won't be sorry if you let me come in." His hands moved on my thighs, up and down. "I've been told I can make a woman pretty happy."

There was no doubt in my mind that it was true. "I'm sure you could make me sing like a canary," I said, and kissed him, then straightened. "But I've had too much to drink. This is not wise."

He bit his lower lip. "Damn."

"Sorry." I pulled away completely, buttoning my shirt, embarrassment creeping in. I picked up my purse, put my hand on the door handle. "Thanks for the ride."

He half grinned. "Not quite the ride I would have given, but you're welcome anyhow." He leaned close and kissed me. Dizzy with wine, I let him.

There we were again, kissing and kissing and kissing. He reached up and pinched my nipple. "Get out of here."

It stung. I jumped out of the truck. He didn't wait for me to get to a safely lit spot before he pulled out, gunning the engine to show his annoyance.

I stood in the mild dark, too much wine in my head, and glared at his taillights as they disappeared into the darkness, and I tasted the ashes of the night on the back of my tongue.

Did I really have to repeat the whole absurd dance of mating again? Wasn't it enough to do it before I found Daniel?

I made my way only slightly unsteadily to the stairs, which seemed very, very, very long by the time I reached the door. Maybe I didn't want a man, not any of them, if it meant having to do all this again, making mistakes, wading into all the messy needs, wishes, desires. Pride and body fluids and possible broken hearts.

My chest felt thick with the weight of it.

At the top of the stairs, I paused to catch my breath, and I snagged on the view. Not of the dark mountains, not at night, but of the glittering city of Colorado Springs visible between two buildings. It spread out to the east, sparkling in white and red and green, and in my inebriated state, it looked unbearably beautiful. I almost wanted to cry over it. When a tear actually welled up in my eye, I got a grip.

"Go to bed, Nikki," I said.

And I did.

10

Nikki's Perfume Journal Entry

Time: 6 a.m.
Date: May 25, 1993

Bottle: a small Aunt Jemima pancake syrup bottle, washed
clean, tied with a pretty cluster of dried lavender
Elements: dew, roses, damp earth, grass, sunlight, crushed
mint, sage, thyme
Notes: Sunday breakfast with Daniel and Giselle

After we got the restaurant set up for the morning rush, I had a
few minutes to go outside and have some coffee and breakfast before we
opened. I carried a plate of quiche and spinach salad with oranges out
to the garden area behind the restaurant. There wasn't a lot to it, just
some trees and rough greenery and a bench that sat close to the back
of the lot, where the land dropped away to the creek that ran through
town. This morning, the swell was high with mountain runoff, and
the air was crisp and light. I sat on the bench with a sense of relief, my
body buzzing.

These were the kinds of mornings I used to like puttering in my
garden. Starting in mid-March, sometimes even a little bit earlier if the
winter had been mild, I began the day by going to the garden, watering

and feeding the plants, plucking off dead leaves, and pulling weeds and omnipresent elm seedlings. It soothed and centered me, and I was missing it already.

The night before sat on my chest like a weight, an exact contrast to that woman who had so optimistically laid out gardens and tended them. A nicer me, I thought now.

In the suburban neighborhood where my mother moved us, it had always been a vague shame to be one of the Bridges girls. The divorcée's daughters. Everyone on our block, and I do mean everyone, was married. There was a father mowing lawns and a mother setting out homework assignments, and family outings to Dairy Queen on summer evenings.

Not in our house. My mother worked two jobs, for one thing—as a secretary for the real estate company during the day, and as a hostess at a steak house in the evenings three times a week. She paid the bills, did the grocery shopping, kept us in school clothes, made it to every single recital, play, or orchestra appearance we made, but never to the PTA. Once a month, she and her girlfriends went out on the town. Sometimes she didn't come home.

I hated her for it.

Sitting in the peaceful garden of the restaurant, I thought now what a little shit I'd been, judging her so harshly. How lonely she must have been! How hard she had worked! And the stigma for her daughters had been difficult, but how much worse for her to live in that neighborhood with all those intact families, and live with their judgments so her daughters would have a better school, a safer world?

I'd have to call her.

A starling whistled from a tree branch overhead, and I tossed out a crumb from my quiche. The bird cocked his head, whistled again, looked around cautiously, and swooped down. I stayed very still. His neck feathers had the iridescent sheen of motor oil, purple and indigo shining in the blackness. He plucked the crumb into his beak and cocked his head at me.

"Good morning," I said.

From beneath the bushes came the stuttering meow of a cat on the prowl. Before I even had a chance to turn my head, a black streak zoomed into the clearing. The starling squawked, launching itself into the tree. The cat, all youthful athleticism, leaped for the retreating tail feathers, and caught one in a claw and slammed back to earth.

It was the kitten from the shop, all black except the patch of white on his chest. Thwarted in his hunt, he all but scowled, shaking the paw with the feather. It didn't come loose immediately, and he spread his toes and yanked it off with his mouth. I could almost hear him say, Phooey!

I laughed.

He hadn't seen me until then, and turned around, hunched, as if to run away. Scenting my eggs, however, he seemed to change his mind, lifting his nose on the air curiously. I picked a piece of egg and cheese from the quiche and held it up, then tossed it gently his way. He didn't move for a minute, but then the bird squawked again, as if in protest, and the kitten glared over his shoulder, then lifted his tail and sauntered over to the crumb.

"It's not bird, but I guess it's better than nothing, huh?" It occurred to me that it was bird, actually.

Not that the kitten cared one way or the other. He ate with the frantic rush of the starving, and looked up for more. Poor thing. I broke off a substantial-size piece, making sure to get some ham into it, and tossed it to him. He attacked it with a growling ferocity.

I nibbled the food too. I had a slight headache, probably as much from being in the smoky bar as gulping all that wine in two hours flat.

Worse than the hangover was the lump of writhing embarrassment lying in my upper gut, wiggling like maggots as memories of the little make-out session in the car came back to me.

"Ugh!" I exclaimed aloud, and rubbed the place between my eyebrows where it seemed the pictures were reeling themselves out, over and over. The worst moments were—

"Hangover blues?" Zara sat down beside me on the bench.

The kitten skittered away, into the bushes. At least he got something to eat. "A little," I said.

"Thought so," she said, and gave me a tall glass of tomato juice. "This will help."

I tasted the mix, juice and lime and Worcestershire and other things. "Thank you."

She held up a thin cigarette and a lighter. Annie didn't allow smoking inside. "Do you mind if I smoke?"

"No, go ahead." Half-heartedly, I tossed another chunk of quiche into the bushes, but it just laid there. Maybe I'd come out after work, see if I could find him.

"Did you go out with Niraj?" she asked.

"Last night? No. With a friend to a bar by the apartments."

She nodded, stretched her legs out in front of her. The long blonde hair was still damp, and in the morning light, she was plainly well past forty. "There's a pretty good blues band that plays Sunday nights over here if you're ever interested. I go a lot."

"Thanks. I might like that." I frowned. "Didn't much like the place we were last night. Grim, really. Everyone just depressed and living on Lean Cuisines."

"Right. Like the old meat markets, remember?"

I smiled softly. "Right. I forgot that term." I yawned. "Are you married, Zara?"

"Nope. Just me and my dogs." She smoked meditatively. "Somehow, I missed that boat when I was off having adventures. Like I woke up one day and went, 'Oops, I meant to get married. Have kids.'"

"Adventures?"

"Yeah. I was a tour leader for about ten years, small-group hiking vacations in Alaska."

"That sounds interesting. Why quit?"

She shook her head. "You get tired of never having a home, you know? I wanted to put things on the wall and have a dog. My dad lives here and he was pretty lost after my mom died, so I came back two years ago. I got a pair of Akitas and rented a little house"—she pointed—"up the hill."

I nodded, put the rest of my food aside. "I wish I'd thought about renting something over here."

"You still can." The phone rang inside and she jumped up. "Duty calls. See you in there."

I nodded and glanced at my watch. Still had almost ten minutes before we opened. I would finish my tomato juice and see if the kitten would come back.

Adventures. Leading hikes. What would that be like? A breeze blew across the folds of my brain, opening doors, throwing back shutters. I was single and free. I could do anything I wanted to do. Anything. Wander across the world, take a job with a cruise ship, apply for the Peace Corps.

Anything.

Maybe travel was the answer.

The kitten crept out from under the bush and reached for the broken piece of quiche. I flicked it closer to him so he wouldn't have to risk coming out again, then picked up my dishes and went inside.

~

The day went smoothly enough. I was beginning to notice that I felt good when I worked hard physically, that my body liked it, and my mind wasn't so glum. Maybe I should have done it a long time ago.

My last table was a trio of women hikers who'd just come down from the mountain. The mountain being Pikes Peak, of course. Every day there were runners and walkers who jogged past the doors of the restaurant, or came in afterward for sustenance. These three dropped their daypacks and wiped their dusty faces and ordered beers to drink, and appetizers and salads. They were not young—ranging in age from mid-thirties to mid-fifties, I'd guess. One per decade. "How was the hike?" I asked.

"Great," said the oldest, a fit, dark-haired woman. "We went to Barr Camp and back."

"Much snow left?"

"None at all. I was surprised."

"Have you been to the top?"

"Not yet," said the youngest one. "This summer, though—right, girls?"

They lifted their glasses of beer. "To the top!"

I put in their orders and wondered, what would that be like? To hike to the top of Pikes Peak?

The sun was bright and hot when I emerged after my shift, and on impulse, I dropped my things off in my car, bought a bottle of water at the taffy stand, and headed uphill on foot. I wasn't dressed properly and didn't have a hat, so I couldn't go far, but there was a funny, growling hunger in me to put my feet on the trail.

Not everyone who walked the mountain was young or thin. They were fit, or it was a miserable experience, but my idea of what an "athlete" looked like had been slowly shifting over the past couple of weeks, watching the people coming into Annie's. There were all ages, many sizes. There were the elite runners, of course, with their tights and socks with labels—"6L" and "6R" to denote which sock it was, and which foot it went on. My favorites were the older women, faces tanned to leather, with their slightly crepey upper arms and cropped curls. One woman walked the trail every day, and made a point of hiking to the top once every summer, just to remind herself what could be done. Zara told me she was seventy-four.

I walked up the street in my ordinary Reeboks, no fancy hiking or running shoes, and my jeans and my green polo shirt had a couple of food stains on it from the day. My legs were tired from working, and my shoulders, and at the base of my skull was the reminder of the excessive wine last night.

But it still felt good. I walked up to the trail, walked another ten minutes up, then came back down.

On my right as I walked to my car was the empty shop. The For Rent sign was quickly fading in the bright sunlight. The kitten, regal as an Egyptian god-cat, sunned himself on the inside of the ledge. He seemed to be smiling. I thought, suddenly, of the perfume cat my long-dead friend Mark had given me.

On impulse, I ducked down an alley and rounded the bank of old brick buildings. These shops, too, backed up to the creek, the cliffsides grown over with greenery and thick grass. I had to beat my way through to the little shop with the cat. I tried the door, and it opened.

Just in case there was someone there, I called out, "Here, kitty, kitty, kitty."

The previous tenants had not done much cleaning on their way out. The back door opened into a tiny room with a sink and cupboards, and there were papers on the floor. It smelled musty, old, as if there had been no one there for decades, rather than just the short time it must have been. I couldn't exactly remember what had been here before. Shops were always coming and going with the seasons.

The room opened into a short hallway that mainly contained the opening to a stairway that led upstairs. I poked my head into the stairwell and called out, "Hello?"

Nothing.

I went toward the front room. "Kitty, kitty?" I called. I wished for food to coax him with, but when I came into the main room, he didn't even move, just stayed right where he was, sleeping in the sunshine. I picked my way over a stack of papers—they looked like musical programs and old weekly newspapers—to the window, worried suddenly at the foot traffic beyond. What if someone saw me in here?

Nervously, I paused. A counter with glass fronts stood facing the door, and a finger of light fell over the glass shelves, giving me a sudden vision of how pretty it could look with some velvet, and jewel-colored and crystal bottles inside. I wondered again what had been in here. I stepped on a piece of thin wood and it snapped beneath my foot.

The kitten finally seemed to hear me. He startled and poised himself to flee, shoulders hunched suspiciously as he stared up at me.

"I won't hurt you, baby," I said. "Remember me? I gave you food?"

Evidently not. He streaked out, knocking over an empty soda can as he fled. It clanged down to the wooden floor and rolled into the wall, bumping into a baseboard as tall as the middle of my calf, carved and ornate beneath a thick layer of aqua paint.

I picked up the can and settled it on the counter. The floor was wide planks of hardwood, maybe only pine, but in pretty good shape. The light was excellent, and would be all day, thanks to the southern exposure. It was tiny, but how much room would I need for perfume?

For one long moment, I allowed myself to consider the possibility. I imagined the window washed clean and stenciled with Scent of Hours in a properly art deco script, and beautiful bottles displayed on shallow shelves throughout the room, and soft music playing—

The can I'd put on the counter fell off again with a hollow clanging. A brush of dust flew into the sunlight, and I saw the actual condition of the room. It would take more than elbow grease to make it attractive—it would need paint and polishing and inventory, all of which cost money, and that was something I didn't have at the moment.

Shaking my head, I turned around and headed back out. The kitten had not fled outside. I saw the flash of his yellow eyes in the stairwell, and slowed my feet to patiently approach. This time I wouldn't talk. He waited in the doorway, bright eyes wary. I thought again of the way he'd eaten the quiche this morning, with that fierce growling at the back of his throat. I eased my hand forward for him to sniff, and he managed to hold his nerve until I almost touched him, then he bolted up the stairs.

I followed him. Obviously the place was deserted. I was surprised by the light cascading down the stairs, some of it colored, and with delight I climbed upstairs into a wide, open room with long casement windows facing the street. This room, too, was dusty and neglected, with a worn-out couch shoved against the wall and an extremely ugly indoor-outdoor carpet on the floor. It smelled, vaguely, of old cooking.

But the space was generous, with a kitchen at the far end, and a door to what must be a bedroom. Feeling slightly guilty but not enough to leave, I wandered around, opened the door, and peeked in. Dark, and somewhat cold, and very dusty. Still, it was pretty enough. A stained-glass window faced north. The walls were bare wood, which was a lot better than the ugly carpet.

I closed the door again and looked through the window in the kitchen area. It overlooked the creek, and through the trees I could see waves of mountains. Another door was tucked over the stairs. I opened it.

The bathroom. And, oh! I stopped in the doorway. In spite of the years of grime on the graying walls, in spite of the dirty fixtures, I was smitten. Tucked below the eaves, it was aglow with amber light from a stained-glass eyebrow window close to the floor. The floor was plain wood planking, and the fixtures were antique—a pedestal sink and an ancient toilet and the biggest, most gorgeous claw-footed bathtub I'd ever seen.

I knew immediately that it didn't matter how much work it took—this apartment was going to be mine. I would do anything for that bathroom. In my mind, I saw a line of strongly scented, feathery French lavender plants in clay pots, and maybe some lemon geraniums for the sun to heat.

Behind me, the kitten squeaked. I turned around and he was poking his head around the door, his eyes big and yellow. "Hey, you," I said in a soft voice. For a minute, he wavered, wanting to come forward, achingly hungry for both food and touch, but when I dared take one step toward him, he bolted. By the time I got through the door, his tail was disappearing down the stairs.

"I won't hurt you!" I said, as if he could speak English. "I promise!"

Taking one last look at the magnificent bathroom—though it, too, would need a lot of elbow grease—I went back downstairs and wrote down the number on the For Rent sign. The kitten was gone, but I figured we'd see each other again. Soon.

~

I found Roxanne by the empty pool when I got home. She was laying out, tanning in a bikini a little larger than an envelope. "That is so bad for your skin," I said, sitting down beside her.

"I know," she said, and put her cigarette to her lips. "So's smoking. I don't intend to live that long."

"Don't say that!"

"Go get some shorts on and lay out with me. You'll like it. And they're saying these days that it's a cancer preventative."

"You know what? I think I'm going to. You want a soda? Or a snack? I have some fruit in the fridge. Grapes? An orange?"

She opened one eye. "You are such a mom, aren't you?"

"No, I'm just nice. Unlike some people here." I stood up. "I'll be back in a few minutes."

It was hard to find anything that would fit and didn't look obscene—there was too much of me spilling over the top and coming out of the behind of the suit. My butt, I noticed with despair, looked like a pair of overripe grapefruits. Finally, I settled on a tank top and some stretchy old shorts I used for painting, and carried a can of soda to the empty pool. I popped the top as I sat down.

"So how did your evening go?" she asked without opening her eyes.

I thought of Wolf. "It was over when I left you."

"You didn't sleep with him?"

I was glad she wasn't looking at me. My ears were hot as I thought of myself undoing my bra and telling Wolf to kiss my breasts. "No."

"I did."

"Slept with Wolf?"

"No, Alan." She smiled slightly. "He was a surprise. Very well hung."

I clapped my hands over my ears. "Don't tell me, don't tell me!"

She laughed.

"I thought you weren't going to do that anymore."

"What? Have sex?"

"No, just . . . you know, sleep with strangers."

"Oh, we aren't strangers. Alan is my boyfriend." She moved her arm to look at me.

I took the hint. "I am now minding my own business."

"Excellent."

The sun really did feel very good, and I stretched out on the chaise longue. Closed my eyes. "When does the pool open?"

"Memorial Day. Just like everything else."

In the small trees planted around the area, birds twittered. Light blazed against my eyelids, turning the world red, and I let go of a breath. "I explored a shop in Manitou after work. I'm thinking of renting it."

"Yeah? What would you sell there? Are you an artist or something?"

"I make perfume. It's a very tiny shop, and I'm sure it wouldn't support me by itself, but I'd still like to try it."

"Go for it."

I turned my head to look at her, surprised by a lightness that bloomed through my chest. "You don't think it's stupid?"

"No, why would I?"

"It's kind of impractical."

"Maybe." She opened one eye a slit. "What has practical gotten you?"

"Good point."

Turning over, like a roasting chicken, Roxanne settled on her elbows and looked at me. "Life is short."

"Jeez, your eyes are really red," I said without thinking, then put a hand over my mouth. "Sorry. That was rude."

She pulled her sunglasses down from the top of her head. "I had to talk to my ex this morning. Usually I can avoid it, but my son had to get stitches in his toe, and he needed the insurance card."

"Ow! Is he okay?"

"Yeah." She settled her face into her elbow, and there was something fragile about the turn of her neck. "It was only a couple. A skateboard injury. He should have been wearing his shoes."

That didn't really explain her very red eyes. "I don't mean to pry, but I don't get it. Did you have a fight with your ex or something? You look pretty miserable."

"We always fight if we talk." She sighed. "No matter how hard I try not to yell at him, something always makes me mad."

I thought of the email I'd had from Giselle. "I know what you mean. My daughter sent me a picture of her and her dad in London, and it was a great photo of both of them, and then I realized she took it, the new little wifey, and I wanted to"—my hands twisted themselves into fists—"strangle somebody."

"Exactly. Grant's wife—Lorelei, believe it or not—"

"Gag."

"I know." Warming to her subject, she raised up on her elbows. "Lora-Lies-a-Lot is what I call her. But anyway, she was going to take him to the ER for the stitches, and I lost it. Why couldn't Grant take him?" She touched her chest, that place of burning. "It just infuriated me to think of some doctor thinking she was my son's mother."

"Oh God! I haven't even thought of that angle." I flung an arm over my eyes. "And it would be so easy to think so. Sometimes strangers don't know she's mine."

"It makes me crazy. How are you supposed to belong to someone and then you don't anymore? How are they supposed to belong to you and then they don't? They just belong to someone else. They get naked together!"

A sharp burn slid across my ribs. It was a picture I tried hard never to allow into my mind—Daniel and his secretary who was promoted to wife. "I know," was all I said.

"It made me crazy at first. I was so intimate with his body, it was like it was just another part of mine, the way you feel about your kids, you know?" She put her head down on her forearm. "Especially his penis. That really belonged to me. I knew it in every single incarnation possible—dead flaccid and lying on his thigh, saluting." She slammed her board-straight hand against her brow. "Gently nudging my bottom. Rolling around in my hand. The vein against my tongue. All of it."

I wondered if she knew there was a tear on her cheek. "I know," I said again.

"Knowing someone else, some other hand or mouth or vagina, was exploring it, touching it, felt like having a hand in my intestines. It made me feel sick, and if I try to ignore it, and I can, the hand is still there, moving around inside of me."

"That's exactly it. Ow. You should write an article or something."

"Thanks." Her voice was muffled. "I should write that the way to get over it is to call his new babe a cunt on the phone."

"Or not."

"I know." She sniffed, wiped away tears from her cheeks. "I hate that word."

We always depersonalized the new women in our exes' lives, I thought dimly. We didn't use their names. We made up insults for them, plays on words, all sorts of things to keep us from recognizing that she, too, was a woman, just like ourselves. "And it's not like she acted alone, right?" I said in a burst of fairness. Truthfulness. "That's what I always come back to: it wasn't just her."

"I guess. That doesn't exactly make it easier, does it?"

"No." I thought of a single, searing moment, when I'd seen Daniel put his arm around his new wife. She was tiny, much smaller than me in every way—height, weight, shoulders, hips, legs, even hands and feet—and I'd felt betrayed because he'd always said he liked me for the Amazon I was. Liar, liar, pants on fire.

"Who was she?" Roxanne asked. "The one your ex married. He married her, right? I think you told me that."

"Yes." I gulped lemon-lime soda. "Oh, she's every cliché in the book—a younger, prettier secretary. How about yours?"

"A neighbor who moved in just after we celebrated our seventeenth anniversary. I never even had the sense to be jealous. It never occurred to me that he'd go with anyone else." A bloody half-moon of color stained each cheekbone. Her nostrils flared. "She was single, had this sexy boyfriend. We used to laugh about them making noise when they had sex. Lorelei." With a low moan, she smashed her fist down on the chair and dug her nose into the protection of her elbow. "God, I hate her so much!"

"I know," I said.

"Sorry. I'm not always like this. I'm just having one of those days. The books all say you have to let them just be there. You'll feel better eventually." She raised red, swollen eyes to me, and I saw the hickey on her neck. "How long do you reckon?"

A vast mothering swell rose in me, and if I'd known her a little bit longer, I would have hugged her. Another part of my brain was sifting through a thousand scent memories for one that would match a tone, a flavor in my mind, the missing element of Roxanne's perfume.

What did anger smell like?

11

Nikki's Perfume Journal Entry

<u>Ingredients:</u> Castoreum

<u>Class:</u> Animal

Castoreum is a dried follicular substance that comes from the secretion of the prepuce glands of male or female beavers. This secretion is stored in a gland that produces an oily substance. The beaver uses the oily substance to waterproof its coat and to mark its territory. The gland is treated with volatile solvents to obtain resinoids and absolutes. Today, beaver secretions are mostly replaced by synthetic substances.

Sundays at Annie's were very busy. She served an organic brunch buffet and it was renowned far and wide. The sideboards in every room groaned with generous slices of orange and green and yellow melons, sliced bloodred tomatoes, steaming trays of free-range eggs and organic meats, overflowing baskets of grainy, fruity muffins and sticky Danishes. Eggs and pancakes were cooked to order, and that was what kept us busy.

It was surprisingly agreeable work. The customers were generally in fine spirits, happy to be breakfasting with family or friends, alive and eating well on a fine Sunday morning in Colorado. The buzz of their voices was a composition of pleasure, men and women and children punctuated with laughter. Hard to imagine a more satisfying sound.

I was off at one, and sat down at the bar to have a soda before I left. I counted tips happily, stacking up bills and quarters in neat piles for Zara to cash in for me.

"Want a mimosa?" she asked, holding up a wine bowl with a liquid the color of dawn. "Somebody ordered one and changed her mind."

"Tempting, but no. I'm driving."

"Oh, please," she said, and put it down in front of me. "It has maybe a half serving of champagne. Live a little."

I plucked the cherry and orange garnish from the rim. "What the heck. I'm going to eat too."

A woman with dark hair sleekly pulled away from her face sailed into the bar. She was strikingly beautiful, with enormous blue plum eyes and high cheekbones, and the lean limbs of a teenager. "Hallo, Zara!" she sang out in an English accent. "How are you?"

Zara slanted a glance my way. I gave her a perplexed glance in return. Was I supposed to know this woman? She shook her head. "Good, Hannah. Tequila?"

"Please—and make it a double, if you would. I'm just home from the Islands, and you know how depressing it is to return from holiday."

That, I thought, would explain the pecan-colored tan on her bare arms and legs. She wore a skirt of pale turquoise, embroidered with beads and glittery things on the hem. I separated dimes from the pile of change and watched Zara pour top-end tequila into a mixing glass with ice, put a lime in the bottom of a martini glass, and strained the now-cold tequila into it. "There you go."

"Thanks." She sipped. "Ooh, perfect. You're always so good."

Zara dried glasses from the rubber matting by her sink. Her body posture was extraordinarily stiff and I wondered what the history was between these two. Clearly, Hannah either did not realize or did not care that Zara found her about as appealing as a woman-size cockroach. "Glad you like it. Do you want a table?"

"No," she said, plucking the lime from the bottom of the glass with her fingers, which she then licked, one at a time. "I was hoping to run into Niraj. Have you seen him?"

I kept my eyes carefully on the pile of coins in front of me. I'd been hoping to see him, too, but if this was an example of the women he ordinarily dated, I was way out of my league.

"Sorry," Zara said, and it was not difficult to read her warning glance at me. I sucked my upper lip into my mouth and looked at the clock. I wanted to remember to get the phone number off the rental sign at the shop. The one I'd written down yesterday had not worked.

"Cash this in for me, will you?" I said to Zara. "I think it's seventy-two. I'll be right back."

She nodded. Pulling the scrunchie out of my hair, I flung off my apron and dashed outside to the shop up the street. This time, I wrote the number down very carefully. The kitten wasn't immediately visible, and I put my hand on the window to block the glare so I could peer into the room.

The same detritus. The same sense of dusty promise. A vision of bottles in many colors flashed over my imagination.

So lost was I in my reverie that I nearly screeched when I pulled away from the window and almost ran into Niraj, who laughed and grabbed my arm before I slapped at him.

"So sorry," he said, and I had forgotten how lyrical his voice was. "I didn't mean to frighten you. I was going to Annie's to see if you would like to come have tea—or maybe a little chai"—he smiled—"with me this afternoon."

"Um." I clenched the pencil in my hand, dazzled by his voice, the look of his very deep eyes with their starry lashes, but mostly by the scent of him, not a waft but a solid arm that reached out and wrapped around me—that roundness of earth and spice and pine. God. I wanted to open my mouth and drink it down. "I . . . uh . . . am not dressed for it."

He smiled, not at all wolfishly. "Just to my house. It is not far, just up the street. I'd like to show you."

I felt frozen—then realized the woman had just returned from the Islands, and he'd just come back from a business trip, and I was going to have a crush on a guy like that? No way. "There's a woman looking for you at Annie's," I finally managed. "She's at the bar, talking to Zara."

His eyes narrowed. "What does she look like?" His voice was tight.

"Her name is Hannah."

He looked down the street toward the restaurant. His hands were quiet at his sides. "What is she doing here, I wonder." He did not sound pleased.

"I don't know." I looked at the number written on my hand, tried to remember my happiness in seeing the vision of perfume bottles in rows. "Maybe you should ask her."

He caught my arm when I started back down the street. "Nikki, please wait a moment."

I looked at him hard, looked at his hand. "Please don't do that."

He released me instantly, put his hands on his hips. "I told you I followed a woman from England to here. That is Hannah. We do not speak, if I can help it." He looked at me seriously. "She likes to cause trouble. I'm sure she has trouble in mind now."

I'd picked up the impression that she had dumped him, but that was a discussion for another day. The truth is, I wanted to trust him, and it wasn't fair to judge him without knowing the facts.

Taking a breath, I said, "All right."

"So will you come have tea?" He folded his hands in a prayer position, oddly respectful, as well as playful. "I have been hoping to see you again since I left. Is it all right to say that?"

I smiled. "Yes."

"So you'll come?"

"I'm not sure about going to your house, Niraj. I'm a little uncomfortable with it."

He raised a hand. "I swear it will only be tea. If you like, you may call Zara and ask her if I am trustworthy. She knows me."

"Did you date her too?" I cleared my throat. "Not that I care, it's just that it's nice to be in the loop."

His eyes glittered. "I did not." His nose twitched, like a rabbit, and I realized he was holding back a smile. "I will not lie, however. She wanted to go out with me, but I felt no interest in her."

I raised my eyebrows skeptically. "Zara?"

He shrugged. "No."

"How could you not like her? She's gorgeous."

"She is pretty," he said, inclining his head. "But a little too much for me, I think. She likes to drink hard and stay up very late."

"And you don't?"

"Not really." He shrugged, as if to say, *You may as well know it.*

"Tea, huh?"

"Yes. Only tea."

"It better be. I smell like a goat." I grinned. "And I'm starving, so you'd better have some cookies or something to go with it."

"That can be arranged." The *r*'s rolled a little, just enough to send a rustling over my nerves. "Can you come now?"

"I have to go get my things."

He threw a frown toward the restaurant. "I will wait."

"Okay. I'll be right back."

"Will you mind if I ask you not to mention that I am out here?"

"I won't." I dashed back inside through the back, stopped in the employee restroom in the kitchen and hurriedly combed my hair. Mary gave me a look. "Must be a man."

"He's just a friend." But suddenly a grin the size of the sky split my face, and I put my hand over it.

Her laugh was earthy. "I can see that."

Wiggling my fingers at her, I dashed through the swinging doors to the dining room, and deliberately slowed down. I picked up my purse, took a long swallow of the mimosa, and folded the money Zara had put on the counter. "See ya in a few days," I said. "I don't work again until Wednesday."

"Have a good one," she said in her cigarette-throaty voice.

The woman—Hannah—was no less gorgeous upon second look. I had not exaggerated her plum-colored eyes, her beautiful shoulders, her amazingly glossy dark hair. She was a knockout.

So was Zara, for that matter. While I was . . . well, "ordinary" was a good word. Round and ordinary and obviously mid-forties. But I thought of Niraj's starry eyes and didn't care. He liked me.

Did. Not. Care.

"See ya!" I sang, and rushed out the door.

~

To reach his house, Niraj and I walked to a staircase made of pinkish granite, cut into the hillside. The steps led steeply to an even steeper ribbon of street, just visible through the low-hanging arms of cotton-woods. At the foot of the steps was a bubbling spring, pouring water endlessly through a spout. I put my hand under it and captured a palm-ful as we went by.

"It's not far," he said, "but it's steep."

"That's how you keep those excellent calves, huh?"

He looked at me. "Are they?"

"Very."

"I'm glad you like them."

The grade felt as if it were straight up, and I gave up talking. It really wasn't very long before he turned down a more level stretch and we walked on an old, multi-squared sidewalk with grass growing in the cracks, to an Arts and Crafts bungalow perched on the hill. Lilac bushes, not yet in bud, clustered in the corners of the grassy yard, and peonies sprouted in front of the porch. Two wicker chairs and a table faced southwest, and I paused to look over my shoulder at what they viewed.

It was only the street, the trees, the house across the street, a furry blue-green elbow of mountain just visible over the roof. "Pretty," I said.

"It is," he agreed. "But it is nicer from the back. Come in."

I hadn't expected homemaking skills from a bachelor computer geek, honestly—maybe utilitarian desks, a computer breathing somewhere in the front room, plain window coverings, anime posters or some other oddity like that on the walls.

Instead, the room was furnished with sturdy mission-style furniture that matched the Arts and Crafts era of the house; good wood; and a soft, nubby, copper-colored fabric with red and gold accents. A figure with the head of an elephant and the body of a human sat in the middle of the mantel, and there was a moody photo of more elephants in a line across a red sky. A glossy pothos spilled over the windowsill and down the wall, leaves shining in the sunlight. The rooms smelled of exotic spices, some cooking I didn't know, vaguely ginger, and something I couldn't name.

Niraj stood beside me. I was aware of the heat of his arm along the outside of my own, conscious of the scent of his skin, of his waiting. I glanced at him. He glanced down at the same moment, a slight lift of his left eyebrow the only expression on his face.

I thought of his sleek ex-girlfriend. Together with this evidence of his homemaking skills, I felt foolish and oversize. "This is in beautiful condition," I commented, since I could tell he waited for my impressions. "Did you have it redone?"

He nodded. "It was not in terrible shape. But I had a man come in and redo all the wood, and the floors." He gestured to the well-tended oak around the windows, the high baseboards, the gleaming floor with an Arabian Nights rug on the floor.

"It's wonderful." I realized it had to also be worth a fortune. "I accidentally blew up my old house."

"Blew it up? How did that happen?"

"I don't know." I met his curious gaze and told the truth for the first time. "I probably didn't really want it and didn't know how else to get out of it. Subconsciously, of course. I didn't do it on purpose."

"It was a difficult divorce?"

I touched the cool green marble of the mantelpiece, a Pikes Peak specialty. "Aren't they all?"

"I suppose they are." He moved, leading the way through the long front room. "Come through here. Let me show you the rest—the view from the back is fantastic."

"All right." I followed him into the kitchen, a broad room with white walls and glass-fronted cupboards. Hexagonal tiles lined the backsplash over the sink, in shades of brick and white, and the floor repeated the color. A plain wooden table sat by the window that overlooked the garden, and a pile of books was stacked there, some in a language with curly letters. "Is that Arabic?"

"Hindi," he said. "I am learning. Slowly." He picked up the book and flipped through it. "We are several generations removed from India now. My mother's family lived in South Africa, and my father's family has been in London a long time."

"So have you ever been to India?"

"Not yet." He put the book down. "Ironically, I was offered a position there—it was thought I might be a good man for the job, supervising other Indians."

There had been much made in Colorado Springs of the outsourcing of computer jobs to India. "That seems as if it might be awkward. The token, right?"

He smiled in surprise. "Yes. And I think I've found my home here." He gestured and we went through the back door. He spread a hand, as if tossing a beautiful scarf across the landscape. "How could a man leave this?"

I put my hands to my cheeks and laughed softly. The wooden porch, braced on very tall stilts, looked out over the valley, the tumble of the town to the right, the climb toward the mountain to the left, and directly in front, a framable view of the Garden of the Gods, nestled beneath the hills. "I can see Annie's!"

"That is just why I purchased the house, so I could admire the restaurant."

I gave him a wry smile. "Ha ha."

He leaned on the railing, relaxed, confident. "I love to sit out here. It is very different from anything in England."

"It really is amazing, Niraj," I said. "I could tumble out superlatives for a year."

"Thank you. Would you like to see the rest? And then I'll make your tea."

"Sure."

He showed me the bathroom, with a tall, deep tub, and a row of African violets on the windowsill, and the study downstairs, reached through a set of french doors. And then upstairs to the bedrooms tucked under the eaves. I tried not to look at the one I knew must be his—a simple frame bed, a bureau, a large, framed sepia photo of an elephant and a boy. Soft north light spilled through the window, making an inviting pool of stillness. His bedspread was white.

A voice whispered in my mind, *You will be happy here.*

The other two bedrooms were unfurnished, just open, empty rooms. "I have not lived here very long," he said.

"So not much time has passed since you broke up with your girlfriend?"

"Long enough," he said. His voice said clearly the subject was off-limits.

We went back down the stairs and Niraj said, "Make yourself at home. I'll make the tea."

Left alone in the living room, I prowled the edges of the room, examining things. Books lined the shelves on either side of the fireplace. Paperback science fiction and fantasy novels took a lot of space, predictably, but there were also many others. Thick historical texts on the eighteenth century; explorations of various sciences—botany and bugs, mainly; financial texts; business; travel. Very smart, this one. I liked that.

His television stood mute against the wall, not as a centerpiece as most were. When he carried a tray into the room and put it on the low coffee table, I pointed. "You don't watch much television, do you?"

"I find it makes me sleepy, except for cricket matches."

"Cricket? They have cricket on TV?"

His eyebrows rose to the middle of his forehead. "Of course!"

He looked so scandalized, I had to laugh. "I'm pretty sure I've never seen cricket in any form, never mind TV."

"Blasphemy!" He spread his hand open on his chest and gave an exaggerated gasp. "It is the finest game in all the world! I'll have to introduce you."

I laughed. "The finest game in all the world?"

He wiggled an eyebrow. "Yes." He waved me toward the seating area. When he settled on the couch, I chose the chair kitty-corner. Then wondered if I should have sat next to him on the couch.

God, Nikki, I thought in exasperation. Grow up.

"It's not so interesting on television. Much better in person—and even better to play."

"Do you play?"

"Oh yes." He shook out cloth napkins, one for me and one for him. "But I will warn you, it is best not to get me going."

I smiled. "Point taken."

On the tray was a fat blue ceramic pot and a pair of mugs, along with a plate of cookies, and another of cheeses, cucumbers, sliced tomatoes, and some thin bread. He passed me a saucer. "I'll pour the tea. Help yourself to everything else."

"Thank you. I am very hungry, I'm warning you."

"Good." He picked up a mug and poured a steaming, fragrant mixture into it and passed it over to me. "My own special chai," he said with a grin.

And for one second, I was snared by the moment, fully living it. Me at forty-three, slightly sweaty after a day working a job I genuinely liked, sitting in a house in Manitou, a town I adored, with a dark-eyed man

I thought might be my lover sometime soon. Against the backdrop of the warm, well-appointed room, he was beautiful, his hair in tumbles, his strong nose so appealing, his full lips. And most of all, the direct expression in his dark eyes—frank appreciation, gentleness, intelligence.

I accepted the cup. "Thank you," I said, and carried it to my nose, inhaling deeply, letting the spices blend and expand in the cavity of my sinuses.

"Ooh, that's fabulous!" I narrowed my eyes. "I can smell the coriander and cloves. Cardamom." The rest melded in a mysterious combination of things I did not know. "What else?"

"Secret things," he said, and his lips quirked slightly. "If I tell you now, how will I ever hope to bring you back again?"

I met his eyes. "Good point. Because, of course, there's nothing at all interesting about you, only your tea."

"Exactly. Did you find the missing element in the perfume you were working on?"

It surprised and pleased me that he remembered. "Not quite. I think it needs to be a note of some dark emotion. Anger, or bitterness, a combination, maybe."

"Fire?" He plucked cookies from the plate, and slices of cheese.

I tested the idea against my memory of the fragrance, redolent of earth and bodies and women's laughter. "Fire might be too much, and smoke seems too little." I wrinkled my nose. "It's hovering right on the edge of my imagination, just not quite there."

"Gunpowder?"

I'd been reaching for a cookie and stopped. "Ooh." I looked toward the leaded windows on either side of the fireplace, let them blur as I imagined the possibility settling into the perfume. Sharp, piercing—a charcoal scent, not a red one. "That's a definite possibility. Not sure how to represent it, but . . . ooh. Nice." I grinned at him. "Thanks."

"My pleasure." He gestured. "Eat!"

Again silence settled. Unlike most men, he had not put music on, and I felt a need to fill up the spaces in our conversation with prattle.

"How did your business trip go?" I bit into a cookie, a grainy oatmeal style with chocolate coating. "Yum! Oh, that's good."

"Mmm. My favorite," he said approvingly. "The trip . . . it was business. No excitement. Just meetings, meetings, meetings. A new program, new ideas."

"Do you like your job?"

"I do," he said without hesitation. "There are days I weary of it, as with anything, but it is creative and challenging."

I found myself watching his lips move, looking at the darkness within, and found a shiver rushing down my neck. I looked away urgently, embarrassed. "That's good."

"Do I make you shy, Nikki?"

I blushed and looked up at him. "A little, maybe."

"How can I make it easier for you?"

"Um . . . I don't know." I laughed a little uncomfortably. Such directness!

"Are you afraid of me?"

"No!" That much I was sure of. "You just . . . I just think . . . I don't know why you like me." I blushed even more, the heat pouring over my face, down my neck. "If you do, that is. Oh God. I'm bad at this."

He laughed softly. "Will you do me one small favor?"

"Of course."

He shifted on the couch to make space beside him. "Sit here instead of there, will you?"

"I can do that." I stood up, bringing my cup with me, and sat down primly, holding the mug on my tightly closed legs. "There."

He pursed his lips, as if considering some difficult problem, and then reached for my cup, took it from my hands, and put it on the table. A ripple of anticipation moved up my spine, settled at the nape of my neck. The scent of him seemed intensified, clove and fir and that wildly arousing astringent note I thought might just be his sweat. I had a sudden vision of myself bending in to press my nose to his throat, to bite him there.

161

God, Nikki, get hold of yourself!

He picked up my hand and turned it over to brush his fingers across my palm. "You are smart," he said. "And healthy."

The descriptions stung. "That sounds like a border collie."

He laughed, the sound robust as the spices in the tea he'd made. "I'm British, Nikki. Often, we are a bit reserved."

I looked at him. "I'm American, Niraj. It's a little hard to know what you're thinking sometimes."

"How's this?" He touched my hair, the angle of my cheekbone. "Your hair is beautiful and your smile is kind, and I love your figure, if it is all right to say that."

I felt like an idiot. Pleased, but idiotic, like a pretend virgin, and I moved my fingers against his. "You have the best lips I've seen in a long, long time."

"Ah, that's better," he said, and made a quiet little noise. His fingers traced the edge of my ear, and my breath caught high in my throat as he leaned in, and then the scent of him was all around me, and I inhaled it, closing my eyes to await the touch of his lips. His hand steadied my jaw, and then his lips met mine.

Oh.

His mouth was as lush as rose petals, and tasted of ginger and honey and chocolate. I liked the fullness of his lips, the thick aggressiveness of his tongue, liked the feeling of his hand on my jaw. I inclined my head, invited him in farther, enjoying a certain receptive passivity that wasn't really my usual style.

One kiss, two. He lifted his head, and I looked at his eyes with surprise and heat, and he smiled slightly, touched a finger to my jaw, bent in once again. This kiss was hotter, deeper, more aggressive, from my part and from his. A bolt of blistering hunger moved through me, dizzying and intense, and I felt as if I would drown in him. I put my hands up, found my palms settling over his ears, my fingers in his thick hair. Hair is not Daniel's strong point, and Niraj's curls were startlingly erotic.

He made a low noise, and at the exact same instant, we both pulled back, and for a long space of seconds stared at each other. "Wow," I said.

"Yes," he said, and gave a perplexed little laugh, shifting suddenly in a way that made me realize with yet another idiotic blush that he was aroused and uncomfortable. Roxanne's rhapsody about penises floated through my mind, and I had to struggle not to giggle nervously.

And then I wondered if he was circumcised and if I would see him naked, and I—

I stood up. "That was intense," I said, and walked to the kitchen, took a breath, came right back.

"Are you all right?" he asked.

"No. Aroused. Alarmed, maybe." I widened my eyes. "You really are very handsome, and I like the way you kiss, and I like your brain, but the weird thing is, the way you smell is making me feel like a vampire."

"A vampire?" he echoed.

"Yeah, I just want to devour you."

He looked pleased. "Devouring is all right."

I smiled. "Yeah. But maybe I should go for today, before this gets all out of hand."

"No, no." He waved his hands. "Stay. Sit over there. I will not kiss you anymore, I promise." When I didn't move, he took my hand, pulled me up, and walked me over to the chair. "There. Have another biscuit."

"This body does not need cookies."

"That body is perfectly fine the way it is," he said, and picked up his tea. "Now, tell me, Nikki-Nicole, about your perfume. About this business you wish to open."

That seemed safe enough. "All right." I lifted my mug from the table and took a sip. "It's something I've been playing with for a long time. The Scent of Hours—perfumes that sort of capture the spirit of a moment, like the day you get married, or when a baby is born, you know?"

"Go on."

"I'll make them in small batches and put them in particular bottles, and then sell them to tourists. I'd also like to be able to blend custom perfumes. I've done a few for people, up till now only friends and family, my sisters, my mother, that kind of thing. And I don't want to sound like a braggart, but anyone I've made a perfume for has loved it."

"Ah, of course. A signature."

"Right. There's a shop not far from Annie's that's for rent." I showed him my palm, where I'd written the telephone number. "I'm playing with the possibility of renting it, but it's kind of scary."

"What makes it frightening?"

"It would need to be done by the time the tourist season starts, and it's a mess, and I don't have any money to speak of—and, well, it seems a little insane to make custom perfumes in a world where there are people who are trying to get perfume banned from public places."

"And yet, what is more powerful than the memories triggered by scent?"

"That's true." Pleased, I sat forward. "Did you know that scent is the only sense that bypasses the brain and thought centers and goes directly to the limbic system?"

"Really. So that does what?"

"It takes us directly to visceral memories, transporting us to a time and place instantly."

"Ah, so that's why I can feel sad when I smell cinnamon, because it takes me to my grandmother, whom I miss very much."

"Exactly. If I smell an apple Jolly Rancher candy, I instantly think of a friend of mine from childhood. Mark." And I realized suddenly that it was the second time I'd mentioned him to Niraj, when I never spoke of him at all. In twenty years of knowing Daniel, I didn't think I'd ever told him about my best friend from childhood.

"Is something wrong?"

"No, just a little odd. That friend of mine is the one who caught horny toads with me. He died when we were seven, and I never usually think of him, but that's twice I've said something about him to you."

"Perhaps I remind you of him." He smiled. "Perhaps there is something in my scent, hmm?"

"Hey! You might be right. Honestly, I can't remember what he smelled like, except maybe—" I narrowed my eyes, thought of the creek where we were forbidden to go, where we caught our horny toads.

I couldn't quite catch it. "I don't know."

In my purse, my cell phone rang, and I jumped. "Sorry, I have to look in case it's my daughter."

The number came up as unavailable, and I flipped the phone open. "Hello?"

"Mom?"

"Giselle! Hi!" I gave Niraj a big smile and a thumbs-up. He pointed toward the back and I stood up and headed toward the kitchen. "Are you home?"

"Yes." She had precise, careful diction, always. "We got back yesterday. That is a long, long plane ride."

"I'm sure." I went out on the back deck, and leaned on the railing, feeling a slight wash of vertigo that went away when I looked up at the horizon.

Giselle told me about her trip to London, about seeing the Tower of London and the Thames and the Tube. I was conscious of a ball of jealousy over her accounts, but I was also very, very pleased that she'd had the experience.

And then, out of the blue, my daughter said, "I really miss you, Mom."

"You do? I miss you, too, babe. Are you still going to come spend the summer with me?"

"At least part of it, but Dad said we might do some more traveling."

"Oh." I tried to keep my voice even, but the gilded happiness I'd been feeling suddenly evaporated. "How long? Where are you going?"

"We don't know yet. Maybe Spain. She wants to go there."

The wife, of course. "Are you getting along pretty well with her now?"

"It's okay. She just tries too hard. I keep telling her I don't need a mom, that I already have one, but she doesn't listen."

"Be respectful, babe."

"I am!"

"Good." Below, a figure in a turquoise skirt and dark hair emerged from the café. Hannah. It seemed as if she looked up to this spot, and saw me. Why did I care? "Are you going to send me some pictures?"

"Yes."

We talked a little bit longer, and then hung up. I leaned for a moment against the railing, feeling dizzy with the changes in my life, the sense of not being able to quite catch up. The worst of it was the giant hollow spot in my chest that sucked all the air out of my lungs, the black hole of missing her.

Niraj, who had obviously heard me hang up, came out on the deck. "Are you all right?" he asked.

I forced a smile. Nodded. "Thanks."

"How old is she?"

"Fifteen. They just got back from London."

"You did not miss anything. It's a big, noisy, grimy city."

"So they say. I'd like to see for myself."

"And so you should."

I took in a breath, blew it out. "Sorry. I'm all right now. I just miss her like crazy."

"I'm sure. I have never had children—I would have liked it, I think."

"It's not too late. Men father children well into their eighties."

He shook his head. "No, it is too late. I am no longer willing to go through all the things that would be required. I do not want to be the sixty-seven-year-old father at the high school graduation."

"I can understand that."

"It is one of the reasons," he offered, "that I did not stay with Hannah, the one you saw this afternoon. She wished to have children."

"Ah." I frowned. "She's very, very beautiful."

"Yes," he said. And that was all.

I didn't push it. Suddenly, though, I felt very tired. "Well, Niraj, I have enjoyed the tea and the conversation, but I think I need to take my leave."

"Very well." He turned and opened the door, holding it so I could pass in front of him. I picked up my purse and tucked it over my shoulder.

He held out his hand with a faintly ironic smile. "Thank you for coming, Nikki."

I took his hand and wondered why I was being so formal with someone I liked, when I'd been so hot to trot with Wolf, who seemed like a bad boy who'd be a big fat pain in the butt. "Thanks, Niraj. I enjoyed it a lot. Especially"—I paused and looked at his mouth—"the cookies."

He grinned. "Me too."

I let his hand go, and hitched my bag higher on my shoulder. "I'll see you around."

"Will you walk with me again soon?"

That was easy. "Yes. Name the day."

"Tuesday?"

"You're on."

12

Nikki's Perfume Journal Entry

Time: 4 p.m.
Date: July 7, 1988

Elements: patent leather, sweaty satin, Aqua Net hair spray, crushed bluegrass, white wine, chicken browned with an onion
Possible ingredients: clary sage, tobacco, grapefruit, ambrette? civet?
Notes: wedding perfume

Experiment #1, 4-12-90
Notes: Not civet. Try costus, very light.

Mark Ruley was my best friend when I was seven, a boy with glossy brown hair and blue eyes, who suddenly and inexplicably woke up sick one day—"A rare blood disease," they said—and died the next. It scared my mother to pieces. She cried and cried and cried. Cried till her eyes were swollen and red and her cheeks had cowlike splotches all over them.

I'd cried over many things, my lost bracelet from the Garden of the Gods, which no one would take me back to so I could get another one; my favorite pink sock that I'd accidentally let go of when I'd been letting it fly like a flag out of the car window; my father shipping out to Vietnam.

I sort of expected that sooner or later I'd get around to crying over Mark. We'd been planning to be married when we grew up. For my birthday that year, he'd given me two things, both of which he'd picked out himself.

The first was a small velveteen cat with a pink feather and glowing pink rhinestone eyes holding a small bottle of Golden Woods perfume. Cat and bottle were protected by a clear dome, and my sisters were keenly impressed and jealous that I should have inspired such a gift. I didn't like to wear the perfume because it seemed to draw mosquitoes, but I did like to take the dome off the cat, open the bottle, and smell it. I liked the name, Golden Woods, and I'd breathe it in, trying to pinpoint the threads that made it smell like the name. Light, I thought, and leaves, and bark. Trees and sunshine and Saturday afternoons.

The other gift, which I'm sure my mother did not remember, was a fistful of pink carnations he knew I'd like for the scent.

I didn't cry over Mark dying, and they couldn't make me go to the funeral because I hid in my closet with the dome and cat for the whole day, only coming out when I finally heard my mother talking in low tones to a neighbor about it.

I didn't cry. Not then and not over the following months. I didn't let my mother wash my tennis shoes, because I'd been wearing them the last time we played outside together, down by the creek, where we were not allowed to go. The reddish mud smeared over the fabric of the shoes reminded me of him every time I looked at it. In the afternoons when I got out of school, I'd walk down there and sit. It smelled of the pine tree that stood over the bridge, and of faint dankness, and cool water and sunshine. It smelled like Mark.

I never did cry. But now, whenever I catch an unexpected whiff of a certain combination of elements—water and woody perfume and that dusty softness of summer—I almost always do.

This afternoon in my beige apartment, I pulled out essences and began to mix them recklessly, blending light and pine and carnations into something that smelled like a Saturday afternoon in the seventies, and a boy who had been gone five times longer than he'd lived.

And as I did it, I felt a thousand things moving in my body. Memories. Losses. A day walking along the river. A moment with Giselle in the middle of the night. The moment of kissing Niraj for the first time, his lips so lush and delicious. I lifted bottles to smell essences and let them call up whatever they would.

Moments, moments, moments. What did that have to do with Mark?

A wisp of an idea swirled around the edges of my brain. He was important to my life, to what was happening now, but how? I didn't see the connection.

It did seem to me that it was strange how much a person could influence your entire path. The smell of him. The carnations. The cat.

What was it? The connection eluded me.

~

After working so hard all week, it was good to have a day off, to sleep in until eight, and amble through breakfast, reading the paper and drinking coffee. Instead of taking a shower, I put on my tennis shoes and headed up to Ute Valley Park, which wasn't a valley at all, but a hilly, wild area not far from the apartments.

The morning was crisp and cool, the sun breaking over pine needles in a wash of aromatic deliciousness. It made me think of Niraj, and I wondered, without trying to solve it, what it was about his particular scent that was so appealing to me. I'd had the same reaction to Daniel, of course. We all do to our partners, but I didn't remember noticing it so much.

I noticed it more when we were splitting up. Daniel has a scent like Irish Spring soap, and notes of lemon and man. Clean and healthy. I liked it on his T-shirts, and ended up throwing a few pillows away after a while, when I couldn't stand it anymore.

The strong scents made me think of the perfume store idea again. What would it really take to make it happen? I had the perfumes. I'd need bottles, names, some branding. The shop. It was dirty and neglected, but the space was honestly just so perfect.

Could the shop be the answer to what I was meant to do?

It seemed it might be worth a try. When I got home, I went online to look for perfume bottles on eBay. There was every sort of bottle imaginable—old liquor and medicine bottles, which I liked a lot, to 1930s atomizers and Avon collectibles. I lingered with yearning over a matched set of blue, ribbed Laliques, and again over a stamped rose bottle in shades of pink and purple that was very beautiful.

That bottle, filled with Wedding Afternoon, would be spectacular, but I would have to charge $75 minimum to make it worthwhile. If I even won the auction.

I had, briefly, considered offering my perfumes on eBay, but people needed to smell fragrances. It wasn't as if they knew me or my product, and although I was quite sure I had a genuine talent for it, they were somewhat unusual fragrances, individual and distinctive. One needed to smell such perfumes.

But it occurred to me that I was procrastinating. Bottles were something I would settle on later. If I seriously wanted to consider the shop, I needed to have an official look at it, find out how much it rented for.

Before I lost my courage, I jumped up, crossed the room, and punched the number into my cell phone. A gravelly voiced man barked, "Hello?"

"Hi, I'm calling about the store you have for rent in Manitou?"

"Yeah. How can I help?"

"I was just wondering how much it is. And how much will you kick in toward cleaning it up?"

"Three-fifty a month for the shop alone, eight-fifty if you take the apartment and the store."

"Really." I was paying nearly $1,000 for my apartment alone. "And what about cleanup?"

"You want to do the cleanup, I'll give you two free months. But I still gotta have a deposit, and you'd have to sign a lease."

I paused, my heart suddenly beating faster. "How much of a deposit? And how long a lease?"

"Two months, and the lease is negotiable. I'd prefer a year."

I twisted a lock of hair around my thumb. "Let me think about it."

"You want to take a look at it? I got time this afternoon."

"Let me check my calendar and get back to you, okay?"

"Sure thing."

After I hung up, I sat with the phone in my lap and mulled the possibilities. Two months, if I took the apartment, would be $1,700. Plus utilities. Plus cleanup costs, which would be substantial. Then decorating and—

My heart swelled in a sudden opening that nearly hurt. If I didn't have to live here, it would be possible, but that would mean I'd have to pour elbow grease into the apartment, too, and there wasn't time before the tourist season started on Memorial Day to get both done. If Giselle was to spend any time with me at all this summer, she would be much happier sunning herself by the pool while I worked rather than knocking around a tiny mountain hamlet she'd always dismissed—along with her father—as baby-boomer last-stand-ville. Were there even two bedrooms in that apartment? I didn't think so, but maybe I could sleep on a futon in the main room and let her take the bedroom.

And I'd need to generate some more inventory. Which meant I'd need to lay in a few supplies, and get very focused about having some labels printed attractively, and—

I jumped up, unable to be still, and paced toward the patio doors, the plants starting to green very nicely now. What if I really did this?

You could fail.

True. Fall flat on my face. Realize that it was absolutely not a way for someone to get ahead, make money.

You could succeed.

And then what? My heart felt as if someone was pounding on it. What if, what if, what if?

Before I could chicken out, I flipped my phone open and hit the redial button. When the same gruff voice answered, I said, "I just called a minute ago. I'd like to see the place, if you still have time to meet me."

"Yep. One o'clock?"

I glanced at the clock. I had a little more than an hour. "Great. I'll see you there."

It wasn't until I was in the shower that I wondered where the hell I thought I was going to get the money. My credit was nonexistent. I'd made a thousand small mistakes during my marriage and then had blown up my only asset, so it wasn't as if there were any savings. The insurance company was still dragging its feet. How much money would it need to be?

I had about three months of savings to cover rent and expenses for that much time, if I fell ill or something, and considering my precarious circumstances, that seemed like an important bit of cushion. What if I sprained an ankle and couldn't work at Annie's? And what if I did that while Giselle was staying with me? How could I even buy groceries without that small savings account?

Scrubbing my face, I thought about it. How much would it really need to be? Five or six grand, all total? It was a huge sum of money to me now, but surely I could find a loan for such a small amount. Sooner or later, the insurance company would give me something.

It wasn't really about money. It was— Oh, I just wasn't sure. What did I know about running a business? What did I know about retail? What did I know about anything?

My thoughts seesawed back and forth like this all the way through my shower, through the drive to Manitou, and the whole way up the street after I parked. The door to the shop was open, and a heavyset white man with a baseball cap on his head was kicking through the papers on the floor. "Sheesh," he said. "There musta been some bums in here or something." He stuck out a baseball mitt of a hand. "Jim Flannigan."

"Nikki Bridges."

"Go ahead and take a look around."

Since I already had—but of course I couldn't say that to him—I looked in a circle around the small shop. It was the same long, narrow area, with the excellent front window. The kitten was nowhere in evidence.

"Utilities are in your name too," the man said. "Wiring and plumbing are in good shape, believe it or not."

"Oh, I believe you."

He picked up a sheaf of papers. "I reckon I'd give you three months free, if you want to do the cleanup, since it's in such bad shape. I'm ashamed to see it, but my wife's just passed. I been busy with her awhile." His rheumy eyes watered, and he took a handkerchief out of his back pocket and wiped his nose quickly.

"I'm so sorry."

He cleared his throat, wiggled his heavy, flying white eyebrows, and moved away, pointing. "Let me show you the apartment, huh? I haven't been up there, so I don't know what it'll be like."

"That's fine." I followed behind him down the short dark hallway to the narrow stairs. We emerged into the main room of the apartment, and I felt the peace in the rooms again. The long windows, the transoms over the doors, the stained glass. It was a wide-open space, with half walls in a couple of spots. I imagined my computer desk near the stairs, with a view toward the mountains, that blue-and-green vista.

"My daughter used to look after this, but she moved to Minnesota," he said.

"Ah." The mention of the daughter made me see the apartment through Giselle's eyes, and my heart sank. Even if I said it was a cool loft, Giselle's sophisticated tastes would never be fooled. She was driven, ambitious, and sophisticated, and I doubted very much if she would like this slightly tattered Victorian apartment in a hippieish neighborhood.

Not to mention, would there really be room for her? I crossed my arms. Even if I put a futon in here—

"I got some nice carpet if you want it," he said. "My son-in-law could lay it for you. It's them big roses, pretty colors. I've been meaning to get it done."

"Cabbage roses?" I said.

"Yeah." He gestured. "You gotta see the wallpaper in the bedroom, and there's a pretty porch there too."

"A porch?" I hadn't seen that. I followed, unable to resist. He flung open the bedroom door to reveal the space, the window overlooking the same high branches as the kitchen and the creek. A door I hadn't noticed the other day was at the other end of the room, and Flannigan opened it to let in a spill of light.

"My knees can't take so many steps in one day," he said. "Go on, take a look."

The steps were narrow, painted white. I followed them up a twisting circle to a small rooftop garden. The air was light and fresh, and it was like a magical, secret thing. "Oh!" I said. My plants would love it here.

Once upon a time, I had been filled with a good many wishes and dreams and hungers—small things, mostly. When I was ten, I wanted to go to camp. At seventeen, I wanted to learn everything there was to know about cooking raspberry desserts, about perfumes, and ached, with a wide vastness of longing, to walk the streets of London and see the sun set in a new sea.

When I met Daniel, all my desires and longings coalesced in the fineness of his strong hands and robust laughter, and I married him with nary a wisp of regret. When Giselle was born, I felt full-up, brimming.

Over the years, the yearnings and wishes returned. I wanted to learn to tango and I burned to collect the best plants for scent, and grow a perfect pocket garden of delphiniums. Soft passions, soft hungers, as warm and peaceful as my life was, but no less rich or pleasing for all that. I never was the kind of girl who wanted to save the world. I just liked making it beautiful and comfortable.

And when the great surprise of my divorce began, when Daniel suddenly turned traitor and broke my heart, over the grim breaking up that seemed to last forever and ever and ever, all my longings had again been focused on him, on trying to save the marriage, the family, the life I so loved. I gave up wanting anything but that.

When nothing I did, no amount of effort or good behavior or prayer, could save it, it was as if my heart just could not stand to wish for anything new. I was numb for months, my limbs dull and heavy, my brain half-dead. I didn't care. About anything.

Standing on that rooftop, with the apartment below my feet, and the shop below that, I felt yearning unfurl. I felt like a warrior who had finally returned to the land of her birth—the losses and tragedies immovable and wearying, but all the same . . . in the past.

I felt a wish for a new life, the possible life I could have in this spot, the dreams I might be able to fulfill, the things I would learn.

I had paid three months down on the other apartment. That would see me through until Giselle came to visit, surely. I'd keep the ugly, cast-off furniture for her sake, and in the meantime sink my desires into this place, into a dream that was all mine, and had been for a long time.

Scent of Hours Perfume.

I stood on the roof, imagining the furniture I would carry up here, and the plants in their pots, and breathed in hope. It smelled of sun-heated pine blowing down from the mountains and the ghost of lavender to come, and marigolds, sharp and astringent.

Marigolds. Hmm. It seemed too early. I inhaled again. No, I was right: distinctly, definitely marigolds. Maybe someone had a pot of them in a windowsill or something.

Marigolds. I let the note expand in my head. Pungent, orange, deep, strong. Maybe that was the undernote in Niraj's skin. I turned in the direction of the hill where his house sat, and looked for it. A large pine obscured it from where I stood, but if I moved—and I did—I could see it clearly.

I went back down the stairs and said, "Okay, I want it. What do you need from me?"

The figure he named took all but $300 of my reserve, but I wrote the check without even a tiny hesitation. I thought of Roxanne, and her droll voice saying, "What has practical gotten you?"

Exactly.

～

"Roxanne!" I cried as I came up the stairs to my apartment. She was standing outside her door, smoking. "Guess what I did?"

She still looked worn, and even thinner, if that was possible. But her voice was encouraging when she said, "Tell me."

"I rented that shop! It's so crazy, I can't believe I did it."

"That's fantastic, babe!" She shivered a little on my behalf. "You should come out with me and Wanda to celebrate."

"Are you guys going out?"

"Tomorrow night. It's her birthday. I was going to ask you anyway. We're just going to have some dinner and a couple of drinks."

I fit my key into my own door, thinking of those dwindling reserves in my bank account. "Where are you going? I don't have a lot of cash."

"She likes Jack Quinn's, the pub downtown."

"That's one of my favorites!" I wondered what I could give up for the evening out. "I could just have soup and bread, I guess. Help you buy Wanda a couple of beers."

"Sure."

"What time?"

"Not until around six-thirty. It shouldn't be busy on a Tuesday, and we'll just have some supper and a beer and come back up here."

"All right. Thanks, Roxanne."

She stubbed out her cigarette in the pot she kept by the front door. "No problem."

Her movements were stiff. "Are you okay?" I asked.

She waved a hand. "Just a little overexertion," she said, and gave me a sly lift of an eyebrow. "Nothing to worry about."

"Alan again?"

"Um." She bowed her head. "No, actually."

"Oh." If this had been my daughter, I would have been very worried. Her body language broadcasted signals of secrets and dismay. Lightly I said, "You wretched slut, you!"

She raised her head, met my eyes. Smiled.

"Come over and have some coffee," I said. "Help me figure out what I'm doing with this shop."

She brightened. "Okay." She pushed the front door open. "Kids, I'm going down the hall to Nicole's. Holler if you need help."

Faintly, they said, "Okay, okay."

"Homework hour," she explained. "If I don't make them do it right when they get home, it never gets done."

"I remember."

"God, you must miss your daughter!"

I nodded, threw my keys on the counter. "I talked to her yesterday, and her dad thinks they might do some more traveling this summer."

"But you have a custody agreement, right? Just say no."

"Right. I could." I pulled the coffee filter basket out. "But bring her to Colorado Springs when she could go to Spain? What kind of sense does that make?"

"The sense that she needs her mother."

I dumped coffee grounds into the trash. "It doesn't seem like it."

"Don't kid yourself—daughters really need their mothers, and even more at her age. Not," she said with a frown, "that I've been doing such a great job of it lately." She scooted onto the barstool by my counter. "Now, tell me all about your shop. What are you going to do? And what kind of help will you need?"

I chuckled. "Oh, you have no idea." I told her about the mess, the challenges, the garden space on top of the building. She listened actively and made the right noises and volunteered to gather a work crew to help clean it one weekend day. "Between me and you and my kids I bet we could get things shipshape in no time."

Cheered, I poured her some coffee. Things were looking up. I had friends, a job, a possible boyfriend, and I was even taking a chance on the thing I'd most wanted to do all my life.

Life wasn't so bad at all.

13

Nikki's Perfume Journal Entry

<u>Definitions</u>

Citrus is primarily composed of scents such as bergamot, lemon, orange, tangerine, and grapefruit, to which other orange-tree elements (orange blossoms, petit grain, or neroli oil) have been added. Floral or even chypre accords are sometimes present as well. These perfumes are characterized by their freshness and lightness, including the first "Eaux de Cologne."

Roxanne stayed for one cup of coffee, then went down the hall for a short nap. I had carefully not asked any more about the man she'd slept with. Clearly, there had been something dismaying about it, and I wondered if she needed some counseling.

Well, obviously she needed counseling. But maybe directly about her need to sleep with so many men. It might have been different if it seemed she was enjoying herself. I didn't buy the idea that promiscuity was always about low self-esteem. Some people really did just want to have sex with a lot of different people at some point in their lives.

But Roxanne, for all her earthiness, didn't seem to be having sex for the fun of it. It felt like there was something else beneath it. Fury, probably. A need to punish. I made a mental note to ask Wanda about it tomorrow night.

I spent the evening making lists. One for the work I'd have to do on the shop. One for the supplies I needed to make perfume in larger batches. One of the inventory I'd need to generate in order to open, and how much I'd need to spend. I thought $5,000 would do it.

I was fairly sure I could still get a loan for that much. If worse came to worst, I could probably ask Daniel. He definitely had it, and I'd be able to manipulate his feelings of guilt fairly easily. The idea brought a grin to my face, oddly. Who knew I had it in me?

Happily, I signed on to the computer. There was a chatty email from Giselle, a follow-up to her phone call, with a long, detailed trip report, complete with pictures. There wasn't a single one of Daniel's wife. I didn't know if Giselle had just taken pains to spare me, or if it was accidental, but either way, it was a kindness.

My favorite was a cameo of Giselle in a Tube station. The light was greenish behind her, and the tiles on the wall were tiny. Next to her was a machine advertising Cadbury chocolates. Giselle had obviously found something enchanting, because there was a bright light in her eyes, and her full, red lips were slightly parted. Her hair was scraped back from her face tightly, showing off her high cheekbones, and for the first time I glimpsed the woman she was going to be. The caption below it read, "Dad said you'd like this one best. Do you?"

I had not realized my daughter would one day be a great beauty, but the evidence was right before me. The strong lines of cheekbone and brow gave way to a delicate chin, which illuminated the tender lushness of her Angelina Jolie mouth, a gift from Daniel's mother. Her eyes were slightly tilted, her eyebrows flying into arches.

TO: gisellegiraffe@hotmail.com
FROM: nikki@scentofhours.com
SUBJECT: trip report

Darling Daughter,

Your dad was absolutely right—I do love the photo of you in the Tube. I will have to have a print made. And THANK YOU so much for that long, detailed trip report. One day, we will go together. If you go there to study in college, I'd have a good reason to come visit, wouldn't I? And then you'd know all the best places to eat and how to avoid the crowds. I'm very happy you had the opportunity, and Spain sounds great too. Please never ever fret about the travel and me. You have to grab all the chances you can in your life. I'm doing the same. Today I did something wonderful: I rented a shop so I can sell my perfumes. I'm going to call it Scent of Hours (surprise, surprise!) and I hope to get it open by the time the tourist season starts. I am missing you tons, though! Ask your dad to send you out for a long weekend. Never mind—I will. ☺ I'm making new friends here, and I have a job—how funny, but I really like it a lot—and I have my eye on a black kitten who is skittish and terrified but obviously needs a home.

I love you, love you, love you! Be good and be careful and call your mom whenever you think of it!!!

Sweet dreams,
Mom

When I finished the email, I hit Send, then opened a second and wrote to my ex:

Hi, Dan. You were absolutely right—that's a gorgeous picture of our daughter. Did you realize she was going to be a beauty?!? Sounds like she had a wonderful time, and it's terrific you can give her such great opportunities. Listen, I am missing her madly—could you possibly send her out to visit for a long weekend sometime soon? I'm still waiting for the verdict on the insurance, so don't have a lot of extra cash, or I'd be more than happy to pay for the ticket. All is going well here. I'm working. The new apartment is boring but clean and neat and has a great view of the mountains. Hope you're well. Nikki

I sent the email, and almost immediately, my phone rang. I smiled, thinking it was probably Giselle or Dan, but another name came up.

Flipping open the phone, I said warmly, "Hi, Niraj."

"Hello, Nikki!" His voice, resonant and lyrical, poured into my ear, down my neck, my back, pooling warmly at the base of my spine. "How are you tonight?"

I tucked the phone closer to my ear, thought of his mouth, moving so close to the phone on the other end. My voice sounded huskier to me when I said, "I'm good. Thank you."

"I forgot to give you the little present I brought you from San Francisco."

"A present!"

"Only a little thing, but I meant you to have it yesterday, and I forgot. I'll bring it tomorrow, if you're still interested in walking." His voice softened teasingly. "If you even like me, that is."

"Ha ha." I grinned as if he could see me. Stopped by the mirror and flipped my hair out of my eyes. "I'd love to. I was even thinking of a walk I'd like to try, if you're up for it."

"I'm sure I will be."

"Let's walk a little way up toward Barr Camp, then. I'd like to get a feel for it. My customers are always running and walking up to it. I'd like to check it out, and I'll be working in the area tomorrow, so that would be a good time to try it." Enough detail, Nikki, I said to myself. In the mirror, my cheeks were flushed.

"Perfect."

"Okay." I paused, trying to think of some way to continue the conversation. "Um. I guess I'll see you tomorrow, then."

"I was just thinking," he said, "of your pretty hair."

"You were?" I brushed a hand through it. "I was thinking a minute ago of your nice mouth."

"Do I have a nice mouth?"

"Oh yes."

"No one has ever said that to me before. Thank you."

I laughed softly. "You're welcome. Why is this so hard?"

"It is. I don't know why. After so many times, you would think it might be easier, hmm? I think it never is."

"Well, it isn't so many times for me. I was married pretty young."

"Not so many for me either. I was too plain and strange for the girls."

"It's still hard."

"Yes. But not so much that I want to stop trying."

"Exactly." My phone beeped at me, and I pulled it away from my ear to see who was calling. "Sorry, I have to take this call. It's my daughter."

"No problem. I will see you tomorrow."

"Bye." I hated to hang up, but I did it. "Hi, Giselle!"

"Wrong," said her father. "It's me this time."

"Dan!" I carried the phone into the living room, discovered I was straightening things on the table before I pulled my hand back and stuck it under my arm. "Is there something wrong?"

"No. I just got your email and thought I'd call for a change. It's been a while since we had a conversation."

My ex-husband has a voice like Barry White. Low, rolling, sexy as a kiss to the hollow of your throat. I don't talk to him on the phone because it always bothers me. Even with the sound of Niraj echoing, it was hard to listen to Daniel without thinking of having sex with him—and he's always been an imaginative and energetic lover.

But I also knew he used that voice and his talents for his own ends, and this was no social call. "What's on your mind?"

"I'm sorry you missed out on the trip to London, and Giselle's visit," he said, and he sounded very sincere. Of course. "I'll be happy to fly her out there for a long weekend. She can check her school schedule and see what would be a good time."

"Great! Thanks." I waited for him to get to whatever this was about. My neck muscles corded, making a minor headache start in the back of my skull. To prod him along, I made a guess at what might be on the agenda. "She told me you might go to Spain this summer."

"Good, good. We'll make sure you have plenty of time together, before and after."

"Okay." Impatiently, I said, "Dan, what do you want? I know you better than this, and you have something on your mind. Spit it out."

He chuckled, and it was the velvety rumble of a knowing Buddha. "You know me too well. Giselle just told me about your perfume store, and I thought it was kind of interesting."

Interesting. "Well, I'm pretty excited. I've always wanted to do this."

"It always was your little hobby."

Little hobby. "Right." A hollow place opened up in my chest. "I'm going to let you go, Dan. Have Giselle call me with the dates."

"London was great, Nikki. I thought of you a lot. I'm sorry we never went."

I shook my head. "Don't, please. You can't have it both ways."

"I know. I'm sorry, that's all."

"Good night, Daniel. Go feel guilty on somebody else's dime, all right?" I hung up, and stood there with my arms across my chest, maybe trying to hold in the burn.

My little hobby, indeed.

TO: niraj.bhuskar@blipdata.com
FROM: nikki@scentofhours.com
SUBJECT: a shop! a shop!

Hi, Niraj. I forgot to tell you this—I am so excited!—I signed a lease on that little shop in Manitou. 😊😊 😊 I've never done anything so rash in my life. And of course it's entirely possible that I'll fall flat on my face, but perhaps I'll succeed wildly. I'm very excited (in case you can't tell). That's what I'm doing in the neighborhood tomorrow, starting the cleanup.

See you tomorrow!!

Nikki

The next morning, there was one email. From Niraj, who wrote:

You'll succeed wildly, I'm sure of it. I cannot wait to hear all about it.

Two sentences that made me feel like the queen of the world, filled with power and light. I put on some old jeans and a T-shirt, and packed a change of clothes and a towel in my bag—it might not be the most elegant of places yet, but I could shower in that beautiful bathroom. Or could I? Maybe there was no shower, only a tub. I couldn't remember.

At any rate, I could freshen up there for my hike.

I stopped in the King Soopers across the street and picked out heavy-duty trash bags, a new broom and dustpan, pairs of rubber gloves, and industrial-size lots of cleaning supplies. I drove across town just ahead of the glut of commuters who'd mob I-25 after seven-thirty, and parked in the little place up the alley, which the landlord had told me was mine, a weedy little lot on the south side of the creek. A narrow path led beneath the trees to the back door of the shop, and I let myself into the cold and gloom, carrying the first load of supplies.

The back area was especially depressing. The sun never shone in these windows, and the sink was ten thousand years old, and the floor was a particularly ugly shade of stained, ancient linoleum. Dirt was in the corners, and a battered door guarded—what?

I pulled it open. Of course. The basement. Like I'd ever be going down there. At least I had a landlord here.

I closed the door and picked up my bags of supplies and carried them down the narrow hallway to the front room. From the corner of my eye, I saw the kitten streak up the stairs to the apartment, and smiled to myself. It did occur to me to wonder how he was getting in here, but for now there were more important things to worry about.

The sun had not yet penetrated into the area in front either. It was cold and shadowy. The faded lettering on the window looked tawdry, and so did the aqua paint on the baseboards.

So much work to do!

An icy panic fell on me—the obligatory, oh-God-what-have-I-done moment—but not even telling myself that's what it was helped. There was trash in the corners, and dust and grime on every surface, and spiders draping cobwebs all over everything, and it all just seemed so stupidly, absolutely insane. There was too much work here for one person—not to mention, what did I even know about running a business? Nothing. I had no idea what I needed to do, if I would have to have permits or permissions or licensing of some sort.

Stop.

The voice came from my gut. Just stop. Breathe. One step at a time. I didn't have to do everything in the next hour, or even in the next day. If I could get everything together for Memorial Day weekend, I'd have a good jump on the tourist season, and a good idea of how things were going to go. How far away was that? I calculated the weeks in my head.

Twenty-seven days.

I could do it. With a determined grunt, I put the bags on the counter, and took things out, one at a time, as if to declare my intentions to the nay-saying voices. Bleach. Thump. Wood soap. Thump. Pine-scented cleaner. Thump. Paper towels, rubber gloves, scrubbers, a bucket. Thump.

I wondered what Madame Mirabou would say about my chances in the shop. Maybe I should ask Roxanne for a reading. Except, what if it was bad? I picked up a scrap of paper from the floor and wrote on the back:

- Find out what licenses and permissions I might need
- Call about phone service
- Call around for a sign painter
- Buy squeegee for the windows

It made me feel better, and the last thing I took out of the bags was an aluminum cat dish and a bag of dry Meow Mix. Shaking the bag, I called out, "Kitty, kitty, kitty!" and went to the foot of the stairs. The kitten came to the top of the steps and peered down at me. He didn't look particularly nervous, but he didn't look as if he was in a big hurry to come down either. "All right," I said. "Have it your way."

I filled the bowl, held it up for him, and put it down with a flourish on the last step. "It's here whenever you want it."

Thus empowered, I rolled up my sleeves and got to work.

~

I worked straight till one, when I stripped off my gloves and stepped back to see how much I had accomplished today. The trash was gone and I'd swept the cobwebs from the ceiling and corners, and I'd washed the counters and the display-window floors with a mild cleanser, and then mopped the main floor. It was now at least possible to see the potential in the room.

Mentally, my list of chores was growing longer, but for the moment, enough was enough. I carried the bucket to the ancient sink in the back room and dumped it, then grabbed my overnight bag and carried it upstairs to the apartment.

The kitten was asleep in the bathtub, and either didn't hear me or didn't care.

"Hello there," I said, and put down my bag. He lifted his head and yawned, showing his tiny pink tongue, then just looked at me. Rather than sending him running away again, I let him be.

What a great tub! It was grimy and stained, but I thought it could come clean with some hard-core cleanser. I'd learned from my old house that this old porcelain didn't respond at all well to Scrubbing Bubbles or anything else so mild. It required powders, with bleach, and elbow grease.

The floor was pine and would need a good soaking with wood cleaner, then a bucket or so of oil to moisturize it, and there was some peeling wallpaper that needed to be stripped and carted away. Still, nothing could blunt the beauty of the honey-colored light pouring in through the amber stained glass. I thought the walls should be a shade of gold. Butter, maybe, or even a light pumpkin. I'd have to enlist eyes with a better color sense than my own. Usually I depended upon Giselle or my sister Molly, but neither of them was immediately available.

For now, I took off my old T-shirt and shorts and had a sponge bath in the sink. I washed my face and hands and torso, put on a fresh blouse and shorts, and combed my hair. In my purse were a few makeup supplies stowed for this purpose, and I brushed some color over my cheeks and lips, added some mascara to my too-light eyelashes, which was always the biggest improvement.

And as I thought sometimes lately, it wasn't such a bad face. For a while, going through the rejection of divorce, I'd wanted a face like my rival, wide-eyed and dark. Every time I'd looked at my face through those months, I felt pale and old and ugly.

But it was my face—the only one I had—and mostly I liked it again these days. I still liked my eyes, a very ordinary color of blue, the same color as the mountains, and my curly hair, which was healthy and naturally very pale blonde. There were lines now around those eyes, and I would pay the price of living in the dry, sunny West by the time I was seventy, but I liked the olive tone of my skin, and the directness of my gaze and the strong angle of my jaw.

Good enough.

Before I headed out to meet Niraj, I wandered through the apartment again, trying not to see the work that needed doing, but the possibilities. The light was wonderful in every room, and most of the windows framed some small, special rectangle of beauty. Tree branches or the edge of a mountain or even the street itself.

In the bedroom, I finally noticed the wallpaper the landlord had mentioned. Pale grays, blues, and roses, it was very old-fashioned and surprisingly beautiful. It wrapped around the door to the roof, and I opened the door, climbed the narrow steps, keeping my head low, and emerged again on my private deck.

A good day. Over the town, the mountains seemed to have stretched out on the horizon to sun themselves. I could barely glimpse the Peak over the shoulder of another. As I stood there, the lady of the mountain rustled her skirts, tossed her hair over her shoulder.

Welcome, child.

I smiled.

~

I stopped in to take Mary a hefty fistful of mint. "This was growing out there by the creek," I said.

"Mmm," she said, "that's nice. What are you doing here today?"

"I'm meeting someone. And wanted to check my schedule." I lifted pot lids, smelled inside. "Ooh, that's wonderful! Nutmeg and pork?"

"Yep. Tomorrow's special." She bruised the leaves of the mint with a flat thumb, smelled it again. "Maybe I'll make a mint sauce. There much more of it out there?"

"Tons!" I peeked in the oven, and a chicken was roasting. "Do you want me to get some more?"

"Nah, I'll go later. What you want to eat?"

I shrugged. "Something substantial. I've been cleaning all morning, and I'm going hiking this afternoon, so bring it on."

"That's what I like to hear." She washed her hands. "Go on, now. I'll send it out when I'm done."

"Thanks."

I sat at the bar and read the new edition of the *Independent*, a weekly newspaper, liberal as the *Gazette Telegraph* was conservative. Jason, the barista who had been behind the bar the day I first applied, brought out my food.

"This is yours, I guess?" He put down a turkey sandwich, piled high with sprouts and extra avocado. "What kind of spell did you put on Mary?"

I bit into the sandwich. "Mmmm. That's so good. I'm starving." Washing the sandwich down with milk, I asked, "What do you mean?"

"She never does super-duper extra-special sandwiches for the employees." He raised a brow. "Especially blonde ones."

I laughed. "We just clicked."

The bell over the front door rang and I looked up to see Niraj come in, his hair freshly cut to show the clarity of the bones in his beautiful face, his square chin drawing attention to his full lips. His beautifully muscled legs were bared by a pair of khaki shorts. A stab of lust twisted in my lower belly and I let it show in my eyes as he came over and sat down.

"Hi," I said, and put a lot of warmth in it.

"Hello." He put his hand on my shoulder, briefly. As if he'd been baking in the warm afternoon, his spicy scent steamed from his torso.

I thought of a ginger cookie, fresh from the oven. He met my eyes, frankly admiring, and for a minute I thought he might kiss me. His hand strayed to the back of my neck, swept over it discreetly, moved away. "How nice to see you."

"I meant to get over here sooner so I'd be finished eating before you arrived," I said. "I just got carried away working."

"No hurry," he said. "Take your time."

"Would you like something?" Jason asked him.

"Tea, please. Iced, with lemon." Settling his elbows on the bar, Niraj looked at me. "So it was a productive morning?"

"Yes. It's a little daunting, how much there is to do, but it felt good to get started."

Jason brought the tea in a tall glass, garnished with lemon and mint leaves. He settled it on the old, polished wooden bar, and Niraj drew it forward with thanks. The bell rang over the door.

I glanced up, my mouth full of avocado and sprouts and free-range organic turkey on the most lusciously seeded, wheaty bread you could imagine. My muscles were pleasantly tired from cleaning work. Niraj's arm rested against mine lightly, a companionable promise, and life was just about as sweet as it had been since the day I walked in from the grocery store and my husband, looking gray and exhausted, said, "Nicole, will you sit down, please? I need to talk to you about something."

Next to me, Niraj swore softly under his breath. "There is going to be trouble," he said.

Into the bar sauntered Hannah, the sultry-lipped Englishwoman, with her long legs and deep bust and artfully cut dark hair. She wore a lime-green shift with very little beneath it, and her eyes were the color of delphiniums. "There you are, darling," she said, and made her way toward us. "I've been looking for you in every pub for miles."

"Hannah—" he began as she sat down next to him.

As if I were invisible, she draped her hand around his shoulders and laid her head against his arm. "All is forgiven, love," she said with a heavy sigh. "You can come home now."

Niraj shoved back from the bar almost violently, ducking away from her arm. "Do not make a scene, Hannah," he said in a dangerous voice. "I am weary of it, do you hear me?"

I was very still, waiting to see what would happen. Hannah rolled her eyes, smiled, and shook her head, as if they'd been down this road a thousand times. "I know you're angry, but we'll work it out. We always do."

She reached for him, and he shook her off, so much revulsion in the gesture that it shocked me. With a quick step back, he gestured a movement like picking up the phone. He took my elbow, his eyes flickering to Hannah, then back to me. "I will not be able to keep our date this afternoon," he said. "I am sorry."

He stalked out.

Hannah grabbed her tiny purse and ran after him. Through the window, I saw Niraj break into a jog. Jason picked up the phone. "I need to report a problem," he said. "Restraining order violation. Yeah. Annie's Organix."

He put the phone down. Met my eyes. His mouth turned up in a wry little twist.

"What was that all about?"

He shook his head, picked up a bar towel uncomfortably. "Let him tell you."

I raised my eyebrows. This man might be a little more trouble than he was worth. "I think I'll pass."

Instead of arguing on behalf of Niraj, Jason said, "That'd be my recommendation."

I looked out the window, up the hill toward the beautiful art deco house on the hill, conscious of a piercing disappointment.

But better now than later. Maybe I'd needed this reminder that love meant risking heartbreak. I'd had enough of the latter for one life, thanks.

"Why don't you wrap that up for me?" I said, pushing my sandwich across the bar. "I'm going to clear out before I change my mind."

14

Nikki's Perfume Journal Entry

Time: 8:02 p.m.
Date: June 4, 1991

Bottle: a patent medicine bottle, pale blue or green
Elements: water from a hose, wet grass, crushed lavender,
astringent geranium leaves, earth, whisper of mountain nights,
twilight . . . what does twilight smell like?
Notes: garden evening

I volunteered to be the designated driver for the birthday outing
with Wanda and Roxanne, but Roxanne had already worked it out.
Her daughter, Amy—a skinny, Goth-pale, black-fingernailed girl
of sixteen—drove her mother's car to the downtown restaurant and
dropped us off. "I'll pick you up at eight-thirty, all right?"

Roxanne kissed her. "Thanks, sweetheart! We'll call you if we need
you sooner than that."

"No problemo," she said, and smiled at me. Her eyes were a daz-
zling blue, and in spite of the pierced tongue, the black, the assemblages
of rebellion, she was very sweet. "Have a good time, and don't do anything you wouldn't want me to do!"

"We can't get in too much trouble in two hours," Wanda said. Her children had gone to a friend's house for the night. "Not nearly as much as I'd like!"

"Wanda!" Amy said. "You're married, remember?"

She laughed. "I'm only kidding!"

As I scrambled out behind the others, Amy said, "Hey. They seem a little hysterical or something. Let me know if I need to come early to keep them out of trouble, okay?"

I touched her wrist, wondering suddenly how much she knew of her mother's promiscuity. Roxanne took care to hide it, but still, the girl was sixteen. "I promise I'll keep an eye on them both, sweetie. Don't worry."

She flipped her tongue ring around and tapped her front teeth with it. "Thanks. See ya later."

Jack Quinn's was one of the ubiquitous Irish pubs in Colorado Springs, downtown in a strip of bars, restaurants, entertainment for the eternally cool, and it was itself almost too self-consciously hip to bear, with dark wood and long tables in the back and lots of stout on tap. I still loved it. The leaded glass and Celtic music and pints of ale made me feel like I might be somewhere in the world besides America.

Wanda tossed her hair back from her face as we walked in. "Oh, I like this!"

Her hair was long and free down her back, shiny and healthy, and she'd taken some time with her makeup. She still had that nameless something that marked her as a soldier's wife, but I'd never noticed that she was so attractive. Her black blouse boasted a square neckline that showed off pretty white shoulders and lots of creamy cleavage. "How old are you today?"

"Twenty-seven!" she said. "Three more years until the big three-o!"

I met Roxanne's gaze and we both laughed. "Enjoy it, sweetheart," Roxanne said. And when the hostess came to seat us, she pointed at the booths. "Can we eat in one of the private spots first, and then move out of there later?" Roxanne lifted a big bag. "It's a birthday dinner."

"Sure!"

As we walked through the restaurant, men turned around to watch us. Or more likely, Roxanne, who was dressed in a slim black skirt and red shoes, her toenails painted fire-engine red. At a distance, she looked thirty, and even up close, it wasn't easy to decide.

Between the two brunettes, I felt pallid and too tall, but it didn't matter. Tonight was for Wanda.

Twenty-seven. It seemed a billion years ago. I thought back. I must have been pregnant with Giselle, alight with hope and anticipation. I stayed home with her, and loved every second of it. A long time ago now.

We ordered pints—mine stout, the other two ales. When the waitress hurried away, Roxanne reached back into the big bag at her side and brought out hats, noisemakers, and little toy harmonicas. "We have to wear them for at least a little while," she said.

I put mine on happily, and blew on the noisemaker. "Happy birthday!" I cried, and blew it again. "Bravo, Wanda!"

She blushed and blew her own rolling whistle. "The hat will mess up my hair! You have no idea how long it takes to get all the kinkiness out."

Roxanne put hers on and said, "No exceptions. You don't have to put the little elastic thingy on, but you have to at least put the hat on your head."

"Okay. I can do that." Wanda perched it on top of her head. "How do I look?"

"Gorgeous. Where's your phone?"

"Right here!" She flipped open a camera phone and handed it to Roxanne, then leaned in close to me. "Smile. We'll send these to Tommy."

Roxanne clicked the picture, then reached back into the bag. "In honor of our talk the other night, I got Nikki presents too." She put down Mylar-wrapped packages for me and Wanda, and her eyes were sparkling. "Open them!"

I ripped mine open, and started to laugh. It was an enormous vibrator, bright blue. A smaller package proved to hold batteries. "So you never run out," Roxanne said.

With a wiggling of my eyebrows, I clutched it all to my chest. "Thank you. I can hardly wait to get it home."

Roxanne beamed.

Wanda, too, had a vibrator, hers red. "What am I going to do with this, Roxanne?" she said in a fierce whisper. "What if my kids find it?"

"Don't be so worried, you silly girl. So what if they do? Do you think they'll understand the vibrator idea just yet?"

The waitress appeared with the pints, and Wanda scrambled to put away her dildo. I put mine down beside me and we all snickered, like girls caught sneaking cigarettes in the bathroom. The woman gave us a little smile and settled our beers on the table. "I'll be back in a little while to take your food order."

Wanda's face was plum with embarrassment. I nudged her, laughing. "I'm sure she has one herself."

"Well, we all have breasts, too, don't we, but we don't go showing them around." She looked at the box beside her. "Still, thanks. It will be . . . um . . . interesting."

"No problem." Roxanne pulled out a big card, and pushed it over the table toward Wanda. "This is the real present. Happy birthday, sweetie."

Wanda opened the card. "A spa day!" She gave a little screech and pounded her feet on the floor. "Oh, that's wonderful, Roxanne. Thank you."

"You bet, kiddo. You can be all sleek and gorgeous when your husband gets home."

"How long is it?" I asked.

"Two and a half weeks!" She widened her eyes, touched her middle. "I'm so looking forward to it."

Roxanne pushed a small box toward me. "This is a little something more for you too."

I ripped the paper off, to discover a box of—"Condoms?"

"Yes. Equally practical. We didn't do the condoms thing when we were young, but it's important now, and it's hard for people to buy them sometimes."

Sincerely, I said, "Thank you. That was very thoughtful."

"What can I say? I'm just a thoughtful kind of girl." She picked up her glass and raised it high. "To a great twenty-seventh birthday!" she cried.

I lifted my glass, too, but I also noticed that when Roxanne lifted hers, her sleeve fell backward and there were some serious bruises on the back of her arm, as if someone had grabbed her very hard.

None of my business. "To Wanda!"

We ordered our food and Wanda's phone rang. She picked it up and grinned, her face transforming. "Hey, baby!" she cried. "What are you doing awake? It's the middle of the night!"

Roxanne and I looked at each other. "Do you want us to go?" Roxanne whispered.

Wanda shook her head adamantly and lifted a finger, and it was true the conversation only lasted a minute or so. She punched a button on the phone to hang up and held it in her hand for a minute, looking down at a picture on the tiny screen.

"Is that him?" I asked.

"Yeah." She passed the phone over to me. "That was taken just a few weeks ago, in Baghdad."

The photo showed a sturdy, muscular man in his early thirties, his neck sunburned above his olive-green T-shirt. Sun blasted down on his head, hooding his eyes, and he was smiling, but it looked more pained than cheerful. "He's handsome," I said, and meant it.

"Can I see?" Roxanne said. She peered at the photo. "He looks worn-out is what he looks."

"Have you met him?"

"When he was home for leave—what was that, about seven months ago? His father died, right?"

Wanda nodded. A small frown creased her forehead. "Yeah. I think he looks tired, too, but more he just seems kind of weird."

"What do you mean?" I asked.

"Kind of cold. Unemotional."

"I had an uncle who had PTSD," Roxanne said, handing the phone back. "When he got back from Vietnam, he was a little crazy for a while. Said he just couldn't get used to things the way they were."

I hesitated, then said, "My father went to Vietnam. His body came back, but never his heart, as my mother liked to say. He disappeared when I was a teenager, and we never saw him again."

They were both staring at me, horrified, and I lifted a shoulder. "Sorry. That was a bit of depressing stuff, huh?" I gulped some stout, hurried on to fill the silence that had dropped. "But back in the day, they weren't treating vets very well for their traumas, were they? I'm sure the army knows what to do with returning vets now."

"Not so you'd notice," Roxanne said with a sigh.

"She's right," Wanda said. "I thought they'd give them all this counseling and stuff when he got back last time, and they didn't really. They had a suicide prevention class"—she widened her eyes to show how crazy that made her—"and that was about it."

And now he'd be back from another tour. That had to be nerve-racking.

"It has to be so weird for them," I said. "I mean, there you are, in some village or some war-torn city for months and months, and you have to be on your toes, and you don't really know who the bad guys are, and you're eating lousy food, and you're hot and dusty all the time, and then all of a sudden, you get on a plane, come back to the world you left, and it's all exactly the same. All sterile and air-conditioned and noisy and squeaky clean." I swigged my beer. "I mean, really. It has to be bizarre."

Wanda looked at me. "I never thought about that. It does have to be really weird, doesn't it? Thanks. That kinda helps."

I shrugged. "Sure."

"Sorry about your dad," she said.

"Long time ago."

Wanda noticed the same bruises I had on Roxanne's arms. "Roxanne!" she said, and her eyes were narrowed.

"What?"

"You swore on a stack of Bibles you wouldn't go back to him again."

"Who?" I asked.

At the same time, Roxanne said, "I didn't. He came over to talk about the kids, and one thing led to another."

"Your ex?" I asked.

"Yes," Wanda said, and she was genuinely angry. "Look at those bruises!"

"You're making too much of it," Roxanne said, and to me added, "We always liked rough sex, and I guess Lora-Lies-a-Lot isn't quite as into it."

"You sleep with your ex?"

She shrugged. "Every now and then."

I remembered how she'd been stiff and tired the day before. Not a big deal—we'd all been there, hadn't we?—but . . . "It doesn't seem like a particularly good idea to sleep with a guy you're trying to get out of your system."

"That's what I say," Wanda said. "Not only that, it seems like every time there's something else that happens. Every time, Roxanne." She looked at me. "He sliced up some of her paintings once. She broke his window—all these little violent things I don't like."

Roxanne shrugged. "He's just another dick."

"If that were true, you'd be okay," Wanda argued. "The truth is, he's the only one you care about, and it's gonna hurt you." When Roxanne looked sullenly into her glass, Wanda said, "Don't forget about Alison."

"Oh, please." Roxanne rolled her eyes. "I'm not the suicidal type."

"Somebody committed suicide?"

"Yeah, in the apartment below yours, last summer. She never got over her divorce, and on the day her husband got remarried, she killed herself."

"Sweet revenge," Roxanne said.

"Don't say that!" I protested. "That's awful!"

"Roxanne," Wanda persisted. "You have to stop it. It's self-destructive."

"Whatever. Okay!" She shook her choppy hair out of her eyes. "Let's party, girls!"

"It's my birthday," Wanda said, "and I get to say what I want to say." She put her white hand around Roxanne's wrist. "It's dangerous when you play with him. You start getting stronger, then you let him get to you, and you have to start all over again."

Roxanne dipped her head.

"You're the one always saying that we have to love ourselves first," Wanda continued. "If your daughter were doing what you're doing, or if one of us did, what would you say?"

Roxanne picked up Wanda's hand and pressed a quick kiss to her wrist. "You're right, sweetie. And I appreciate it. I know that you care about me."

"Good. Promise you'll talk to the counselor about this?"

"Yes. Cross my heart and hope to die. Stick a needle in my eye." She raised a hand, like a Girl Scout giving an oath. "Promise."

"All right." Wanda raised her glass. "To loving ourselves first!"

"Amen!" I said. We clinked and drank.

~

Two hours later, I helped pour the more than slightly inebriated Wanda into the back of Roxanne's car, and climbed in beside her. Roxanne slid into the front seat, and even I could see her daughter was annoyed with her. "Who was that guy you were kissing?"

Roxanne had half picked up a lonely soldier at the bar, and flirted with him, let him buy us shots—which I did not drink—and ended up giving him a giant kiss at the door on the way out. He had to be at least fifteen years younger than her, and I was both shocked and impressed. The woman had what it took.

To do what? I wondered to myself. Get laid? Get any man in the room? I didn't know.

In answer to her daughter, she looked at her rings. "Nobody," she said. "Just a friend."

"A friend? Ha!" Amy pulled into traffic smoothly, bouncing a little in her annoyance. "That's a funny word for it."

I looked out the window.

"Everybody else okay?" Amy asked.

Wanda put her head back on the seat. "I drank shots! I never drink shots."

"When you get home, you should drink a bunch of water and take some aspirin, or you'll feel like shit tomorrow." Roxanne yawned. "How was your night, kiddo?"

Amy said shortly, "Fine."

"Don't be mad at me. I didn't mean for you to see that."

I kept my attention on the traffic outside. What would Giselle think if she saw me kissing someone?

"I'm not mad," Amy said.

"Yes, you are."

"Okay, maybe I am. Why do you have to do anything like that? You already had your family and a long marriage. Isn't that enough?"

I had to stifle a snort, but Roxanne was wiser. "I'm sorry you saw me kissing someone," she said again.

"I wish you guys would all get some boundaries, you know? Kids do not want to think of their parents like this. It's disgusting."

"It's uncomfortable for you," Roxanne said, echoing like a good counselor. "I do apologize."

Amy let go of a breath, looked over her shoulder to change lanes. "It's okay." She turned up the radio. Dido's "White Flag" filled the car. Roxanne looked at her hands.

Wanda reached for my hand. "Am I a terrible person for getting drunk?"

I laughed, patted her cold fingers. "No. And you can call me in the morning, so I can tell you again."

"It's not that I don't want my husband to come home," she said. "I do. I'm just worried about the whole thing."

"It's okay."

"This friend of mine? Her husband said he can't stand it at home now. And she says he has bad nightmares, and she thinks he's going to leave her, or make her leave."

"That's pretty sad."

"It is. And some of the wives say they don't even know who their husbands are when they get home. Like, they're so different, they're somebody else."

"Wanda!" Roxanne said sharply from the front seat. "Don't borrow trouble."

Wanda recoiled, which of course Roxanne couldn't see. "I'm not!" she protested. "It's just scary, you know?"

I touched her wrist with the tips of my fingers, brushed the delicate skin there. "It's normal to feel nervous, kiddo. I grew up in this town during Vietnam. Soldiers' wives worry about their returns."

She nodded.

"There are lots of counselors out there if he needs to talk to somebody," I added. "If you need it."

Amy pulled up in front of our stairs. "If you guys want to get out, you won't have to walk so far."

"Thanks, hon." I touched her shoulder.

"You're welcome."

When we got out of the car, Wanda hugged me. Fiercely. "Thanks," she said. "You really did help tonight."

"No problem. Remember the water and aspirin."

She waved backward over her shoulder, and I turned to go up the stairs. I was reaching into my purse as I rounded the last bend, so when a figure stood up, I was startled and ready to fight or flee, as necessary.

It took a long moment to sink in that it was Niraj standing there. Looking sober and splendid in a thin cotton shirt of the palest possible shade of purple. My pleasure in seeing him stung, and that made me wary.

"Oh," I said. "It's you." I moved to go around him.

"Nikki, you have a right to be angry."

"Thanks for giving me permission." I brushed by him, and kept going, headed for my door on the dizzyingly high steps.

"It would be very nice if you could give me one moment to explain."

I shrugged, pulled myself up the last turn. "Go ahead."

"May I come in?"

He stood right behind me, that freshness of his skin blowing over me on the breeze. I thought of his mouth and his tongue, and the hope I'd been feeling.

Then I thought of how crushed I'd felt when he left with no explanation, abruptly breaking our date. "You don't owe me anything, Niraj. We've only just met."

He brushed a finger over my arm. "I was very rude, and I would like to apologize."

I turned the key in the lock, still undecided. From the stairwell came the sound of Amy and Roxanne's voices. They were climbing the stairs behind us, and the one thing I did know for sure was that I wasn't ready for anyone else to see him.

Pushing my front door open, I turned around and grabbed his sleeve. "Quick," I said, and he tumbled into the foyer. I pushed the door closed behind us.

15

Nikki's Perfume Journal Entry

THINGS I LIKE TO SMELL
June 10, 1976

Ponderosa pine bark — like butterscotch
Cabin bathroom at La Foret Church camp. Herbal Essence
shampoo, Irish Spring soap, toothpaste, pine trees
The smell of scrub oak leaves rotting on the forest floor Water
rushing through Cheyenne canyon. Bananas

I felt Niraj behind me, warmth and presence. My flesh rippled with wanting him. I turned. He put his hand on my shoulder.

And then we were tangled up, and he was kissing me, and there wasn't a single cell in my body that resisted. His arms looped around me, and our chests and bellies and thighs pressed tight, the wall hard against my back, and that luscious mouth was on mine, and my tongue hurried into his mouth, and my hands were in his hair, and we were kissing like the fate of three island nations depended upon it. It made me dizzy. His scent. The taste of his lips. The press of his body against mine. I wanted to rub against him and resisted.

I pushed against his shoulders. "Okay, okay. Hold on. Let me catch my breath."

He pulled away somewhat, but his lips grazed the end of my nose, a gesture I found almost unbearably tender. I ducked under his arm, reached for the light switch, and dove into the circle of reality contained in the middle of the beige, bland room.

"Start talking," I said, and faced him, my hands on my hips.

Good. God. His hair was mussed a little, the curls sticking up on his crown, a lock falling on his forehead. His eyebrows were arched and dark, and those red, lovely lips were slightly moist.

This, I thought, was exactly how Lucifer should be painted.

He said, "Do you want the long version or the short one?"

"Short. Then I'll decide."

"Hannah is crazy. She will not leave me alone and keeps causing trouble, and I have a restraining order against her. I left so quickly so that you would not become a target."

I frowned. "You couldn't say something? Warn me? Call my cell phone?"

He took a breath. "I handled it poorly. I apologize."

I could feel the beer I'd drunk. "I need some coffee." I headed for the kitchen. "I'm not inviting you to stay over, but since I'm making some for me, do you want some for yourself?"

A slight quiver moved on his lips. "Yes, all right. That would be nice."

"You can come sit down at the breakfast bar here if you like," I said, and went to the kitchen. The perfumery was open on the counter, along with the thick, battered leather-bound journal of perfume recipes and notes. I closed the book but left it there. I took the coffeepot off the burner and filled it with water. "It's going to have to be high-test. I've had a bit to drink."

He smiled. "I can tell." He settled at the breakfast bar, the open organ in front of him. He folded his brown hands and took a deep breath. "That smells wonderful."

I nodded, gestured toward the three tiers of essences and absolutes and various ingredients. "Perfume ingredients."

"May I open them?"

"Absolutely. Smell away."

He came around the counter as I busied myself with measuring coffee grounds and pouring water, and taking out cups and spoons and a pitcher for milk. He opened several bottles and smelled them, grunted, frowned, once inhaling deeply. "Intriguing," he said. "Where is the one you were making? Might I smell that?"

I nodded, and took a small brown bottle from the lowest rung. Opening it, I wafted it under my nose, again was taken aback by the fierceness of it. "Not for everyone," I said, and handed it to him.

He smelled it carefully, then held my hand steady so he could smell it again. "This is the one you wanted gunpowder for?"

"Yeah. Anger."

He held it there, not directly under his nose, but to one side. "It is very powerful. I like it very much."

"Still not quite there," I said, and brought it back to my own nose. "It needs a teeny bit more edge." I narrowed my eyes, looked in the distance, thought perhaps it might be—

I put it down and gave him a smile. "It will come to me. Best not to start experimenting with it tonight. I'd hate to ruin it."

"It smells," he said, "like something Hannah should wear."

"Why is she so angry with you?"

He shook his head. "I have a history of attracting women who are . . . somewhat damaged. She is badly damaged, and I could not help her anymore." He met my eyes. "I would rather not tell her secrets, but she is wounded."

Every time I spent even five minutes with him, I liked him better. He never said what I thought he would. "Am I damaged?"

He inclined his head. "Are you?"

"I'm divorced. Badly. I feel pretty mad."

"I don't know if that always means damaged."

In my slightly tipsy state, I liked thinking about me. "No, as dramatic as it is, I don't feel damaged. Not entirely sane, of course, but just slightly battered, as we all are."

His eyes crinkled when he grinned. "Yes."

"So am I out of the running, then? Because I'm not particularly wounded?"

He chuckled. "On the contrary. I am quite weary of damaged women."

"Good." I smelled Roxanne's perfume again, then put it aside and picked up one of my favorites. "Try this. Tell me what it makes you think of."

He obligingly bent down to smell it. Light looped through his hair, skated down the high bridge of his gorgeous nose. I wanted to put my palm against his crown, and resisted.

"It smells like summer," he said. "Like a sunny summer afternoon."

I laughed, the sound throaty and delighted, even in my own ears. "You have a nose! That's wonderful!"

"Do I?"

"You do!" I turned toward the counter to flip open the book of recipes. On the page for Wedding Afternoon, I stabbed my finger down. "Look at the list of ingredients!"

He moved closer, looking over my shoulder. I felt him against my back, and went still, wishing for things I didn't know if I should want. The beer made it seem too easy to just turn around and—

As if he'd read my thoughts, he brushed my hair to one side and pressed his lips to the back of my neck. "You seem suspicious of my reasons for wanting to spend time in your company," he said quietly.

I closed my eyes. His lips were warm and moist on my skin, brushing sweetly over that very sensitive place. Gooseflesh rose on my entire body, and he put his hands on my hips, moved a little closer. Kissed my neck again.

"You're making me dizzy," I whispered.

"Do you want me to stop?"

I closed my eyes. "No."

He pressed his body against my back and trailed his tongue over my nape, and I shuddered almost violently. "Oh, that's so nice!" I said helplessly. His hands slid upward, edged around my breasts, and when I did not object, he moved higher still and cupped them in his hands, kneading gently as his mouth and tongue made patterns on my neck. I bore it as long as I could—so much pleasure!—then turned in his arms and pressed upward to kiss him, my arms around his neck.

He made a soft noise of relief and then we were kissing, elaborately, lips shifting, moving, slipping, sliding, fitting and not. It was such a luscious moment that I wanted to imprint every detail in my memory—I felt the skin of his neck against the thin flesh on my inner forearm, and his thighs were close against my own. I moved my hands downward, gauging his back and waist as our hips pressed hard together. He moved his hands again, his fingers lightly grazing my nipples. I kneaded his hips. Our tongues lashed and laced.

He raised his head. "We will be lovers," he said matter-of-factly. He rubbed his thumbnail over the aroused tips of my breasts, and looked me in the eye as he did it. "But not when you are drinking and can blame it on that. When you are sober and you want me because it is me."

I blinked. Beneath my hands, his back was hot, and I reached beneath his shirt to touch his skin. It was surprisingly silky. "You have very soft skin."

"Not all of it," he said, and raised an eyebrow.

"That part I know too." I laughed.

He took a breath, moved a little away. "Will you make me some coffee now?"

"Yes. That would be a good idea." I tried to shake off the shivers. "And then you can go home."

"Will you go with me on a picnic Saturday afternoon?"

"I work Saturday."

"Sunday?"

"All right." I hadn't yet been anointed into the Sunday shift every week. I'd have to work up a little to claim the best tip shifts. "Do you want me to bring something?"

He smiled in a secret way. "No. I think it will be a little surprise."

"All right," I said. Then I made the coffee and sent him on his way.

$\sim$

Since moving to the new apartment, I hadn't had as much trouble waking up in the middle of the night as I'd had in the old house. But when three a.m. rolled around, I found myself wide awake, thinking of the fact that I'd just spent most of my cash reserves on a harebrained scheme to sell perfume to the public, and I didn't have enough inventory or any idea of how to run a business, or anything else.

I nearly gave myself a panic attack, and finally decided to just get up and at least worry productively.

In the fluorescent-lit kitchen, I made a cup of herbal tea, ruby-colored and smelling of peaches, and sat on a barstool at the clinically designed counter. I put on a CD my sister had made for me, a collection of all kinds of things from our youth, and while "Vincent" played, I started jotting down some notes.

One thing at a time. Inventory. For the first time, I realized I was going to have to standardize some of the perfumes. I'd need a signature line for Scent of Hours Perfumes—establish the flagship set, and offer them on the website, and that way I could offer samples of new blends and experiments to intrigue potential customers.

That way, too, I could have bottles of my own created. There was no way to be able to fill enough antique bottles with my own scents to make enough money. I could, again, still offer some perfumes in those exquisite little lots, in the beautiful bottles. I'd charge an arm and a leg for them. A slogan flashed into my mind: *Rare scents for a rare woman.* I wrote it down. Maybe *A unique scent for a unique woman*?

Think about that. In the meantime, if this was going to work, I'd have to figure out my product line, and what scents would go in which bottles. Scents first.

Flipping through my notebook, the years and years of notes and perfumes I'd made—some seriously, some slapdash, I wondered how to choose.

From the box I'd shown Niraj, I took several two-ounce amber bottles with labels I'd hand-lettered. These were my own favorites, things I'd been blending for a long time. Wedding Afternoon was a fresh and breezy perfume, with notes of grass and lavender, and the crispness of grapefruit. It wasn't a rough draft—it had been through a dozen refinements, and I'd reproduced it many times. It also did not require blending in small amounts—I could make it in amounts large enough to market easily. I smelled it now, let it expand in my head, thought about what sort of bottle it would require. Maybe a pale green bottle, a two-ounce size. An atomizer? I wrote those thoughts on my tablet.

Another favorite, an evening-weight perfume, was the musky Tuesday at Midnight, civet and patchouli lightened by notes of lemon, vanilla, and hay. It was actually a fairly long list of ingredients, and it had been through a dozen experimental stages, but this version was one I'd been reliably making for five or six years, and it was quite stable. What sort of bottle? Something sensually shaped, maybe cobalt glass. No, too obvious.

Or was it? I thought about some of my favorite bottles over the years—Avon had created some beauties. What if I tried to find something along those lines—blue pillars with a label of starry nights?

Brainstorming further, what if the essence was blue, and the bottle white or soft pink? Hmm. I made notes on the tablet by my arm. It might stain, but maybe not. Maybe I could find some colorant that would evaporate upon contact with the skin.

What other perfumes had I standardized? Lots of them, actually—it just happened if you did this long enough. I flipped through the recipes, things I'd experimented with over the years and loved, things I did not love. Things I'd forgotten. Some were exotically rewarding, but too difficult to make in large batches, or too unstable to reliably reproduce.

I took out a third bottle, and grinned, pulling a cork out to smell the cologne within. This was a light, playful scent—Picnic with My Sisters. There were notes of sassafras, forest, and chocolate, running water and tobacco—not a cigarette-smoke sort, but the aroma of walking into a cigar store.

Yes. That would be a nice balance. I thought of the Moody Blues album *Days of Future Passed*, a composition of songs that followed a day, from "Dawn," to the very famous "Nights in White Satin." I lined up the three bottles—two afternoon perfumes, one night. I could change the name of Wedding Afternoon to Wedding Morning. That might work, especially with the hint of grapefruit, and a sense of breakfast—

Resistance rolled into a ball in my chest. No. All right, then. Wedding Afternoon. Picnic in Cheyenne Canyon. Tuesday at Midnight.

Did I have anything that would work as dawn, or at least as a base for beginning to create one? I flipped through the journal, scribbled a couple of possibilities.

Leave it for now.

Next, I'd need a label, bottles, a unifying design idea. Who did I know who could help me with this? There was really only one person: Evelyn, with whom I'd been very annoyed for no particular reason aside from her smug, plump marriedness. How dare she be so happy when I was so miserable?

Not fair. I got up to send her an email. When I opened the program, there were two emails in the lineup. One was from Giselle, one from Niraj. My stomach jumped. I glanced at the clock. It was nearly four—I'd be going to work in an hour anyway. Whatever the news, it wouldn't keep me from sleeping.

First I wrote the note to Evelyn. Very quick and sweet: Help! I need your elegant eye for design. Urgent! Call me and I'll buy you lunch and pick your brain. Love, Nicole.

The one from Giselle was all in the subject line: COMING NEXT WEEKEND!!!!!! ☺ ☺ ☺ ☺ I opened it, noted the times and flight numbers, and wrote back a giant smiley face of my own, drawn with exclamation points. I'll have to work some, but will try to get things lined up for you to do. LOVE YOU!!!!!

TO: nikki@scentofhours.com
FROM: niraj.bhuskar@blipdata.com
SUBJECT: reasons

Dear Goldfingers,

There are many reasons why I "like" you. You have a beautiful, shy smile. Your hair is like cotton candy. And you are intelligent, which is more rare than you can possibly imagine. You do not take yourself or life too seriously. You look at me as if I am dashing, a pirate or someone exciting like that, instead of a man who does such a boring thing as computers. You are sexy and kind and I want to touch you and listen to you talk, and those seem like very good reasons for wanting to spend time with someone.

We men do not ask for such reassurances, but we sometimes would not mind hearing them ourselves, you know.

Niraj

~

TO: niraj.bhuskar@blipdata.com
FROM: nikki@scentofhours.com

SUBJECT: re: reasons

Dear Niraj,

Because you have eyelashes that look like they were dipped in ink. Because you have very nice calves, and you knew the name of Marin Marais, and flirted with me by offering knowledge. Because you have a sexy accent and kiss very well and smell like something just out of the edge of my memory.

And you like to walk.

Nikki the Needy, who likes to know

P.S. You forgot to bring my present again. Just saying.

16

Nikki's Perfume Journal Entry

SCENT OF HOURS

Time: 11 a.m.
Date: April 30, 2006

Scents: The smell of rain, sweet and salty, grass, and the
sharpness of Branston Pickle, and that elusive piney scent of his
skin, root beer
Notes: picnic with Niraj

Over the next few days, I was very busy. Between work, trying to
get the shop cleaned up, and preparing in whatever ways I could think
of for Giselle's visit, I hit the bed at nine-thirty and slept like the dead
until four, when it was time to start over again.

Every day, there was email from Niraj—at least one, usually two
or three. Not long or involved, but pleasant. Amusing. Touching base.
I heard from Giselle every day, too, which made it seem as if she really
did miss me. In idle moments, while I waited for a pot of coffee to finish brewing at work, or as I scrubbed a wall at the shop, I wondered if
things were okay out there. It had been a little odd that even Dan said

he missed me while they were in London. Had things not gone well with Ms. Wife?

There was little time for mulling it all over. Giselle could tell me soon enough. I hoped she would like her new bedroom. I wondered what she would think of my new job, of the shop and my new circle of friends. I wondered what was going on with her life, if she had a boyfriend, if there were new good friends or if she missed the old ones. Did she even keep in touch? She didn't talk about them much. At Christmas, the last time she'd been here, we'd both been so miserable knocking around the old house with the ghosts of Happy Christmases Past that we didn't even bother to celebrate—we watched movies on TBS and ate microwave popcorn and pie. "This is cool in a sick kind of way," she had commented at one point.

I laughed. "I guess it is."

"Not that I particularly want to repeat it."

"No."

This year at Christmas, I'd be in the apartment over the shop. The thought gave me a happy little rush. I knew exactly where I'd put my tree—at the top of the stairs, near the first big window in the living room.

Providing this whole scheme worked out, of course. At the moment, that seemed as if it would be a miracle in itself.

~

Kit and Evelyn met me at the shop Saturday afternoon. I managed to get off work, clean up, and change clothes before they arrived, so my secret waitress life was still safely tucked away.

A good thing, because they were a little dismayed about the condition of the shop, I could tell. All polite smiles and nods, but when I turned my back, they were exchanging horrified glances, I knew.

Evelyn was, however, enthusiastic about coming up with some ideas for my labels and logo. She liked the possibility of using an art deco font, both for the storefront and the bottles themselves, and in a flash of brilliance suggested the possibility of ocean-liner decor as a possibility. "Or no!" she said. "How about those seagoing things that brought back plants from all over—"

Kit, listening as she gazed around the shop, said, "But then you lose the art deco connection, and that really works with the perfume angle, and the whole spirit of the Pikes Peak region." She put the last phrase in quotes with her fingers.

"Right. Good point." I pursed my lips, peered toward the mountains.

"How about a conservatory theme?"

Evelyn's eyebrows rose. "Good! What do you think, Nikki?"

A ripple flew over my skin as I imagined orchids and scented geraniums filling the room. "Yes, I like it. Wrought iron, painted white?"

"Or wicker, which is cheaper."

"Good. Yes." I thought of clear shelving, and perhaps some palms. "Oh, I love this idea!"

Evelyn paced forward, then back. "Green and white stripes on one wall, the rest white to make it seem bigger."

"We could paint the floor in a faux flagstone design," Kit offered. "I just did it a couple of weeks ago and it was so much fun!"

"Love it."

We batted around a host of possibilities and came up with a general strategy. Evelyn promised to come up with some sort of solid plan by midweek, and then we could all get busy next weekend. Saturday was the only day they were both free, and I felt my heart plummet. Giselle would be here, at my request, and she'd probably hate being stuck in the shop all day. There was a lot going on in my life, but the one thing I truly did not want to lose sight of was how badly I wanted to spend time with my daughter. Whatever else happened, that had to be my first priority. "Giselle's going to be here, but let me see what she thinks, and I'll call you."

~

Sunday, Niraj picked me up at eleven. It was thrilling to open the door of my apartment to a man, and I felt a soaring sense of possibility in looking at him. He wore a pale orange polo shirt that made his skin look admirably rosy, and a pair of shorts and walking sandals instead of boots. His ankles showed a faint tan line, but I loved the look of his fine-boned, high-arched feet.

The big shock was his hair, which had been shorn into a close short cut, leaving behind only hints of the waviness. I blinked in surprise. "I would have said I loved your curls, but wow, that haircut suits you."

He rubbed an open palm over it. "Summer, I like to wear it shorter. By spring, I look like a sheep."

"Both are very good."

He took my hand, bent in to give me a kiss. "Thank you. You look very pretty too."

We headed to his car, and I shaded my eyes, looking to the west. A bank of clouds bubbled up over the mountains, light and dark. Iffy, for a picnic. "Did you check the weather report?"

"It may rain a little, but no thunderstorms."

"A picnic in the rain?"

He shrugged. "I am an Englishman. If you wait for sunny days, you will never do anything."

I laughed. "Fair enough. Where are we going?"

"It is a surprise."

"You're being very mysterious." I ducked into his Land Rover, thinking it was oddly ironic and appropriate that he should drive something with that whiff of the colonial to it. "I feel odd not bringing anything at all."

He rounded the car and got in. "It's nothing so much. I hope you'll like it."

We headed southeast, which intrigued me, and I was slightly disappointed when we did not end up at the Garden of the Gods or

Cheyenne Canyon or any of a dozen—a hundred—picturesque places there were to picnic in and around the city, but at Memorial Park, a wide grassy park, mainly devoted to various sports fields. Baseball diamonds, tennis courts, and of course the war memorials. There was a nice lake at one end, but it had had to be drained for some reason, and the whole area was covered with construction equipment and earthmovers. There were various field games going on, and intrepid Rollerbladers resolutely circling the drained lake. A bus from a monolithic local church was parked by one end.

Niraj pulled his car into a small lot at the northwest end of the park. Catching my expression, he grinned. "Do you mind helping me carry things?"

"Not at all."

He gave me a blue plaid blanket, and a small canvas bag that was heavier than it looked. He picked up a proper wicker basket with wooden handles, a plastic bag, and an umbrella. It wasn't some fold-up model, either, but a tall, classic, green one.

"Do you know, I don't even own an umbrella?"

"I have many." He gestured with it to a small hill, near a cluster of men in white shirts and pants. "There, I think. Where we can see."

"See what?"

His smile quirked on one side. "That," he said, pointing with the tip of the umbrella to a strip of sandy-looking ground with a gatelike contraption at each end, "is a cricket field."

I remembered that cricket was one of his favorite things. Pleased, I grinned. "And those, I assume, are the cricket players?"

"Yes." He stopped and looked back to the field. "I think this will do. Will you spread out the blanket?"

The players, milling in little knots around a picnic table piled high with various bags and equipment and chairs and such things, looked at us curiously as we settled in. There didn't appear to be any other spectators. "Do you know those men?"

"I sometimes come to watch them play, but no, not really. Acquaintances."

Niraj sat down and started taking out all sorts of small plastic dishes from his deep bag. I could see lettuce and tomatoes, each in their own separate container. A glass bottle of Branston Pickle, another of pickled beets. Plastic utensils and plates, paper napkins. More containers. I chuckled. "Quite a lot of food for two of us."

"This," he said with some satisfaction, "is an English salad." He started taking thin blue plastic lids from the containers—sliced cucumbers, tomatoes, iceberg lettuce, sharp white cheese. There were brown rolls and sliced white bread with butter, and thin ham and sausages sliced into little rounds.

"I am about to make a pig of myself, I'm afraid." The wind whipped my hair into my eyes, and impatiently I pulled it back and tied it into a knot. I could smell the rain, and looked toward the mountains. "I hope we don't get rained out."

He handed me a plastic plate. "Please begin."

I watched him, and imitated his combinations, lettuce with tomato, buried in salad cream, which tasted—I sampled it—as if mayo had been mixed with mustard. The sausage, ham, and cheese were grouped with the pickle, which was next to the grocery store deli potato salad. "Sorry, I'm going to skip the beets." A raindrop splashed my ankle, and I wiped it away. "They make me think of school lunches."

"All the more for me." Busy with his own plate, which he arranged with great concentration, he did not seem to notice that there was rain splatting in little spots around us.

I put down my plate and opened the umbrella, which was enormous and spread over both of us easily. "Better?"

He smiled. "Yes."

We covered the food and pulled the bread under the umbrella, and he moved closer, then reached for the handle. "Shall I hold it while you eat?"

"No, hold it for one minute," I said, "and let me get settled." He held his groaning plate in one hand and the umbrella in the other, and I shifted my plate into my lap and took the umbrella into my left. Our bodies touched and I raised an eyebrow. "Cozy."

"It was all part of my plan," Niraj said, and bent in to kiss me lightly.

The rain splatted against the umbrella, a little more and a little more, but in my sweater I was warm enough. "It's so rare to have rain without lightning and thunder," I commented. "I've never had a picnic under an umbrella before."

"Do you like it?"

"Yes." The smell of rain, sweet and salty, mixed with the scent of grass, and the sharpness of Branston Pickle and that elusive piney scent of his skin. "It would make a good perfume, this moment."

"Would it?" He popped a tomato in his mouth. "That is a high compliment." His attention was snagged by the players. "Oh, look. They're about to begin."

"They won't wait until it stops raining?"

"Ordinarily, they would, but they've traveled a long way and do not have much time."

"Where did they come from?"

"I'm not sure about one of them, but the team going to bat is from Fort Collins."

It was at least a hundred miles. "Good grief."

"Not many cricket pitches in Colorado."

"I guess not." Even in Colorado, that was a long drive. "Who plays it? Besides Indians, that is."

He smiled. "No one so well as we do, of course, but it's a game played in all the old Empire countries—India, the West Indies, South Africa. Now watch this and I'll explain what they're doing."

It was a little like baseball, in that one man threw the ball and another tried to hit it. The pitcher was called a bowler, and the action used to bowl the ball was quite athletic. The batter both tried to knock the ball a long way, as in baseball, but also to prevent the ball from knocking down a little fence behind him.

I watched and ate, enjoying the polite little claps Niraj broke out in now and then. "Well done," he called.

More, I liked the pure pleasure of sitting with him on a plaid blanket in a park I'd never think of as boring again, having a picnic in the rain.

When we finished eating, Niraj took my plate and put it aside, and put his arm around me. "Is this all right?"

"Very." Our thighs touched. I wished mine were thinner, but his were so lean and lovely I didn't waste much time mourning my own shortcomings.

We simply sat there, close, umbrella overhead blocking the soft misty rain, and he made comments sometimes and rubbed my arm now and then, and shifted to hold my hand. And I had the sense to think, Uh-oh, but not enough to do anything about it.

At the end of the day, he walked me to the door of my apartment and I struggled with what to do—invite him in? Not invite him in?—and we were silent as we went up the stairs. "I had a great time, Niraj," I said.

"Am I forgiven now for deserting you at Annie's?"

"You already were."

He squeezed my fingers. "Good."

At my door, he paused. "I will not come in today."

Which spared me the problem of deciding for myself. "All right."

"But I'm going to kiss you."

"That's all right too." In fact, my whole body gave a shout of delight when he stepped close and put his arms around me, and our chests pressed together, and our thighs, and then our lips. His body fit mine exactly, our limbs lacing the right way, heads the right heights, his sturdiness balancing my softness. His tongue slipped inside my mouth, exploring, inviting, and he knew how to dance and tease, to play. As the kiss deepened, he pressed me into the door a little and his erection nudged my pelvic bone in the most ancient of greetings. I pressed back, my hands on his buttocks, and the electricity between us exploded. He made a little sound and tilted his head and our kiss was suddenly a lot hotter, a lot deeper. His hands moved on my shoulders, my back, my hips. My nipples awakened. I wanted to rub against him.

I don't know how long we stood there kissing like that. A long time. Long enough that my hips were softening and I was in a seriously hot fantasy of what it would be like to feel my naked breasts against his chest.

But not yet. I pulled away a little, put my hand on his face. "Thank you. I have to stop now. You're making my blood boil."

His eyelids were heavy, making his eyes look as seductive as melted chocolate. His lips brushed mine once more. "Mine too," he said.

Our eyes met, all in silence and vivid connection, and his thumb moved on my ear. "I have not met someone I liked so much in a long time, Nikki. It's not anything I can name, either, not your hair"—he brushed a lock away from my face—"or your beautiful lush breasts, which I do hope to see without their coverings one day"—a river of desire rushed through them, through me, at the idea—"or your intelligence, which is very appealing to me."

I waited, feeling a buzzing electricity rushing through my veins. His lips, so full and well cut, were above mine, and I thought of his understated *Well done* at the match, and the heady, narcotic deliciousness of his scent.

"It's just you," he said. And smiled. He took a breath and released me. "Will it be too much to ask you out for dinner next week? There is a wonderful restaurant I like very much, Mona Lisa, and I would love to take you there."

Mona Lisa was a fondue restaurant with a wine bar, and I'd wanted to eat there for ages. "Oh, I'd love to."

"Will Wednesday be all right?"

"Yes, perfect." I frowned. "What shall I wear? Will you dress up or not? Colorado is so casual, I never know."

"I'll wear a jumper and nice slacks. Will you wear a skirt?"

I smiled. "Would you like me to?"

He lifted a shoulder. "American women never wear skirts enough for me."

"Consider it done."

"I'll pick you up at six-thirty." He kissed me once more and was gone.

⁓

Monday, I found myself fretting about money, and called the insurance company. Again.

I already owed Daniel money he'd loaned me for living expenses after the house blew up. My income from Annie's was not as terrible as I'd feared, but there wouldn't be much left over, month to month. The shop would likely not be self-supporting for a while—that was what I needed the cushion for. The person handling my claim was not in her office, and I tried dialing through to a supervisor, but was put on hold for thirty minutes, and sighed with exasperation before hanging up. It had been sixty days already. Surely they had sorted it all out by now.

Without that claim, I would be in dire straits.

There was only so much tension a person could stand. This week, Giselle's visit and getting the shop ready had to be at the top of the list.

I did spend several days in the apartment, both getting things ready for Giselle's visit and preparing perfumes to use as inventory. My cash flow was very small—minuscule—so I set aside a certain amount of tips per day to use toward the purchase of bottles and labels, and I would have an order ready to go when the capital reached $400. I'd earmarked $100 flat to paint the walls of the shop, and bring in plants. The shelving was still not an idea I'd solved.

I brought groceries into the house, all the things Giselle used to like but I didn't know if she did these days. Some of it was very expensive, something I'd never noticed when Daniel was paying for our groceries and all I did was hand over the debit card. The sweet cereals, the frozen goodies, all of them cost a fortune, and I decided to set aside a little bit of cash for her arrival, and we could go shopping when she got here. And, too, I planned to bring her to Annie's, which was the food I mainly ate these days. Breakfast when I got there, lunch before I left, some day-old baked goods or almost-ready-to-spoil meats and cheeses. The rest of the time, it was ramen noodles, which are surprisingly filling and cost about a quarter per meal.

The night before I was to meet Niraj for our dinner date, I was aware of a low-level anxiety floating through my body, landing in my chest—What if Giselle hated everything in my life? In my gut—What if this perfume shop was a bust? What would I do then? What if Niraj—I couldn't think what I feared about him, about that situation, at least not specifically. It was all terrifying. Or maybe I did know what that fear was: What if I fell in love?

Stop.

To stave off all my fears, I got busy and sat down at the organ of my perfume trade. With a sure hand, I took a clean two-ounce bottle and filled it halfway with jojoba oil. Then, without even any hesitation, as if some Being beyond me was doing the choosing and mixing, I added sunshine and pine trees and dew, the ginger scent of a man's skin; coffee, bar cleaner, a kitten's clean black fur.

Dawn, I would call it.

17

Nikki's Perfume Journal Entry

<u>Ingredients</u>: Ambergris
<u>Class</u>: Amber
Not to be mistaken with yellow amber (fossilized resin of plant origin), ambergris is a sperm whale secretion. Sperm whales produce it to protect their stomachs from the beaks of the cuttlefish they swallow. Once released, it must stay in the water for a long while before developing its characteristic odor. Ambergris is used in herb teas and dyes. Nowadays it is mostly replaced by a synthetic version.

Mary joined me outside when I took my breakfast early Wednesday morning. It was cool outdoors, overcast and threatening a storm, but the quiet of the creek appealed to me more than going to the break room upstairs.

"How you doin', girl?" she said, settling next to me on the wooden bench. Her apron was covered with flour and she spatted at it. "How's the special this morning?"

I widened my eyes in a swoon, nodding, my mouth full. It was a Southwestern-style quiche, with fresh guacamole on top and whole-grain muffins with raspberry jam in the center. It sounded like an odd combination until you tasted it, and then you wondered why avocado and raspberry were not obviously married all the time, like bagels and cream cheese.

"It's unbelievably good," I said finally. "Have you ever put the raw fruits together? Avocado and raspberry?"

Her lips turned down in contemplation. "Can't say that I have. Sounds interesting. Wonder what we could mix it with? Olive oil? Pineapples?"

I chewed the muffin meditatively. "How about a nut of some kind? Almonds . . . no, maybe pecans?"

"Not quite. Maybe mint. Maybe . . . pears."

"Ooh!"

"I'll have to play with it. The trouble is, both are real soft, bruise easily. Keeping them in good shape for presentation might be a challenge."

"Mmm. True."

"You keep thinking, though. There might be a way. It's a good idea."

"Thanks." I examined the texture of the muffin and broke a piece off. "How's life anyway? Heard from your son yet?" She had a son who'd been invited to a music camp.

"He's happy as a pig in slop. I'm glad it worked out. I think he might really try to get the courage to apply to Juilliard."

I grinned. "That would be something, huh?"

"Yeah." She snorted. "'Specially considering all I got was my GED."

"I'm pretty sure my daughter will end up in some Ivy League school. She's absolutely driven."

"Yeah? Why doesn't she live with you?"

I tossed crumbs to the birds. "There are extenuating circumstances."

"Like what? You a drug addict?"

I laughed. "Hardly." I waved a hand, not willing to discuss it with Mary this morning, for sure. "It's just complicated."

"Huh."

"She's coming to see me this weekend."

"Is that right?" She twirled her towel into a whip. "So you seeing old Niraj?"

I blinked. "Um. Kind of, I guess."

"Zara said it's more than kinda. That he's hot for you."

"She did? How would she know?"

"A friend of hers works with Blip Data too. They been on a project or something. Friend said Raj is grinning ear to ear over his new girlfriend."

In spite of myself, I grinned. "I was just sitting here wondering what to wear tonight. He's taking me to Mona Lisa."

She whistled. "Fancy!"

"I've never been there. And I really don't have anything to wear. I'm not the same size I was when I got divorced, and I haven't needed any fancy clothes."

"Well, if it's a little big, that's not such a problem, right?"

"Yeah, if that were the problem. I'm bigger, not smaller."

"He liked you small and you rebelled when you divorced?"

Startled, I gave her a look. "You know, I never thought about it, but I bet you're right. I was this size when we met, and he said he liked it, liked a woman with curves and all that, and then the minute we moved over to that damned house, he was nagging me all the time." I narrowed my eyes. "He's now married to a skinny woman too."

"Lost himself. They just do."

"Whatever. I'm not interested in solving it. He's gone, I'm done. That's that."

She chuckled. "And there's Niraj, making things better. That's a fine-looking man."

"Absolutely." I touched my diaphragm. "I'm nervous."

She wrapped her hands in her apron. "Be careful with that one, all right? I'm fond of him and he seems all brazen and full of himself, but he's had a hard road, and he's the real deal."

"Hannah?"

"Not just her. The one before broke his heart."

"I thought he followed Hannah here."

"Yeah. There was one he nearly married, back at home in England."

I gave her a perplexed look. "How do you know so much about him?"

"He's my boy," she said mysteriously, and winked. "Don't you worry about all that. Just be good to him, a'right?"

"We haven't been going out long, Mary. It's still very casual."

"Is it?" She met my eyes. "You think he's your rebound guy."

"Maybe. Or a transition person or whatever. I haven't been with anybody else. What are the chances that my marriage ends and the first guy I meet is the one I want to be with?"

"It happens. And honey, you oughta see your face when he comes in a room."

"Oh." I blushed.

Her laughter was low and rich. "C'mon, baby, let's get our bottoms to work."

~

Niraj arrived at my apartment about five minutes early. I dashed to the door and flung it open. "Come in, come in. I'm not quite—"

I halted. He wore a camel-colored silk shirt and raw silk slacks. He looked elegant and pulled together and somehow still relaxed. In his hands he carried a bouquet of pink carnations.

"You look like an advertisement for something really expensive," I said. "Cognac, maybe, or a very fast car."

He grinned. "Has anyone ever told you that you give wonderful compliments?"

"No. Thank you." I waved him into the living room. "Come in."

"These are for you," he said, offering the carnations. "And I wish I were as talented with words as you are, but all I can say is that you look wonderful."

"I will be better in one minute. Please sit down, I'll be right with you."

He came closer. "Will I ruin makeup or anything if I kiss you hello?"

"No."

He bent down and pressed his lips to mine lightly. "Hello, Nikki."

"Hello, Niraj."

A little flustered, I headed back to my bedroom and carried the flowers with me, then realized what I was doing and brought them back to put on the counter. He gave me a smile. "Shall I find something to put those in?"

"If you wouldn't mind." I laughed lightly. "Check over the sink."

In the bathroom, I leaned in to finish putting on my mascara, then flipped a comb through my curls one more time. The lipstick was a sheer copper glaze—I'd never really gotten the hang of anything more than that.

I stepped back. The dress was one I'd found in one of the summer storage boxes, just a simple black dress with no sleeves and a square neckline. My middle was bigger than it had been, but so were my breasts, and I was pleased by the way they filled the neckline. My hair looked good, the legs were still in good shape, and there was a man out there who wanted me.

I tossed a beaded black shawl around my shoulders and slid into my shoes, a pair of forties-style slingbacks that made my legs look longer. "Okay. Are you ready?"

Niraj stood up, and his gaze washed me from head to toe. "I can't decide whether to first admire your cleavage or your legs."

I struck a pose with one hip cocked. "Take your time."

~

The restaurant was cozy and quiet, with classical music playing and little alcoves all through the restaurant. The wall by our table was lined with empty wine bottles, with notes written in honor of the celebrations they'd marked. *Karl and Anna Fredrick—10th Anniversary Dinner. Harold Thomas—55th Birthday. Hale Family Reunion.* Several engagements.

The food was wonderful. The service was excellent. But it was Niraj I admired and enjoyed. He entertained me with stories of his brothers and sisters, of his adjustment to living in North America. In turn, I gave him stories of my youth, which I'd spent partying, and the delights of my old garden.

But all I could think about was leaving the restaurant to go back to his house or mine, and putting my hands on his skin. Every time his gaze flickered over my shoulders or arms, I felt it all the way down my spine. And I wasn't alone. He stumbled in conversation, apologized, did it again.

After fondue of every course, we arrived at the last, a chocolate fondue with raspberries, angel food cake, tangerines, and bananas, all served with a marvelous coffee. "I am not going to be allowed to eat for a week after this," I said.

"Me either. But it was worth it, was it not?"

"Yes. Very much so."

He paid and we held hands as we went out to the street, where we paused in the mild night. A soft breeze ruffled my wrap, tickling the backs of my arms. His hand was warm.

"Well, now we have some choices," he said.

"Yes?"

"I can drive you home."

"Mm-hmm."

"We could go for a nightcap somewhere."

"Mm-hmm."

His fingers shifted in mine, tightening. "Or we can go to my house—either for a little while, or a longer while."

I smiled. "Will you hold my wine-drinking against me?"

"It depends on what you hold against me."

"Ah, I see." I leaned closer. "What would you like me to hold against you?"

His eyes were heavy-lidded. "Everything. Naked."

"That sounds good to me."

He kissed me. "My house, then?"

"Yes."

It was only up the street, and we were inside his living room in five minutes. The scent of fir and ginger, the particular perfume of his skin, silkily wrapped me up as we came into the room. Niraj took my purse and put it on the table by the door. A small Van Briggle lamp stood there, a woman shining light into the foyer. He turned back and took off my wrap. "Come," he said, "into the living room with me."

We sat on the mission-style couch, sank into the big cushions, and he said, "Would you like some coffee or tea or chai?"

I met his eyes. "No."

"Good." And then he was kissing me, and I put my hands in his hair. I tugged his shirt from the band of his pants and put my hands on his back, feeling the swoops of muscle on either side of his spine, the sleekness of skin, the extraordinary heat.

I tumbled backward, and he kissed my face, my chin, my jaw. His hands were in my hair, and his lips moved all along my neck, a heated thrust of moist tongue making a trail down my throat, along the wing of collarbone, down lower to breasts spilling up into the neckline of my dress. He opened his mouth there, hot and hungry, and suckled in a way that made me ache for him to do it lower. I made a soft noise, pulled his head up to my mouth, and he plunged in with a furious hunger that lost none of its skill. "Let's go upstairs," he said. "Let me take off your dress."

"Yes."

In his bedroom, he said, "Wait one moment," and he lit a fat pillar candle. The flame was just enough to illuminate without making me feel too exposed. I reached for his shirt buttons, and he stood there and simply allowed me to unbutton them, to skim off his shirt, and put my hands on his skin. Rounds of shoulder, warm-colored flesh over his chest, scatters of hair between very dark nipples. I swayed forward and kissed his chest, his nipples, my hands on his waist, his arms, his back.

"My turn," he said quietly, and turned me around so he could unzip my dress.

Before it fell, however, I said, "Wait," and I shimmied out of my pantyhose. "Too awkward."

"You're right." His nostrils flared as he skimmed the dress from my shoulders, revealing a strapless black bra that served up my breasts like sweets in black lace. He turned me so that I faced him, then he raised his hands to the lace, rubbed his thumbs over my nipples, slowly peeled the lace away. "More beautiful than I imagined," he said, and there was a satisfyingly raw note to his voice.

And in that second, I found myself filling the moment entirely, living it, knowing as it happened that I would remember it always. Niraj, with his bare shoulders and beautiful head, lifting my breasts with reverence in his palms, cupping them together and touching his thumbs to the tips, rubbing them into furious points, his face glazed with the pleasure it gave him. And then the sight of his mouth, full and hot, taking that aroused point all the way into his mouth.

I moaned.

And we stripped out of the rest of our clothes, kissing wetly, rubbing our skin together, arms and chests, thighs and feet. We stood naked in his bedroom in the light of a single candle and kissed and kissed and tasted and touched until we were both nearly mad with it.

And then, something in me woke up and screamed: You are naked with a complete stranger!

One minute we were kissing, and I felt his thighs against mine, and his belly, and his arms on my naked back. I was lost in the pleasure and comfort of being skin to skin, feeling that after such a long dry spell. Our bodies meshed, just right, skin and arms and legs and lips, and then, as if someone poured water over me, it was suddenly not okay. Maybe he did something a little alien or new in some small way that made me remember—Hey! I'm naked! He is seeing all of me. All the middle-aged skin, the not-so-perky lift of my breasts, the dimpling of my thighs. Oh God. What am I doing?

And it struck me—no one else had seen me naked in close to twenty years. Only Daniel, who had then judged my nakedness unworthy.

Panic rose in my throat. I tried to remember that this was Niraj, whom I'd been aching to have naked, be naked with. I liked the feeling of him. His hands were in my hair, tight and fierce, and his breath smelled of fennel and sugar. I kissed him again.

He raised his head, cupped my face. "What is it?"

I stepped back suddenly. Abruptly. I was naked except for my panties. Niraj wore nothing at all, which had seemed perfectly normal and even quite fantastic a second before, but that slight difference, that ten inches between us, made it all seem . . . if not tawdry, at least embarrassing.

I raised my arms over my breasts. "I don't know." I could feel my hair brushing my naked shoulders and it was at once sensual and a reminder of how uncovered I was. "I don't know," I whispered again.

His expression fluidly moved through a dozen emotions—dismay and hunger and regret and finally steadied on patience. "All right." He lifted his hands toward me, but I couldn't seem to meet them, and he dropped them, and I ducked my head in absolute mortification.

"God, Niraj, I'm really sorry." To make it even worse, I found tears welling up in my eyes, and not the sort that could be hidden by ducking my head, either, but flowing like a river right over my cheeks. Keeping one arm around my breasts, which were really not all that coverable with one forearm, I shakily raised a hand to my face, trying to hide the sudden tears. I didn't know him well enough to fall apart with him. "I'm so embarrassed. I'm sorry."

He disappeared for a minute, and I stood there trying to pull myself together, and he returned with something he wrapped around my shoulders. It was soft cotton and smelled richly of him. A robe. He put it around my shoulders and pulled me into him, and I was still struggling so hard to avoid having hysterics, I could barely speak. My hands were shaking violently. He stroked my hair. "It's all right."

"No, it's really not. I should be more sophisticated than this."

His fingers wove over my scalp, over the edge of my ear. I leaned into his chest, my forehead pressed into the hollow of his throat. "Should you?"

"I don't know."

"What don't you know?"

"Nothing. I don't know anything about anything. I woke up one day in somebody else's life and she forgot to leave the rules on what I'm supposed to be doing with it, and none of the old rules make sense, and this wasn't supposed to happen."

"That would be frightening."

"It is." My voice sounded thin and violet, the talcum voice of a six-year-old.

As if he heard that as well, he said, "Shall I make us a cup of hot chocolate?"

I raised my head. "I don't think chocolate will ease my terror enough to get me to sleep with you tonight. Would you rather I just went home?"

He touched my jaw. "I would still like to make you some chocolate. If you wish to go, that's all right too."

That brought a fresh wash of tears, pouring out of my eyes like someone had poured a bucket on my head. "Yes, chocolate. I'm going to wash my face."

He kissed my forehead. "I will be downstairs. Take your time."

I raised my arms and hugged him. It was only then that I realized he'd not bothered to cover his own nakedness, and I was filled with a swift, biting regret. What was I doing? Turning this man away?

Gently, he disengaged. "I'll be downstairs."

I fled to the bathroom.

18

Nikki's Perfume Journal Entry

Time: 4 a.m.
Date: February 2, 1991

Bottle: a small, squareish, milk-colored bottle
Elements: stale breath, breast milk, oranges, cloves, sweat,
baby lotion, peaches
Notes: nursing my daughter in the middle of the night

Feb 4

Maybe orange flower, cloves, peach, musk to suggest that
middle-of-the-night feeling. What for the sweetness of milk, of
adoration? Vanilla? Jasmine?

Feb 22

Result: A floral with peach notes, and the slight muskiness
of the middle of the night and baby sweetness. The scent of my
daughter.

I came down the stairs, reassembled in my sexy black dress, which now felt like the costume of a foolish young girl. The house was very quiet. I noticed things on my way down that I had not seen before—a collection of black-and-white photos of elephants along the stairs, a whimsical-looking stuffed bear sitting beside the computer, an empty glass on the desk. He was neat but not fussy. Warm, but not too over the top.

In the living room, I paused, a swelling feeling of dismay in my chest that protested the very idea of having to go in there and face him. A huge part of me wanted to just slip out the front door, walk in my stocking feet down to someplace along the main drag and call a cab.

But that would be awful, a terrible way to treat a man who had been very patient with me.

Still, I stood there, my shoes dangling from my fingers. In the kitchen, Niraj clinked cutlery against a dish. On the mantel was an elephant god with four arms, looking happy and prosperous, and something about his face cheered me. I touched a knee, took a breath.

"That is Ganesha," Niraj said from the threshold. "He is most beloved, the god of new beginnings."

"No wonder he looks so happy," I said.

His gaze was steady. "Yes." Gently, he reached for my hand, lifted my fingers to his mouth, drew me into the kitchen. "I made chocolate."

The table was set with a fat white teapot and cups to match, and tiny silver spoons on patchwork place mats colored pink and green, magenta and blue, all woven with gold thread. A heady scent of chocolate and cinnamon filled the room, and I sat down with my hands in my lap. "I'm really sorry, Niraj. I feel very embarrassed."

"No apology is necessary," he said, and poured a cup of the chocolate. Steam rose from it. He nudged the dish toward me and said, "Now, there is a perfume."

I bent my head into it, smiling. "It is." I raised my head and met his eyes. "Thank you, Niraj."

"You are quite welcome."

"I haven't met anyone like you."

"No," he agreed. "You have not." He passed me a plate of nutty brown bread covered with jam. "Now we will forget it all and eat something soothing and sweet, and I will drive you home."

I wanted to make it all right, to talk it around to some place of normality, to ask if he thought I was really wounded, and if that was going to make him crazy. The sentences ran through my mind, all noise and bluster, little girls trying to trumpet themselves into more importance to hide their terror.

Instead, I decided to just accept the moment, my own flawed self, the fact that sometimes things were just not perfect. "All right."

~

It was one-thirty when I closed the door to my apartment. I flipped on the light in the kitchen, and my bravado collapsed in the grim greenish fluorescent light.

Niraj had driven me home and kissed me lightly before I got out of the car, but I felt his reserve. It made me want to cry, that I'd wrecked things with a guy who had genuine potential.

But maybe I didn't care about potential. Maybe it was just too hard to start over at this age, hard enough to keep myself together without adding a man into the mix. On the counter were the carnations he'd brought, and I bent my head into them, breathing in the spicy deliciousness. Carnations are so common, but the absolute is very expensive, and mostly people use a substitute of black pepper and ylang-ylang.

This was the real thing. It did not comfort me. It only drew a line under the strangeness of this life I was living, where I did things like go to happy hour and come in from a date at one-thirty in the morning.

I stared with loathing at the space around me. All the beigeness, the khaki and white, nothing out of place, nothing to offend or jar. Why had I rented it?

Throwing my keys on the counter, I turned in a circle, taking in the heavy wooden table, the cast-off furniture, the peaches and greens I would never have chosen in a thousand years, the bare walls.

I didn't want this life. I had never asked for it. I liked the old one. I liked my beautiful gardens with all the roses and scented plants. I loved the graceful dimensions of the old house, the moldings and wainscoting. I loved sitting in the kitchen while brownies baked, reading a magazine or a newsletter or emails from my sisters as the scent of chocolate filled the house with love.

As if someone kicked me, I doubled over and sank to the floor. It felt as if someone was slicing me open, from the base of my throat to my pubic bone, and I curled like a fetus in the middle of the plain white tile floor.

I wanted the old life back. I didn't want to be forty-something, trying to date and figure out where I fit in, starting over with new friends in a new life. I was lonely. I felt lost and frightened. It wasn't an adventure, or at least not the sort I wanted, or had ever desired. I didn't want hand-me-downs and insecurity or a new lover.

I'd loved the old life! A lot. I loved being a mom, even a despised soccer mom. I liked bake sales and going to lunch in the middle of the week. I liked consulting with my friends about what to wear for a school function, or to a neighborhood Christmas party.

The tears that had started in Niraj's gentle arms spilled out of me. I lay there and sobbed, hard, for a long time. It wasn't that I wanted to. I just couldn't do anything else. I laid on the cool kitchen floor, and sobbed in purest, deepest, wildest grief. I had loved my husband and my marriage and being a mother, and absolutely hated that I'd lost it all.

The irony was, it was only because I'd lost everything that I felt free enough to lie in the middle of my kitchen floor, sobbing. It was this ridiculousness that finally wormed its way into my sorrow. I didn't quite laugh, but it wasn't exactly a frown either.

Wearily, my body exhausted from hard work, my spirit depleted from all the challenges, I picked myself up off the floor and went to bed to sleep for three hours before it all began again.

~

I got off early on Thursday to make sure everything was ready for Giselle, and promised everyone at Annie's I'd bring her in for breakfast Saturday morning. Annie had insisted I take Friday, Saturday, and Monday off, and promised to give me more hours next week so I could make up the time.

I was predictably exhausted when I headed for the airport the next afternoon, which befuddled me even more than I was already. I'd changed clothes three times, trying to find something that looked a little less down-market than the jeans and V-neck T-shirts I'd been living in. I found my good leather clogs in the back of the closet, and they only smelled a little of house-burning-down smoke. I'd had several boxes of summer clothes in the garage when the house blew, and I tossed through them urgently, trying to find something that still fit. I couldn't button the blouses across my expanded chest, and the pants absolutely would not zip over my tubby tummy—you would have thought the extra-hard work would have at least earned me a little weight loss!—so I abandoned them and rushed to Target, where I found a duo of sundresses that seemed mom-like and at least somewhat an imitation of the old me. There were some flowered sandals on sale for ten bucks, and I threw those in too. The whole lot cost half my precious paint-stash money, but which was more important?

Daughter, definitely.

At the airport, I was there a little too early, and even after I looked at all the magazines in the gift shop and paced around the whole upstairs, end to end, I still had time to burn. I felt jumpy and kept getting a strange little hitch in my throat, like I had an allergy. I went into the bathroom to put on lipstick, which I didn't wear too often these days, but Giselle had been living in the Marin County area, had just returned from London. She also lived with a size-six stepmother with breast implants—this irked me more than any other single thing, since mine are a hundred percent natural, and very pretty still, thank you—who probably knew all about designer labels.

Of course, the bathroom lights did nothing to reassure me. The greenish tint made the circles under my eyes look like I'd taken up with zombies, and the lipstick shade looked off, and my hair had not been properly cut in quite some time, so the once-attractive messy cut was now just shaggy, and the curls were frizzy today, and it was too long, and I hoped people didn't think I was trying to be too young.

The worst of it was the dress, though, which had looked all right in the dressing room and now the turquoise flowers looked like something Daisy Mae would wear.

My chest constricted so much, I could barely breathe. Was I having an asthma attack or something? I took hitching little breaths and told myself to relax. I paced out to the hallway again, and the hitch in my throat eased.

I just kept pacing, and pulled out my cell phone. First I tried Kit, and then Roxanne, but neither was home. I thought Wanda might be too young to relate to a full-blown panic attack born of too many things changing in a person's life.

Then again, she had a husband in Iraq.

Finally, I called my mother. She answered, sounding a little weary. "Hello, Nicole."

"Hi, Mom, are you busy?" To my horror, my voice broke on the last two syllables, and the wretched tears were back.

"Honey, what's wrong?"

"Nothing. Everything. I feel like an alien and I have no idea who I am, and why did I have to do this at forty-three?"

"It sucks, sweetheart. I'm sorry. It gets easier."

Tears welled up in my eyes, and I had to go stand by the window to hide my face. "Do you promise?"

"Yes. And remember, honey, the only person you have to be is yourself."

"But I don't know who that is!"

"Just be who you are today."

Something broke, an egg full of terror. The contents spilled away harmlessly. "Oh."

She chuckled. "I knew this was going to be really hard on you. Either one of your sisters would have managed better than my little homemaker."

"I'm at the airport. Giselle is coming for a visit. Just for the weekend, but I think it scared me. I miss her so much. I want the weekend to be good."

"Just be honest. Be who you are, even if that's all mixed up."

"Thanks, Mom." I wiped the tears away. "I'm sorry—I've been totally self-centered. How's Bob?"

"He's doing very well. Much better. It was a big help to have his daughter here, and it cheered him up a lot."

"How is it for you?"

"Oh, it's fine. One thing you learn when you get to my age is that life is long. It's hard to hold a grudge forever."

I smiled. "I'm glad, Mom."

"Cheer up, honey. Giselle loves you. You enjoy yourself this weekend."

"I will. Thanks."

When I clipped the phone closed, I turned around and passengers were spilling up the ramp. And in the midst of them was my daughter, loping and lovely, her knees and elbows too prominent, her hair scraped back from her face. She was peering around people in front of her, and I knew the exact moment she caught sight of me. Her whole face burst into sunshine, and she—my dignified teenager—broke into a run. She hurled herself into my arms with a giant bear hug. "Oh, I miss you so much, Mom!"

Everything that had felt off-center suddenly didn't matter at all. I hugged her tightly in return, smelling the particular milk and morning freshness of her skin, and for once, it was perfectly fine to be just in this minute.

This very one, right now.

~

"I thought," I said, pulling into traffic, "that we could have some supper at my apartment, then do whatever you like with the rest of the evening. Are you tired?"

"No, not at all."

"How does delivery pizza sound for supper?"

"Not that great. I honestly haven't been eating very much junk food." She lifted one brown shoulder. "It's a different world in California."

"Ah—well, you'll like the restaurant I'm working in, then." I changed lanes. "It's all organic food."

"You're a waitress?"

I gave her a sidelong look. Measured her reaction when I said, "Yes."

She tilted her head. "Do you like it?"

"I do, actually. We'll go over there tomorrow for breakfast and you can see what it's like."

"Okay. And your cat? Did you get him yet?"

"No. I'm feeding him, but he's still very scared." I paused. "You might see him tomorrow—we're going to spend some time at the shop I told you about. Kit and Evelyn are going to meet us and help me get things cleaned up. I don't have to spend the whole day, but they don't have any other time to meet me, and I need to get the place open by Memorial Day."

"That's fine, Mom. Really. I'm just happy to see you."

Something huge welled in my heart, and I managed to barely avoid saying, *Really?* I looked at her. "I glad to see you too. I miss you insanely."

She was quiet for a little while, looking out the window. "I miss Colorado. I thought it would be so cool to live in California, and I like the ocean, but it's different there. I miss Pikes Peak."

"My uncle Joe used to say that you could never really leave the mountains, that they'd always call you home."

We were traveling through the middle part of the city, on the interstate. "Can we drive by the old house?" she asked.

I didn't immediately reply. "It's not really there anymore, you know."

"I know. I just . . . I guess I just want to see what it's like now."

"All right," I said. "Before I go there, let me say there are times in life you might want to remember what was, instead of what is. You know?"

She looked at me, biting her lip. Her eyes were always more serious than a child's, and that was true right now. "I know what you're saying. And actually, that's kind of why I want to see it. To remember that things really have changed."

"Okay." I signaled and slid across several lanes of traffic to take the Bijou exit, which took me almost directly downtown. I turned north on Cascade, and as we drove, I made small talk with Giselle, asking about school—fine; friends—a few; boyfriends—none. A few blocks down, I turned west, then turned again, onto Wood Avenue.

It was a revered little strip of houses, with ancient trees and mansions of the old school—built when labor was cheap and the silver money was flowing. These houses boasted three and four floors, servant staircases and quarters, bedrooms by the dozen. The lots were generous, with deep gardens of thick bluegrass and old peonies and roses, and porches overlooking the serenity.

Daniel had grown up about a mile south, in what had been one of the worst neighborhoods in town in those days, though it was gentrifying in a big way now. His mother had been a domestic all of his life, so he'd had the opportunity to glimpse both sides of the stairs, and then he'd been bused to high school—my high school—in the suburbs, where he'd been in class with colonels' daughters and lawyers' sons, and he'd made up his mind he'd make his way into their world.

And he specifically wanted Wood Avenue. The first decade of our marriage, we drove the area at least once a month, dreaming. Everything he had was poured into becoming successful enough to make it happen. Most of the occupants of these places were surgeons, lawyers, other professionals of that nature. He was a contractor, and not necessarily of their educational levels, but he made a fortune in his contracting business by knowing what they wanted. Our little family, when we moved in, gave the neighborhood a little cachet, a little bohemian flair, so they welcomed us.

"I never did like this neighborhood," I said.

"Why?" She sounded shocked.

"It's kind of stuck-up. Everybody is always so worried about keeping up appearances."

"I guess," she said, and went quiet as we pulled in front of the lot where our old house had been. The old property had been razed, and eventually a new one would be built here. The area was exquisitely valuable.

Our house had been built by a silver millionaire in 1888, and it had had three full floors, plus an attic for the servants—or in our case, offices for Daniel and me. It had had fourteen rooms, a sunporch, a front porch, and a balcony over the back garden. I'd always found it dark and cold, and spent whatever time I could outside in the gardens.

"The tulips look great," Giselle commented.

I nodded.

"All right," she said. "I'm done."

"That's it?"

"Yes."

When we were back on the highway, I said, "So what's your new house like?"

She shrugged. "Big. Pretty. Perfect."

"Are things okay?"

"They're fine," she said in a weary voice. "I just wish . . ." She sighed.

"Wish?"

"That we could go back to the old days."

I touched her hand. "I know." I would have added, Me too, but it would have been a lie. Seeing the empty ground where the house had been standing, all I'd felt was a sense of relief.

"I think Dad misses you," Giselle said. "He talks about you all the time."

In spite of myself, there was a little frisson of spiteful pleasure over that. "I'm sure that goes over well."

"Oh, he's careful when she's around, but when we're by ourselves, he's always mentioning things about you—like, 'This is like your mother's garden,' or 'That looks like something your mom would wear.'"

I carefully kept my eyes forward, sorting through the possible replies. I wasn't sure what her agenda was, or if she had one. Finally I said, "That's natural. We knew each other pretty well, after all."

"Do you ever miss him, Mom?"

"I missed him the night I didn't want to go downstairs and check the pilot light on the furnace, that's for sure."

"Not like that. You know what I mean."

There was strong emotion in her voice, a slight unsteady fierceness that told me my answer mattered. To choose it properly. What did she need? Hope for? Was it reassurance?

I took the Fillmore exit toward the apartments, mulling it over. Carefully, I said, "I miss things about our old life. Saturday mornings, going to garage sales. That was fun. And Sunday morning breakfasts."

"I mean Dad. Do you miss him?"

"Sometimes," I said. It was not entirely a lie. "But we have to accept that the past is over, capiche?"

"I know that, Mom." She shifted irritably. "You're not dating or anything, are you?"

I thought of Amy, complaining to her mother that kids just didn't want to know certain things about their parents. I wasn't sure where I was with Niraj after Wednesday night—and anyway, Giselle didn't need to know anything right now. Without directly lying, I said, "My life is pretty full without men to make it complicated."

"Good."

TOP NOTES

I have perfumed my bed with myrrh, aloes, and
cinnamon. Come, let us take our fill of love until
the morning.
—Proverbs 7:17–18

Happiness is a perfume which you cannot pour on
someone without getting some on yourself.
—Ralph Waldo Emerson

19

Nikki's Perfume Journal Entry

THINGS THAT SMELL GOOD
August 3, 1989

Raspberries
Pomegranates
Bread baking
Clothes dried outside on the line
Baby hair

When we arrived at the apartment complex, there was a swarm of traffic in the parking lot, including what I thought was a television news van. For one searing second, I wondered if something bad had happened with Roxanne, and in the next split second, I was reassured by noticing there were no police cars or ambulances. And no, no police tape.

The fact that I should have that reaction told me I was more worried about Roxanne's stability than I'd realized. I would have to talk to her.

"What's going on?" Giselle asked.

"I'm not sure. It looks like happy news, since there's no cops."

She looked at me with alarm. "Do you get cops in here?"

"Sometimes." I shrugged. "Look around, Giselle. It's a few hundred apartments, probably. There's bound to be trouble in a village now and then."

I parked in my usual place and only then did we see the army khakis, obscured by the suits of the newspeople. "Soldiers," I said aloud, and my heart leaped again, this time for the possibility of happiness. "I bet some soldiers have come home."

"Oh, cool!" Giselle said, and peered curiously toward the knot of people. "Can we go over there?"

"Sure. A welcome is always a good thing." I wondered if it might be Wanda's husband.

We walked up the sidewalk, and there were a dozen soldiers or more, along with their young wives and little kids looking somewhat apprehensive over the men holding them so happily. I saw Wanda standing next to a burly man with swarthy features. She looked stunned and happy, her cheeks blooming with delight. He had his arm around her, his other hand on his five-year-old son's head.

It was the merest glance, but in that second, I saw something I recognized from long ago. A mask of pretend politeness, and beneath it, panic.

And I was suddenly nine years old, and we were having a welcome home party for my father. There was cake and flashbulbs going off, and too many people crowded into our tiny house in Stratton Meadows, and I found my father in the backyard, drinking a beer, staring at the peach tree, all alone.

"Come on," I said to Giselle. "She's my neighbor. We can greet her later."

I thought she was going to protest. Instead, she looked at me and followed without a word.

〜

Inside the apartment, Giselle looked around with no expression. "Isn't that the couch from Mrs. Vargas's basement?"

"Yep. All of it is stuff people gave me."

She nodded, accepting that, and I felt ashamed for misjudging her. Curiously, like a dog, she moved around the perimeter of the apartment, looking out windows, pausing at various spots. "It's nice to see all these plants in here. My stepmother doesn't care for houseplants."

"I see." It didn't surprise me, somehow. She with her lacquered nails and pedicured toes. "Let me show you your room."

"Cool." She grabbed her backpack and followed me down the short hall. I pointed to the bathroom, moved with no small amount of apprehension into the back room. "Oh, wow," she said. "Cute! It's like French provincial or something. Isn't that what this white stuff is called?"

"Maybe. I'm not sure. We don't have to keep it, but for now at least you have some furniture."

She turned, eyes bright. "Could we paint it? Maybe a bright coral with thin bands of yellow? Or . . . turquoise with bands of red or—" She looked back at it. "Something like that anyway."

"Absolutely," I said with a laugh. "I love your color sense, girl. I've been floundering without you to steer me in the right directions."

"I can tell," she said, flipping a pointed finger up and down at my dress. "You look like you did *The Sound of Music* with that dress."

I laughed and spread the skirt out. "What, you don't like it? I was trying to look like a mom or something."

"How can you not look like a mom?" She was genuinely bewildered.

"I'll get rid of the dress," I promised. "Now, what for supper? If not pizza, some Chinese? I think there's a Chinese close by too."

"Nah. We eat way too much Chinese. I get tired of it."

"Oh, I bet you do." I waved my hand. "Let's go to the kitchen. I need something to drink."

I padded into the narrow little room and kicked off my shoes, took out some store-brand sparkling water, and poured a glassful. I waved it at Giselle, and she shook her head. I took a long, satisfying swallow and felt a tiny bit refreshed. "No Chinese. No pizza. What sounds good?"

"Anything?" she asked.

"Within reason. We're not doing seafood, if that's what you mean, or Red Lobster." She could eat her weight in crab legs.

"You know what I'd love?"

"What?"

"Your spinach quiche and those little brown rolls."

I struggled to keep a straight face. Part of me was delighted, already checking things off to get at the store. She loved me, loved my spinach quiche! Proof, right there, that I was the superior mother.

Another part of me was using an invisible hand to slap me soundly. My feet and shoulders were tired from the short night, the long day. My eyes, my legs were tired. Even my hair was tired. I opened the fridge to see what there was. "Hmm," I said, stalling.

There was pretty much nothing in there. A quarter inch of cheese. Two lemons. A half-gallon of milk, an orange, and some lettuce stuff. I had planned to get takeout tonight, then shop tomorrow, and there was only some breakfast food in the house. Quiche had a lot of steps and a lot of ingredients.

Then again, how often was my only daughter in my house, asking for anything? I smiled. "I can't do the rolls because they have to be started early, but I can do the quiche. I'll run across the street and get a few things. Anything else you can think of that you'd like to have?"

"Hanson's soda? Can I check my email while you're gone?"

"Sure."

I got her settled with the computer, scribbled out a grocery list, and headed down the stairs. Grimly, I must admit. It was five-thirty. The store would be packed. It was a headache to get across the street, and it always made me feel guilty to drive across the street anyway, but the traffic this time of day would make crossing the street on foot a very dangerous undertaking.

But there were things you did for your children.

On my way down, I stopped impulsively at Wanda's apartment and knocked smartly. Her husband, still in uniform, opened the door with a scowl. "No more interviews."

I waved a hand with a smile. "No, no. I'm your neighbor, Nikki, and I'm headed to the grocery store and thought I'd stop and see if you guys needed anything from the outside world."

"Nikki!" Wanda cried, coming out of the back bedroom with a freshly changed baby on her hip. "That's so nice of you!" She pushed her husband gently aside and he looked confused. Then irritated. "Tom, this is Nikki Bridges from upstairs. Nikki, this"—she beamed—"is my husband, Tom. They sent them home early!"

"How you doing?" he said gruffly. His hair was brush cut, the sides nearly bare, the top an exact quarter inch long. His face was darkly tanned, and there was weariness in his eyes. "Sorry about that. They've just been hounding us all day."

"It's all right," I said. "Understood. It's nice to meet you." I held out my hand and he shook it with firm formality. I let go. "So you need anything, kiddo?"

"I would love a gallon of whole milk, and some bacon for breakfast. Can you give her some cash, honey?" She dashed for the back when one of the other children started to cry. "I'll get the kids fed and we can have a nice, quiet supper when they go to bed."

He reached into his pocket and peeled off a couple of twenties. "There's a liquor store over there, isn't there? I'd kill for a quart of vodka and some orange juice."

"Sure." I met his eyes. "Welcome home."

For an instant, I thought he might cry. He wiggled his nose. "Thanks."

~

It was a delicious luxury to sleep in the next morning. I managed to stay in bed until seven, which was very late for me these days. Giselle was tucked like a flat little frog beneath the covers, her long legs sticking out of the blankets. I covered her and went back out to have coffee and check my own email.

Nothing much going on there. Which meant there was nothing from Niraj, a fact I felt with a rippling disappointment. He'd obviously decided I was wounded after all, and who could blame him?

But damn. I liked him. In only a few weeks—maybe a month—I'd grown to enjoy his emails, his little nicknames for me, the possibilities he represented.

It occurred to me, sitting there in my bathrobe in the cool morning, that maybe he was waiting for me to make the next move. I'd been the one who pulled back, after all. Should I send him an email or an e-card or something?

I didn't know the answer. Maybe, at any rate, I should wait until Giselle went home, since she was obviously fretting about the idea of me dating.

I showered, drank a second cup of coffee, and put together a plan for the cleaning later in the day—with any luck, we could get everything all the way clean so I could start painting after I took Giselle to the airport. I'd take her to the restaurant today for breakfast, then either run her back here until later, or talk her into going to the pool in Manitou. She'd have to go alone, but it would be a lot easier on me, and it would be more interesting than sitting around the shop while we cleaned.

Combing out my hair, I poked my head into her room. "Giselle, how long do you need to get ready?"

"Go 'way," she said, and pulled the pillow over her head. "It's not a school day."

I grinned. Some things did not change. Just as I'd driven my mother crazy with my early-bird habits, Giselle drove me nuts with her nocturnal ways. I tugged the pillow off her head. "We talked about this last night, sweet potato. How long do you need?"

"Twenty minutes."

"Okay. I'm coming back to roust you at eight-thirty."

"Fine! Can I just sleep now?"

Chuckling, I put the pillow back down over her head. She snatched it and burrowed in deep. The rustled sheets made the smell of her, milk and oranges, rise into the air in almost visible waves, and my heart felt like it would burst.

I hated her being gone! Hated missing her all the time, pining away for her phone calls.

And yet, as a mother, I still felt I'd made the right decision. Daniel had advantages to offer that I simply could not. Because he was black and so was Giselle, painful as it was to go there. Because he did love his daughter madly, and maybe he'd made some points about the desirability of his being the primary parent.

But sometimes I wondered if I wasn't a coward. What was I afraid of? What was I afraid I couldn't give her?

I tossed *The Sound of Music* dresses into the Goodwill pile and riffled through the closet for something remotely appealing. There was a plain red button-down blouse and a khaki skirt I liked all right. My hair was too long, but I made an attempt to smooth it out, and it ended up looking like something from 1978.

A sensation of tears built at the back of my throat, and I stepped away from the mirror. What was that about?

Who was I now? I didn't even know what I was supposed to wear, much less how to direct a young woman of color through the traps and difficulties she might face.

Would they really be so different from my own? From my mother's? Were women so different, color to color, or did we all have mostly the same issues?

I didn't know. I didn't know who to ask. I didn't know how much of this was my lack of confidence from the devastation of divorce and how much was real. It made me furious that I had to ask the questions at all, that we lived in a world so divided—still—that worries about race could divide a family.

Before I could choke on my rage or my tears, I glared at my face in the mirror. "Get a grip."

Then I went to Giselle's door. "Time to get up, kiddo."

~

It was nearly nine-thirty by the time we parked on the hill in Manitou Springs. Giselle had not yet really awakened, and yawned all the way across town, but she looked pretty in a low-slung short skirt and a cropped top that showed off her slim brown tummy and long legs. She'd left her hair loose and it tumbled in copper-and-brown ringlets that fell around her shoulders and elegantly angled face. What a pretty thing she was becoming!

I'd parked in my shop space, and as we walked on the path down the creek, I said, "The shop I rented is right here. Do you want to see it before we go to Annie's?"

"Right here? This shop?" She looked dubiously at the weedy back area.

"I got it cheap because it needed so much work. Sweat equity."

Her eyelashes, long and spiky, fanned upward as she looked at the brick building. "Let's go in."

I opened the back door, letting the scent of cool dust out. I'd cleared most of the junk from the back room by now, and there were only cleaning supplies stacked up on the shelf over the sink, and leaning neatly against the wall. A quiet spill of green north light came in the bank of multipaned windows. I gestured Giselle in front of me. "Remember. It's still in raw shape. Kit and Evelyn, and maybe one of the women from my apartment building, are coming over this afternoon to help me get it ready to paint."

She moved through the narrow hallway into the front shop area, and turned in a circle. "Oh, Mom." She sighed. "This is so great."

I grinned. "You like it?"

"It's perfect for a perfume shop." She smoothed a hand over the wooden counter, eyed the high ceilings. "Do you have decorating ideas in place yet?"

"Some." I told her about the brainstorming for a conservatory feeling, the green and white to lighten the small space, the idea of painted wrought-iron accents. "What do you think?"

She wrinkled her nose. "It's not a bad idea. But maybe a little bland?"

I tossed my Farrah hair out of my face. "Okay. So what are you thinking?"

"Well . . ." She pursed her lips, narrowed her eyes. "Perfumes are . . . vivid, right? Like, I think of cloves and spices as red and strong. You don't make a soft kind of perfume, really. You like patchouli and musk and rose, and I've never ever smelled a perfume that you made that would be right for a lady to wear to tea, you know?"

"Giselle!" I grinned ear to ear. "I had no idea you paid so much attention to my perfumes."

"I love the one you made for me. And when I miss you, I smell the one you helped me make for starting junior high. Remember?"

"I do. You wanted it to smell like Constant Comment tea." I laughed. "Which is where I got the idea for the one I made for you."

"Are you going to sell that one? Mine?"

"I hadn't planned to."

"I think you should. It's just a really good fragrance, and not like anything else." She gave me a coy glance. "But you have to name it Giselle's Perfume."

"Done." My stomach growled. "We can come back here after breakfast. I'm starving."

"Okay." She noticed the litter box in one corner. "Is your cat here?"

"I don't know." I went to the base of the stairs and called, "Kitty, kitty, kitty." A little patter of paws on the floor over our head made me smile. He was coming around. I shook food into the dish at the foot of the stairs. "There he is."

He stood at the top of the steps, blinking yellow eyes owlishly down at Giselle and me.

"Ooh, he's so cute!" she cried. "I want to come back after breakfast to see if we can catch him, okay?"

"You can at least see if he'll let you pet him."

"Is that an apartment up there?" she asked.

I nodded. "We can look at it later too. It really needs a lot of work."

"Are you going to live here?"

I met her dark gaze. "I hope so. Eventually. We'll see." I glanced at my watch. "C'mon. Let's go eat. I want you to meet everyone while it's kind of slow."

We walked down the green path toward the back of Annie's. The silvery creek was full of snowmelt and roared down its narrow channel. Dozens of birds sang, and the high-altitude sun stretched bright fingers through the tree leaves.

Giselle inhaled. "God, that smells so great! Can we go for a picnic, maybe?"

With an unexpected ping of loss, I thought of Niraj, the cricket picnic we'd shared last weekend. "Did I tell you I saw a cricket match last Sunday?"

"No! Was it cool?"

"A little slow, but it was fun to do something different."

"I've been really interested in lacrosse lately. I found out I'm good at it."

"That's fantastic, kiddo."

"So can we have a picnic tomorrow?"

"I have to work in the morning, unfortunately, but how about after I get off work?"

"A late-afternoon picnic?"

"Sure, why not? By the creek in Cheyenne Canyon?"

She shrugged. "Okay." Light danced in her dark hair, brought out the copper shimmer, showed the warmth of her skin tone. I was suddenly overwhelmed with happiness to have her with me, to be in her company. I flung my arms around her from behind. "I'm so crazy about you, you know that?"

"Why?"

I laughed. "Because you're smart and strong and quirky and very good with color and you're mine, mine, mine."

Instead of struggling against my arms, she leaned backward into me and put her hands on my forearm where it looped around her chest. "Nobody says things the way you do, Mom. It's one of the things I like best about you."

"Thank you." I rubbed her arms. From the back door of Annie's, a pair of figures emerged—Annie and Mary. "Good morning!" I cried, and tucked my chin into my daughter's shoulder. "Here is my devastatingly fantastic daughter."

"Mom!" she cried, and rolled her eyes. I let her go with a chuckle.

Annie's eyes crinkled up. "If your mother will not sing your praises, who will?" She reached out a slim hand. "It is lovely to meet you, dear. Your mother speaks of you every day."

"Thanks," she said.

Mary raised her eyebrows at me, over the top of Annie's head. "You're just full of surprises," she said, and I knew she was talking about Giselle's obvious mixed-race background.

"So they say." I shrugged. "Giselle, this is Mary, who is the dragon of the kitchen, but you know what she cooks? The sweet potato salad from *Spoonbread & Strawberry Wine*."

"Oh my God," Giselle said. "That is my favorite, favorite food in the world."

Mary smiled. "Is that right? As it happens, I'm making it for the lunch special today."

"No way!"

She nodded. "Way. I'll send some home with your mama, and you can have it for supper."

"We're going in to have breakfast," I said.

They nodded, and we all moved through the kitchen. From behind me, Mary said, "Niraj is there, by the way."

Butterflies leaped, swirled, fluttered. Anticipation? Fear? He had not called or anything. "Oh." I glanced back over my shoulder at her, wondering if there was a warning. Was he with someone? I frowned at her. What?

"Just saying."

I put my finger to my lips, cocked my head toward Giselle. Mary nodded. Giselle pushed through to the dining room and I rushed back to the kitchen. "Is he with someone or something?"

"Not that I saw. What's up? I thought you had a hot date with him the other night."

"I did." I sighed. "It's . . . oh, I'll tell you later."

"All right." She picked up a stalk of celery. "That ain't the only story I want to hear, now."

"Right. There's not much to tell, really. I'd better get out there." Mary nodded.

I went into the restaurant, my tummy full of fluttering. Giselle stood by the bar, looking around curiously. In this world, against the orchids and ferns and Victorian styling, she was so plainly not white.

But it also would be very hard to say just what her background was. She could have been Turkish or Cuban or Greek; East Indian, West Indian, or America Indian; Puerto Rican or Maori. A woman of color, as they say. Which was why her father had pushed so hard for her to live with him.

And why I'd given in. Maybe it had been cowardly. I still wasn't sure.

But just now, that beautiful girl was with me, here and now, and in her narrow shoulders and deep bust, in the quirk of her distinctive smile, I could see myself. She was my daughter too. "Ready?" I said.

It was only then that I saw Niraj, sitting at the other end of the bar. I started, and didn't know whether to stare until I met his eyes or rush away. He looked wonderful with his hair shorn and his shoulders covered in a pale green shirt that brought out the warm brown tone of his skin. I felt my spine soften, as if in insistence that we should lie down together right now.

"Mom!" Giselle said. "You are so staring at that guy! Do you know him?"

At that moment, Niraj looked up. He didn't smile. He did not look away. He raised his hands in front of him and put them together, as if in prayer, bowing slightly: namaste. A spiritual greeting, he'd told me. The spirit of me greets the spirit in you.

Pierced, relieved, I brought my hands together, too, and bent to greet him, a silent namaste in return. "I know him," I said. "Let me introduce you."

"You lied, didn't you?" she said. "He's your boyfriend."

"Not exactly."

"I don't want to meet him."

For a moment, I wasn't sure what to do. There was no manual of dating to which I could refer. I gave him a look, shrugging a little, and let Zara seat us in the west alcove. As I sat there, a sucking sensation made my chest feel hollow, and the back of my neck burned. I felt torn exactly in half. Daughter and man. To whom did I owe allegiance? She had been born from my body, and I would know her all my life, spirits willing. He was new, and perhaps only in my life for a moment. By that measure, I should respect my daughter's wishes.

But Niraj had been kind to me, very patient, and I did not want to wound him. And after all, wasn't I the elder between my daughter and me, the person who supposedly knew some of the answers?

From a mysterious place inside of me, a voice said, *What do you want, child?* It sounded like the voice of the mountain, the spirit mother who had drawn me into this job, into the shop.

"I'll be right back," I said to Giselle, and I rushed into the bar.

Niraj was already gone. Damn. "Where did Niraj go?" I asked Zara.

"He left. Seemed a little put out." She put down a package on the bar in front of me. "He asked me to give this to you, and said to say it was . . ." She paused, and gazed up toward the ceiling. "Oh yeah. A gift between friends."

I picked up the box. "For the record, I really screwed up with him." And now my daughter was pissed at me. "When you get a chance, can I get some coffee?"

"Absolutely."

Before I went back to the table, I stood at the bar and opened the package he'd wrapped in soft fabric. It was a smaller version of the statue on his mantel, the elephant-headed god who looked so happy and fat.

I wished, very much, that he was here to thank.

20

Nikki's Perfume Journal Entry

Roxanne

Time: 5 p.m.
Date: spring, 2006

Elements: camaraderie, the heavy grape smell of wine, a hint of smoke from Roxanne's cigarette breaks, the lurking promise of snow in the air, women laughing, pizza, Roxanne's Ode to Penises
Notes: What does anger smell like? Red pepper? Gunpowder?

At the end of breakfast, Giselle was beginning to come out of her funk. At least she wasn't glowering at me the whole time, and had managed to engage in a couple of civil exchanges about weather, a book she was reading, and a friend who had had her eyebrows lasered. "I have really awful eyebrows," she said. "Do you think I should do that?"

"Well, the thing is, eyebrow styles change. I'm not against permanent hair removal, but eyebrows seem a little iffy."

"I never thought about that." She showed me her arm. "Do you think my arms are hairy?"

"Not really." I rubbed my fingers over the downy softness. "A little hair is normal."

"Not if you're totally coolly African," she said with a snotty tone in her voice.

I made a derisive noise. "I suppose you mean Keisha." At her annoyed expression, I narrowed my eyes. "She's not doing the superiorly black thing with you, is she? Because she's about as mixed blood as anyone in America."

"Dad says I got your Irish hairiness."

I burst out laughing. "Probably. But you also got my great legs and nails, so count your blessings. Tell him I said so."

She grinned. "It's okay, Mom. I just wanted to tease you a little. Keisha does sort of play up her unwhiteness, but I don't care. Everybody in California is mixed, so it ends up being totally cool. I like what I look like."

"So do I."

I looked at the check, across which Mary had written: FREE. I grinned. "Now we need to decide what we're going to do. Do you want to come with me to the shop, or go back to the apartment? I have friends coming to help me clean, so it shouldn't take that long."

"I'll go with you. Can I try to catch the kitten?"

"Sure." I pushed back from the table. "It's only a one-bedroom apartment, by the way, but I figured you could have the bedroom and I could take the living room when you come to visit."

"What if I wanted to live with you again?"

I paused. "Do you?"

"Sometimes, I do."

"Well, maybe I'd just keep the apartment I have, then."

She chewed her lip. Lifted a shoulder. "I guess we can cross that bridge when we come to it."

"Good idea." I paused. "You know I'd love to have you, don't you?"

"Yeah." She bowed her head. "I want to go to the shop now."

~

As we approached the front door of the shop, I noticed Roxanne and Amy were waiting by their car, both of them smoking cigarettes.

"Gross," Giselle said.

"Be nice."

"No one smokes in California. Nobody."

"I know. But these are my neighbors and they're here to help me, so you'd better be nice. Got it?"

"Whatever."

Roxanne was dressed in tiny black jean shorts and a bandanna-style halter top. All of her was tan and lean and riot-worthy. Large sunglasses hid her eyes. In contrast, Amy wore oversize pants, a big T-shirt, and several thousand pounds of silver chains—necklaces, bracelets, a belt. Her hair sported red streaks today. "Hey, you guys!" I said. "I'm so glad to see you! Amy, this is my daughter, Giselle."

"Hey," Amy said.

"Hey," Giselle said in return. "Want to help me find the kitten?"

"Where is it?"

"Upstairs, I guess."

Amy shrugged. "Sure."

"Let me unlock the front door," I said, and I flipped through the keys, realizing this was the first time I'd ever opened it from this side. "So," Amy said, standing behind me. "Like, my mom said you were going to paint a sign in the window? And I do a lot of silk screening, so I could, like, probably make you a stencil if you want."

"Really?" I pushed the door open and turned around to look at her. "Would you be willing to do it on spec? I don't have a lot of cash."

"Sure." Her hands were in her pockets, and she gestured with her elbows. "If you want, I'll make some sketches first."

"Okay. I was thinking something sort of art deco, you know?"

"Like those French posters? Lautrec and those guys?"

"A little later than that. The 1920s or so?"

She nodded. "I'll make some drawings, pull up some fonts on the computer."

"That's great." I touched her arm. "Thanks."

To my surprise, Wanda was coming up the sidewalk, and with her was her husband, Tommy, looking a lot more comfortable and relaxed, in a pair of worn-out jean shorts and a plain blue tank top. He was still unmistakably a soldier, with the dog tags and haircut and sunglasses, but he looked cheerful. "How ya doing?" he said.

"I'm so amazed to see you guys! You don't have to help, Wanda! You didn't know your husband was coming home so soon!"

"I was going to have Tommy hang out with the kids, and cancel the babysitter, but he remembered you were the one who helped me with the boys when they were sick, and he wanted to come help too."

I grinned. "Cool. Well, heaven knows, I'll be able to use you."

Roxanne joined us. "Hi, Tom," she said, pushing her sunglasses on top of her head. "You might not remember me, but I'm one of your neighbors too."

The spark in the air was almost purple, the length of time they held eye contact a bit too long for my comfort. "I remember you," he said, and shook her hand.

I glanced at Wanda, but she was smiling benignly. Maybe I was imagining things. "Don't be silly, Roxanne. You had dinner with us three times."

Roxanne tilted her head and smiled in her slow, seductive way. "Well, it's been a long time."

"I remember you," he drawled, and looked away.

Danger, Will Robinson, I thought. Danger, danger, danger.

No. I was not imagining things. I didn't know if they'd had a little fling before, or if there was just a lot of sexual tension between them, but I didn't like it. "Let's start. It gets hot in there once the sun moves."

As we headed into the shop, Kit and Evelyn came from the other direction. Evelyn dragged a red wagon full of supplies—I thought I even saw paint. "Oh, you angel!" I cried, and hugged her. I introduced everyone to everyone else. Kit and Roxanne greeted each other stiffly, the two most beautiful women in a room now jockeying for who was the fairest of them all for today.

I shook my head and ducked into the shop. At least I didn't have to compete.

~

It was an embarrassment of riches. Evelyn, the taskmaster, had drawn up a list of necessary steps—remove all trash, sweep floors, scrub walls, wash windows—and assigned tasks. The girls were put on window detail, and once they polished the shopfront, they washed the tiny panes in the back room, then went upstairs and washed the ones in the apartment. Kit got to work on drawing patterns for the floor according to a grid Evelyn had mapped out. Roxanne, Wanda, and I were put on washing duty, then polishing details. Tom was sent to the basement to check wiring, plumbing, heating, and pronounced it all fine. He brushed spiderwebs from his body as he emerged, however, and I winced. "It must be awful down there," I said.

"Not that bad, really. You probably need to know where everything is. Let me show you."

I shuddered inwardly. "Can you draw me a map?"

"I guess so."

"For God's sake," Roxanne said in her smoker's rasp. She was high atop a ladder, scrubbing off what appeared to be a couple of centuries' worth of grime from the upper-level walls. A hundred miles of legs were displayed. "Just go with him, then you'll know where it is."

From the middle of my chest came a dull, froglike glub. Maybe it wouldn't be so bad to at least see it, and if I went one time with somebody else, it wouldn't scare me so much the next time. "All right."

He didn't grin at my wimpiness, and I remembered he'd just come back from a war, where people carried guns all the time and little children lost arms and the next car could hide someone who'd blow himself up. "I'm sure spiders are way down your list of things people should

267

be afraid of," I said as we came to the open cellar door, "but I swear to heaven, I get hives thinking about spiderwebs."

"You'd be surprised at the things I'm afraid of, ma'am," he drawled.

I stood at the top of the stairs, and a gust of cool air billowed up from the darkness. I thought of buried bodies and ghosts—and unexpectedly, of lying in the grass with a jammed finger, smelling damp earth and fire while the ashes of my house drifted down out of the sky around me like snow.

I swayed dangerously, and gripped the threshold. "I don't know if I can do this," I said.

"You look bad." He touched my shoulder. "Take long, slow, deep breaths. In through your nose, out through your mouth."

I put my hand on my upper tummy, and met his eyes, trying to follow directions. He had good eyes, very dark blue with dark lashes, and I saw his children would all look like him when they grew up. In, out, I breathed.

"That's it. Keep at it." He reached around me, and clicked on a switch. "This is what we're gonna do," he said. "There's a set of stairs, then we're going to turn right to look at the furnace. I'll show you where the pilot light is."

A little voice screamed inside of me, and I scrambled backward. "I can't."

He seemed to get that I meant it. "All right." He touched my shoulder. "Really scares you, doesn't it?"

I snorted in uncomfortable laughter. "You could say that."

"Remind me in a few days, and I can show you some things to let that go."

"Can't a person just have some things they don't want to do?"

"Sure can. But what if you're here all alone and the water line breaks? Better to know how to turn it off."

I breathed out. "Yeah. Well, I'll work on it."

For now, though, I was saved.

~

By the end of the day, not only was the shop clean, but two walls had been painted white, and the entire grid for the floor painting had been laid out and begun. The apartment upstairs was clean, the bathroom scrubbed, the kitchen ready to be used eventually. I made plans to bring a few things over tomorrow—some plants for the roof, maybe something to sit on up there, a few things for the bathroom.

When we got back to the other apartment, Giselle and I had showers and made some salads for supper to go with the pie Mary had sent. While I tossed greens and cheese and tomatoes, she sat at the breakfast bar, bent over her phone, sending text messages. She'd done the same thing at breakfast, off and on.

"You know," I said finally, "that gets a little old, that you have that thing going sixteen hours a day."

She looked up, her attention still on the phone. "What? It's just that a friend of mine is having trouble with her boyfriend."

"Can you put it away until after we eat?"

"I guess so. If it bothers you." She thumbed in a message and closed the phone. It made a little musical noise as it shut down. "I won't even turn it on until after supper. How's that?"

"Better." I spread place mats on the bar. "Don't you get tired of being in touch all the time?"

"No. It wasn't pleasant when I was in London and couldn't talk to anyone at all for weeks."

"You know," I said, "you might try doing it on purpose, just one day a week or something."

"Why?" She was aghast.

"It's not natural for people to be in touch with one another all the time like that."

She lifted her fork. "Why? Humans are pack animals, you know. We're like dogs, wanting to sleep on top of one another."

"Maybe. You just might try it once in a while, and see what happens if you're not talking to someone all the time."

Clearly, she thought it was an idiotic idea, and I let it go. "Do you want to rent a movie or something?"

"Not really. Maybe I'll just go to my room and hang out, if that's okay."

"Is everything all right?"

She gave me a classic teenager look, that half sneer that says you're crazy. "Yes. Why?"

"Just curious."

"I'm a teenager, Mom. We don't like to be with adults all the time. Two days in a row is a lot."

I laughed. "All right."

Her retreat gave me time to catch up on a few chores that had been neglected. I started a load of laundry and mopped the kitchen floor and turned the computer on to check email, only realizing as I sat down that I was extremely tired. It had been a very long week, and I had to get up and open the restaurant tomorrow morning. Sundays were not such an early start—we didn't open until eight-thirty—but it was still another workday.

It felt good to just sit down and let go of things. I told myself I was checking to see if my sister had put anything together, but I was really looking for something from Niraj.

There was nothing from either of them. In the other room, I heard Giselle talking on the phone, and shook my head. It was amazing how much time she spent on that thing. I sat there, bemused, thinking I ought to send an email to Niraj, at least thanking him for the Ganesha statue. As I thought about him sitting at the bar today, my thoughts wandered back to the night at his house, the feeling of his arms around me, his chest against my breasts, the sound of his breath in my ear—

He scared me. It would be okay to have a fling, but all this emotion filling me was too much, too sudden, too everything for a rebound thing.

"Mom!" Giselle said behind me, and it sounded like it was the second time she'd said it, with that slight impatience. "Dad wants to talk to you."

She held her phone out, and I took it without much excitement. "Hello?"

"How you doing?"

"Fine. What's up?"

"Nothing, really. Sounds like Giselle's having a nice time there."

What was this about? "Good, I'm glad."

"She said you're opening a shop?"

Giselle hovered in the room, pretending to pluck dead leaves out of the pots on the floor. "I told you that the other day. A perfume shop."

"She said you're seeing someone too. A dark guy."

I narrowed my eyes. He sounded . . . jealous. "That's none of your business."

He chuckled, as if he knew me better than I knew myself. "Ah, baby, you always did have a streak of independence I liked."

Something in me snapped, a vial containing some acidic emotion. "That's why you didn't want me to work or have my own income or have any kind of life?"

"It wasn't like that. I wanted to take care of you."

He didn't even seem to hear the dichotomy in the two desires. And maybe that was the whole trouble. I thought about making a sharp comment about him dumping me, but I would not fight with him. Not with Giselle in the room.

Actually, not at all. I didn't care enough. "You know, Daniel, I'm tired tonight. If there's something you want to talk about regarding Giselle or anything like that, I'm happy to discuss it, but otherwise, I'd just like to go."

It was quiet on the other end of the line. "Baby—"

"Stop calling me that."

"I'm sorry. I just wanted to tell you that I made a big mistake."

I felt punched. "I have to go, Daniel." Without waiting for his reply, I handed the phone back to Giselle.

"Jeez," she said, her little cheery face sliding away. "You don't have to be mean."

I didn't answer. "Go talk to him in your room. I'm not part of that any longer."

~

Giving in to my weariness, I let Giselle have the computer so she could talk some more to her friends, via Instant Messaging and email, and went to watch television in the living room. Despite the awful colors of the couch, it was deliriously comfortable, and I dozed off watching a rerun of *ER*. When my phone rang, I thought it was part of the show at first, and I didn't stir. It stopped, then started ringing again.

I grabbed it off the coffee table and peered hard at the caller ID. EL PASO COUNTY POLICE DEPARTMENT. Alarmed, I picked up. "Hello?"

"Oh, thank God," Roxanne said. "Nikki, this is Roxanne, and I need a little favor."

"Are you in jail?"

"Um, yeah, but don't worry. There's not money involved."

I sat up straight. "What do you need?"

"Can Amy spend the night with you?"

"You're in jail for the night? What did you do?"

"It's a long story, and I don't have much time, but can you take care of my daughter and we'll talk about the rest tomorrow?"

"Of course. She'll be here."

"Thank you."

"Roxanne . . ." I paused, not sure how to express my concern for her. It wasn't as if we'd known each other a long time, after all.

"I know," she said. "I need to get my act together. I know I do."

"I'll take care of Amy tonight," I said. "You take care of yourself."

When I hung up, I padded to Giselle's room and knocked. "I'm going down the hall to get Amy," I said.

She yanked open the door. "Get her? What do you mean?"

"Her mom is in jail, so she's going to spend the night here. On the couch, I guess."

"It's like ten feet down the hall!" she said with a curl of her lip. "She can't handle it?"

"I'm not asking your permission. But I do expect you to be nice."

"Mom." She rolled her eyes. "Have you noticed that she's a Goth? That she cuts herself? That she smokes? I don't hang out with people like that."

"You are not to make judgments, and you are not to be unkind, do you hear me? I won't hesitate to soap your tongue if necessary."

"What am I, five?"

"She's a nice girl who is doing the best she can under difficult circumstances. Not everyone has a father who sweeps them off to London and Spain."

She ducked her head. "Fine."

Barefoot, I went down the hall. Through the front door of Roxanne's apartment, I heard shouting, one-sided, as if Amy was yelling into the phone. I knocked hard.

Amy swung open the door as if she were a hurricane. Her mascara was smeared, and it was plain she'd been crying. She put the phone on her shoulder, fury coming off her in pale red waves with a scent of gunpowder. "What do you want?"

"Your mother called me. She wants you to come over to stay the night with us."

Her eyes on my face, she lifted the phone and said succinctly, "I hate you." She clicked it closed. "You know who that was? My loser dad!"

With a wild cry, she turned around and knocked everything off a table that stood in the foyer, and when that crash wasn't enough, she kicked the table over too.

Then she stood in the middle of the room, her arms at her sides, looking like she was three and had lost her kitten. "He didn't want me to come over because his wife is afraid of me, but not because of me, because my wacko mother is stalking them! My mother is in jail, and all my dad can say is, 'Sorry, you can't come here.' My brother is there, he can be there any time he wants, but I can't! You know why? Because Lorelei doesn't like me! Would he send me to a foster home rather than let me live with him?"

There was such anguish in her voice that I moved forward and took her into my arms. "It's awful. I'm sorry."

She clutched me, her hands in fists, a deep keening cry coming up from her chest. "I hate them all."

"I know."

"I want everything to be normal. How long does this part have to last?"

"I don't know, sweetie." I rubbed her back. "I don't know."

~

Giselle sulked into the room and sat at the breakfast bar while I fixed some french toast for Amy. She had her phone in her hands, however, and kept tip-tapping text messages as we sat there. I finally turned around and snapped, "Giselle, that's enough. It's rude!"

"At least I'm not talking on it all the time!"

"I wouldn't like that either." I scowled. "If you can't stay off it, you're going to have to give it to me for the duration of the weekend."

She huffed, but pushed the off button. "I'm the only kid I know whose noncustodial parent disciplines her at all."

"Maybe that's what's wrong with the world," Amy said.

"Discipline?" Giselle asked.

"Custodial and noncustodial parents. Don't you get sick of it?"

Giselle had to duck her head very fast. "Yeah."

"Come on, guys," I said, blinking back tears. "I'm not saying we can't talk about that at some point, but could somebody please tell a joke? I'm going to start bawling my eyes out."

Giselle said, "What did your mom do to go to jail?"

"Giselle!"

"I'm just asking."

Amy flipped a penny in the air, over and over. "Not that much. She just goes and sits across the street from their house, which used to be our house, and smokes cigarettes in her car."

Despite herself, Giselle let go an earthy giggle. "That could drive you crazy, all right."

"Which person?" Amy said. "I think it's hurting my mom more than it's hurting my dad."

Giselle glanced at me. "Yeah."

~

The girls settled in to watch a movie on HBO. I had to work in the morning, and they had their instructions for breakfast, reaching me, what to do and not do. They weren't toddlers. If they stayed awake all night, so be it.

But I was stirred up by the excitement and decided to go play computer games for a little while. Check email.

When there was still nothing from Niraj, I realized I was being an idiot, and opened up a new message.

TO: niraj.bhuskar@blipdata.com
FROM: nikki@scentofhours.com
SUBJECT: thanks and apologies

Hi, Niraj,

Thank you so much for the Ganesha statue. He's wonderful, and it's fortuitous that you bought him in San Francisco before I ever even thought of opening the shop. I'm going to put him in a special place of his own.

What's funny is that my daughter suggested this morning that my idea of white and green for the shop was too bland, and I might want to think of tapping into the idea of spices, the faraway. Red and gold, and tigers and elephants. I think she's right.

I also want to apologize on two counts. The first is for my strange behavior on Wednesday night at your house. I don't know what got into me, why I felt so frightened all of a sudden. I just did.

And I'm sorry about not coming to talk to you at Annie's this morning. My daughter was with me and she's still not over the divorce, and she picked up right away that I "like" you and was kind of upset, especially as I'd told her I had no boyfriend (not that you are, but you know—and also what a weird word for a woman in her forties to use!) and then it seemed as if I was lying to her. Since I'm new to all of this, I sort of panicked and let her set the tone, and by the time I realized I'm the adult, and therefore I get to set the tone, you were already gone.

You may have come to the conclusion that I'm crazy or more wounded than you expected at first, and you don't want to keep seeing me, but if you're interested, I'd love to see you again. Maybe I could show

you the shop. It looks good. We did a lot of work
today!!

Take care,
Nikki

I punched the Send button, went to the kitchen to pour a glass of
white wine, which I thought I'd more than earned, and came back to
play Zuma, which I liked mainly for the music. I played one round and
my email icon flashed. Putting Zuma on pause, I opened it.

TO: nikki@scentofhours.com
FROM: niraj.bhuskar@blipdata.com
SUBJECT: you charm me

Beautiful Nikki,

It is hard for me to keep my pleasure in check here
in this email. I had been worrying and worrying for
three days that I put you off, that you would not want
to talk with me anymore, and that would have made
me sad. Not that I'd want to go into the jungle and
kill myself or anything so dire as that, but sad enough
that I was wondering how to make it up to you for
being so forward, pushing you maybe a little more
than you wished.

I am very happy you liked the Ganesha statue, but
he is not the gift I brought back from San Francisco.
I only bought him on Friday, downtown, because I
thought you would like to have him in your shop as a
blessing for a new venture. The other thing—it's only
a little bauble—I will try to remember to bring to you

the next time we meet. I am not usually forgetful. I sometimes think this thing has a life of its own, and is hiding from me sometimes. ☺

Mary told me about your daughter's feelings. She's beautiful, just like her mother, and just the age to be surly. It is not easy to manage these things, and I understand how it could be awkward. Take your time.

It seems to me there is chemistry between us—not only physical, but mental and emotional, and I would like to see where it leads us. Seeing that you are new to this world of dating, I will attempt to be mindful of your limits, if you will be mindful of my truth, which is that I have dated more women than I'd like, and you are rare and fine.

As for the word "boyfriend," I've always preferred the French frankness of "lover." It encompasses the adult nature of a budding connection, doesn't it? I would like to be your lover, but I am content for now to be your companion and friend.

I would very much like to see you. And your shop. I will leave it to you to let me know where and when.

Is your daughter here for long? Leaving you with a single kiss, set at the junction of your shoulder and neck,

Niraj

Sitting there in my quiet office, with only the sound of the computer breathing, and the low sound of the television in the other room, it was almost as if Niraj were present. I felt him all around me, his lips ghostly over mine. I remembered with a wash of heat how he had looked in the dark, bending down to kiss me, his shoulders smooth in the candlelight, his lips so very talented.

Before I could chicken out, I wrote:

TO: niraj.bhuskar@blipdata.com
FROM: nikki@scentofhours.com
SUBJECT: Monday

Dear Niraj,

Your email gave me shivers. You are a very, very appealing man and I am aching to kiss you again. My daughter will be leaving Monday afternoon. Would you like to meet me at the shop around four? I'll buy your supper afterward.

A very warm kiss in return,

Nikki

His email came back in five minutes, and contained one line:

I shall be thinking of it every minute until then.

21

Nikki's Perfume Journal Entry

THINGS I LIKE TO SMELL
September 2, 1973

My mom's hair spray
Dryer sheets in the air when I'm riding my bike home
Hamburgers on grill
Nail polish
Comet cleanser
My sister Molly's shirts after she's worn them

Sunday morning, I left the girls sleeping, with instructions for breakfast on the counter. Since we opened a little later, I stopped at the shop on my way to work, carrying in a small stack of towels and a bagful of toiletries—shampoo, soap, bath salts, and oils—which I settled in a wicker basket on the chest against the wall of the apartment bathroom. I hung the towels, and arranged the soaps in a little fan on a shelf beneath the window. The walls still needed paint, but the bathtub was gleaming, and the light was wonderful.

I would be happy here.

At Annie's, Penny and I set up the buffet, set the tables, and got the restaurant ready for the day. I took a pot of tea to the kitchen. "You need help, Mary?"

"There's my girl!" She grinned. "Just full of surprises, aren't you!"

I grinned. "One or two, one or two."

"If you wouldn't mind, babe"—she gestured with her knife to a pile of fruit—"slice the oranges and cut the apples into cubes."

"Got it."

The music was playing softly—the Beatles Brunch, which got on my nerves after a while most days, but this morning was tracing the story of the song "Let It Be."

"One of my top ten songs of all time," I said.

"Me too."

"So," I said, and carefully sliced the end off an orange, "can I ask you, a 'woman of color,' a political question?"

"Yes. As long as you know I'm gonna tell you the truth."

"One of the things my ex said about Giselle living with him and his new wife was that she needed to be connected to the black community."

"Good idea in theory, I guess. Is his new wife white?"

"No. She's black, too, which he said would make a difference to Giselle. But I don't think they're getting along all that well."

Mary gave me a measuring look. "Got too blonde for the brother, did you?"

An unexpected rush of emotion hit the back of my eyes, and I had to duck my head. "Exactly," I said.

"Bet that stings. But I don't have to tell you that you're better off without a man who sways with the wind like that."

I took a breath. "I know. He broke my heart, but I'm over it." It wasn't until I said it that I realized it was true.

"As for your daughter," she said, and put her hands on her hips. "You're her mother, Nicole. Use your head."

I met her eyes. "Right. She's so smart, you know? The schools are better out there. But I need to be sure she doesn't turn into a little snot."

"That's right. You're her mama."

"You can be her auntie."

"It'd be my pleasure."

"Now," I said, "tell me about you and Niraj."

She paused, smiled, and shook her head. Which made me realize they'd been lovers at some point. My mouth opened. Mary laughed. "What? I'm not that old!"

I waved a hand. "I never said you were."

She started humming a song under her breath, a blues song by the Sapphires, about a woman who wants a young, young man. I laughed.

"We got each other through a bad time," she said.

"I'm glad."

"He's a man worth having," she said. "The real thing."

"I'll keep that in mind."

～

Roxanne got out of jail, promised Wanda and me that she would call her therapist, and seemed to settle down. Amy was furious with her, but when Roxanne dressed up as Madame Mirabou and gave readings for everyone to thank us, Amy relented. A little.

On the way to the airport, Giselle asked if I thought Roxanne might be anorexic. I had to admit ignorance. "I don't know what to look for."

"She's awfully, awfully skinny."

"I'll pay attention."

We discussed our arrangements for the summer. It was true that Dan offered her more advantages in terms of her education, but I wanted her with me on the off months. Period. She could travel to Spain later, when her character was formed. In the meantime, I needed to have plenty of access to forming that character into one of compassion, honor, and integrity.

After seeing her off, I went to the Manitou apartment to wash up. I gathered the food I'd made into a brand-new wicker picnic basket, and took it to the roof, where I'd spread a thick blanket I'd brought from home, and set up a bucket filled with ice and root beer and wine. A portable CD player was plugged into the outlet by the door.

I was waiting inside, the front shop door open, when Niraj came up the street. He wore a white Henley with the sleeves shoved up on his arms, a pair of jeans, and sandals.

Wow. He was so gorgeous, I almost couldn't breathe. And he was looking at me as if I did the same thing to him.

What had I been thinking—he'd been completely naked and I'd left him! When he came in the door, I said, "You look so good, you make my knees weak."

His expression blazed. With one hand, he caught my head and pulled me forward into a deep, luscious kiss. My skin flamed. "I have a surprise for you," I said, and took his hand. "Let's eat."

I led him to the rooftop, and he murmured properly all the way through the building, commenting on the light, the walls, the little beauties. On the roof, however, he paused and smiled, very slowly "It is very private up here."

"Yes." I opened the picnic basket. "I have made an American picnic," I said, and sat down on the blanket. I punched the CD player to let a low stream of blues roll out of the box. "First, we have B.B. King."

He grinned. It made me look at his lips. "Do you know, your eyes are dilated?"

"Are they? What does that mean?"

"It means," he said, coming over to me and sitting on the blanket, "we don't need the food just yet, do we?"

"No," I whispered, and leaned backward as he kissed me. He tumbled to the blanket with me, pressing our bodies together in the same heat they'd discovered each time we'd touched. "I am ready to make love to you this time, Niraj."

"I am more than ready to be your lover, Nikki," he breathed, and kissed my throat. "But we will just go as far as we like, and no further."

"I would very much like you to take off your shirt."

"Would you?" His eyes twinkled. "I will if you will."

"You first."

Niraj sat up and unbuttoned his shirt, quickly, then shucked it off, leaving his shoulders and chest bare in the warm spring sunshine. His skin was polished and smooth. Dark hair spread in a triangle over his chest, and I raised a hand to my own shirt.

"Allow me," he said, and lifted his hand to my blouse. I dropped my arms and watched his brown fingers unfasten the buttons, push away the fabric, reveal my bra, this time a more ordinary thing. He drew a finger down over the aroused right nipple, circling it twice before raising his hands to the straps at my shoulders. Slowly, slowly, he peeled it downward until my breasts were bare in the sunlight, and he bent his beautiful head and pressed his face into the softness with a sound of gratitude and delight. His hands cupped me from beneath, his tongue swirled around one, then the other. He raised his head. "Beautiful," he said, and kissed me. I laughed, low in my throat, and reached around to unfasten it completely.

We tumbled backward, the bareness of his chest rubbing against my own, our mouths locked in heat and dance. I ran my hands down his sleek sides, down the bones of his spine. He traced the edges of my breasts, suckled my lip, then my neck, then put his entire attention on my breasts. Fingers, lips, tongue. Suckling, releasing, tracing, teasing. His hips were hard against my own and we moved in an old, old motion, an easy bump and grind, his legs between mine.

"Niraj," I whispered, aching. "I want you. In me."

"Oh yes," he said, and we stripped away our jeans.

And this time, I paused to look at him. All of him. And this time, I didn't panic, but felt a deep, wild rush of pleasure. I held out a hand. "Come here," I said.

And this time, he knelt between my legs and I was shivering with anticipation. Just as he nudged the entry, I said, "Wait one second," scrambled for the condom Roxanne had given me, and rolled it into place. "There."

He raised his head. Put his hands on my face. "Are you all right?"

Our eyes met, and I felt the blinders and protections fall away. I let him see me, the real me. I saw into his heart too. "I just wanted," I said, lifting my hips to meet him, "to be looking at you as we joined."

So he did not look away, nor did I, while he slid into me, and for one long, long moment, we were locked there, eyes and bodies joined. "Chakras aligning," I said, and he said, "Uh-huh," and bent down to join our lips.

And that was the end of control. Light burst in my limbs, through my lips and heart and hips and head. He moved slow and hard and I came like I was splitting out of my skin, and remembered, all in a rush, why it was such a good thing to have a lover, to make love, to have sex. "Oh," I whispered, clutching him to me. I put my hands on the small of his back and gripped him close to me and bit his shoulder, his neck, and he, too, found his release, pressing himself so deeply, tightly into me that it felt as if we were fused.

Then he raised his head and kissed me.

And I kissed him back. "Thank you for bringing me back to myself," I said.

His grin tilted to one side. "Anytime."

We made love for a long time, in the open air of my rooftop garden. Then I fed him cookies and bananas and we drank root beer and listened to the blues, and made love again. His body was not perfect, but it was beautiful anyway.

Just as the sun was going down, my cell phone rang. I let it go, but it rang again, a full series, and then again. I finally picked it up and saw Roxanne's phone number on the caller ID. "Hello? Roxanne?"

"No, it's Amy," she said, and I could tell she was crying. "All hell is breaking loose here, and I'd really like it if I could come over to your house and stay with you."

"What's going on?"

"I don't want to say over the phone. It's awful."

"Amy, what's wrong? Are you hurt?"

"No one's physically hurt. She's not arrested, either, but my dad came and got my brother, and he wouldn't take me."

Bastard. "I'm in Manitou, so it's going to take me a little while to get there. Hang on, okay?"

"I'll be here."

I looked with regret at Niraj. "That was my neighbor's daughter. She's upset—and her mother really has been on a tear lately. I have to go see what I can do."

He skimmed his fingers over my collarbones, down the slope of a breast. "I am glad I can now call you my lover," he said quietly.

I bent over and kissed him. "Me too. I'd love to do this again very soon."

"I shall look forward to that."

~

By the time I got to the other apartment, the drama was ending. Unfortunately, I didn't need anyone to tell me what had happened. Wanda's red eyes, Tom's hangdog face, and Roxanne's stony, smoking silence told the tale.

"Hey, Wanda," I said. She shook her head and pushed by me. Tom followed behind her, looking winded and bewildered. He glanced up, met my eyes, looked away, color flooding his face.

Roxanne stood outside the apartment, smoking. She wore a little black skirt, with bare legs and bare feet. No bra beneath a blue T-shirt. She was so thin I could almost see her thigh bones. "Roxanne?"

She bent her head, pressed her fist to her forehead. "I don't know," she said. "He just seemed so lost. Or maybe it's me. I don't know." She raised her head. "Why did I do that?"

"What did you do?"

Her face was blotchy from crying, her eyes hopeless as she lifted her cigarette and smoked, furiously. "I seduced my best friend's husband."

"Oh, Roxanne."

"I know." She blew out smoke. "I know."

I wanted to slap her, shake her. Something. And yet, there was something so devastated about her, as if the marrow of her bones had been sucked away, that I also felt pity. I crossed my arms, mute in the face of the disaster.

Amy came out with a rucksack on her left shoulder. "I'm not living with you anymore," she said to her mother. "You make me sick."

Roxanne reached for her daughter. "Don't, baby. Please." Tears leaked from her eyes. "I'll make it up to you, I promise."

"I have to go, Mom," she said. "You just can't get your shit together, and I'm tired of it."

"Amy," I said, "maybe just spend the night in Giselle's room, huh? Just one night, let your mom have some time, and we'll all talk tomorrow?"

She shook her head. "I called my friend Yvette and she's coming to get me. No offense or anything. I just need to get away."

I nodded. Amy plodded down the stairs. Beside me, Roxanne moaned softly, pressing her fingers to the spot between her eyes. "I can't make it stop hurting," she said. "Nothing I do stops it. I can't live like this anymore."

"You need some help, Roxanne. You need to get yourself together for the sake of your kids, but mainly for yourself."

She lifted her head, and I thought of the Day of the Dead skeletons—her eyes were hollowed, her movements jerky and odd. "Look what he's turned me into," she said, and put a fist to her heart. "I can't stand myself. I can't stand him." She moaned. "I can't stand any of this! I don't know what to do."

I reached for her, and she crumpled into my arms, all angles and overheated skin and tears. "You have to let him go, Roxanne. It's going to kill you."

"How could I have done that to Wanda?" She squeezed my upper arm so hard, I winced. "How could I betray my best friend? She's been so good to me!"

I felt scared, suddenly, of the agony in her voice. It made me remember a night not long after Dan had moved out, when I couldn't stop crying for nearly six hours. Every time I'd sort of stop, another giant sucking howl of loss would wash through me, and I'd be back to it. I cried until I couldn't breathe, until my eyes were swollen practically shut.

I stroked Roxanne's hair.

"I just want to die," she whispered.

"I know, honey," I said. "But you have to live."

A keening, husky moan came out of her, almost like a living thing. "I can't. I can't."

"C'mon," I said. "Let's get you to bed. Things will look better in the morning."

"Will they?" she asked.

I ignored the bristling of dread over my spine. "They will," I said. "I promise."

And I guess she decided to make it so, one way or the other.

22

My phone rang early. I was still asleep when I stumbled into the living room and tried to find the cell phone. Tugging it out of my purse, I flipped it open, tossed my hair out of my eyes, and croaked, "Hello?"

Wanda's voice said, "Turn on the television. Channel 13."

"Wanda?" I peered at the microwave clock. It was only six a.m. "What's wrong?"

"Roxanne."

My stomach dropped, but it was that odd clunking of expectation. Without a word, I found the remote control and clicked on the television. Nighttime video, shot through with blinking red lights and yellow police tape, showed an ordinary suburban house with a sloping grassy lawn.

On fire.

Roxanne's car was parked in front. "Shit," I whispered. "Is she okay?"

"Police have taken a suspect into custody for the fire," a grave, female reporter's voice said, "rumored to be the ex-wife of the resident. Apparently, no one was at home when the fire started, and no injuries are reported, but the house is expected to be a complete loss. Back to you, Kara."

More video, of Roxanne, looking pale and dull, being escorted down the driveway, wearing the same blouse and skirt she'd been wearing the afternoon before.

"I feel so guilty," Wanda said. "Even though I am so mad at her, I wish I could have done something."

"Oh, sweetie, don't. Be mad at her, it will be easier."

Wanda wept softly. "But I love her."

"I know."

"Will you see what you can find out?"

"Yes. Wanda, I'm so sorry."

Her voice was thick. "Me too."

~

It took some doing, but I finally pieced the details together. Sometime after midnight last night, Roxanne, stone-cold sober, drove to the home she had shared with her ex-husband for twelve years and used a key to go quietly through the back door, into the kitchen—where she'd cooked a thousand meals for her now-fragmented family—and calmly, deliberately, set fire to the kitchen, the bathroom, and the bed in the master bedroom. She walked back outside and waited for firefighters to come, too late to save it.

The news was full of it for days. A classic triangle tragedy, piercing anew each and every time.

It haunted me. All of it. The layers and layers of betrayals—Grant, then Roxanne with the married men she'd seduced, over and over again, Wanda and Tom.

In some ways, it was a relief. In some dark part of me, I'd been afraid she would kill herself. Or one of the others.

What was frightening was that I understood what she'd done. Not only the impulse, but the satisfaction it must have brought. It would have been so much easier to kill Daniel than to live with his betrayal, to recognize, in small ways and large, how enormously he'd let me down. There had been days through those first months after our break that I would have happily tied Keisha up and pulled out her fingernails, one by one. When I would have gladly tortured each of them in front of the other.

When I would have been deeply thrilled to shoot bullets into their bodies and watch them die.

Vicious. Brutal. Not at all civilized. I know all that. But it doesn't matter. The betrayal is too.

So why did I manage to get through it, and Roxanne didn't? The question haunted me.

One night, too unsettled to sleep, I went to the shop. It was past midnight. No one was out in the streets of Manitou, unless you counted the homeless man asleep beneath the streetlamp. A big moon, not quite full, shone down over the mountains, huddled around the town in the dark.

I unlocked the front door and flipped on the light. It was bald and too bright—for winter, I would need lamps. For now, it suited my needs, which were simply to get busy, do something productive. I locked the door behind me for safety and got to work. For the one red wall, Evelyn, with her eye for detail, had found some fantastic shelving of dark wood that had little relief carvings of tigers and elephants along the edges. She said she'd found them cheap at a garage sale, which might well have been true, though I suspected not. She had not let me reimburse her. Against the red, they looked spectacular, and I could hardly wait to put beautiful bottles of perfume on them. With little paper blossoms?

Mmm. Maybe not. I did think black-and-white photos of elephants would be an excellent addition. The movie *Green Card* crossed my mind, and I wondered what the soundtrack to it had been—Enya, maybe? Might be good to get a lot of things like that to help facilitate the mood for shoppers.

Kit had taped off the floor in a simple diamond pattern, and started filling it in so I could follow along. The colors were an earthy red and softer gold, which sounded too extreme until I saw how she used it on the aged pine floor. It gave it a feeling of old and elegant, a faded ballroom in a faraway land. Filling in the squares was an ideal task tonight.

As I painted, I kept seeing blips of Roxanne the night she'd betrayed Wanda. Her glazed eyes and bruised chin and swollen face. Her dull voice saying, "I just can't do this anymore." The fragility of her collarbone, so modishly extreme.

Wanda, Roxanne, Tommy. Daniel and Keisha and me. Roxanne and Grant and Lorelei.

Good sex. Bad sex. Roxanne, for all her blithe posturing, had been having a lot of bad sex, and sex with Tom had been the worst, most self-destructive act of all. Wanda loved them both, and the marriage might survive, but it had taken a pretty serious blow. The friendship would not survive. The betrayal was too severe.

I thought of Niraj. Tender, open, passionate sex with no painful edges attached. That was how it was supposed to be. I was free, so was he. We were old enough to know what we were doing. Our connection brought no danger to anyone else.

I sighed. Filling dark yellow paint in a diamond drawn so painstakingly by Kit, I thought of myself at the top of the basement stairs that night, afraid to face the darkness. The spiders. The ghosts. So convinced I couldn't do it that I'd let a hundred-year-old house that somebody would have loved blow up. I'd been absolutely resigned to going with it.

Wouldn't they all be sorry then?

My lungs constricted painfully, and I reared back on my heels, paintbrush in hand. Putting my other hand to my chest, I tried to ease the awful recognition.

God! I nearly killed myself that night! It had been passive, a refusal to face the present, to take responsibility for my life as it was, rather than the actively self-destructive things Roxanne had been indulging in. But if I'd gone up with the house, the result would have been the same—Giselle's mother dead, an ex-wife who couldn't handle the transition.

I couldn't breathe. My heart raced and I put the paintbrush in the can, choking. I had been willing to die rather than change.

Die, rather than change.

Wanda said our husbands had all shown bad character, and maybe they had, but where was our own strength of character, mine and Roxanne's? Where had we gone astray ourselves? It scared me, not knowing.

Character, Wanda said. It was not okay for a husband to betray his wife. It was not okay. Things happened and that was life, but it was an awful thing to do to someone, and I wanted to say that out loud.

Without much thought, without even much guilt, Daniel had waltzed away into another life, leaving mine in a zillion tiny pieces and no map for me to put them back together again.

Something started dissolving, the pressure in my chest turning to tears that ran unchecked down my face. Grief, recognition, a certainty that I had to learn to face up to my life just as it was, in all its messes and mistakes and losses, all its joys and surprises and delights.

I had to face myself. First.

And weirdly, I knew exactly what it would take. Standing up, I wiped my cheeks with my palms, then dried them on my soft, old jeans. I marched down the hall to the back room. It was dark. The moon shone through the bank of windows, and I could imagine I was back eighty years. Flipping on the light didn't make it a lot better—it was just so stark, so obviously ancient. I sniffed, braced myself, and pulled open the basement door.

The light switch was on the wall just inside the door, and I flipped it on. Below, at the foot of those rickety, open-slat wooden stairs, was a swept concrete floor.

A spider rushed up the wall toward the ceiling. A plain brown spider, not very big, but I felt an involuntary ripple down my neck. Every cell in my body said, *You've got to be kidding*.

I went into the shop and picked up one of the old towels scattered around. It was fairly clean. I shook it and put it on my head like a veil, clutching it tight beneath my chin. I could tolerate a spider on a foot or arm, but it caused me serious trauma to imagine them in my hair or inside my clothes. Ick.

I gripped the towel hard and took a breath, then took the first step.

And the second. And the thirdfourthfifthsixth, fast, all the way down. I rushed into the open area of the cellar, and blew out like a hard-working athlete. Whispers of air brushed my ankles. Warily, I looked around. There were cobwebs overhead, and I kept the towel tight over my head. I didn't see any other live spiders, but I felt their eyes from hidden spots, imagined the troops ready to—

"Stop." I said the word aloud. A single word. It helped, and I said, "Look around."

The furnace was to my right, fairly new-looking. To my surprise, I could actually see the pilot light, which was burning just fine. In the other direction was a good-size hot-water heater, also fairly clean and new looking. Next to it, against the wall, were water pipes with large knobs for turning them off and on. I assumed one was hot, the other cold.

I turned in a circle. There was really nothing else in there. It was old and plain and clean.

Behind me, I heard a footstep. I startled and whirled around, my skin crawling in terror.

"Meow-p!" said the kitten, who'd followed me down. He stopped and "meow-p"ed again, his eyes a vividly bright yellow. Trotting down the rest of the stairs, he came all the way over, and rubbed against my ankles.

"Well, it's about time!" I bent down and picked him up. His fur was as silky as mink, his lean young body strong and giving at once as he tucked his head under my chin and began to purr. I forgot to hold on to the towel, and it fell down around my shoulders, but it suddenly seemed okay.

Jammed beneath the step was a tarot card. I recognized the bright yellow background and long rectangular shape of it. I bent down to pull it out—the three of cups, which showed a drawing of three women dancing.

Here was my life. Right now. It didn't matter what had come before, what I'd believed it might be, where I thought I might go. The only thing that mattered was where I was right now. The path, my choices, external forces had brought me here, to this night, grieving my friend's devastating choices.

And celebrating my own.

Because, somehow, I'd survived.

It was only as I turned and headed up the stairs that I remembered Mark, and the basement in his grandmother's house. He swore there were ghosts down there, and went to great lengths to terrify me about it. We crept down there one day and he kicked over a can, and out of it came a gigantic black widow. We both screamed and ran up the stairs, and we never went back down there again.

Mark had been a gift. His loss, at such a vulnerable time, had taught me early about the capriciousness of life, and the power of grief. But most of all, it had taught me to value the hours of life.

Every hour.

Carrying my kitten upstairs, I felt only a small wash of dread, that horror of things chasing you up from the darkness, and I doubted very seriously that I'd go down there again if I could find a way out of it, but I'd done it.

I'd done it.

Flipping off the light, I closed the cellar door and put the kitten down. "Let's go take a bath, huh?"

He sat on the lip while I filled the giant tub. I didn't have any clean clothes, and I'd have to sleep on the roof with a quilt and a flat pillow, but that was all right. The room, with its dormers, made me feel cozy, the amber windows full of promise. I climbed into the tub and sank to my neck in copious hot water, and rested my head against the back of the tub. The kitten hopped up and peered at me curiously, then jumped down and made himself comfortable on my discarded clothes. He licked a paw.

I closed my eyes and thought of all the paths that had had to converge to get me here. How do you love yourself?

You just do.

23

Nikki's Perfume Journal Entry

Time: 4 p.m.
Date: April 25, 196—

Elements: mud, water, sweet young sweat, sunbaked hair,
scrub oak rotting in the undergrowth, fir, hope
Notes: Mark and me

The Thursday night before Memorial Day weekend, I had a small party in the Manitou apartment, which was slightly less horrendously furnished than the one in Splitsville. I had a futon, but it was a solid wooden one, my own taste, a dark wood with a red-and-yellow patchwork. I'd hung curtains made of old saris woven together in pink and green and gold at the windows, and since chairs were expensive, there were cushions on the floor. Since both places were paid for, there was no reason not to keep them through July. The insurance company had reluctantly approved my claim, and when the money came through, I'd buy new furniture. Eventually, maybe I'd invest in a new home, but not until I knew what shape my life was taking. The patchwork on the futon, the curtains, the pillows reflected my feelings about my life: it was assembled from bits and pieces, but I wasn't entirely sure where I wanted to live permanently, who I wanted to live with. An apartment was a good way to just be with that transition.

The one thing I did know is that my perfumes were important. The shop, Scent of Hours, would have a grand opening tomorrow. I'd had it open for a couple of weeks—staffed by Amy when I couldn't be there, and Giselle was going to work there, too, over the summer. We'd asked the landlord to divide the large bedroom in the apartment into two, and he'd agreed. She very badly wanted to stay in Marin County to go to school, and I'd finally given in because she was so focused on becoming a doctor, and schools were better out there. But we had all—including Daniel and Keisha, whom I'd made have regular conversations with me—agreed Giselle would also spend a lot more time with me.

Everyone was here tonight. Kit sat with Wanda near a table with crudités and I knew Wanda was pumping her about how to go to school with children. Tommy was not in evidence. He'd stayed home with the boys. The marriage was shaky, but in some ways the wreck of his single crash of infidelity had served to throw him right into counseling to manage the losses he'd faced in combat. Maybe it would help.

Roxanne wasn't there either—nor was she in jail, exactly. A court-ordered evaluation had resulted in a need for further diagnosis, and she was in a Denver facility for anorexics. She wasn't doing particularly well, but I went to see her every other week.

Happily, a whole group of restaurant friends came too: Mary, Annie, and Zara, who'd brought a gigantic pitcher of mimosas so we could toast the opening. She sat with Evelyn and Pamela, talking dogs, I thought. They were all big dog lovers.

The last person to arrive was Niraj, who entered the gathering of women without even a flicker of consternation. He carried a small package with him. "I finally remembered to bring you the little present I bought in San Francisco after we first met."

I laughed. "I forgot!"

He lifted a palm, cautioning me. "It is only a little thing, remember."

"That's fine." I tore the paper off. Breath left me. "Niraj!" I said, and started to cry.

"What is it?"

I covered my mouth, my view of my little present blurring as life, or the universe or somebody, offered me proof that they cared, that they knew me, that I mattered.

It was a small flocked black cat inside a plastic dome that was a bit worse for the wear. A pink ribbon held a golden heart around its neck, and its pink rhinestone eyes matched the pink feather boa behind it. The small bottle of perfume it held was Golden Woods.

"Thank you," I whispered to Niraj. To the universe.

To Mark, wherever he was. I flung my arms around Niraj's shoulders and let him hug me. "I'll explain another time."

He kissed my ear.

Zara raised her glass. "I'd like to propose a toast to Manitou's newest enterprise, Scent of Hours. May the Lady of the Mountain bless it and keep it, and let it prosper for many years to come."

I raised my glass. "To the future!"

ACKNOWLEDGMENTS

Some books are harder to write than others, and I'm grateful to the angels who flew in when I needed them on this one. Thanks go to Cathi Stroo, because only your sister knows you well enough to bring over a CD for a bad day and then it ends up being the soundtrack for the book in progress; Meg Ruley, Linda Marrow, and Charlotte Herscher for guidance; and Arielle Zibrak, who flew away to adventure; Christie and Teresa for reading and cheering me on and calling to say, "Have you done your pages today?"; Mandy Aftel for writing *Essence and Alchemy*, a magical, evocative book about the perfumer's art.

ABOUT THE AUTHOR

Photo © 2009 Blue Fox Photography

Barbara O'Neal is the *Washington Post, Wall Street Journal, USA Today,* and Amazon Charts bestselling author of more than a dozen novels of women's fiction, including the #1 Amazon Charts bestseller *When We Believed in Mermaids* as well as *The Starfish Sisters, This Place of Wonder, The Lost Girls of Devon, Write My Name Across the Sky,* and *The Art of Inheriting Secrets.* Her award-winning books have been published in over two dozen countries. She lives on the Oregon coast with her husband, a British endurance athlete who vows he'll never lose his accent. For more information, visit barbaraoneal.com.